本书是国家社科基金重大项目"弥尔顿作品集整理、翻译与研究"（19ZDA298）阶段性成果

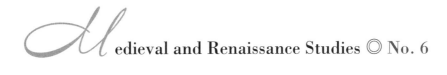

*M*edieval and Renaissance Studies ◎ No. 6

中世纪与文艺复兴研究

（六）

郝田虎　主编

Edited by Hao Tianhu

ZHEJIANG UNIVERSITY PRESS

浙江大学出版社

主编的话

从篇数上说，《中世纪与文艺复兴研究（六）》仅有 16 篇，但其分量是沉甸甸的。作者阵容可谓强大，青年学者和资深学者兼备，包括意大利中世纪学者劳拉·伊赛比·德·菲立比斯，以及多位著名学者如张隆溪、陆建德和邱锦荣等。其中，陆建德、伊赛比·德·菲立比斯和阮婧的论文是英文的。陆建德教授翻箱倒柜，在暑热中找到了 40 年前的手稿，这是他在复旦读大学时的文章，当时得到加拿大籍外教许美德的激赏，而其论题——古希腊悲剧作家欧里庇得斯对美国现代戏剧家尤金·奥尼尔的影响，似乎至今仍未过时。这篇论文完成于 1981 年春天，恰好是中国比较文学在当代复兴的时节。1981 年 1 月，北京大学成立了比较文学小组，成员有五位，包括季羡林、杨周翰、李赋宁、乐黛云和当时刚刚研究生毕业的张隆溪。几十年过去了，张隆溪教授在他的老师杨周翰先生的激励下，作为首位担任国际比较文学协会主席的华人学者，早已成为国际学术界的知名学者。孔子曰："三十而立，四十而不惑。"复兴的中国比较文学在不惑的年纪，究竟明白了什么？杨周翰先生 1986 年提出的任务，"使比较文学学科真正成为一门世界性的学科……特别是用我国的丰富的文学遗产和文学实践去充实世界文学"[①]，我们完成了多少？2022 年 3 月，杨周翰先生的另一名学生，王宁教授在"跨越·比较·汇通：外国文学与比较文学高端论坛"上应邀做主旨发言，他依然在呼唤比较文学中国学派的兴起。《中世纪与文艺复兴研究》特设立两期专栏，刊登四位重量级学者（陆建德、王宁、张隆溪和张哲俊）的文章，隆重纪念中国比较文学复兴 40 周年。此举不仅意在回顾和总结，更是在展望未来，期

[①] 杨周翰，1986，《国际比较文学研究的动向——国际比较文学协会第 11 届大会述评》，《国外文学》第 3 期，第 10 页。

许在下一个 40 年里，中国比较文学能够"鲲鹏展翅九万里，翻动扶摇羊角"，巍然屹立于世界学术之林。

跨越和传播是第六辑的关键词。张隆溪教授强调比较对于东西方文化交流的重要性，重新探讨了 17、18 世纪东西方交往中的智性接触，他认为比较是跨文化研究的核心方法。翻译也是跨文化交流的重要媒介，举凡黄必康译莎士比亚诗剧体《牡丹亭》、华明译《马洛戏剧全集》、朱世达译《文艺复兴时期英国戏剧选》等，都用翻译的桥梁沟通了东西方文化之间的鸿沟。而戏剧翻译由于其体裁的可表演性，尤其得到了本辑作者的关注。伊赛比·德·菲立比斯从文学跨越到了历史，并尝试了跨文化比较。张亚婷和张炼的论文概述了英国中世纪文学在中国的跨文化旅行。陆建德讲的文学影响、邱锦荣讲的莎士比亚十四行诗教学、张薇讲的卞之琳对 A. C. 布拉德雷莎学观的接受，都属于传播的领域。杨林贵、李伟民主编的《云中锦笺——中国莎学书信》即将由商务印书馆出版，此书从书信的角度记录了中国莎学的历史，即莎士比亚在中国的传播史。青年学者杨开泛在德国出版了英文专著《盎格鲁-撒克逊英格兰的时间观念》，有利于中国学术走出去。以沈弘、许展等为代表的中国学者对早期英国文学的解读，展现了中国学人的良好风貌。《中世纪与文艺复兴研究》一如既往，连接着中国和世界、过去和现在，它憧憬着未来汇通的美好愿景和崇高目标。

我们在此鸣谢浙江大学世界顶尖大学合作计划"浙大-耶鲁中世纪与文艺复兴研究合作计划"的慷慨资助。感谢审稿专家们的无私援手，感谢诸位特邀编辑和责任编辑张颖琪老师的勤奋工作。期待读者的反馈和意见建议，以便论丛越办越好。编委会热忱欢迎相关领域的各位同仁踊跃投稿，大作请惠寄 cmrs2016@163.com; 稿件体例详见本辑论文，切勿一稿多投。

郝田虎

2022 年 4 月于紫金港

目 录

Contents

纪念中国比较文学复兴 40 周年专栏

Commemorating the 40th Anniversary of the Revival of Comparative Literature in China

【编者按】中国比较文学在当代的复兴，已经走过了整整 40 年。1981年 1 月，北京大学成立了比较文学小组，成员有五位，包括季羡林、杨周翰、李赋宁、乐黛云和当时刚刚研究生毕业的张隆溪。1985 年 8 月，杨周翰当选国际比较文学协会副主席；10 月，中国比较文学学会成立，季羡林出任首任会长。2016 年 7 月，张隆溪当选国际比较文学协会主席。2019 年夏，国际比较文学协会第 22 届大会在澳门成功召开。2021 年 12 月，华东师范大学成立比较文学系。中国比较文学在当代复兴，并产生世界性的影响，是几代学者努力奋斗的结果。为了纪念中国比较文学复兴 40 周年，在郝田虎的组织下，中世纪与文艺复兴研究中心在线上举办了"跨越·比较·汇通：外国文学与比较文学高端论坛"（2022 年 3 月），《中世纪与文艺复兴研究》特设立两期专栏，著名学者张隆溪和陆建德为首期专栏分别贡献了一篇论文。张隆溪教授的论文是一篇英文新作，发表于 2020 年，由张炼译成中文，经作者授权发表；陆建德教授的英文论文是一篇旧作，完成于 1981 年春，由王瑞雪整理，经作者授权首发。这两篇文章，向我们示范了如何做跨文化研究和影响研究，希望对读者有所启迪。让我们继往开来，接力完成杨周翰 1986 年提出的任务，"使比较文学学科真正成为一门世界性的学科……特别是用我国的丰富的文学遗产和文学实践去充实世界文学"①。

---

① 杨周翰，1986，《国际比较文学研究的动向——国际比较文学协会第 11 届大会述评》，《国外文学》第 3 期，第 10 页。

比较与 17、18 世纪东西方的相遇①

张隆溪

张 炼 译，郝田虎 校

内容提要：作为文化和传统的东方和西方这两个概念，只有通过比较，通过商贸、旅行及其他各种交往形式的相遇才可能产生。如果说 13 世纪的马可·波罗代表了欧洲在商贸和地理知识拓展方面的东西方交往的早期阶段，那么，随着耶稣会传教士的介入，以及启蒙运动时期欧洲文化和社会的内部发展，17、18 世纪成了东西方交往中智性接触的重要时期。不仅"中国风"的流行改变了欧洲人物质生活的趣味和美学，而且莱布尼茨和伏尔泰等哲学家通过中国找到了他们正在寻求建构的国家和社会。这一国家和社会建立在理性基础上，而非基于宗教信仰。再次探讨当时的东西方相遇，将有助于我们更好地理解跨文化交流中的比较和差异，而这一议题对于我们当前所处的时代显得尤为相关和重要。

关键词：跨文化交流；比较；东方和西方；欧洲；中国；17 世纪；18 世纪；马可·波罗；莱布尼茨；伏尔泰；耶稣会士

作者简介：张隆溪，北京大学英语文学硕士（1981），哈佛大学比较文学博士（1989），曾任教于北大、哈佛和加利福尼亚大学河滨分校，现任香港城市大学比较文学与翻译讲座教授。2009 年获选为瑞典皇家人文、历史及考古学院外籍院士，2013 年获选为欧洲学院外籍院士。2016—2019 年，任国际比较文学协会主席。长期以来专注于东西方跨文化研究，曾以中英文出版 20 多部专著和多篇学术论文。主要著作有：《二十世纪西方文论述评》（生活·读

---

① Zhang Longxi, "Comparison and East-West Encounter: The Seventeenth and the Eighteenth Centuries," in Angelika Epple, Walter Erhart, and Johannes Grave (eds.), *Practices of Comparing: Towards a New Understanding of a Fundamental Human Practice* (Bielefeld: Bielefeld UP, 2020), pp. 213-227. 中译文已经作者审定。

书·新知三联书店，1986）、*The Tao and the Logos: Literary Hermeneutics, East and West* (Duke UP, 1992; 韩译本 1997; 中译本《道与逻各斯》1998)、*Mighty Opposites: From Dichotomies to Differences in the Comparative Study of China* (Stanford UP, 1998)、《走出文化的封闭圈》（生活·读书·新知三联书店，2004）、《中西文化研究十论》（复旦大学出版社，2005）、*Allegoresis: Reading Canonical Literature East and West* (Cornell UP, 2005; 日译本 2016)、*Unexpected Affinities: Reading across Cultures* (U of Toronto P, 2007)、《比较文学研究入门》（复旦大学出版社，2009）、《灵魂的史诗：失乐园》（台北大块文化，2010）、《一毂集》（复旦大学出版社，2011）、《文学—历史—思想：中西比较研究》（香港三联书店，2012）、《阐释学与跨文化研究》（生活·读书·新知三联书店，2014）、*From Comparison to World Literature* (SUNY P, 2015; 日译本 2018)、《文学—记忆—思想：东西比较随笔集》（中国社科出版社，2019）、《什么是世界文学》（生活·读书·新知三联书店，2021）等。

译者简介：张炼，湖南师范大学博士，浙江大学外国语学院"百人计划"研究员，主要研究中古英语文学。

校者简介：郝田虎，哥伦比亚大学博士，浙江大学外国语学院教授。

Title: Comparison and East-West Encounter: The Seventeenth and Eighteenth Centuries

Abstract: East and West, as cultures and traditions, become possible to conceptualize only in comparison and in the encounters of trade, travel, and other kinds of interactions. If Marco Polo in the thirteenth century represented an early stage of the East-West encounter in trade and the expansion of geographical knowledge in Europe, the seventeenth and the eighteenth centuries became the important time of intellectual contact in East-West encounters through the mediation of Jesuit missionaries and because of the internal development of European culture and society during the time of the Enlightenment. Not only did the trend of chinoiserie change European taste and aesthetics in material life, but philosophers like Leibniz and Voltaire found in China what they were seeking for a state and society, built on reason rather than religious belief. To revisit the East-West encounters of that time may help us attain a better understanding of comparison and difference in cross-cultural interrelations, which remains an issue of particular relevance and importance for our time today.

Key words: cross-cultural interrelations, comparison, East and West, Europe, China, seventeenth century, eighteenth century, Marco Polo, Leibniz, Voltaire, Jesuit missionaries

Author: Zhang Longxi holds an MA in English from Peking University (1981) and a Ph.D. in Comparative Literature from Harvard (1989). He has taught at Peking, Harvard and the University of California, Riverside, and is currently Chair Professor of Comparative Literature and Translation at the City University of Hong Kong. He is a foreign member of the Royal Swedish Academy of Letters, History and Antiquities (inducted 2009) and of Academia Europaea (inducted 2013). He was elected President of the International Comparative Literature Association for 2016—2019. He serves as Editor-in-Chief of the *Journal of World Literature* and Advisory Editor of *New Literary History*. He has published more than 20 books and numerous articles in both English and Chinese in East-West comparative studies. His books in English include *The Tao and the Logos: Literary Hermeneutics, East and West* (Duke UP, 1992); *Mighty Opposites: From Dichotomies to Differences in the Comparative Study of China* (Stanford UP, 1998); *Allegoresis: Reading Canonical Literature East and West* (Cornell UP, 2005); *Unexpected Affinities: Reading across Cultures* (U of Toronto P, 2007); and *From Comparison to World Literature* (SUNY P, 2015). Email: ctlxzh@cityu.edu.hk

Translator: Zhang Lian, Ph.D. (Hunan Normal University), "One Hundred Talents Project" researcher at the School of International Studies, Zhejiang University. Her main research field is Middle English literature. Email: zhanglian_hn@zju.edu.cn

Reviser: Hao Tianhu, Ph.D. (Columbia University), professor at the School of International Studies, Zhejiang University. Email: haotianhu@zju.edu.cn

　　贝内迪克特·德·斯宾诺莎（Benedict de Spinoza）有一句名言："限定即否定。"（Spinoza, 1951: 2.370）事物不是基于自身被定义的，其定义也不仅仅只关于其自身。只有通过比较和区别，它们才变得明确和可识别。通过否定及与其他事物的辨析，我们才可能确定我们思忖的是什么。换句话说，从本体论和认识论的角度来看，比较对于理解和诠释是必要的、有用的方法。"比较还是不比较，与生存还是毁灭不同：它不是个问题。"这是我在其他地方阐述比较这一概念时说过的一句话。"在最基础的层面，从本体论来讲，我们无法不比较。我们总是比较，以便辨析、认知、理解，做出判断和决定，再按决定行动。无论从认知思考还是从身体举动的角度来看，我们所有的行为都依赖比较，除了比较，我们别无他选。"（Zhang, 2015: 11）一与多、统一与多样、阴和阳、男和女，这些基本概念在东西方智慧中都有清晰的表述。中国古代哲人老子在其名著《道德经》里说："天下皆知美之为美，斯恶已，皆知善之为善，斯不善已。"一切事物都有别于其对立面，也会产生其对立面。老子接着说："故有无相生，难易相成，长短相较，高下相倾，音声相和，前后相随。"（李耳，1985: 171）像所有这些二元对立的基本概念和术语一样，"东"与"西"也形成了一对基本概念。二者的比较使我们定位自我，以获得方向感。但是，当我们说的东西方指全球范围内的地理区域和文化体系时，这种方向感极大地扩展到亚洲和欧洲大陆的广大区域，以及它们不同的文化、历史和传统之中。从这个意义上讲，只有像古代丝绸之路这样的旅行和贸易路线将彼此隔绝的世界各民族汇聚起来，东西方的概念才能建立起来。东方和西方的比较自然产生了对二者分歧和契合关系的阐述。不过，丝绸之路的历史距今如此遥远，我们几乎无法将之与一个特定的名字、一个用生动而可信的故事揭示生命真相的活生生的人联系起来。

　　这就是马可·波罗（Marco Polo, 1254—1324）的意义所在。他是以其东方之行闻名的第一位欧洲人，用某种程度的细节叙事方式，给我们带来一种真实经历的感觉。马可·波罗是威尼斯人，他赴中国的行程有一定时间背景。成吉思汗领导无往不胜的蒙古军队，以武力征服了大片区域，开辟了从西伯利亚到欧洲东部，横跨欧亚大陆的路线，穿越了曾是东亚和基督教欧洲之间屏障的中亚和西亚地区。马可·波罗与父亲、叔叔一行，经历了长时间的冒险行程，来到了中国。此时成吉思汗的孙子——忽必烈已经登上了皇位。约翰·拉纳（John Larner）认为，马可·波罗的重要贡献是拓展了欧洲人的地理知识。他说："事实上，在中世纪的地理文化中，从索里努斯（Solinus）到伊昔多（Isidore），再到戈苏因（Gossuin），都找不到类似马可·波罗之书那样的著作。"（Larner, 2001: 77）"在他之前和之后都没有人把如此丰厚的地理新知识传授给西方人。"（Larner, 2001: 97）欧洲人获得了这些新知识，其表现之一就是最早向欧洲人展示外面广阔世界的《加泰罗尼亚地图集》（the Catalan Atlas），其中展示的许多亚洲地名，显然就是从《马可·波罗行纪》（*The Travels of Marco Polo*）的描述中获取的。

然而，马可·波罗算不上是一个知识分子，他到中国的时候，忽必烈已经建立了元朝，南宋已经回天无力，这使他并没有多少机会与占人口多数的汉族人打交道，也无法仔细观察中国传统文化。这也是马可·波罗中国之行的真实性不时受到质疑的部分原因。①然而，在我看来，最让他的欧洲同胞感到不舒服和怀疑的，莫过于马可·波罗书中对蒙古帝王的高度赞扬。马可·波罗对比了亚洲和欧洲的财富、权力和繁荣程度，展示了大多数欧洲人想象不到的华夏或中国的图景。比方说，在说到忽必烈时，马可·波罗认为："全世界所有的皇帝、所有基督徒和撒拉逊人②的国王，他们一起拥有的权力或取得的成就都无法超过大汗忽必烈。"（Polo, 1968: 78）这样的表述对于当时及此后很久的欧洲读者来说都是不可思议的，但是马可·波罗的叙述仍然给欧洲人留下了深刻的印象，激发了他们对于一个极其富饶的东方的想象。至今各大图书馆和博物馆仍存有很多用各种欧洲语言写成的、图饰华美的《马可·波罗行纪》手绘本，这证明了他"在当时就享有盛誉"。在拉纳看来，"作者生前其作品就有多个译本出现，这在中世纪是一个无与伦比的记录"（Larner, 2001: 44）。从历史角度来看，特别是以今天带着后殖民式的敏感来看，我们可以看到马可·波罗作为东西方交流的先驱的重要性，从而认可他东方行程和冒险的意义。他的东方之行为人们提供了构想东西方相遇的一种截然不同的方式，迥异于一直以来以东方主义话语占据论述主体的方式。马可·波罗的中世纪游记与影响深远的东方主义和后殖民主义理论模式完全不同，其写作的年代早于 19 世纪欧洲殖民扩张时期，提供了一种不同的东西方相遇模式。就像我在其他地方论述过的，它

---

① 质疑马可·波罗游记的人不少，其中吴芳思（Frances Wood）是最有名的一位。她写了一本带有反诘标题的书：《马可·波罗到过中国吗？》。见：Wood, 1995.
② 撒拉逊人（Saracens）是古代阿拉伯游牧民族的一支。——译者注

不是基于"征服或占有"的欲望，而是基于"认识和理解"。这一东西方相遇的替代模式，对于我们当今世界特别有价值（Zhang, 2008: 295）。

在 15、16 世纪的文艺复兴时期，《马可·波罗行纪》受到更多读者的欢迎，它与但丁（Dante）的《神曲》（Comedia）、托马斯·阿奎那（Thomas Aquinas）的《神学大全》（Summa Theologica）一样，是受到当时人文主义者广泛阅读的最重要的著作之一。它的名声甚至超出了学术界。当哥伦布航行寻找亚洲大陆时，他携带了一本《马可·波罗行纪》。如拉纳所言，这是一本"实用的教科书"（Larner, 2001: 140）。在现代历史学家看来，中国不仅对于哥伦布是一个鼓舞人心的目标，对于当时很多有抱负的冒险家和探险家也是如此。卜正民（Timothy Brook）认为，由于马可·波罗的游记，"中国在大众想象中占据了很重的分量。欧洲人将之视为一个拥有超越任何已知规模的权力和财富的地方"，寻找中国的探索成了"一股强烈的持续力量，对于 17 世纪历史产生了重要影响，在欧洲、在中国、在二者之间的大多数地方都是如此"（Brook, 2008: 19）。中国瓷器、丝绸、茶叶、墙纸和其他物品激发了 17、18 世纪欧洲艺术家的灵感，他们创作出有"中国风"和洛可可风格的创新性装饰作品，而青花瓷和其他东方主题则常常出现在荷兰静物写生画和弗美尔（Johannes Vermeer）的室内装饰中。像安托万·华托（Antoine Watteau）、弗朗索瓦·布歇（François Boucher）这样伟大的法国画家都曾绘画一些想象中的中国人物，他们推动了"中国风"的流行。对此，我在分析西方人心中的中国形象时曾经谈到过："布歇的绘画、素描和挂毯中出现的是他想象中的中国人的生活形象，集快乐、平和、和谐、陌生于一体，是一片色彩明艳、细节迷人的乐土，以典型的欢乐和练达的方式描绘，展示了布歇的典型艺术特征。"（Zhang, 1998: 32）17、18 世纪欧洲的中国形象与近两百年来中国在欧洲的形象非常不同。

在 17 世纪，关于中国的梦幻般的、富于想象的形象开始出现在诗歌和大众想象中。约翰·弥尔顿（John Milton）是他那个时代最博学的英国诗人，他曾提到：

> 途中，它（指撒旦）降落在塞利卡那，那是
> 一片荒原，那里的中国人推着

　　　轻便的竹车，靠帆和风力前进。①（杨周翰译，1981: 60）

这样的中国加帆车形象在今天欧洲的一些"世界地图"（mappa mundi）里仍然能够找到，中国与 17、18 世纪审美情感的变化联系起来。用风帆驾驶的"轻便的竹车"与中国事物的形象完美相符，它们轻盈、精致、灵巧，也很脆弱。例如，在亚历山大·蒲柏（Alexander Pope）的英雄体滑稽诗篇《夺发记》（*The Rape of the Lock*）里，"一个脆弱的中国瓷器罐"被打碎，这是一个预示性的标志，预示着喜剧和情节剧的主要情节（Pope, 1988: 71）。塞缪尔·泰勒·柯尔律治（Samuel Taylor Coleridge）在一首美得出神入化的诗里，梦到忽必烈汗和他那"庄严的欢乐穹顶"（Coleridge, 1965: 115）。这表明，马可·波罗对蒙古皇帝的描写，到 19 世纪仍能深深唤起浪漫主义诗人的想象力。伊塔洛·卡尔维诺（Italo Calvino）的《看不见的城市》（*Invisible Cities*）意大利语版本首先在 1972 年出版，此后出现了多个不同译本，盛名远扬。书中写到了忽必烈与马可·波罗交谈、马可·波罗提到他的行程和他到过的许多城市。在一个全球各民族和城市相互联通的时代，此情节是一个极好的例子，它表明马可·波罗的游记对 20 世纪的人们进行世界构想时的重要性。

　　实际上，在 17、18 世纪欧洲对于中国和东方的想象里，耶稣会传教士发挥了比马可·波罗更重要的核心作用。13 世纪的马可·波罗代表的是贸易和欧洲地理知识拓展方面的东西方相遇早期阶段，重要的文化交流和互动要等到几百年以后。16 世纪晚期和 17 世纪初期，基督教传教士——比如范礼安（Alessandro Vilignano, 1539—1606）、罗明坚（Michele Ruggieri, 1543—1607）、利玛窦（Matteo Ricci, 1552—1610）三位意大利耶稣会士——来到东方，与中国及东方进行了首次实质性的知识和文化交流。正是这一波东西方文化和宗教的交锋，使跨文化比较脱颖而出。在明朝万历皇帝（1573—1620 年在位）的特别允许下，利玛窦于 1601 年抵达北京，此时他见到的中国社会和文化与当时的欧洲完全不同。当时的中国富足、组织有序，其悠久的历史可追溯至基督诞生之前很久的远古时代。当时的中国给利玛窦和其他基督教传教士留下了深刻印象。利玛窦采取耶稣会本土化的传教策略，学会了中文，用中文写了一篇关

---

① 英文原文来自：*Paradise Lost*, III.437—439，参见：Milton, 1993: 76.

于基督教教义的论文，即 1604 年出版的《天主实义》。这些耶稣会士认为，中国人创造了如此成熟的文明，在中国和基督教传统之间寻找相似之处是可取的，如此才能达到使中国人皈依天主教的目的。

传教士必然是比较主义者。利玛窦比较中欧文化时认为，中国文化和习俗中有"基督教的痕迹"，"中国人的生活中有很多十字架元素"（Ricci, 1953: 110, 111）。他阅读中国经典文献，从中国古代文献中找到翻译"Deus"及其他基督教概念的合适中文词，比如"天""主""上帝"等。利玛窦曾在自己的日记里写道，自己将"Deus"一词译为"天主"（Lord of Heaven），传教士们"几乎找不到更合适的词儿了"（Ricci, 1953: 154）。在他看来，中国和欧洲文明尽管在语言、文化、历史方面存在明显差异，但它们是完全可比和兼容的。他用中国古代的概念和术语讨论基督教教义，用汉语写作，将之视为完全合宜的媒介。他说，《天主实义》一书"完全从自然的理性之光得出结论，而不是基于《圣经》权威"，书中"为此引用了中国古代作家的作品，含有一些不只是装饰性的段落，这促进了其他中国图书的、爱探索的读者对此书的接受"（Ricci, 1953: 448）。在 17、18 世纪，利玛窦和其他耶稣会士描述的中国的"自然的理性之光"与欧洲的知识氛围产生了显著的共鸣。此时许多启蒙运动哲学家都在寻求将理性确立为组织社会生活的方式，以摆脱天主教会的阴影。利玛窦充满信心，将比较作为理解不同文化和传统的一种有效方式。他是东西方跨文化理解的又一先驱，为亚洲和欧洲的跨文化关系的发展做出了巨大贡献。

利玛窦和其他耶稣会传教士在中国的事业极为成功，因为他们使一些高级官员甚至皇家成员皈依了基督教。最突出的例子是徐光启（1562—1633），他是一位受洗的重要官员，教名保禄，利玛窦和他合作翻译了欧几里得（Euclid）的《几何原理》（Elements）前六卷。另外两个显耀人物是李之藻（1565—1630）和杨廷筠（1557—1627），他们与徐光启一起构成了中国天主教的三大支柱，他们的家乡——上海和杭州——也成了中国晚明时期传教士活动的中心。此时已经到了明朝末年，不久，到了 17 世纪中期，中国经历了动荡的王朝更迭，清朝取代了明朝。不过，清朝的满族皇帝顺治（1643—1661 年在位）、康熙（1661—1722 年在位）仍然友善地对待耶稣会传教士，对他们带到中国的欧洲新知识十分感兴趣。康熙皇帝对数学和几何知识很有兴致，与一些耶稣会士交善，这在基督教传教士及其在欧洲的通信人心中激起了一个充满希望的愿景。他们希望将中国转化为基督教国家，把康熙暗暗地视为另一个君士坦丁大帝。

比如，格特弗里德·威廉·莱布尼茨（Gottfried Wilhelm Leibniz, 1646—1716）就曾热情洋溢地提到康熙皇帝。"谁对这样一个帝国的君主不感到惊奇呢？"他这样写道，"然而，他在美德和智识方面受到传统的教育，以对法律的特别尊重和对智者建议的极为倚重来管理自己的臣民。他如此卓越，似乎确实适合做裁决。"（Leibniz, 1994: 48）克里斯蒂安·沃尔夫（Christian Wolff, 1679—1754）是莱布尼茨的后继人，他的态度更为热烈。他认为，康熙皇帝和中国的其他统治者是君主的范例，他们实现了柏拉图的"哲学王"理想。沃尔夫认为，为了用"自然的理性之光"统治，君王应该有哲学家的头脑。"中国人正是如此，他们的君王是哲学家，哲学家是君王。"（Wolff, 1992: 193）这些想法源于胡安·冈萨雷斯·德·门多萨（Juan González de Mendoza, 1545—1618）、李明（Louis Daniel Le Comte, 1655—1728）、让-巴普蒂斯特·杜赫德（Jean-Baptiste Du Halde, 1674—1743）等欧洲旅行者和耶稣会传教士颇具影响力的早期作品。面对 17、18 世纪欧洲学者，这些作品发挥了重要作用，它们将中国展示为一个理想政体。"中国实现了柏拉图的梦想——它是一个由哲学家统治的国度。"阿瑟·洛夫乔伊（Arthur Lovejoy）在一篇博学的重要论文里这样写道。他还引用阿塔纳修斯·基歇尔（Athanasius Kircher）的《中国图说》（*China Illustrate*, 1670）作为例证。基歇尔说，中国帝王"讲究哲理，至少是允许哲学家教诲和指导他"（Lovejoy, 1948: 104）[①]。将中国帝王塑造为哲学王这一正面形象，其重要佐证来自耶稣会士对中国科举考试的报道。学子们的学识通过科举考试得到检测，国家从这些学子中招募精英统治者。科举考试始于 7 世纪的隋朝，在 9 世纪的唐朝被规范化。它不论学子们的家庭背景、财富或社会地位，为他们提供了一个改变命运、用自己的学识效力于帝国官僚体系的机会。因此，中国的科举制度产生了两个对于欧洲现代性相当重要的概念，即贤能政治（meritocracy）和社会流动性。

---

① 基歇尔的话引自法文译文。

　　莱布尼茨比较了中国和欧洲，认为二者是相辅相成的。他在致信来华耶稣会主管克劳德·菲利普·格里马尔迪神父（Father Claude Philip Grimaldi）时曾提议，"在相隔遥远的民族之间应该进行新的知识交流"；耶稣会士给中国人带来了"欧洲知识的概貌"，他想要看到的是，"中国人关于物质（世界）的神秘知识，在繁盛了许多个世纪的中国传统里持续保存累积，现在也应该被我们所知道"。因此，莱布尼茨呼吁中欧之间的相互启迪："让我们交换礼物，用光点亮光！"（Leibniz, 1992: 64）在《中国近事》（*Novissima Sinica*, 1697/1699）的前言里，他重提这一理念："当然，我们的情况正陷入越来越严重的腐败，看来似乎需要来自中国的传教士教导我们如何运用和实践自然宗教，就像我们派人教他们启示神学一样。"（Leibniz, 1994: 51）卜正民认为，17 世纪的欧洲是带着尊重和渴望看待中国的，这一点可以在欧洲生活的很多方面清楚地看到。"因此，到 17 世纪初，在欧洲人眼中，中国人首先是政府管理艺术的大师，"阿瑟·洛夫乔伊说，"他们在此后近两百年的时间里都是同样的形象。"（Lovejoy, 1948: 103-104）很快，中国人也因其完美的道德而受到赞扬。"到了 17 世纪末，"洛夫乔伊接着说，"人们普遍认为，仅凭自然之光，中国人在政府管理艺术和伦理方面就已超过了基督教欧洲。"（Lovejoy, 1948: 105）接下来我们也会看到，这就是 17、18 世纪欧洲对于中国的主要看法。

　　但洛夫乔伊的要点是研究中国对 17 世纪末和 18 世纪欧洲审美情感和艺术实践的影响（此时早期浪漫主义已经出现），表现之一包括"对中国园林的艳羡，也有对中国建筑和其他艺术成就的认可"（Lovejoy, 1948: 101）。他认为，威廉·坦普尔爵士（Sir William Temple）是英格兰"最早和最热切的中国狂"。坦普尔爵士认为，中国人在政治理论和实践上胜过"欧洲哲人的一味沉思默想，胜过色诺芬的社会公共机构，胜过柏拉图的理想国，也胜过我们现代作家笔下的乌托邦或者大洋国"（Lovejoy, 1948: 110）[①]。坦普尔爵士在《论伊壁鸠鲁花园》（*Upon the Gardens of Epicurus*, 1685）一文中，赞扬中国美学理念注重自然，并不强加人为的秩序和整饬。对此，洛夫乔伊认为，坦普尔爵士不知道自己"正在为未来

---

① 坦普尔的引文参见：William Temple, *Upon Heroick Virtue*, 1683. 这里采用了作者自己的译文（张隆溪，2004: 98）。——校者注

的'英国花园'制定原则"（Lovejoy, 1948: 111）。18 世纪，在威廉·梅森（William Mason）、约瑟夫·艾迪生（Joseph Addison）、亚历山大·蒲柏等英国作家和诗人的笔下，自然美的观念，尤其是"如画"的理念，构成了"浪漫主义的前奏"（Lovejoy, 1948: 114）。坦普尔用的一个怪词，"sharawadgi"（疏落位置）①，大约取自中文，是一个表达中国美学理念的术语，用艾迪生的话说，是一种"天然野趣"。1750 年，霍勒斯·沃波尔（Horace Walpole）在写给朋友的信中说，他对"'sharawadgi'或者说中国式的不对称在建筑、庭院、园林中的运用都同样感兴趣"（qtd. in Lovejoy, 1948: 120）。洛夫乔伊还引用了其他很多作者，包括威廉·钱伯斯爵士（Sir William Chambers），后者是"18 世纪下半叶中国园林的主要爱好者和宣传者"（Lovejoy, 1948: 122）。从这些例子我们可以看出欧洲人品味的改变，对新古典主义审美标准的反叛，因而也构成了 18 世纪末和 19 世纪浪漫主义的前奏。洛夫乔伊称："当规律、简洁、一致和易于理解的逻辑之类的观念首次受到公开质疑时，就到了现代审美史上的一个转折点，此时，真正的美是'几何'的假设，不再是'所有人都同意的自然法则'。""在英国，无论如何，对这一假设的否定几乎贯穿了 18 世纪始终，被公认为是由于最初受到了中国艺术范例的影响。"（Lovejoy, 1948: 135）即便对中国园林的理想化最终在 18 世纪下半叶的英格兰发了馊，如洛夫乔伊所言，浪漫主义的"中国渊源"仍然是思想史上的一个重要插曲，在我们的时代，它对于我们仍然有认识和欣赏的价值。

在法国，伏尔泰对于孔子和中国文化的仰慕众所周知。他写了一个剧本《中国孤儿》（*L'Orphelin de la Chine*, 1753），该剧取材于一部 13 世纪的中国剧作。他还在《风俗论》（*Essai sur les moeurs*, 1760）里盛赞中国是"宇宙中最睿智的帝国"（Voltaire, 1963: 224）。在伏尔泰的时代，中国也许没有欧洲那么先进的机械学和物理科学，但他认为，"他们完善了道德，而这是首要的科学"（Voltaire, 1963: 68）。他极为钦佩孔子以极其清晰的方式教导美德，在"纯粹的格言中，你不会发现任何琐屑和荒谬的寓言"（Voltaire, 1963: 70）。对于伏尔泰和百科全书编纂者而言，中

---

① 此处采用了钱锺书的译法（"散乱位置"或"疏落位置"），张隆溪同意钱锺书的观点（2004: 98-99）。方重将这个怪词译为"洒落瑰奇"（1988: 26），可以参照。——校者注

国不仅是马可·波罗描述的财富的典范，也是建立在理性思维基础上的政治国家典范。"随着 1760 年伏尔泰的《风俗论》出版，对中国的仰慕达到了高峰。"阿道夫·赖希魏因（Adolf Reichwein）在他对中国与欧洲思想和艺术交流的开创性研究里这样说道（Reichwein, 1925: 79）。赖希魏因甚至认为，孔子是"18 世纪启蒙运动的保护神。只有通过他，启蒙运动才能与中国连接起来"（Reichwein, 1925: 77）。

　　如此，中国和孔子在欧洲启蒙运动时期的道德哲学和政治哲学方面都有非常积极的形象和影响。在物质生活方面，中国因其丝绸、瓷器、墙纸、漆器和其他商品等出口物资而为欧洲人所熟知，这不仅影响了欧洲人的品味，也创造了"中国风"的艺术时尚。修·昂纳（Hugh Honour）认为，这种中国风"可视为欧洲如何看待华夏的视角表达"（Honour, 1961: 7-8）。"……在易碎瓷器的精致色调中、在微微闪亮的中国丝绸的蒸腾色度中，产生了升华，"赖希魏因也说，"向 18 世纪欧洲的上流社会展示了一种幸福生活的景象，就像他们自己的乐观主义曾梦想过的那样。"（Reichwein, 1925: 25-26）中国、孔子在伏尔泰和其他启蒙运动时期哲学家笔下的正面形象，一部分是基于从中国传回的耶稣会士报道，另一部分则是基于他们自己的社会想象。中国没有占社会主导地位的教会，而其科举制度从不同家庭背景、社会地位的学子们中招募官员和统治精英。由此，中国提供了一种世俗、理性的生活样式，以及基于学识和知识的社会流动模式。这正是启蒙哲学家为欧洲设想的生活方式。此时欧洲仍处于教会的深刻影响之下，由严格的世袭贵族制度统治着社会各阶层。于是，与中国的比较成为一种方法论，被运用在 17、18 世纪许多作家的作品里，以了解一个遥远而不同的文化和社会，但更多的是对欧洲的生活进行社会批判。米歇尔·德·蒙田（Michel de Montaigne）以同样的方式，用巴西食人族来比照批判看似文明的欧洲人的腐败。孟德斯鸠（Montesquieu）借两个波斯贵族之口评判法国社会。奥利弗·哥尔德斯密斯（Oliver Goldsmith）的作品《世界公民》（*The Citizen of the World*）从一个虚构的中国哲人的局外人角度进行写作，借此嘲讽英国人。

　　利用中国进行自我批判，这在约翰·韦布（John Webb）于 1669 年出版的《历史论文——试探究中华帝国的语言为原初语言之可能性》（*An Historical Essay Endeavoring a Probability That the Language of the*

Empire of China Is the Primitive Language）一书中有一个奇异的体现。正如翁贝托·艾柯（Umberto Eco）所观察到的，很多欧洲神学家、哲学家、作家、学者都痴迷于"语言混乱的故事，以及试图通过重新发现或发明一种全人类共有的语言来弥补其不足之处的故事"（Eco, 1994: 1）。寻找完美语言的背景是《圣经》里关于语言混乱的巴别塔故事。在这个故事里，欧洲所有语言都被上帝诅咒为彼此无法理解，因而被排除在候选名单之外。这一寻求的动机是，如果人类能够重新发现上帝创造的、在人类堕落之前亚当在伊甸园说的原初（意谓第一、初级、"最早"）语言，人类可能会找到一条回归纯真和天堂的路。17世纪耶稣会传教士关于中国的报道，以及中国远远早于《圣经》年代的远古历史，使人们能够在希伯来语、古埃及语、古希腊语之外构想亚当的语言。韦布在1668年5月29日呈献给查理二世的献辞书信里写道，他写文章的目的是"促进发现那个学识的金矿，从远古时期开始，它就隐藏在原初语言或'第一种语言'中"（Webb, 1669: ii-iii）。韦布演绎出的论点以《圣经》的权威和"可信的历史"为牢固的基础，因此他的观点一定给同时代人留下了逻辑简洁有力的印象。他说：

> 《圣经》教导说，直到建造巴别塔的谋乱之前，全世界都通用同一种语言；历史又告诉我们，当初世界通用同一种语言，巴别塔尚未建造之时，中国就已有人居住。《圣经》教导说，语言混乱的判决只是加在造巴别塔的民族身上；历史又告诉我们，中国人早在这之前已经定居下来，并未到巴别塔去。不仅如此，不管参考希伯来文或是希腊文的记载，都可以知道中国人在巴别塔的混乱之前早已使用的语言文字，一直到今天他们仍然在使用。①（Webb, 1669: iii-iv）

韦布不懂中文，只能依赖耶稣会传教士的报道和当时的其他材料，以及《圣经》的权威。他认为，"中国要么是在洪水之后被诺亚建立起来的，要么是被闪的一些儿孙们在到示拿之前建立起来的"，"很有可能的是，中华帝国的语言是人类的原初语言，在洪水之前在全世界广泛使用"（Webb, 1669: 31-32, 44）。像沃尔夫和当时其他作家一样，韦布也宣称，

---

① 这里采用了作者自己的译文（张隆溪, 2009: 9）。——校者注

中国人"是上帝之城的公民"，"他们的国王可以说就是哲学家，而他们的哲学家就是国王"（Webb, 1669: 32, 93）。在当今社会，所有这些论断听起来都显得怪异和荒谬，就像一个无知的亲华者的幻梦。但是，瑞琪尔·兰姆塞（Rachel Ramsey）指出，韦布是一个保王派人士，也是一位建筑师，他由于未能获得自己所希望的测量员的职位而深感失望，他本来认为自己在王朝复辟之后完全有资格获得这个职位。因此，考虑到英国王朝复辟的政治现实，以及韦布的个人经历，我们就不难理解他的奇怪言论。他的话其实是对英国社会和那个时代幕僚制度（patronage）的一种变相的批评，也是他个人怨恨的一种表达。不仅如此，作为 17 世纪思想史上一个有趣的插曲，韦布的著作表明了"当政治上的保守派眼看自己对复辟后君主制的希望不断落空时，他们如何把中国作为一个有效手段，对时政展开一种间接的批评"。兰姆塞这么认为："也许更重要的是，像韦布的《论文》这样一部有点古怪的书可以告诉我们，在 17 世纪欧洲关于历史、政府和幕僚制度等概念的诸方面，中国曾发生过的影响甚至比大多数汉学家们所认识到的还要复杂和细致得多。"[①]（Ramsey, 2001: 503）实际上，当今西方对于中国的普遍的负面看法，更多地是由近代欧洲殖民主义和帝国主义历史的影响造成的。因此我们需要一种历史考古学家的眼光，才能重新发现 17、18 世纪欧洲人心目中中国和东方的形象。

当然，就像任何其他复杂现象一样，民族和文化的相互交流、东方和西方的碰撞总是包罗万象的。在欧洲历史上，中国的形象从来不是单一和统一的。在 17、18 世纪，莱布尼茨和伏尔泰代表了对中国和儒学更积极更热心的观点；与此同时，也有让-雅克·卢梭（Jean-Jacques Rousseau）、孟德斯鸠、弗朗索瓦·费奈隆（François Fénelon）等哲学家对中国政治体系和文化影响持怀疑和批判的看法。到了 18 世纪，已经有丹尼尔·笛福（Daniel Defoe）这样的英国作家从好战的帝国主义者视角贬低中国人。然而，总的来说，我们可以得出结论：在 17、18 世纪，中国在很大程度上以相当正面的形象衬托了欧洲；中国从伦理和政治角度提供了一个社会想象的模型，而这与启蒙运动哲学家们所希冀的相当吻

---

① 这里也采用了作者自己的译文（张隆溪, 2009: 10）。——校者注

合。他们想要建立一个基于理性而非宗教信仰的社会，为学子们提供社会流动的渠道，使他们用知识和学问，而非通过贵族血统继承的权力来参与政府治理。与欧洲相比，中国因其不同而展现出吸引力，而这一不同的形象，不管它是真实的，还是被理想化地扭曲了的，都符合了启蒙运动的社会和政治想象，从而产生了非常积极的影响。

在当今世界，中国作为一个古老的文明古国，正在重新崛起。尤其是经过改革开放，中国巨龙发生了彻底改变，经济快速发展，庞大人口的生活条件迅速改善。这成为全世界最引人瞩目的事件之一，让所有人感到震惊。同时，作为一个由共产党领导的国家，由于意识形态因素，中国的崛起被大多数欧洲人和美国人当作对西方民主体制的挑战甚至威胁。如何理解中国这样一个既古老又现代的国家和民族，在今天成了一个迷人的重要议题。因此，我们回顾早期的东西方接触，以及中国在帝国主义和殖民主义时代以前在欧洲的形象，远远不只是为了满足稽古的兴趣。此期的中国，与国民弱小愚昧、国家衰败昏沉的形象截然不同。历史不就是一面照见当下的镜子吗？它帮助我们更好地认识今天的世界，让我们本着平等和富有同情心的理解精神，本着开放的世界主义精神，重新审视一个完全不同时代的世界。我们世界的未来在很大程度上取决于这种跨文化理解和东西方关系的改善。因此，比较，特别是东西方比较，对我们今天的世界具有社会和政治意义，对未来的世界也是如此。

引用文献【Works Cited】

Brook, Timothy. *Vermeer's Hat: The Seventeenth Century and the Dawn of the Global World*. London: Bloomsbury P, 2008.

Coleridge, Samuel Taylor. "Kubla Khan: Or, A Vision in a Dream, a Fragment." *Samuel Taylor Coleridge: Selected Poetry and Prose*. Ed. Elisabeth Schneider. New York: Holt, Rinehart and Winston, 1965. 114-116.

Eco, Umberto. *The Search for the Perfect Language*. Trans. James Fentress. Oxford: Blackwell, 1994.

Honour, Hugh. *Chinoiserie: The Vision of Cathay*. New York: J. Murray, 1961.

Larner, John. *Marco Polo and the Discovery of the World*. New Haven: Yale UP, 2001.

Leibniz, Gottfried Wilhelm. "Letter to Father Grimaldi (1692)." *Moral Enlightenment: Leibniz and Wolff on China*. Ed. and trans. Julia Ching and Willard G. Oxtoby. Nettetal: Steyler Verl, 1992. 63-69.

---. "Preface to the *Novissima Sinica* (1697/1699)." *Writings on China*. Gottfried Wilhelm Leibniz. Trans. Daniel J. Cook and Henry Rosemond, Jr. Chicago: Open Court, 1994. 45-59.

Lovejoy, Arthur O. "The Chinese Origin of a Romanticism." *Essays in the History of Ideas*. Arthur O. Lovejoy. Baltimore: Johns Hopkins UP, 1948. 99-135.

Milton, John. Paradise Lost*: An Authoritative Text, Backgrounds and Sources, Criticism*. Ed. Scott Elledge. 2nd ed. New York: Norton, 1993.

Polo, Marco. *The Travels of Marco Polo*. Trans. Ronald Latham. London: Folio Society, 1968.

Pope, Alexander. *The Rape of the Lock. Selected Poetry and Prose*. Ed. Robin Sowerby. London: Routledge, 1988. 63-85.

Ramsey, Rachel. "China and the Ideal of Order." *Journal of the History of Ideas* 62.3 (2001): 483-503.

Reichwein, Adolf. *China and Europe: Intellectual and Artistic Contacts in the Eighteenth Century*. Trans. J. C. Powell. New York: Barnes & Noble, 1925.

Ricci, Matteo. *China in the Sixteenth Century: The Journal of Matthew Ricci, 1583—1610*. Trans. Louis J. Gallagher. New York: Random House, 1953.

Spinoza, Benedict de. *The Chief Works of Benedict de Spinoza*. Trans. R. H. M. Elwes. 2 vols. New York: Dover Publications, 1951.

Voltaire, François M. A. de. *Essai sur les moeurs et l'esprit des nations et sur les principaux faits de l'histoire depuis Charlemagne jusqu'à Louis XIII*. Ed. René Pomeau. Vol. 1. Paris: Garnier frères, 1963.

Webb, John. *An Historical Essay Endeavoring a Probability That the Language of the Empire of China is the Primitive Language*. London, 1669.

Wolff, Christian. "On the Philosopher King and the Ruling Philosopher (1730)." *Moral Enlightenment: Leibniz and Wolff on China*. Ed. and trans. Julia Ching and Willard G. Oxtoby. Nettetal: Steyler Verl., 1992. 187-218.

Wood, Frances. *Did Marco Polo Go to China?*. London: Secker & Warburg, 1995.

Zhang, Longxi. "The Myth of the Other." *Mighty Opposites: From Dichotomies to Differences in the Comparative Study of China*. Zhang Longxi. Stanford: Stanford UP, 1998. 19-54.

---. "Marco Polo, Chinese Cultural Identity, and an Alternative Model of East-West Encounter." *Marco Polo and the Encounter of East and West*. Ed. Suzanne Conklin Akbari and Amilcare A. Iannucci. Toronto: U of Toronto P, 2008. 280-296.

---. *From Comparison to World Literature*. Albany: State U of New York P, 2015.

方重，1988，《求学时代漫笔》，载《外语教育往事谈——教授们的回忆》，上海：上海外语教育出版社，第 18—34 页。

李耳撰，王弼注，1985，《老子道德经》，《丛书集成新编》第 19 册（共 120 册），台北：新文丰出版公司，第 170—189 页。

杨周翰，1981，《弥尔顿〈失乐园〉中的加帆车——十七世纪英国作家与知识的涉猎》，《国外文学》第 4 期，第 60—69 页。

张隆溪，2004，《〈17、18 世纪英国文学中的中国〉中译本序》，《国际汉学》第 2 期，第 93—102 页。

张隆溪，2009，《约翰·韦布的中国想象与复辟时代的英国政治》，《书城》第 3 期，第 5—10 页。

（特邀编辑：厚朴）

黑暗内心的探索：
略论欧里庇得斯对尤金·奥尼尔的影响

陆建德

内容提要： 戏剧研究界谈及古希腊悲剧对尤金·奥尼尔的影响时，通常会提到埃斯库罗斯，因为奥尼尔的《悲悼》的故事框架来自埃斯库罗斯《奥瑞斯忒亚》中的阿伽门农神话。但是奥尼尔的悲剧创作也让读者联想到欧里庇得斯，一位致力于描写生活中诸多不那么高尚、光彩的感情和冲动的古希腊剧作家，比如《美狄亚》《希波吕托斯》和《酒神的伴侣》都以刻画非理性的黑暗力量见长。奥尼尔的剧作旨在揭示人世的本来面目，即使令人不快，也绝不退缩。本文认为，奥尼尔在某些方面继承了欧里庇得斯的创作风格，并以他的代表作之一《榆树下的欲望》为范例，加以论证。古今两位杰出剧作家都不顾社会习俗的禁忌，以悲剧的语言呈现了他们对于某种植根于人的黑暗内心的欲望的深刻认识。

关键词： 欧里庇得斯；尤金·奥尼尔；影响；《榆树下的欲望》；悲剧；人性

作者简介： 陆建德，1982 年毕业于复旦大学，1990 年获英国剑桥大学博士学位后就职于中国社会科学院外国文学研究所和文学研究所，现任厦门大学比较文学与跨文化研究中心主任。著作包括《麻雀啁啾》（1996）和《破碎思想体系的残编：英美文学与思想史论稿》（2001）等，主编《艾略特文集》（五卷本，2012）和《现代化进程中的外国文学》（2015）。近年关注世界文学的翻译与中国现代文学兴起的联系以及 1894 年至 1930 年的中国文化转型。这篇论文作于 1981 年春季学期，指导教师是加拿大学者许美德（Ruth Hayhoe）教授。

Title: Exploration into the Heart of Darkness: A Study of Euripidean Influence on Eugene O'Neill

Abstract: Students of drama usually associate Aeschylus with Greek influence on Eugene O'Neill, for one of O'Neill's masterpieces, *Mourning Becomes Electra*, is based on the Agamenon myth as found in Aeschylus' *Oresteia* trilogy. However, O'Neill's tragic writings are also highly suggestive of the spirit of another Greek tragedian Euripides, whose uncompromising devotion to the task of portraying aspects of ignoble, debased and irrational life is fully shown in plays like *Medea*, *Hippolytus* and *The Bacchae*. This undaunted openness is shared by O'Neill, whose final aim is to present life not as it should be, but as it is, no matter how shocking and unpleasant it means. This paper tentatively draws a parallel between Euripides and O'Neill, and uses *Desire under the Elms*, O'Neill's most representative tragedy, to argue that the two dramatists defied the conventions and taboos of their societies by visions of some tremendous and mysterious forces immanent in human nature that would eventually shape man's destiny.

Key words: Euripides, Eugene O'Neill, influence, *Desire under the Elms*, tragedy, human nature

Author: Lu Jiande graduated from Fudan University in 1982 and received his doctoral degree at the University of Cambridge in 1990. After working for years at the Institute of Foreign Literature and the Institute of Literature in the Chinese Academy of Social Sciences (CASS), he is now Director of the Centre for Comparative Literature and Transcultural Studies at Xiamen University. His books include *"Dr. Zhivago" and Other Essays* (1996) and *Fragments of Broken Systems: Essays in Anglo-American Literature and History of Ideas* (2001). He is also the editor of *T. S. Eliot: Poems, Plays and Critical Essays* (Chinese edition, 5 vols., 2012) and *Literature in the Process of Modernization* (2 vols., 2015). In recent years he has written extensively on the genesis of modern Chinese literature and its active interaction with world literature, and also the cultural transformation that took place in China from 1894 to 1930. This paper was written for Prof. Ruth Hayhoe during the spring term in 1981 when the author was a student at Fudan. Email: lujd@cass.org.cn

I have been trying to seek the transfiguring nobility of tragedy, in as near the Greek sense as one can grasp it, in seemingly the most ignoble, debased lives.

(O'Neill, 1927: 199)

Students of drama usually associate Aeschylus with Greek Influence on Eugene O'Neill, the greatest playwright America has ever produced, for one of O'Neill's masterpieces, *Mourning Becomes Electra*, is based on the Agamemnon myth as found in Aeschylus' *Oresteia* trilogy. Yet a careful comparison between the two tragedies will undoubtedly indicate that in *Mourning* the classic situation is bodily transferred to a modern setting and details of the plot are altered to conform to the new complex of O'Neill's tragic thought. The contrast between the two endings will reveal the two dramatists' difference in *weltanschauung*: when Orestes is set free and the Eumenides are reconciled at last to a new and kindlier ruler at Athens (in *The Eumenides*), O'Neill carries his story with a greater daring to a tragic ending— Lavinia (Electra's counterpart in *Mourning*) locks herself in the family mansion, tortured by the ghosts of the past (in *The Haunted*). Imbued with the optimism of Marathon and Salamis, Aeschylus' plays are often characterized by happy endings. In *The Danaïds* Aphrodite intervenes like Athena in *The Eumenides* for acquittal; in *Prometheus*, Zeus, first cruel and mean, at last mellows into benign wisdom. This belief in divine justice cannot be found in plays by O'Neill.

To bring this point for ponderation is not to discredit the belief that Aeschylean influence on O'Neill is obvious. That influence is undeniable so far as literary form and subject-matter are concerned. But the study of literary indebtedness is much more delicate and complex. We cannot focus our attention exclusively on the external and the apparent as the 18th-century classicists, who missed the genuine spirit of classical literature. The working of the literary creations of a great writer is a silent and subtle thing, and with the passing of years it becomes an imperceptible part in the intellectual tradition of the world. Influence on content, thought and general world outlook is often far more pervasive and persistent than outward influence, but the study of the influence of this nature demands from students of literature keener attention and the willingness to run the risk of making "niggardly" or "pettifogging" comparison.[1]

With this aim in mind, when we dig into O'Neill's tragic thought as made manifest in his dramas, we will find his tragic thought very suggestive of the spirit of another great Greek tragedian, Euripides. Unfortunately, Euripidean influence on O'Neill is still a lacuna in the study of modern drama.[2]

In a comparison between Euripides' writing and his own, "Sophocles said that he drew men as they ought to be; Euripides, as they are" (Aristotle, 1895: 1460b). The validity of this statement can be proved by their works. In Euripides there was always uncompromising devotion to the task he set himself: to present in terms of tragedy what he saw and felt in human life.[3] His portrayal of "ignoble and debased life" only shows his unblinking courage in facing stark reality. This attitude toward dramatic writing is shared by, or has made a notable impact on, Eugene O'Neill, whose final aim is also to present life not as it should be, but as it is, no matter how shocking and unpleasant it means. "I would never be influenced by any consideration but one: 'Is it the truth as I know it—or better still, feel it?'" (Heiney and Downs, 1973: 199)

It is just this fundamental attitude, this unmistakably urgent quality of sincerity that makes the two tragedians alike in rejecting the ideals of the societies into which they have been, in defying the conventions and taboos of their age, and especially in expressing by means of tragic language their visions of some tremendous and mysterious forces immanent in human nature that shape man's destiny. These phenomena might be a case of chance

---

[1] Professor Ruth Hayhoe's comment: a delicate and subtle argument, a very promising beginning!

[2] In all the materials that I have access to, no comparison between Euripides and O'Neill has been made, or even mentioned.

[3] Use of *deus ex machina* only explains that he was aware of certain random force that did exist in the order of the world.

parallelism, but when O'Neill's familiarity with Greek tragedy and the fact that a writer's thought can be unconsciously influenced are taken into consideration, the study of O'Neill's indebtedness to Euripides must be indispensable to understanding and evaluating some of his tragedies as well as his tragic ideals.

A survey and analysis of one of O'Neill's most representative tragedy *Desire under the Elms* (1924) will establish the comparison that we are considering. As our main attention is confined to studying literary influence on content and thought, discussions about the anatomy of character and structure, about contrivance of stage-mechanism are outside the scope of this paper.

With New England in the period around 1850 as its background, the play opens on the farm of Ephraim Cabot, a mean and avaricious materialist but also a hard-working, God-fearing patriarch. In the first act Cabot has just left to bring home a third wife, the young Abbie Putnam. Cabot's two elder sons, despairing of ever inheriting the farm, depart for joining the Californian gold rush. Abbie instantly proves to be as possessive as her old husband. The second act describes the increasing hatred of Abbie for Cabot and her devouring desire for the young Eben, a psychologically complex personality, son of Cabot's gentle second wife. In her "seduction" of him there lies the intention to produce an heir who will inherit the farm for her. After the birth of the child, a raucous celebration party is held in the third act. Cabot now signs over the inheritance to the child. Eben suddenly gets the idea that he has been most wickedly utilized. He denounces Abbie, but Abbie has already inadvertently fallen in love with him. At the mercy of her passion, Abbie smothers the infant as proof of her devotion. In his disbelief in Abbie's motive, Eben informs the sheriff of the crime. But he finally realizes he cannot live without Abbie. When the police come he admits complicity in the crime and the two culprits are led to their punishment. Old Cabot is left alone on his stony farm, still in the conviction that "God's hard an' lonesome" (Act III, scene iv).

When the play was first staged in 1924, the hatred and vengeance of the sons, the incest of mother and son and the infanticide incurred harsh criticism from conservative critics and theatre-goers. Fred Niblo Jr. passed into verdict that "*Desire* is also gruesome to the *n*th degree… it is impossible for anyone who cares anything about the theatre at all to approve it" (Niblo, 1924). The play was banned in Britain and Boston—the citadel of American "highbrow" intellectuals. Later in Los Angles the entire cast of the road company was even arrested, tried on the charge of obscenity. But gradually the play won recognition. No matter how "revolting" it might be, the elemental violence of *Desire* is reminiscent of the old Greek myths.[1] In its total honesty of emotion, in its challenge to the traditional sense of decency, the play is a resonant echo of an ancient voice, the voice of Euripides.

Superficially or accidentally the play resembles the Theseus-Hippolytus-Phaedra story as it is found in Euripides' *Hippolytus*. But similarity in dramatic pattern is not our major concern. The greatness of *Desire* is not what its rational framework can suggest.

When the play begins Abbie is highly "rational," she marries Cabot with a hard determination to take over the farm. As soon as she joins the family, she makes her aggressiveness felt by calling everything "my" or "mine." In Eben that possessive proclivity is by no means less obvious. His shrewdness and business acumen are fully exposed when he steals his father's money to buy the inheritance of his two elder brothers. But in both Abbie and Eben there are "a fierce repressed vitality" and "the same unsettled, untamed desperate quality," which are symbolically suppressed by the two enormous elms on Cabot's farm, two humane elms "with an aspect of crushing, jealous absorption." The play develops with their mutual hatred, their ambivalence and at last their love. In the process of change in the relation between the two, the vaporization of their rationality takes place. Toward the end of the tragedy, that "repressed quality," an unknown element in man that has been cabined

---

[1] Professor Ruth Hayhoe's comment: true.

in the nut-shell of New England Puritanism explodes with the most destructive irrational violence. When Abbie is "seducing" Eben, she is also ready to do anything for him, potentially a Medea:

> I'll sin fur ye! I'll die fur ye! (Act II, scene iii)

Here we can hardly distinguish whether she is doing it on purpose, or simply at the dictation of that nameless lord of the dark heart.

> It's agin nature, Eben. Ye been fightin' yer nature ever since the day I come—tryin' t' tell yourself I hain't purty t' ye... Hain't the sun strong an' hot? Ye kin feel it burnin' into the earth—nature—makin' thin's grow—bigger 'n' bigger—burnin' inside ye—makin' ye want t' grow—into somethin' else—till ye're jined with it—an' it's your'n—but it owns ye, too—an' makes ye grow bigger—like a tree—like them elums... Nature'll beat ye, Eben. Ye might's well own up t' it fust's last. (Act II, scene i)

What is "nature" here? It might be sweeping desire, but it is far above sexual implications: it is also the sun and the earth. Abbie herself is not certain, yet her assertion is short and simple, a typical Dionysiac one: "Nature'll beat ye, Eben" (Act II, scene i). Driven by this force, mother and son rush toward their incest and infanticide. When at the end they "stand looking up raptly in attitudes strangely aloof and devout," they become actually in a tragic exaltation the impersonation of what the modern Bacchant D. H. Lawrence called:

> The dark potency of blood acts; ...the genuine dark sensual orgasms, which do... obliterate the mind and the spiritual consciousness, plunge them in a suffocating flood of darkness. (1923: 124)

Old Cabot is in the grip of another force, seemingly antipodal to that of the two perpetrators of incest, but essentially also irrational. That force is expressed in his almost fanatic faith in a puritan God, a faith articulated in his reasonless commitment to his stony land. When there is gorgeous prospect in the West he still sticks to his own farm and preaches:

> God's in the stones! Build my church on a rock—out o' stones and I'll be
> in them! …I'd made thin's grow out of nothin'—like the will o' God, like
> the servant o' His hand. (Act II, scene ii)

And those who want to make quick money are contemptible to him:

> God's hard, not easy! Mebbe they's easy gold in the West, but it hain't
> God's gold. It hain't fur me. I kin hear His voice warnin' me agen t' be
> hard…" (Act III, scene iv)

His sense of possession and property seems to transcend vulgar materialism
in that it is enveloped in an irrationally religious atmosphere.

Thus we see it is under the control of the terrible and also great passions
that Abbie and Eben, and Old Cabot fight blindly toward their tragic finality
on different planes and in different directions.

Both Aeschylus and Sophocles had a glimpse of certain blind, arbitrary
forces in the world, yet they recognized them as external realities instead of
intrinsic quality of human identity. The awareness of the power of the
irrational, which shape man's destiny and at the same time take deep roots in
man's heart as is shown in *Desire*, had its articulate expression in Euripidean
plays, particularly in *Medea, Hippolytus* and *The Bacchae.*[①] Even a rough
analysis of the plays will suffice our present comparative need.

The Aristotelian theory of tragic character cannot help us if we are to
find out the hamartia in Medea. In the play Euripides did not depict her as a
good but betrayed passionate wife, who hurls herself into horror only when
stung by deadly ingratitude. Euripides was too sober to ignore that in human
beings there are non-rational emotions which may run wild, blotting out our

---

① In *Andromache, Hecuba* and some other plays, there are also descriptions of the
primitive fierceness of human passions.

reason and bringing disastrous results.① So when Medea blazes her way through life leaving behind her ruin and death, Euripides makes her the tragic flaw of mankind at large, the embodiment of terrific vindictiveness and of the universal truth that:

> But passion overmastereth sober thought;
> And this is cause of direst ills to men.②

The goddess of love in *Hippolytus*, though capricious and irresponsible, is also a fundamental and familiar element that is organic in the natural order of conditions in which man lives. Wanton Aphrodite is not something that can be vanquished by rationality which poor Phaedra ironically is in possession of. In Abbie's terminology she is just "nature" that demands obedience. The Greek tradition, the Greek aristocratic tradition in particular, stressed the value of moderation and self-control (or *sophrosyne*, which cramps spontaneity). The Nurse in *Hippolytus* is the spokesperson of this thought:

> I praise, past all that seeks excess,
> The middle way—
> And the wise will witness what I say. (ll. 263—265)③

The old nurse contrived to worm the secret from her (her love to Hippolytus) & treacherously, under an oath of secrecy, told it to Hippolytus. Because the nurse is rather an object of ridicule in all her worldly wisdom and cunning, Euripides' progressiveness in thinking as compared with his contemporaries is obvious. He has seen in our human situation an invisible world in which man's rationality does not work. And that world is the very Olympian world

---

① This point is well-treated in E. R. Dodds' "Euripides the Irrationalist."
② Trans. Way (Line number is not available in *Medea* in *Greek Literature in Translation*).
③ Trans. F. L. Lucas. Wodhull's translation seems more illustrative:
　　A foe to all excess, I rather praise
　　This sentence, "Not too much of anything;"
　　And in my judgement will the wise concur.

as painted by Artemis, in that chaotic world "what these deities represent, instinctive passions, is independent of reason and morality" (Kitto, 1939: 206-207).

The dominant thought in *Medea* and *Hippolytus* is carried further in Euripides' last masterpiece, *The Bacchae*. Here the god of wine is Nature itself—including human nature—in its blind instincts and impulses and intoxications and destruction. Powers of deep-lying desires in the heart of human darkness are granted full scope. These violent elements have strange power in its own right to make life beautifully fantastic as well as terrible. We cannot but accept them and sit amazed before their presence by the grandeur and meanness of our deeds. Like Hippolytus, Pentheus is honest, but his hubris, his rationalistic infatuation and his ignorance of the irrational side of human nature make him march unconsciously towards the doom that awaits him. The chorus sings:

> Fool, that wars with wanton spirit
> And lawless anger against the rite
> Of Thy mother and of Thee!
> O Dionysus, he shall merit
> Death, for his blinded heart that fights
> Invincibility. (ll. 995—1000)[1]

The idea underlying *Medea, Hippolytus* and *The Bacchae* can be summed up as Euripides' affirmation of the existence of some irrational and invincible powers personified in Medea, Aphrodite and Dionysus that formulate inexplicable but inexorable human law. This tragic thought has been explicitly reflected in O'Neill's plays.[2]

This notion needs further explanation because some might contradict it by harping on Euripides' attack on religion. They hold that these immoral

---

① Trans. F. L. Lucas.

② Not only in *Desire*, but also in *The Great God Brown, Long Day's Journey into Night*, etc.

Olympian immortals are repulsive to him, contrary to his aspirations, so he deliberately portrays gods in an unfavorable light in order to destroy belief in them, and that many of his plays are pieces of atheistic propaganda, merely impotent protests against the absolute tyranny of Olympian dictatorship that is sheerly outside mankind.

It is true that gods in Euripidean plays are often jealous and lustful, moved by meanest motives.[①] But reading too much in the appearance of these gods is dangerous. It will give rise to the opinion that absolute pre-determination is the keynote in Euripidean plays. If forces that are external to human affairs directly determine human actions and tragedy, the inevitable conclusion will be that the freedom of human beings is severely, or totally, restricted by divine control. Here a troublesome question will arise: if man is merely a helpless puppet manipulated by outsides forces, can he have enough status to achieve tragic significance?[②] Why should Euripides delineate with profound psychological insight the inner conflict of his tragic figures (for instance Medea and Phaedra)? Trivial characters sunk in dreary hopelessness claim no presence in Euripidean dramatic writings.

Besides, people are so influenced by the Hebrew concept of religion that the word "god" greets our eyes with very strong Christian connotations. The word "god" in Greek, θεός (theos), has much richer implications. Primarily it means something eternal, so it can be freely applied to all that is greater than man because it lasts forever.[③] Goodness therefore does not belong to the divinities by definition. Thus in Euripidean plays gods are often forces within the heart of man which are also greater than the individual because it is eternal, shared by all individuals. Ambition, equality, struggle, hope, sorrow as well as many other dark intrinsic forces in man are all called

---

① In *Ion* Apollo is almost a lawless ravisher, utterly selfish and ready to lie.

② Even in Sophocles' *Oedipus Rex,* Oedipus' struggle against his fate can be regarded as the tragic process of gaining self-knowledge.

③ Professor Ruth Hayhoe's comment: fine.

"gods."[1] So, when Euripides wrote:

> we are slaves of gods, whatever gods may be. (*Orestes*, l. 418)[2]

he did not mean we are slaves of exclusively Olympian gods. Hecuba knows fully well the subtlety of the issue when addressing the lord of the world:

> Sustainer of the earth, o'er earth enthroned,
> Whoever thou art, so dim to our conjecture—
> Zeus, or the Law of Nature, or Man's own Mind,[3]
> I cry to thee! (*The Trojan Women*, ll. 884—887)[4]

More admirable is that Euripides not only gave many possible interpretations to the word "gods," but also depicted gods—in our context they are human passions: love, vindictiveness or blissful Dionysiac madness—as they are, not as they ought to be. It is the human tragic drama that is reinforced or universalized by the appearance of these gods in anthropomorphized form, not the other way round.

When we reach this point, a comparison with O'Neill becomes easier. It will throw fresh light on the topic we have been discussing if we place O'Neill's theory of tragedy in juxtaposition with Euripides' understanding and description of "gods."

Greek tragedy, born of primitive wonder & desire, has its religion, or religious emotion, about it: that it is always concerned with man's relation to great world forces (in Euripides, they can be intrinsic in us), the whole permeating atmosphere is always that of religion.[5] O'Neill belonged to a generation in rebellion against the artificialities of a society that glorified

---

① This issue is exhaustively and convincingly explored by G. M. A. Grube (1941: 41-62).
② Trans. Gilbert Murray.
③ Professor Ruth Hayhoe's comment: a well-chosen quote.
④ Trans. F. L. Lucas.
⑤ I owe this point to Gilbert Murray's "Greek and English Tragedy."

material success, and against the romantic conventions of a theatre dedicated to entertaining rather than troubling. He wanted to write something deeper and bigger. His reading of Greek tragedy strengthened his determination to restore that great Greek tradition. At the beginning of his literary career he stated:

> Most modern plays are concerned with the relation between man and man, but that does not interest me at all. I am interested only in the relation between man and God. (Krutch, 1932: xvii)

Yet O'Neill is clearheaded enough to know that in our modern world there was no "ready" God for our surviving primitive religious instinct. Though he is convinced that a playwright must dig at the roots of the sickness of his day to give a new God that will render our life meaning and death comfort.[①] Thus life's feel and colour and nuance did not attract his attention, and the "great inscrutable forces are his interest" (Trilling, 1936: 177).

When the crux of the problem comes—what is that "God," or the "great inscrutable forces" or the relation between the two, O'Neill (like Euripides) can offer no answer. Under these complex influences, O'Neill in a somewhat not very consistent manner identified, or at least blurred the distinction between, the amoral, irrational dark forces with God:

> I'm always acutely conscious of the Force behind (Fate, God, our biological past creating our present, whatever one calls it—Mystery certainly) and of the one eternal tragedy of Man in his glorious, self-destructive struggle to make the Force express him... this is the only subject worth writing about. (O'Neill, 1927: 199)

Again the two great tragedians meet: neither of them are certain of the nature of those forces of God (or gods).[②] But both of them, Euripides the classical modern mind and O'Neill the modern classical mind, in their literary

---

① O'Neill expressed this idea in a letter to G. J. Nathan regarding Dynamo, May 7, 1923 (qtd. in Krutch, 1932: xvii).

② Professor Ruth Hayhoe's comment: good.

creations tried with the same single-minded tenacity to explore that terra incognita, the dark nature of these eternities. This spirit of exploration may very properly account for their broad mind and deep insight as shown in their compassionate love for and sympathetic delineation of human beings in the grip of overpowering irrational forces.

F. L. Lucas once observed:

> In the ocean of modern literature, it becomes of course more impossible than ever to trace with any completeness this diffusion of ideas often "indistinct as water is in water." (1928: 153)

This remark illustrates very well our difficulty in tracing Euripides' influence on O'Neil's tragic thought. Direct indebtedness O'Neill owes to Euripides still stands in need of more concrete details and higher scholastic analysis. But in his passion for truth—even the dark truth concerning irrational forces in human soul and in the order of our universe as shown in *Desire under the Elms*, O'Neill is no doubt the greatest and closest American counterpart of Euripides in our modern playhouse. In his pioneering exploration into the heart of human darkness, Euripides was distrusted, disliked, and became a constant butt for attacks from "the aristocracy of philologists, led by the buffoon Aristophanes."[1] Compared with his prophet's fate, it is a consoling fact that though human heart remains dark, the modern world, except a few prig critics, did not grudge O'Neill literary recognition and a Nobel Prize (in 1936) when he carried on that exploration.[2]

Works Cited and Consulted

Aristotle. *The Poetics of Aristotle*. Trans. S. H. Butcher. London: Macmillan and

---

[1] Goethe, *Diary*, Nov. 22, 1831 (qtd. in Murray, 1913: 10).

[2] Professor Ruth Hayhoe's comment: A+ Wonderful. I have been totally swept along by your argument and feel... uplifted and at the same time strangely and deeply moved by your combination of genuine scholarship and a deep sense of humanity and its griefs.

Co., 1895.

Aycock, W. M., and T. M. Klein, eds. *Classical Mythology in 20th Century Thoughts and Literature*. Lubbock: Texas Tech Press, 1980.

Baldry, H. C. *Greek Literature for the Modern Reader*. London: Cambridge UP, 1959.

Bogard, Travis. *Contour in Time: The Plays of Eugene O'Neill*. New York: Oxford UP, 1972.

Bowra, M. *Ancient Greek Literature*. London: Oxford UP, 1933.

Carpenter, F. I. *Eugene O'Neill*. Boston: Twayne Publishers, 1979.

Dodds, E. R. "Euripides the Irrationalist." *The Classical Review* 43.3 (1929): 97-104.

Downer, A. S. *Fifty Years of American Drama 1900—1950*. Chicago: Henry Regnery Company, 1951.

Euripides. *The Plays of Euripides in Two Volumes*. London: J. M. Dent & Sons Ltd., 1947.

Falk, D. V. *Eugene O'Neill and the Tragic Tension*. New Brunswick: Rutgers UP, 1958.

Fleischmann, W. B. *Encyclopedia of World Literature in the 20th Century*. New York: Frederick Ungar Publishing Co., 1971.

Floyd, Virginia, ed. *Eugene O'Neill: A Worldview*. New York: Frederick Ungar Publishing Co., 1979.

Gassner, John, ed. *O'Neill: A Collection of Critical Essays*. Englewood Cliffs, NJ: Prentice-Hall Inc., 1964.

Gould, Jean. *Modern American Playwrights*. New York: Dodd, Mead & Company, 1966.

Grube, G. M. A. *The Drama of Euripides*. London: Methuen & Co. Ltd., 1941.

Hamilton, E. *The Greek Way*. New York: W. W. Norton & Company, Inc., 1942.

Heiney, Donald, and L. H. Downs. *Recent American Literature to 1930*. New York: Barron's Educational Series, Inc., 1973.

Howe, G., and G. A. Harrer, eds. *Greek Literature in Translation*. New York: Harper & Brothers, 1924.

Kitto, H. D. F. *Greek Tragedy*. London: Methuen & Co. Ltd., 1939.

Krutch, J. W. "Introduction." *Nine Plays by Eugene O'Neill*. New York: Liveright, Inc., 1932. xi-xxii.

Lawrence, D. H. "Nathaniel Hawthorne and *The Scarlet Letter*." *Studies in Classic American Literature*. New York: Thomas Seltzer, 1923. 121-147.

Lucas, F. L. *Euripides and His Influence*. New York: Longmans, Green & Co., 1928.

---. *Greek Drama for Everyman*. London: J. M. Dent & Sons Ltd., 1954.

McCollom, W. G. *Tragedy*. New York: The Macmillan Company, 1957.

Melchinger, S. *Euripides*. Trans. Samuel R. Rosenbaum. New York: Frederick Ungar Publishing Co., 1973.

Miller, J. Y., ed. *Playwright's Progress: O'Neill and the Critics*. Chicago: Scott, Foresman & Company, 1965.

Murray, Gilbert. "Greek and English Tragedy." *English Literature and the Classics*. Ed. G. S. Gordon. Oxford: Clarendon Press, 1912. 7-24.

---. *Euripides and His Age*. New York: Henry Holt & Company, 1913.

Niblo, Fred, Jr. "New O'Neill's Play Sinks to Depths." *New York Morning Telegraph* Nov. 12, 1924.

O'Neill, Eugene. "Letter to A. H. Quinn." *A History of the American Drama: From the Civil War to the Present Day*. Vol. 2. A. H. Quinn. New York: Harper & Brothers, 1927. 199.

---. *Nine Plays by Eugene O'Neill*. New York: Liveright, Inc., 1932.

---. *The Plays of Eugene O'Neill*. New York: Random House, 1954.

---. *Long Day's Journey into Night*. New Haven: Yale UP, 1977.

Quinn, A. H. *A History of the American Drama: From the Civil War to the Present Day*. Vol. 2. New York: Harper & Brothers, 1927.

Sinclair, T. A. *A History of Classical Greek Literature: From Homer to Aristotle*. New York: The MacMillan Company, 1935.

Stallknecht, P., and H. Frenz, eds. *Comparative Literature: Method and Perspective*. Carbondale: Southern Illinois UP, 1973.

Thomson, J. A. K. *The Classical Background of English Literature*. London: George Allen & Unwin Ltd., 1950.

Trilling, Lionel. "Eugene O'Neill." *The New Republic* 88 (1936): 176-179.

龙文佩，1980，《尤金·奥尼尔和他的剧作》，《外国文学》（复旦大学外国文
学研究室编）第 1 期，第 1—23 页。

罗念生译，1958，《欧里庇得斯悲剧二种》，北京：人民文学出版社。

袁鹤年，1981，《〈榆树下的欲望〉和奥尼尔的悲剧思想》，《外国文学》（北
京外国语学院外国文学编辑部编）第 4 期，第 29—33 页。

朱虹，1980，《尤金·奥尼尔》，载中国社会科学院外国文学研究所编《外
国文学研究集刊（第 2 辑）》，北京：中国社会科学出版社，第 329—
350 页。

（责任编辑：王瑞雪、郝田虎）

中世纪研究

Medieval Studies

地狱里的工作：记忆术与萨里的查尔顿的壁画《末日审判》对行业的描绘

劳拉·伊赛比·德·菲立比斯

内容提要： 收藏于萨里的查尔顿的壁画《末日审判》是 12 世纪的作品，其特别之处在于描绘了制造商和商人在地狱的情景。通过分析涂鸦、罗马墓碑、后期的意大利壁画等其他艺术样本，本文认为，查尔顿的末日描绘可以被当作旨在激发回忆和创造力的记忆术工具。

关键词： 查尔顿；末日审判；中世纪壁画；修辞；记忆术；罗马墓碑；对行业的描绘

作者简介： 劳拉·伊赛比·德·菲立比斯是西安外国语大学欧洲学院教授。2004 年在纽约大学获得英语专业博士学位，是富布莱特奖学金获得者。曾在纽约大学、维罗纳大学、维罗纳美术学院担任兼职教授。其研究领域为：中世纪与文艺复兴文化、记忆术、视觉及语言建构、修辞学。曾发表多篇论文和翻译作品，其中包括主编《独辟蹊径：向玛丽·卡拉瑟斯致敬的中世纪修辞学研究》，该书是诺丁汉中世纪研究系列第 56 辑（Brepols, 2012）。

Title: A Hell of a Job: Mnemotechnics and the Depiction of Trades in the Last Judgment at Chaldon, Surrey

Abstract: The twelfth-century Last Judgment at Chaldon, Surrey, is unique because it includes a depiction of manufacturers and tradespeople in Hell. Through the analysis of other artistic specimens including graffiti, Roman tombstones, and later Italian wall paintings I suggest that the Chaldon Doom could be used as a mnemotechnical inventive tool meant to stimulate reminiscence and creativity.

Key words: Chaldon, last judgment, medieval wall paintings, rhetoric, mnemotechnics, Roman tombstones, depiction of trades

Author: Laura Iseppi De Filippis is a Professor at the School of European Studies, Xi'an International Studies University. She holds a Ph.D. in English from New York University (2004). She is the recipient of a Fulbright Scholarship and has previously taught as Adjunct Professor at NYU, Università di Verona, Accademia di Belle Arti di Verona. Her research interests include Medieval and Renaissance cultures, mnemotechnics, visual and verbal constructs, rhetoric. Her publications include numerous essays and translations, among which the editing of *Inventing a Path: Studies in Medieval Rhetoric in Honour of Mary Carruthers*, Nottingham Medieval Studies 56 (Brepols, 2012). Email: li203@nyu.edu.

For the carpenter with his chisel [life] is utterly vile

covering the roof in a chamber, measuring ten cubits by six […].

All the work on it is done,

but the food given for it

could not stretch to his children.

Teaching of Khety ("Satire of Trades"), 13th century BCE[1]

I knew a brother myself […] who resided in a noble monastery, but lived himself ignobly. He was frequently reproved by the brethren and elders of the place, and admonished to adopt a more regular life; and though he would not give ear to them, he was long patiently borne with by them, on account of his usefulness in temporal works, for he was an excellent carpenter.

Bede, *Historia Ecclesiastica Gentis Anglorum*, 8th century CE[2]

---

[1] Papyrus Sallier II, column VI, lines 5—8, 19th dynasty, British Museum (transliteration and translation from https://www.ucl.ac.uk/museums-static/digitalegypt/literature/satiretransl.html, accessed 10 March 2021).

[2] Book V, ch. 14: "*Novi autem ipse fratrem […] positum in monasterio nobili, sed ipsum ignobiliter viventem. Corripiebatur quidem sedulo a fratribus ac majoribus loci, atque ad castigatiorem vitam converti admonebatur; et quamvis eos audire noluisset, tolerabatur tamen ab eis longanimiter ob necessitatem operum ipsius exteriorum; erat enim fabrili arte singularis*" (English translation from http://www.heroofcamelot.com/docs/Bede-Ecclesiastical-History.pdf, accessed 10 March 2021).

On the walls of many British medieval churches, wall paintings and graffiti are far from uncommon. Recent surveys have shown the wealth of materials available and some of the findings are truly remarkable. Apart from the classic painted stories depicting the saints, the life of Jesus, Dooms, geometrical patterns and arboreal decorations, common graffiti range from crosses to compass-drawn designs, charms, curses, vessels and animals. Among them, the tracings of shoe soles stand out as rather puzzling. There are many questions as to their meaning and symbolic role, especially when they appear in significant numbers, such as in the cloister of Canterbury Cathedral. Their presence in this particular site has led to hypothesizing that shoe outlines, like hand tracings with which they are often associated, might be related to the notion of pilgrimage, which would involve leaving a trace of one's passage, or to the practice of donating *ex-votos* as thanksgiving for a safe journey. Their appearance in different parts of churches' precincts have spurred suppositions that they might have a symbolic link to weddings or to apotropaic practices.[①] The base of the baptismal font in Morston church (Norfolk) is, for instance, "covered in several dozens of inscribed outlines of shoes" (Champion, 2012: 115) which continued to be carved over centuries, possibly in order to revive this symbol's magical power to shield from evil.

Two undated graffiti versions of the typically medieval Poulaine shoe[②]

---

① According to Gilchrist (2013: 94) and Champion (2014: 247), it seems that brides during the ceremony "were presented with shoes, or their fathers presented a shoe to the groom." While also visible on "early bridges, gravestones and funerary monuments," shoe outlines often decorate porches, towers and chancel arches like at St. Andrew's in Coleby, St. Catherine's in Ludham, All Saints' in Litcham, St. Mary's in Troston. For an overview of the corpus of graffiti in the British Isles see Champion, 2015.

② According to the Hampshire History website (https://www.hampshire-history.com/medieval-shoes-in-selborne/, accessed 10 March 2021) "The pointed toe shoe was popular across Europe from the twelfth to the fifteenth centuries. As with all fashions, it became exaggerated in its form and its popularity waxed and waned. The higher the status of the person, the longer the toe. Women and men both wore the shoe but the men shoe had the longer toe. [...] The toe was kept rigid by stuffing it with packing. The Museum of London has examples of shoes stuffed with moss."

(Figures 1 and 2) are particularly striking and suggest an additional interpretative line.

Figure 1　Two Poulaine shoe outlines next to a chalice. Graffito. Church of St. Mary,
Selborne, Hampshire. Fifteenth century. Photo by Helen Banham. Reproduced with
permission.

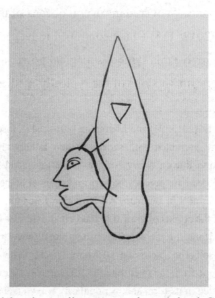

Figure 2　A Poulaine shoe outline next to a demon's head. Graffito. Church of
St. Mary, Troston, Suffolk. Fifteenth century. Pen drawing reproduction
by Rolando De Filippis. Reproduced with permission.

Figure 1 presents two shoe outlines—one of them realistically showing the cross-stitching of the sole[①]—scratched next to a chalice at St. Mary's in Selborne, Hampshire, while Figure 2, representing a shoe tracing with a faint superimposition of a demon's head, is incised on the walls of St. Mary's in Troston, Suffolk—about one hundred and fifty miles away. The odd juxtaposition of a shoe sole with another object—chalice and demon—is noteworthy not only because it appears in two instances some distance from each other but also because of the simple directness of the representation. Both images seem to stem from an impromptu wish to fix in the stone a thought, a symbolic association which must have been, if not self-evident, at least intelligible to those who would have seen them at the time when these rough outlines were etched. The fact that these graffiti do not seem to be the work of skilled artists and that they clearly do not belong to a carefully planned decorative scheme adds to their uncanniness and, possibly, to their meanings as especially evocative *imagines*. If conceived as apotropaic symbols these drawings might simply reaffirm a protective role in warding off evil, as has been speculated. I wonder, though, whether they might also have a larger and more complex role as rhetorically charged icons. Their link to the profession of shoemakers situates them in a chain of associations in which economic and religious matters are presented in an abbreviated, condensed form that might have served a number of rhetorical purposes. After all, professional guilds were a powerful force in late medieval Britain, and their preeminence was felt in both civic and religious practices. Since shoemakers—*cordewaneres* or *corvisars* in Middle English—were tasked with the representation of Judas-related moments in the fifteenth-century Chester and York mystery cycles, the graffiti could also represent a latent cultural link between

---

① See https://www.hampshire-history.com/medieval-shoes-in-selborne/ (accessed 10 March 2021). For an example of cross stitching on a real shoe sole see an item from the Museum of London collections at https://collections.museumoflondon.org.uk/online/object/30541.html (accessed 10 March 2021).

the profession and the notion of betrayal,① or its opposite, loyalty. Is it possible that these coarse graffiti served as extempore reminders to traders and manufacturers of the possible damning consequences of cheating their customers? Or, on the contrary, of the sacredness of honest trade? In other words, can the association of a trading and manufacturing symbol with a chalice and a demon's head, such as we find sketched on the walls of two English parish churches, also have a mnemonic value?

A striking, unique late twelfth-century Last Judgment visible on the west wall of the parish church dedicated to SS. Peter and Paul in Chaldon, Surrey (Figure 3), in which references to manufacturing and trades instead

Figure 3　Last Judgment. Wall painting. Church of SS. Peter and Paul, Chaldon, Surrey. End of the twelfth century. Photo by the author.

---

① The Corvisars were in charge of Play 14 "The Coming of Christ to Jerusalem" in the Chester cycle in which "Judas is put up to betray Jesus by the Jerish priests after causing comic havoc in the temple by throwing the goods (possibly shoes) of a pair of merchants about" (http://chester.shoutwiki.com/wiki/Chester_Mystery_Plays#14-_The_Coming_ of_Christ_to_Jerusalem_.28Corvisars.29, accessed 10 March 2021), while in the York cycle the Cordewaneres set up Play 28 "The Agony and Betrayal" (https:// d.lib.rochester. edu/teams/text/davidson-play-28-the-agony-and-betrayal, accessed 10 March 2021). According to The Worshipful Company of Cordwainers' website "[t]he Company's roots date back to 1272, and the first Charter in 1439 licensed Cordwainers to control the shoe trade within the City of London" (http://cordwainers.org/, accessed 10 March 2021).

of crowns and tiaras are visible among the rungs of the damned might serve to underscore this connection and to shed light on the iconographic origins and purpose of the image.

The Last Judgment at Chaldon, found and uncovered in 1870, is a large mural of 17ft × 11ft. In it, yellowish silhouettes against a rust-coloured background vaguely recall the colour palette and stylistic traits of the wall paintings belonging to the so-called Lewes group in proximate Sussex.[①] It is divided spatially into two registers and four quadrants. The lower tier represents Hell and includes several devils tormenting the damned souls, while the upper level symbolizes Purgatory/Heaven, as made clear by the cross-holding Christ in the top central roundel and by the presence of angels counterbalancing the demons shown below. All of the figures in the mural are painted with stylized or no features, which resemble some of the Romanesque traits with which Last Judgment characters are depicted in the coeval Winchester Psalter (MS BL Cotton Nero C IV, mid twelfth century).[②] The static frontal postures and elegant, pleated drapery of the angels' vestments in the upper tier also appear thoroughly Romanesque. The souls are portrayed in an almost gravity-free environment, climbing on and falling off the central ladder that clearly serves

---

① See Baker, 1942: 1-44, on the stylistic common traits of the decorative schemes "which exist or are known to have existed" in the churches of Clayton, Hardham, Plumpton and Westmerton not far from the Cluniac Priory of Lewes. On the parallelisms with the Chaldon Doom, see Johnston, 1901: 72: "[The West wall of the Hardham church] is the worst preserved of all. Only the upper tier remains and it has been half-destroyed by the insertion of [a] large window. The subject is 'The Torments of Hell', apparently. Large figures of demons are shown hacking the arms and legs of lost souls [...]. The demons are grotesquely ugly and bear some resemblance to those in the famous twelfth-century painting at Chaldon—also on a West wall. The figures are of flesh-tint against a dark red background."

② In particular, see the resurrected souls on fol. 31r, the claw-footed grinning demons boiling the damned with sticks in a fire lit cauldron on fol. 38r, and their mauled capsized bodies on fol. 39r (http://www.bl.uk/manuscripts/FullDisplay.aspx?ref=Cotton_MS_nero_c_iv, accessed 10 March 2021). For an overview of medieval Doom art see Baschet, 1993.

the purpose of connecting two opposed worlds. The small figures engaged on the ladder impart a sense of endless, circular movement to the whole composition and communicate remarkable vividness.[①]

Soon after the uncovering of the wall painting, J.G. Waller described its features in a seminal essay in which he highlighted its relevance with passionate words: "When the time comes for a history of the ecclesiastical art of England to be written, this work at Chaldon must find a prominent place" (Waller, 1871: 306). While some attention has been paid to it more recently,[②] especially in light of its rarity, this work of art has not been the subject of dedicated art historical studies. Waller's detailed and learned analysis highlights the different aspects of the narrative depicted, all considered under the Byzantine-inspired theme of "Ladder of the Salvation of the Human Soul, and the Road to Heaven." He provides textual references for this and a number of other themes detectable in the four different quadrants, offering hypotheses along interpretative lines that might help the understanding of the general composition. He suggests, for instance, that the squatting figure in the lower right corner should be identified with "Usury" thanks to thematic parallelisms with three anecdotes recounted in the fifteenth-century devotional compilation of sermons, *Promptuarium Exemplorum* by the German Dominican John Herolt. Other textual references include, among many others, Herrada's *Hortus Deliciarum*, the works of St. John Climacus, the *Chronicle* of Matthew Paris. The mid twelfth-century *Visio Tnugdali* provides the most apt early

---

① Mural paintings, including this impressively well-preserved specimen, are not as uncommon in medieval English parish churches as the intense whitewashing activities which took place at the time of the Reformation would suggest. The whitewashing actually helped conserve and protect them through the centuries from the aggression of time, vandalism, and bio-attacks. See Rosewell, *Medieval Wall Paintings in English and Welsh Churches* (2008) and *Medieval Wall Paintings* (2014) for a general overview of extant art. The Courtauld Institute in London supports an ongoing Survey of Historic Wall Paintings in the British Isles as part of its Wall Painting Conservation MA (https://courtauld.ac.uk/research/sections/wall-painting-conservation/survey-of-historic-wall-paintings, accessed 10 March 2021).

② See Malden, 1912; Nairn, Pevsner, and Cherry, 1971.

medieval reference to the "bridge of spikes" (Waller, 1871: 288) held on the shoulders of two demons. Souls must perilously cross it in an ancient form of punishment that can be traced back to the *Koran* and beyond, but that also reverberates in the bridges' trials found in chivalresque literature.

Waller's description of the damned shown on the spiky "bridge" is particularly relevant to this essay and needs to be quoted in full: "[...] those who robbed from 'holy chyrch,' as well as from others, were thus punished. They were obliged to carry over their ill-gotten goods. In the painting we probably have represented a number of culprits against 'holy church,' specialized by the emblems of their trades" (Waller, 1871: 290). Thus, he continues, the blacksmith on the far right is "condemned" to "forge a horse-shoe without an anvil;" the next figure is a mason carrying a "mason's pick" whose punishment is unspecified, followed by two females, one of whom carries a ball of spun wool and may represent a "dishonest spinster," while the ascending figure on the left "is, most probably, one who had stolen a tithe of milk" given the whiteness of the vessel's contents. Since the message that needed to be passed on to the parishioners had to be immediately intelligible— "simple and direct"—Weller concludes that "to expect anything deep or mysterious" in such compositions "is quite out of the question" (Waller, 1871: 290). Elaborating on his intriguing research and scholarly references, my suggestion is that investigating the rhetorical aspects of this composition may reveal unexpected interpretative depths.

The rare and exceptional Chaldon wall painting stands out from conventional pictorial representations of the Last Judgment and presents striking compositional peculiarities akin to those visible in the early fifteenth-century Doom at St George's in Trotton, Sussex (Iseppi De Filippis, 2009: 103-114). Some of the features of these two wall paintings in fact suggest that their renditions of Doomsday were used practically, as visual schemes for remembrance, *inventio* and meditation. Their location, for instance, on the west wall quite unusually presents the *memento mori* in front of the altar instead of above it as a fruitful *summa* and as a token to be remembered on the way out.[1] The inclusion of visual schemes to "allude" to lists of vices, virtues, penances and blessings is also uncommon in Last Judgments: at Trotton the unconventional presence of "personifications" of the seven deadly sins and of the seven works of mercy is used to briefly outline topics that can be recalled and amplified in sermons. At Chaldon, a ladder and a tree, which might serve as mental pegs to discuss a wide range of devotional themes, figure as prominently and symbolically as they would in any moral treatise. The ubiquitous Last Judgment "saved on the right/damned on the left of the Christ" spatial dichotomy established in the Gospel of Matthew (25: 31—41)[2] is also challenged: at Trotton, the positions are conveniently swapped to serve the right and left of the preacher who would presumably have faced the wall painting as he sermonized, while at Chaldon a thick horizontal "nebuly" band "representing clouds" according to heraldry (Waller, 1871: 282) starkly separates upper Heaven from lower Hell.[3] The depiction of "damned tradesmen" in the lower right quarter, as we shall see, adds to the rhetorical complexity of the composition and, along with continental stylistic echoes, marks the mural at Chaldon as a fine example of painted inventive rhetoric.

The rhetorical structures that characterize the Chaldon Doom suggest the same, though elusive, relation that connects apparently unrelated artistic genres such as sermon literature, religious drama and devotional wall paintings.

---

① In medieval Britain Last Judgments were frequently painted on the chancel arch, see Christe, 1999: 317.
② *Nova Vulgata Bibliorum Sacrorum Editio*, http://www.vatican.va/archive/bible/nova_vulgata/documents/nova-vulgata_nt_evang-matthaeum_lt.html (accessed 10 March 2021): "*Cum autem venerit Filius hominis in gloria sua, et omnes angeli cum eo, tunc sedebit super thronum gloriae suae. Et congregabuntur ante eum omnes gentes; et separabit eos ab invicem, sicut pastor segregat oves ab haedis, et statuet oves quidem a dextris suis, haedos autem a sinistris [etc.].*"
③ As Christe (1999: 46) points out, the horizontal division in registers clearly marked by separating bands is a common trait of Western versions of the Byzantine Last Judgments as visible in the eleventh-century mosaics at Torcello, in the coeval wall paintings at Sant'Angelo in Formis or in the eleventh- and twelfth-century versions of the *Beatus*.

After all, the iconographic preference for the tree/wheel diagram to illustrate lists of virtues and vices, for the *schemata* of the "seven works of mercy" and the "seven deadly sins," for the visual ordering of the *exemplum* of "*les trois vifs et les trois morts*," commonly visible on the walls of many British parish churches, is tangible evidence that the rhetorical structuring that characterized the composition of medieval texts was far from alien to contemporary image layout. General parallels are detectable, for instance, in sermon literature and wall paintings of the later British Middle Ages, as I demonstrated in the case of the rhetorically "active" Doom at Trotton or in the use of truncated syllogism, or *enthymeme*, in the fifteenth-century depiction of the "Warning to Swearers" at Broughton, Buckinghamshire (Iseppi De Filippis, 2010: 133-147). As we can see from the Chaldon Last Judgment, traces of this structuring are also noticeable in earlier times. Mural paintings of the sort visible at Chaldon, Trotton or Broughton, I suggest, did not only share with the sermons or mystery cycles plays a didactic or moralistic purpose, as it is plain from their common contents, but also a schematic structure echoing the *artes memoriae* that contributed to making these media complementary, if different, thinking tools in the hands of preachers, civic guilds, and their often illiterate or semi-illiterate audiences.

The contemporary *artes praedicandi*, for instance, clearly suggest modes and techniques derived from the arts of memory and often relied on the formal structuring of pictorial compositions to enhance the efficacy of sermons.[1] Thus, while it is important to note that wall paintings and sermons do not directly illustrate each other, tracking the common patterns through which the formal mnemotechnical ordering and the need to remember in order to behave well and consequently be saved at Doomsday develop in these distinct media may reveal the hidden traces of an otherwise baffling

---

[1] Alberic of Montecassino, Thomas Bradwardine and Francesc Eiximenis, among others, repeatedly refer to rhetorical structures and their painted representations as basic tools for composing and remembering sermons; see Iseppi De Filippis, 2009: 104-105.

relation.[1] During a sermon, the preacher and presumably also the parishioners—who at the time stood scattered and not seated in pews—might have glanced at the mural paintings to remember, meditate, elaborate, and literally visualize the words in the preacher's devotional stories. A "concise" wall painting—just as "enigmatic" graffiti, or a rounded twelfth-century Doom table painting in which only three of the seven Works of Mercy are depicted leaving the recollection of the rest to well-trained memories[2]—could therefore be practically used as a tool for "remembering" and composing or, as ancient Roman rhetoricians would call them, as *imagines agentes*.

Though the Pardoner in Chaucer's *Prologue* seems to prefer in-church preaching[3]—where glancing at wall paintings and graffiti would be useful for remembering and improvising extempore his suasive homilies—the rhetorical configuration of these images means that they would echo in the mind even when people were physically removed from the ecclesiastical building. The little evidence we have on sermonizing in England shows in fact that it took place not only indoors, but also in churchyards, market places, chapels, and at crosses.[4] Thus, sermons in all of these venues—often preached

---

① As Gill (2002: 179) notices, the relation between sermons and wall paintings, though "hard to demonstrate," is undeniable: "It is the combination of evidence from medieval sermons and late medieval wall painting which helps us to understand how both contributed to 'the persuasion of many…to meritorious conduct'."

② The unusually shaped Vatican Museums table, attributed to Nicolaus and Johannes, comes from the Oratory of S. Gregorio Nazianzeno in Rome. In it themes from the Last Judgment and the Apocalypse are mixed in superimposed bands. The representation of Paradise and Hell on the rectangular lowest rank is remarkable: opposing a group of damned souls in a flaming cave on the right is a portrait of a praying Virgin on the walls of the Heavenly Jerusalem (see http://www.museivaticani.va/content/museivaticani/it/collezioni/musei/la-pinacoteca/sala-i---secolo-xii-xv/nicolo-e-giovanni--giudizio-finale.html, accessed 10 March 2021).

③ Chaucer (1987): "Lordynges […] in chirches whan I preche" (l. 329); "Goode men and women, o thing warne I yow: / If any wight be in this chirche now / That hath donne synne horrible […]" (ll. 377—379).

④ For an overview of preaching in medieval England, see Owst, 1933; Leith Spencer, 1993.

by a visiting friar, monk, or pardoner—would have been enhanced by the mental retention of visual schemes such as those depicted on churches' walls. After all, mental designs and schemes had been known since Antiquity as preferred means for remembering long and complex matters, and sermonizers, like ancient public orators and lawyers, would have relied heavily on them in whatever circumstances they had to deliver a speech.

Still, the Last Judgment at Chaldon is mnemotechnically striking in more ways than might simply be revealed by its position inside the church and by its crux-shaped spatial division. In Waller's words, this is indeed a "clever and ingenious composition" (Waller, 1871: 304). A large tree in the lower right quadrant is a potent mnemonic device, clearly referring to the Garden of Eden's Tree of Knowledge, the slithering serpent detectable among its leaves and fruits adding legitimacy to the association.[1] It could nonetheless be employed to elaborate on various biblical topics—not only the ones connected to the theme of the Last Judgment—and it could easily "metamorphose" into a Jesse tree, an *arbor amoris*, an *arbor vitae*, the tree of religion etc. These images would normally succeed one another in later moral treatises such as the early fifteenth-century copy of a Carthusian miscellany, MS BL Add 37049.[2] Solely through chains of mental associations, *amplificatio*, hyperbaton or synecdoche, themes such as the creation of man and woman, the notion of original sin, the concepts of deception and knowledge, could become topics for innumerable sermons. As Miriam Gill points out, "[…] preachers might refer to details familiar from visual art, without stating that they would refer to an image" (2002: 173). And the visual

---

[1] For an iconographic description of the Chaldon Last Judgment, see O'Reilly, 1988: 349-350.

[2] Even a quick look at the description of contents of MS BL Add 37049 on the British Library website will reveal the abundance of tree-related references and schemes, for instance on fol. 19v, fol. 25r, fol. 26r, fol. 27r, fol. 38r, fols. 46r-66v, fol. 67v (http://www.bl.uk/manuscripts/Viewer.aspx?ref=add_ms_37049_fs001r, accessed 10 March 2021).

arts in turn adopted schemes and "graphs" from moral and didactic treatises without necessarily acknowledging the borrowing. The rhetorically allusive role of the Chaldon tree is further underscored by the fact that its leaves— differing in shapes and dimensions perhaps to indicate degrees of importance, age, gravity—are painted facing both ascending and descending directions just as on fols. 48r and 55r of MS BL Add 37049 upward leaves are employed to represent virtues and downward ones to indicate vices.[①] The tree at Chaldon could likewise have been a painted chart that served as an *aide-mémoire* for extempore *inventio* on a number of moral issues.

The theme of the Harrowing of Hell, complete with a huge and scary beastly mouth, is depicted in the upper right quadrant of the Chaldon Doom, featuring a triumphant, banner-holding Christ. The open jaws, ready to swallow or regurgitate the sinners, arc powerfully symbolic and could have led to many thematic homilies. Equally evocative, the prominent central ladder seems to allude to the motif of the Ladder of Jacob. It may also represent the ladder of wisdom and perfection, or, as Waller notices, a "road" to Heaven, which, also recalls the rhetorical notion of *ductus*. The popular motif of the Ladder of Jacob is mentioned in the fifteenth century by Mirk in what must have been a common and long-standing homiletic *imago*, eerily echoing the Chaldon angels ascending and descending the ladder: "And as he [Jacob] slepte, hym þoght he saw a laddyr þat right from þe erth to Heuen; and God joynut to þe laddyr, and angyll goyng vp and don þe laddyr."[②] Additionally, the intersection of a central horizontal "nebuly" band and

---

① See the "Tree of Vices" with downward leaves on fol. 48r and the "Tree of Virtues" with upward leaves on fol. 55r of MS BL Add 37049 at http://www.bl.uk/manuscripts/ Viewer.aspx?ref=add_ms_37049_fs001r (accessed 10 March 2021). The British Library holds two more copies of the treatise, MS BL Cotton Faustina B.vi Part II and MS BL Stowe 39.

② Mirk (1905) [ed. Susan Powell, 2 vols, 2011]: 94. On fol. 37v of MS BL Add 37049 "þe mounte of perfection" is reproduced "with Christ holding seven saved souls in heaven, which is at the top of a ladder" (http://www.bl.uk/manuscripts/Viewer.aspx?ref= add_ms_37049_fs001r, accessed 10 March 2021).

ladder delineates a giant cross, which is often depicted, with the instruments of the Passion, in standard medieval Last Judgments.[1] Tree, mouth, ladder and cross in the Chaldon Last Judgment could have constituted mental "pegs" to elaborate on otherwise familiar tales and moral values. Combined, they could really work as a repository for mental and verbal *inventio*.

The lower right corner quadrant (Figure 4) constitutes a striking example of the rhetorical structuring described above and reveals a particularly suggestive superimposition of mnemonic layers. The events and figures depicted here seem to refer to different iconographic topics that are, in perfect mnemotechnical style, conflated, made "*breves*": we can see references to the "seven works of mercy," to the "seven deadly sins," to the Sunday Christ (linking various working tools to the *arma Christi* and to the prohibition to work on Sundays), to the civic roles of the various trades, and to the political, economic and social condemnation of dishonest trading and usury.[2] Contemporary eyes were certainly more apt than ours to approach such a conflation of themes and "unpack" the many superimpositions and references that crossed the lines of genres and settings. This notwithstanding, rhetorical structures and mnemotechnics would have aided considerably in the attempt to unravel such complex, and at times puzzling, images.

In the lower part of the scene, a pair of smaller demons are hovering in the air, holding what looks like a deformed human figure above an open fire by means of hooks attached to the figure's ears (Figure 5). This may well be an embodiment of Usury, as Waller guessed, but it could also incarnate a "diagram"

---

[1] See Christe, 1999: 316-317, who notices the presence of the cross and its addenda particularly in British and Italian pre-twelfth-century items.

[2] Usury and fresco wall painting seem to intercept each other in the commission that Giotto received to decorate the Scrovegni Chapel in Padua. See Frugoni, 2008, who confutes the myth according to which Enrico Scrovegni had his famous chapel built and decorated by Giotto as a penance for his father's and his own indulgence in usury, but also highlights the excellent business transaction through which he assured his place at the highest levels of artistic accomplishment.

Figure 4　Last Judgment. Lower right quadrant. Wall painting. Church of SS. Peter and Paul, Chaldon, Surrey. End of the twelfth century. Photo by the author.

Figure 5　Last Judgment. Lower right quadrant. Detail of the squatting figure. Wall painting. Church of SS. Peter and Paul, Chaldon, Surrey. End of the twelfth century. Photo by the author.

representing a conflated version of several of the personified seven deadly sins that are sometimes depicted in mural paintings and described in sermons as growing out of the branches of the tree of Evil, aptly painted nearby. Gluttony, for instance, is suggested by the bead-like pieces of food that the figure seems to be vomiting; Wrath is alluded to by the deranged expression of the face and by the unseemly long tongue hanging out of the figure's mouth; Avarice is recalled by the pouch fastened to his chest and by the bags hanging from his belt; Lust is implied by the fact that the figure is plunging his invisible genitals in the fire; and, finally, Pride may be hinted at in the seemingly arrogant gesture by which the figure shows a round object to the viewers, which may indicate a coin, as speculated by Waller,[1] thus possibly opening up the moral "chapters" of usury, Judaism and infidelity. Lust and Wrath are also alluded to in the two groups of figures on the left and right of the squatting sinner, one of which seems to portray a couple embracing and the other a person engaged in a fight. Far from representing a single sin or punishment, such schemes seem to deploy latency as their organizing principle: just as in the Doom at Trotton, where virtues are implied by vices, here the tracing of some of the vices would be enough to recall the other vices and their contraries. Indeed, ancient and medieval *artes memoriae* mention "outlining" and "allusion" as some of the most sophisticated ways of constructing thought.[2]

---

[1] Waller (1871: 283): "[...] in his right hand he holds a coin, and pieces of coin are falling from his mouth, out of which lolls his tongue."

[2] See Iseppi De Filippis (2004: 15-16): "[one of the schemes consists in] the process of 'outlining' a discourse so that the hearers can infer its full extent from only a few references. Quintilian mentions this process in Book IX of his *Institutio oratoria* (ii, 97) where he is describing 'allusion,' which he calls 'the *most intellectually* refined [of the rhetorical] devices.' Interestingly, he uses a visual metaphor to explain what rhetorical outlining is: he writes that it is like drawing the first lines instead of a full figure and leaving the viewer to complete the *imago* mentally (IV, ii, 120). 'Allusion' is also mentioned with 'coloring,' '*amplificatio*,' and '*brevitas*,' in Robert of Basevorn's fourteenth-century *Forma praedicandi*, as one of the twenty-two fundamental ornaments of speech. In a rhetorical 'allusion' each figural tableau would not need to be developed in full but instead would rely on the outlining of a series of well-known traits that would make the content both immediately recognizable and memorable to the audience."

The larger scene, whose comprehensive organization is rather compelling, also shows two giant devils holding what looks like a large saw, or a "spiky bridge," to quote Weller, on their shoulders (Figure 6). Lined up on the saw are five smaller stylized figures engaged in various activities and facing opposing directions. From the left, one holds out what looks like a bowl or a vessel; two seem to be exchanging a piece of cloth and a round object; another holds a pointed object in his right hand and an object rounded on one side and pointed on the other in his left hand; while the last in the line, apparently engaged in a gesture distinctive of blacksmiths, raises a hammer in his right hand and holds in his left a bent object with a pair of pincers. Because of the activities they seem to be engaged in, these figures may represent a conflation of the traditional representation of some of the "seven works of mercy" (the one holding a bowl could recall the act of "feeding the hungry" and the two next to him that of "clothing the naked"). They may also refer to some of the professions alluded to in the motif of the "Christ of the Trades," and to trades in general: one looks like a blacksmith shaping what appears to be a horse shoe; another resembles a shoemaker apparently using a knife on a piece of leather vaguely shaped like the sole of a Poulaine shoe; the one holding the vessel might refer to innkeepers; the two sporting shoulder-length headdresses or coiffures and holding pieces of fabric possibly represent dressmakers, dyers, cloth merchants or, as imagined by Waller, spinsters. The overall composition could thus be a reference not only to the punishments implied in having to cross a "spiky bridge" but also to the dangers of practicing a trade dishonestly: after all, a little later Dante, in *Inferno* 28 (ll. 22—63), would condemn those who sow discord (i.e. cause a schism) to be sawn in two. But, in antithesis, the design could also be used to praise the virtues of honest trading. If I am correct in reading these figures as an example of the superimposition of different *schemata*, then such intertwining would suggest as wide a variety of human activities as possible, a range that would certainly have been familiar to the vast majority of parishioners who would have seen it in church. Placing these figures on the cutting edge of a saw could suggest that failing to perform "works of mercy" and honest trades could damn the parishioners. And if they were, for instance, to sin by working on a Sunday, they could metaphorically lose their balance and fall from the saw into the hellish fire below. The "bridge of spikes" and the "saw" could be inventive sources of inspiration for those who used the wall painting as a thinking map.

Figure 6   Last Judgment. Lower right quadrant. Detail of the saw/bridge. Wall painting. Church of SS. Peter and Paul, Chaldon, Surrey. End of the twelfth century. Photo by the author.

While Dooms typically include references to the social status of sinners, the depiction of trades and manufacturing activities, especially as early as the twelfth century, is quite rare. In the early Middle Ages, celebrated decorative programs commonly present a straightforward association between earthly status and afterlife condition. The magnificent twelfth-century mosaics depicting the Last Judgment on the west wall of the basilica of Santa Maria Assunta in Torcello and the image of a harrowing Hell's mouth in the contemporary Winchester Psalter are just two examples of a very common practice. In both, the crowding of tonsured heads, bishops' tiaras, royal crowns and elegant female features clarifies the fate reserved for those who immoderately revel in earthly pleasure and power. The inclusion of Eastern-style, jewel-studded turbans and long-haired male heads sporting massive earrings and long moustaches in the lower tier at Torcello, and of an unmistakable Jewish nose and hat in the midst of the crowd roasting in Hell's mouth on fol. 39r of the Winchester Psalter add to the potency of the political and ethical message conveyed against all kinds of "infidelities." And, starting from the mid-fourteenth century, *dances macabres* all over Europe paraded grinning skeletons alongside representations of the powerful and wealthy in rich robes and precious headgear.[①] Still, no trading tools or tokens are part of these portrayals, which were meant for the edification of all, but in particular of well to do audiences.

As Roger Rosewell notes, mid-fifteenth-century Last Judgments may include "easily recognized attributes such as head-dresses which identify the sex and status of their wearers or clues which reveal the sins of the damned, such as dishonest ale wives clutching tankards or misers being forced to swallow their hoarded gold" (Rosewell, 2014: 75) as may be seen at Holy Trinity Church in Coventry. But depictions of tools, trades or the artisans practicing them are nowhere to be found, even in late medieval British Last Judgments. The turn from the glittery version of damnation for a high-end audience to depictions of common, modest trades in Hell, such as those at Chaldon as early as the twelfth century, thus constitutes an impressive example of rhetorical discourse register adaptation to the local, limited manufacturing and trading economy of an English medieval village and its

① On fols. 31v-32r of MS BL Add 37049 "marginal images of grinning skeletons waving and wearing first a crown and then a tall hat illustrate 'The Dawnce of Makabre'" (http://www.bl.uk/manuscripts/Viewer.aspx?ref=add_ms_37049_fs001r, accessed 10 March 2021). One of the best preserved such parades is the one painted in 1539 by Simone Baschenis on the outer walls of S. Vigilio church in Pinzolo.

non-urban surroundings.[①]

The staging of an intriguing instance of the inclusion of manufacturing and trade rather than high status amongst the damned, makes the Chaldon representation of Doom, as far as I am aware, unique in twelfth-century Britain. Perhaps the motif was more widely present in the British high Middle Ages than it is given to know today, and perhaps other examples have been lost or are still to be retrieved from oblivion. However, no trade-related depictions are present in what is left of the possibly cognate Lewes group wall paintings. The authorship and possible cultural references of the Chaldon mural remain unknown, as do the stylistic influences that may have shaped its composition at the time of the flourishing of Romanesque models on the continent and of their Norman variations in the British Isles. Since the "mental part" of the composition is so engaging, Waller hypothesizes that the painter was a learned "brother of some religious house": either a migrating monk from the continent or an Englishman who had studied in "monastic schools abroad" (Waller, 1871: 304-305). Philip Mainwaring Johnston attributes the realization of the stylistically similar decorative program at St. Botolph's church in Hardam to "the work of a traveling guild who had inherited the traditions of the school of painters of Poitou, and blended them with English ideas" (Johnston, 1901: 89-90). Given that the two locations are less than thirty miles apart, advancing the hypothesis that the same, a similarly trained guild or an individual somehow connected to it could also have been responsible for the Chaldon Doom is perhaps not too farfetched.

Along with Byzantine archetypes also detectable at Chaldon, Johnston suggests that the cycle at Hardham was influenced by Lombardic, Frankish, Italian models blended with "native Saxon and Norman-Romanesque" (90). Interestingly enough, the overall "crusading spirit" characterizing the wall

---

① As early as the 1086 *Doomsday Book*, Chaldon, Surrey—"Calvedone" comprising 2 ploughlands (200 acres) and a church—had no recorded population; see the Open Doomsday website (https://opendomesday.org/place/TQ3055/chaldon/, accessed 10 March 2021).

paintings at Hardham may be echoed in the banner held by Christ in the Harrowing of Hell quadrant at Chaldon, since the pennon closely resembles those stitched on the English-made Bayeux Tapestry (Musset, 2005: 140-141, 214-223) and that visible in the early twelfth-century sculptured doorway at Fordington, Dorchester. Curious iconographic resonances may likewise include the stylized wrought iron Adam and Eve silhouettes on the (probably) tenth-century doorway at Stillingfeet, Yorkshire, which may represent a Viking paradise complete with the still detectable traces of a tree and a beautiful longship.[①] Manuscript illumination, including luxurious productions such as the above-mentioned Winchester Psalter, could perhaps also be part of the cultural and iconographic climate which produced the wall painting at Chaldon. As far as I am aware, though, none of them includes explicit references to trades and/or their tools. Apart from the punishing attitude which became typical after the "invention" of the Christian Hell and Purgatory and which in certain instances included the *ex ante* condemnation of professions,[②] it would be interesting to fathom the extent to which depictions of trades and their tools are in any other way related to death and the afterlife, and what could be the cultural tradition which originated the peculiarly rhetorical composition visible in the lower right quadrant of the Chaldon Last Judgment.

A closer look at some of the sculpted bricks positioned on tombs at the

---

① See http://www.greatenglishchurches.co.uk/html/stillingfleet.html (accessed 10 March 2021): "The generally accepted theory seems to be that the door is as early as tenth century and was brought to Stillingfleet from some other location."

② Textual sources include *St. John's Apocalypse*, the *Book of Daniel*, non-biblical apocalyptic writings such as *The Prick of Conscience* and contemporary visions of Heaven and Hell. See Bernstein, 1993; and Gardiner, 1989. According to Le Goff (1981), the Roman Catholic church's perception of trading evolved from a generalized condemnation in the high Middle Ages especially of the trades linked to different kinds of taboos (*ex natura*) to a new consideration of urban and mercantile sins and sinners between the eleventh and the thirteenth centuries in which the new providers of wealth and well-being are no longer condemned *en masse* but according to the way in which they conduct their trades (*ex intentione*).

necropolis of *Isola sacra* near Ostia Antica reveals that in Roman Antiquity manufacturers and traders often maintained their professional qualification as an identifying mark after death.[①] Archaeological findings have shown that a number of the plaques or bricks—some of which are still visible on the façades of the sepulchers—were originally fixed to the front of the deceased's workshops and depicted typical manufacturing and/or vending scenes. Butchers, bakers, blacksmiths, water and herb vendors, millers and shoemakers are shown in the act of performing their arts and surrounded by the tools of their trade in scenes that were originally meant to publicize and advertise their commercial activities. At the moment of death, the plaques were detached and repositioned on the front of the tombs (Morbidoni, 2017: 255-256; Baratta, 2009: 270) as a sort of signature and, presumably, also as a mnemonic icon summing up the "story" of a particular citizen now passed on to the other world. Some of the scenes present a striking rhetorical use of tools of trade, for example one showing a compass, an axe, a rule and oars to "allude to" the activity of one Publius Celerius Amandus as a ship builder on his funerary stone (Morbidoni, 2017: 257), and another "summing up" the profession of shoemaker by juxtaposing two kinds of sandals (Floriani Squarciapino, 1941: 61).

Rhetorical display based on allusion was also employed in trade-related mosaics, such as the ones still visible on the floors of the *stationes* in the *Piazzale delle Corporazioni*—or Trade Guilds Square—in Ostia Antica. The repeatedly depicted *modius* and *rastellum*—measuring vessel and rake used to smooth out its contents—were a visual "reference to the *mensura* and the *probatio*," i.e. measurement unit and quality control, by which the merchants meant to allude to, and thus advertise, their probity (Morbidoni, 2017: 264). Advertisements similar to those animating the medieval guilds which produced and performed the mystery cycles in Britain are also detectable in

---

① See Floriani Squarciapino, 1956—1958: 183-204, and 1961—1962: 112-115; Floriani Squarciapino, 1941; Morbidoni, 2017: 255-269; Baratta, 2009: 257-276; Taglietti, 2018: 395-398; Grimaldi Bernardi, 2005.

the iconographic representations of *negotiantes* (artisans) and *venditores* (merchants) who enacted sophisticated marketing strategies meant to assure the success of their business. Time and again on their workshop banners they are shown gesturing towards their goods to highlight freshness and quality, establishing eye-contact with the viewers in well-furnished emporia where the typical tools of trade are prominently displayed. In typical rhetorical fashion, reality is thus manipulated in service of self-promotion, as in the bricks repositioned on Tomb 29 at *Isola sacra* in which the tools are—disproportionally—as big as the artisans (Morbidoni, 2017: 261). Trades, and rhetorical strategies, were obviously considered an inheritance mark to be displayed on funerary art because professions could, just as they can today, be a family affair. A wealthy sepulcher in Nocera belonging to a shoemaker, or *sutor*, bears the same patronymic—Atilius Artemas—as that of the owner of a similar tomb in Ostia whose advertising plaque shows him in the act of resoling (Conticello de' Spagnolis and Zevolino, 2000: 73-74). It seems therefore that the rhetorical references to trades in the afterlife we have detected in the Chaldon mural may belong to a longstanding, though forgotten, cultural and iconographic tradition.

But where this early example is unique in Britain, traces of this praxis are still visible in a number of later Dooms in central and southern Italy. Along with some exemplars which are heavily damaged and no longer fully legible, such as those at Assergi (L'Aquila) and Leonessa (Rieti), an impressive piece is the Last Judgment visible on the counterfaçade of the church of the SS Annunziata at Sant'Agata dei Goti near Benevento (Palleschi, 2004: 29-93). Dating to the beginning of the fifteenth century, this Last Judgment is structured according to tradition, but the lower right corner of the fresco (Figure 7) contains a few striking thematic and mnemotechnical parallels with the mural painting at Chaldon. Here too there are references to the seven deadly sins, and by osmosis to their virtuous counterparts, and a rhetorically multipurpose tree, in which down-facing leaves are substituted with hanging sinners, figures prominently. A triregnum-wearing figure labeled *Julian(us) apostata* is being sawn in two,[①] a possible source for innumerable homiletic topics. Hell is here also populated by tradesmen and professional figures (Figure 8): a *ferraro* (blacksmith), a *bancherius* (banker*)*, a *iudex* (judge), a *notarius* (notary), a *sutor* (shoemaker), a *molinator* (miller), a *buccerius* (butcher), a *tabernarius* (innkeeper).

Figure 7   Last Judgment. Hell. Wall painting. Church of the SS Annunziata, Sant'Agata dei Goti, Benevento. Beginning of the fifteenth century. Photo by the author.

---

① Palleschi (2004: 49-54) proposes a convincing interpretation of the puzzling figure being sawn in two by the devils: how could it be "*Julian(us) apostata*" if it wears the papal tiara? Palleschi suggests that the label originally read "*Urbanus papa*" and referred to Urbanus VI (1378—1389) who, held responsible for having caused the Great Schism (1378—1449), is rightly being subjected to the appropriate *contrappasso*. This depiction originates from the controversies that involved, on opposing sides, Urbanus (a Neapolitan by birth) and the family that ruled Naples at the time, the di Durazzo. The censorship that presumably was imposed on the original label confirms that murals of this kind had not only a religious, but also a political, social and dynastic relevance.

Figure 8　Last Judgment. Hell. Detail of the damned tradespeople. Wall painting. Church
of the SS Annunziata, Sant'Agata dei Goti, Benevento. Beginning of the fifteenth century.
Photo by the author.

A similar superimposition of trades and otherwordly damnation is painted on the walls of a chapel annexed to the ancient church of the Santuario della Madonna dei Bisognosi near Pereto-Rocca di Botte (L'Aquila).[1] The walls of the large chapel—built between the end of the fourteenth and the beginning of the fifteenth centuries and composed of three adjacent areas which are thought to have constituted a small shrine adjoined to the bigger one and equipped with an independent entrance way—are completely covered by devotional paintings that include a Crucifixion, a Deposition and a Visitation "signed" by one "Maestru Jacobv pintore de Arsoli" ca. 1420—1440. They are astonishingly well preserved considering the high seismic activity characterizing this region, including the devastating 2009 L'Aquila earthquake. The Last Judgment covers the upper part of a double archway which was originally a chancel arch separating the altar area from the entrance hall where churchgoers presumably stood during Mass. It would have hovered above their heads throughout the office.

Hell (Figure 9) takes up a large section of the right part of the wall painting. In it, Satan figures centre stage, almost double the size of the enthroned Christ at the top. Positioned on six orifices on his body are as many deadly vices (*lussuria, avaritia, gola, ira, svuberbia, acidia*) with the seventh (*invidia*) being held in his arms. As usual, they may be used to recall the opposing virtues. Radiating off the sins are a plethora of professional categories and traders such as *sartore* (tailor), *[ca]lsolaro* (shoemaker), *mercatti* (merchants), *carpentero* (carpenter), *ferraro* (blacksmith), *macellaro* (butcher). Some are apparently connected to specific wrongdoings: *tabernaro* (innkeeper), for instance, is painted close to *ira* (wrath) and *maccabei* to *avaritia* (avarice). A couple of "special" trades are also included: *meretrice* (whore) and *femina de prette* (priest's woman). Other categories of

---

① The Sanctuary was originally erected in the seventh century to house a sacred wooden effigy of the Virgin, which, after a daring flight from Seville, finally reached a safe haven on a hilltop in Abruzzo. A twelfth-century copy is still venerated in the Sanctuary and is believed to generate miracles to this day.

sinners stud the packed space: *ipocriti* (hypocrites), *miciari* (homicides), *biastimatore* (swearer), *traditore* (traitor). Along with Turks and Maccabees, infidels include *iodei* (Jews), *tartari* (Tartars), *soldati* (soldiers, perhaps in the sense of mercenaries). A solitary trespasser is held upside down by a demon and a caption simply describes him as *desperato* (desperate). Under the feet of the central Satan, a group of tonsured and tiara-wearing wretched are roasting among hellish flames. Tools of trade feature grimly in the *contrappasso* tortures to which the professionals are subjected. The *ferraro*, for instance, is being blinded by a devil using a blacksmith awl and hammer while the *[ca]lsolaro*'s back is being incised with a scalpel similar to the ones shoemakers used to cut leather and the *sartore*'s breast is being mutilated with a pair of scissors.

Figure 9 Last Judgment. Hell. Wall painting. Santuario della Madonna dei Bisognosi, Pereto-Rocca di Botte, L'Aquila. First half of fifteenth century. Photo by the author.

Yet another example of the inclusion of damned tradespeople in an infernal context was frescoed on the mid fifteenth-century counterfaçade of the Santa Maria Assunta church in Sermoneta (Latina). The wall painting is unfortunately heavily damaged but what can be made out reveals the features of the mnemotechnical construct being traced. Surrounding a central and gruesome Satanic figure, some of the seven deadly sins are explicitly depicted and inscribed (*gola, ira, svperbia, lvsvria, acidia* and *invidia*), along with *meritrix, ipocriti* and *soldati*. Among them a lacuna in the wall painting bears the caption *sertvri* (tailors) as a trace of the trade-related tradition described above (Figure 10). The same hint appears among the damned in the Last Judgment we find in the end of the fifteenth-century SS. Annunziata oratory in nearby Cori (Latina) where, among others, a triregnum-wearing pope, a crowned king, an upside down hanged *traditore* (traitor), a cauldron boiled *affatochiera* (sorceress) and a profusion of snakes accompany a *macellaro* (butcher) and a *tabernaro* (innkeeper).

Figure 10　Last Judgment. Hell. Wall painting. Church of Santa Maria Assunta, Sermoneta, Latina. Middle of fifteenth century. Photo by the author.

A further intriguing instance of this tradition is the Doom painted on the right nave of the Santa Maria in Foro Claudio Basilica near Ventaroli (Caserta). Dating to the eleventh century, the present basilica was built on the site of an ancient Roman settlement along the *Via Appia* and the *Via Sacra Langobardorum* which ran nearby. Its decorative scheme includes Byzantine inspired wall paintings, both in the apse and on the nave, which may have been influenced stylistically by the decorative programs at the proximate Benedictine monasteries of Montecassino and Sant'Angelo in Formis. The Doom (Figure 11) is unfortunately heavily damaged and only partially legible.[①] Still it is possible to detect a sort of "bubble" structure recalling that of Romanesque illuminated manuscripts which divided the Last Judgment action into different scenes connected through bands or *ducti*. A possibly non-coeval stripe running at the bottom shows, in niches divided by slight columns, manufacturers and traders at work (Figure 12). Those still discernible, from the left, are "localzolaro" (the shoemaker); an innkeeper; a butcher; "lopotecaro" (the apothecary); "loferaro" (the blacksmith). A lower unfinished additional row shows on the left a partially ruined panel where the caption "lomulinaro" (the miller) can be still made out. Hovering above the shoulders of "lopotecaro" and "loferaro," and thematically connecting the upper bubble structure showing the torments of Hell and the lower niches dedicated to the *mestieri* or trades, are little winged devils which might have been scraped off from the other trading scenes.

Figure 11   Last Judgment. Wall painting. Basilica of Santa Maria in Foro Claudio, Ventaroli, Caserta. Eleventh century. Photo by the author.

---

① Rescio (2010: 5-32) dates it to the fifteenth century.

Figure 12　Last Judgment. Detail of the tradespeople. Wall painting. Basilica of Santa Maria in Foro Claudio, Ventaroli, Caserta. Eleventh century (?). Photo by the author.

It is impossible, at the moment, to establish with any degree of certainty whether the same iconographic tradition which produced these later Italian wall paintings is also accountable for the Chaldon Doom's unconventional depiction of trades. Earlier Italian instances might have been painted over, just as later British ones might have been lost or hidden under layers of whitewash. Further, I may simply not be aware of additional northern European examples that might help delineate the transition. The long-standing Roman habit of recycling rhetorically styled mercantile insignia on funerary monuments, though alluringly suggestive, is perhaps not even related to this tradition. The connection cannot, though, be excluded *a priori*.

Two beautiful jade shoe soles dating to a period between the 8th and the 5th centuries BCE were for instance excavated from a noble's tomb in China (Figure 13) possibly suggesting that a connection between the symbol of a trade and the afterlife was also part of other ancient cultures.

Figure 13　Jade shoe soles. Excavated from the No. 1 Tomb of Duke Jingong. Fengxiang
County, Baoji City. Shaanxi History Museum, Xi'an. Spring and Autumn Period
(770 BCE—476 BCE). Photo by the author.

And in his discussion of the Chaldon upper left scene depicting the
Archangel Michael's "Weighing of the Souls," Waller instinctively links it to
the soul-weighing he admired on a number of papyri rolls of the Ritual of the
Dead in the British Museum and to the 1370 BCE sarcophagus of Sethi I in
Sir John Soane's Museum.[①] In the latter, "Osiris is seated holding […] in his

---

① See http://collections.soane.org/object-m470?_ga=2.212637652.1352902824.1607426094-
1962840435.1607426094 (accessed 10 March 2021).

left hand a pastoral crook, in no way differing in principle from that of the bishops in early ages" while "Horus" holds the balance standing "on the top of a flight of grades of nine steps on which are souls representing, according to Champollion, the nine grades of society; but may it not be rather, the 'Ladder' to heaven?" He goes on to note that "in the religion of the Zenda-Vesta, Mithra and Rashné-Rast weigh the actions of men on the bridge Tchinevad which separated earth and heaven." As Waller puts it, these assonances "teach us a lesson; that, however separated by time, the disruption of empires, the passing away of one religious creed, and the acceptance or progress of another, certain thoughts survive through all, only taking other shapes, or rather being clothed in other colours" (Waller, 1871: 299-300). If we consider the examples of trade-related Dooms described above in terms of mnemotechnics, then the metamorphoses, the persistent features, and the cultural references could well be signs of a larger thinking map or, to use Mary Carruthers' words, of a *machina memorialis*.

The opening paragraphs of this essay considered a couple of intriguing graffiti—shoe soles linked to a chalice and a demon's head—which sparked the inquiry leading from "recycled" ancient Roman funerary art to medieval instances of trade-related topics in Dooms. The leitmotif has been the characteristic organization of images to permit remembering and inventing through abbreviating, amplifying, and substituting tropes. The ability of these *imagines agentes* to morph repeatedly to suit the needs of extemporary oratory suggests a widespread perception of rhetoric as a basic organizing principle informing texts, visual displays, and ideas, a perception which we have continued to preserve in certain aspects of contemporary culture, for instance in advertising.

The wall painting at Chaldon, as described above, is divided vertically by a prominent ladder and horizontally by a band which serve a number of rhetorical purposes, including that of *ductus* or "way" connecting not only the underworld to heaven but also different ideas in a discourse. As mentioned, their intersection also delineates a giant cross, yet another possible source of rhetorical invention on a wide range of topics. Additionally, the trades and their tools, including what looks like a shoe sole, are alluded to and not explicitly labelled as in the later Italian examples, making for a particularly subtle, intriguing rhetorical construct. A twelfth-century graffito from Sardinia (Cau, 2016: 35-42) (Figure 14), which brings together a number of these elements in a striking graphic form, may offer an additional instance of the pervasiveness and permanence of certain rhetorical organizing schemes that reveal, time and again, unconventional links between apparently unrelated objects like chalices, demons' heads, ladders, saws, crosses and shoe soles.

The graffito is incised on the walls of the Cistercian church of Sant'Antioco di Bisarcio, whose isolated position "in agro di Ozieri" adds to its uniqueness and peculiarity. The graffito is rather large (6.7ft × 8ft) and incised on a chapel wall on the second floor of the porch. As cleverly shown by Gian Gabriele Cau, it mirrors the now partially lost *tau*-shaped façade of the church (Cau, 2017: 251-288). Eight symbolic drawings (cross, church, bell, ladder, bull, radiating light, finger and shoe sole) representing a *summa* of the architectural aspects and dedication of the church are discernible in it. Whereas a possibly coeval consecratory epigraph is deeply incised halfway through the ladder, the graffito is lightly etched *a sgraffio* and now almost invisible to the naked eye. The inscription celebrates the commission and, though marred by afterthoughts and overwrites, it reads "1190/95 H(AEC) ME FECIT XP PETRI P(ISCOP)U E(T) Q(UOD) MAGI(S)T(E)R P(AT)ER PAULU EXCRYAUYT B(ASILICAM) (DICATAM) S(AN)C(TO) A(NTIOCH)O ET M(ART)IRUM S(ANCTAE) ECCLESYAE † (CHRISTI)."[①] The final dedication is not spelt out but suggested by what looks like a bull's head pierced by a spear to evoke the sacrificial Christ.

---

① Transliteration by Cau, 2016: 39; English trans. mine: "In the period between 1190/95 Bishop Peter made me these things and for these the master father Paul enlarged the cathedral of St. Antioco and of the martyrs of the sacred Church of Christ."

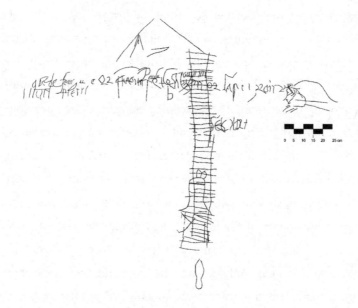

Figure 14　Celebratory epigraph with ladder and Poulaine shoe outline. Graffito. Church of Sant'Antioco di Bisarcio, Ozieri, Sassari. Twelfth century. Drawing by Gian Gabriele Cau, based on his own tracing. Reproduced with permission.

The wealth of hints detectable include the intertwining of a cross and a *chrismon* to express a *Signum Christi*, which may also double as a *Signum Petri*, and light beams to "illuminate" the names of Peter and Paul, which could obviously give way to a chain of reminiscences ranging from the local bishop and magister who were "enlightened" in their church renovation work to the illustrious Apostles whose names they are commemorating (Cau, 2016: 40).[1] At the foot of the long, impressive ladder a single shoe sole, uncannily similar to those etched on the walls at Selborne and Troston might, according to scholarly speculation, refer to pilgrims[2] or, in this particular case, to

[1] On the rhetorical value of the *chrismon* and radiating light, see Iseppi De Filippis, 2018: 137-152.

[2] Cau was able to detect numerous graffiti footprints in this church, accompanied in some cases by initials. As in England, graffiti footprints are common in Sardinian churches and are normally understood to be pilgrims' signatures. See Dore, 2001; Grecu, 2006: 149-190.

someone who purposely decided to initial the graffiti in a distinctive way. The combination of symbolic elements—such as we have seen at Chaldon— and the position of the shoe at the bottom of the ladder may however, represent a "thinking map" whose rhetorical use is made all the more likely by its imposing dimensions. If this reading is correct, the shoe sole might recall devotional "pilgrimages" that lead the penitent up a graduated ladder of salvation to the epigraph at the top representing the divinity through its inlaid references to the cross, the Apostles and Christ. It could also represent a mnemotechnical *ductus* in which a tool of trade and manufacturing is positioned at the bottom of a ladder leading from lower, terrestrial sinning to heavenly salvation. This Sardinian graffito, in other words, could be an abridged version of a Last Judgment in which only the essential elements in a well-known representation are made visible while the rest could be mnemotechnically retrieved by adding details and establishing connections and oppositions. Potentially damning trade-related sins or the exaltation of virtuous artisanal activities, the redemptive ability of holy pilgrimages, and meditations on the ascension or descent of the heavenly ladder, on the theme of the cross, on the notion of sacrifice, on the salvific power of radiating divine light, on the sacredness of Christ's name are just some of the wealth of references a well-trained rhetorical mind could extrapolate from this graffito. Far from being a simple erratic decoration or an odd way of bringing together significant words and symbols, the etched signs would instead be the result of a precise rhetorical intention driven by the necessity of roughly outlining a thinking scheme used to reflect, compose, and communicate.

Puzzling graffiti such as the ones at Selborne and Troston, just as the Last Judgments in which trades are used as a source of *inventio*, seem to contain the very same rhetorical determination. The globalized digital culture we currently experience, with its "explicative" drive, might not be best suited for perceiving the subtlety of such allusive schematizing. The ancient rhetorical tradition reminds us, however, of the fruitful possibilities inherent in the partial telling of a well-known story to allow for extempore creativity.

Since church audiences needed to be repeatedly reminded to be terrified in case they had sinned, and pilgrims kept having to be consoled for the wearing out of costly footwear by the mirage of heavenly pathways represented by shoe soles, persuasive homilies had to be constantly updated with new and enticing details only rhetoric and mnemotechnics could supply.

Works Cited

Baker, Audrey. "Lewes Priory and the Early Group of Wall Paintings in Sussex." *The Volume of the Walpole Society* 31 (1942): 1-44.

Baratta, Giulia. "La 'bonne addresse'. Trovare un'attività artigianale o commerciale in città." *Opinione pubblica e forme di comunicazione a Roma: il linguaggio dell'epigrafia*. Ed. Maria Gabriella Bertinelli Angeli and Angela Donati. Faenza: Fratelli Lega Ed., 2009. 257-276.

Baschet, Jérôme. *Les Justices de l'au-delà. Les représentations de l'enfer en France et en Italie, XIIe —XVe siècles*. Rome: Ecole française de Rome, 1993.

Bernstein, Alan E. *The Formation of Hell: Death and Retribution in the Ancient and Early Christian Worlds*. Ithaca: Cornell UP, 1993.

Cau, Gian Gabriele. "Epigrafia Giudicale. Sant'Antioco di Bisarcio: un'epigrafe commemorativa (1190—95)." *Sardegna Antica: Culture Mediterranee* 50 (2016): 35-42.

---. "'VICIT!' Il grande fregio della Esaltazione Della Santa Croce (1190/95) del cistercense Magister Paulu, nel Sant'Antioco Di Bisarcio (Parte I)." *Theologica & Historica. Annali Della Pontificia Facoltà Teologica Della Sardegna* 26 (2017): 251-288.

Champion, Matthew. "The Graffiti Inscriptions of St. Mary's Church, Troston." *Proceedings of the Suffolk Institute of Archaeology* 43, Part 2 (2014): 235-258.

---. *Medieval Graffiti: The Lost Voices of England's Churches*. London: Ebury P, 2015.

---. "The Medium is the Message: Votive Devotional Imagery and Gift Giving amongst the Commonality in the Late Medieval Parish." *Peregrinations:*

Journal of Medieval Art and Architecture 3.4 (2012): 103-123.

Chaucer, Geoffrey. *The Riverside Chaucer*. 3rd ed. Ed. Larry Benson. Boston: Houghton Mifflin Company, 1987.

Christe, Yves. *Jugements derniers*. Yonne: Ateliers de la Pierre-qui-Vire, 1999.

Conticello de' Spagnolis, Marisa, and Giovanni Zevolino. *La tomba del calzolaio: dalla necropoli monumentale romana di Nocera Superiore*. Roma: L'Erma di Bretschneider, 2000.

Dore, Gianpietro. *Sulle "Orme" dei pellegrini. Testimonianze dei percorsi penitenziali medioevali nell'Isola*. Cagliari: Zonza Editori, 2001.

Floriani Squarciapino, Maria. "Piccolo Corpus dei mattoni scolpiti ostiensi" I. II. *Bollettino della Commissione Archeologica Comunale in Roma*, 76 (Roma, 1956—1958): 183-204, and 78 (Roma, 1961—1962): 112-115.

---. *Civiltà romana: Artigianato e industria*. Roma: Casa Editrice Carlo Colombo, 1941.

Frugoni, Chiara. *L'affare migliore di Enrico. Giotto e la Cappella degli Scrovegni*. Torino: Einaudi, 2008.

Gardiner, Eileen. *Visions of Heaven & Hell before Dante*. New York: Italica P, 1989.

Gilchrist, Roberta. *Medieval Life: Archaeology and the Life Course*. Woodbridge: Boydell P, 2013.

Gill, Miriam. "Preaching and Image: Sermons and Wall Paintings in Later Medieval England." *Preacher, Sermon, and Audience in the Middle Ages*. Ed. Carolyn Muessig. Leiden: Brill, 2002. 155-180.

Grecu, Igniazio. "Le 'orme' dei pellegrini nelle chiese della Sardegna medievale." *Culti, santuari, pellegrinaggi in Sardegna e nella Penisola Iberica tra Medioevo e età contemporanea*. Ed. Maria Giuseppina Meloni and Olivetta Schena. Genova: Brigati, 2006. 149-190.

Grimaldi Bernardi, Grazia. *Le Botteghe romane: L'arredamento*. Roma: Quasar, 2005.

Iseppi De Filippis, Laura. "*Exhibete membra vestra*: Verbal and Visual Enthymeme as Late Medieval Mnemotechnics." *The Making of Memory in the Middle Ages*. Ed. Lucie Doležalová. Leiden: Brill, 2010. 133-147.

---. *Memoria Agens: Verbal and Visual Rhetoric in Late Medieval English Lay Culture, c.1300—c.1500*. Ph.D. dissertation. New York University, 2004.

---. "Remembering Doomsday: *memoria* in Late Medieval English Drama and Iconography." *Word & Image* 25.1 (January—March 2009): 103-114.

---. "Une Esteille Issi Est: The Star as *Imago Agens* in the Chester and Coventry Cycles." *Il dialogo creativo. Studi per Lina Bolzoni*. Ed. Maria Pia Ellero, Matteo Residori, Massimiliano Rossi, and Andrea Torre. Lucca: Pacini Fazzi, 2018. 137-152.

Johnston, Philip Mainwaring. "Hardham Church and Its Early Paintings." *Sussex Archaeological Collections* 64 (1901): 61-92.

Le Goff, Jacques. *La naissance du Purgatoire*. Paris: Gallimard, 1981.

Leith Spencer, Helen. *English Preaching in the Later Middle Ages*. Oxford: Clarendon P, 1993.

Malden, Henry Elliot. "Parishes: Chaldon." *A History of the County of Surrey*, vol. 4. Institute of Historical Research. Westminster: A. Constable and Co., 1902—1912. 188-194.

Mirk, John. *Festial*. Ed. Theodor Erbe. Oxford: EETS, 1905.

Morbidoni, Pier Luigi. "Il commercio e l'artigianato nelle raffigurazioni e nelle testimonianze epigrafiche ostiensi." *Emptor e mercator. Spazi e rappresentazioni del commercio romano*. Ed. Sara Santoro. Bari: Edipuglia, 2017. 255-269.

Musset, Lucien. *The Bayeux Tapestry*. Trans. Richard Rex. Woodbridge: Boydell, 2005.

Nairn, Ian, Nikolaus Pevsner, and Bridget Cherry. *Surrey*. New Haven: Yale UP, 1971.

O'Reilly, Jennifer. *Studies in the Iconography of the Virtues and Vices in the Middle Ages*. New York: Garland Publishing, 1988.

Owst, Gerald Robert. *Literature and Pulpit in Medieval England: A Neglected Chapter in the History of English Letters and the English People*. Cambridge: Cambridge UP, 1933.

Palleschi, Roberta. "Il Giudizio Universale." *Lavorare all'inferno. Gli affreschi di Sant'Agata de' Goti*. Ed. Chiara Frugoni. Bari: Laterza, 2004. 29-93.

Rescio, Pierfrancesco. "L'influenza cassinese nelle più antiche chiese medievali della Campania. Fonti storiche, architettoniche e archeologiche." *Rassegna Storica dei Comuni: Studi e Ricerche Storiche Locali* 162-163 (2010): 5-32.

Rosewell, Roger. *Medieval Wall Paintings in English and Welsh Churches.* Woodbridge: Boydell, 2008.

---. *Medieval Wall Paintings*. London: Shire Publications, 2014.

Taglietti, Franca. "Un nuovo rilievo fittile con scena di mestiere dalla Necropoli dell'Isola Sacra." *Mélanges de l'École française de Rome—Antiquité* 130.2 (2018): 395-398.

Waller, John Green. "On a Painting Recently Discovered in Chaldon Church, Surrey." *Surrey Archeological Collections* 5 (1871): 275-306.

（特邀编辑：张炼）

试论乔叟《学者的故事》之深层次蕴意

沈 弘

内容提要：《学者的故事》是乔叟《坎特伯雷故事集》中长期以来颇有争议的故事之一。这主要是由该故事中男女主人公的个性刻画所引起的。男主人公侯爵沃尔特娶了贫女格丽希尔达为妻，但又对她不够信任，于是便想出了各种极端的方式来考验妻子的忠贞。格丽希尔达虽然成功地经受住了考验，但她对于丈夫的盲目信任和忠诚几乎达到了泯灭人性的地步，很难为现代读者所接受。对该故事主题的阐释，评论家们众说纷纭，但并未达成一致的意见。本文作者认为，像这样一个中世纪的民间传说，并不能单从字面上去理解，因为它往往含有深层的基督教训诫意义。如将它跟《旧约·约伯记》中的故事加以比较，我们便可窥见乔叟塑造这两个人物的用心之一斑。

关键词：乔叟；《坎特伯雷故事集》；《学者的故事》；《约伯记》；人物塑造

作者简介：沈弘，浙江大学外国语学院荣休教授，博士生导师，兼任浙江省翻译协会副会长、浙江省哲学社会科学规划学科组外国语言和文学组成员。研究兴趣：1）英国文学（尤其是中世纪和文艺复兴时期英语诗歌）；2）中外文化交流（尤其是外国人拍摄中国的老照片）；3）非物质文化遗产。出版了45本书，发表了100多篇论文，代表作有《弥尔顿的撒旦与英国文学传统》（2010、2019）、《英国中世纪诗歌选集》（2019）、"遗失在西方的中国史"丛书（2014—2018）等。

Title: On the Biblical Interpretation of "Clerk's Tale" by Geoffrey Chaucer

Abstract: "Clerk's Tale" is for a long time one of the most controversial stories in Chaucer's *Canterbury Tales*. This is mainly caused by the characterization of the two protagonists in the story. Lord Walter marries Griselda, a poor girl from the countryside. Yet he is not sure about her loyalty and chastity, so he tries every possible way to test her. Although Griselda has successfully stood the tests, her blind loyalty and passive submissiveness to her unreasonable husband have invoked aversion among modern readers. In order to give a rational explanation of the characterization of both Walter and Griselda, critics have provided many different interpretations, yet they have never achieved a critical consensus. Nevertheless, to the author of the present paper, a medieval folklore like the "Clerk's Tale" cannot be understood only on the literal level, for it may have a Christian implication of exemplum. If we compare Chaucer's "Clerk's Tale" with "The Book of Job" in the Old Testament, we can have a glimpse of Chaucer's real intention in the creation of the above-mentioned two characters.

Key words: Geoffrey Chaucer, *Canterbury Tales*, "Clerk's Tale," "The Book of Job," character portrayal

Author: Shen Hong, Professor Emeritus at the School of International Studies, Zhejiang University. His research interests are English literature, Sino-Western cultural relations and exchanges, and missionary studies. He earned his B.A., M.A., and Ph.D. from Peking University, and has been a visiting scholar at University of Oxford, Harvard University, University of Toronto, and University of Bristol. He has published altogether 45 books and more than 100 articles. Email: hshen_72@126.com

乔叟《学者的故事》讲述了醋意丈夫考验圣洁妻子这么一个情节极为简单的民间故事，然而它却是《坎特伯雷故事集》中长期以来最有争议的故事之一。20 世纪初，一位不太知名的学者哈蒙德首先指出了一个事实，即婚姻关系是前往坎特伯雷朝圣的香客们拌嘴的重要话题，同时也是他们所讲述的故事中不断再现的主题（Hammond, 1908: 256; Scala, 2009: 50）。《学者的故事》就是"婚姻组合"故事中较为典型的一个。但现代文学评论家们对于该故事的真正含义各执一词，其阐释往往大相径庭。例如基特里奇和卢米亚恩斯基等权威学者认为它有效地反驳了巴斯妇对于美满婚姻中夫妻关系的偏激看法（Kittredge, 1912: 435-437; Lumianski, 1955: 141）。可是也有为数不少的评论者从各自不同的角度出发，对上述观点持完全否定的看法，如欣克利力主该故事的主旨与婚姻本身毫无关系（Hinckley, 1917: 297）；科萨以为，学者在故事中基本肯定了女性在婚姻中的重要位置，因而与巴斯妇并无观点上的分歧（Corsa, 1970: 153）；而惠托克则干脆认为，作为叙述者的香客学者对于故事中男主人公沃尔特的谴责实际上是重申了巴斯妇对于基督教婚姻中夫权至上的抨击（Whittock, 1968: 149）；更有人断言，格丽希尔达的人物形象难以令人接受，并由此认定该故事在某种程度上是一种失败（Bronson, 1960: 103）。面对这种众说纷纭的复杂局面和有趣现象，我们该如何梳理该故事的寓意结构，并对其做出合理解释呢？本文作者认为，要做到这一点，我们首先得承认，《学者的故事》并不像其表面看上去这么浅显，该故事的简单情节中实际上蕴含着一个深奥而微妙的意义结构。

罗曼·英加登在《对文学的艺术作品的认识》这部经典文论中将文学作品的最基本结构视为一个由多种异样意义层次所组成的形态。文学作品的外部表现空间中似乎充满着许多缝隙，英加登将这种意义层次之间的缝隙称为"不确定点"。读者在对作品进行阅读和审美欣赏时，往往会根据自己的丰富想象力和阅历来填补这些"不确定点"，以沟通不同的意义层次，进而从各方面补充完成作者所意欲达到的表现目标。文学作品的艺术魅力和价值有时就在于这种"不确定点"的设置独特和巧妙（1988: 52-53）。

由于其特殊的作品结构，乔叟《坎特伯雷故事集》中的每一个故事都具有两种基本的虚构意义层次：首先，乔叟的每一个故事都被植入一个有机整体框架之中，即它是身份和性格不同的朝圣者在结伴赴坎特伯雷途中轮流讲述的故事之一；其次，每个故事本身又是自成一体的独立叙述单元，它可以根据叙述者的背景和性格，以及他们之间的互动，从不同角度或用不同方式来加以阐释。这种特殊的复合型作品结构决定了故事文本的多层次蕴意。这正是我们用以分析《学者的故事》这一特定作品意义结构的理论基点。

一

《学者的故事》描写的是侯爵沃尔特与贫女格丽希尔达之间的婚姻波折。沃尔特生性多疑，曾几次三番地以极端的方式来考验妻子的忠贞和纯洁；而虔诚善良的格丽希尔达则以无条件地忍耐和顺从夫君至高无上的权力而最终获得了美满的幸福。就故事主题而言，它归属于《坎特伯雷故事集》中一个被称作"婚姻故事"的特殊叙事类别，因为婚姻的主题在乔叟的好几个重要故事中都占有突出的位置，例如《巴斯妇的故事》《商人的故事》《船手的故事》，以及《自由农的故事》。它们都从各自不同的角度审视了婚姻这一主题，并且在不同程度上揭示了夫妻关系在现实社会中错综复杂的矛盾和变化。在某种意义上，《女尼教士的故事》和《磨坊主的故事》也可归属于这一类别，因为它们也都间接地反映出了婚姻的不同侧面。只有把《学者的故事》放在所有这些故事的背景下来进行分析，我们才能更好地理解其真正的思想内涵。

著名的乔叟专家李·帕特森（Lee Patterson）教授 1992 年 3 月在哈佛大学的一次讲座中曾精辟地指出，由于故事叙述者之间的互动，《坎特伯雷故事集》中的绝大部分故事往往都是成双成对的，由此构成和突出了框架故事情节的戏剧性。他认为，表现妻子百依百顺的《学者的故事》与反映媳妇偷汉的《商人的故事》显然是主题上平行对应的。作为当时在现场的听众之一，我觉得他的这种解释不无道理。然而，从朝圣者讲故事的顺序来看，我认为牛津学者的旁敲侧击似乎更应该被看作针对巴斯妇的论调有感而发的，因为当时商人还没有机会轮到自己来讲故事。

从整部作品的框架结构来看，学者和巴斯妇这两位故事讲述者之间也有着众多的对应联系。巴斯妇在其故事引子中就已表现出对教会憎恶妇女的传统恨之入骨，对被培养作为教士的牛津、剑桥学生也普遍持敌视态度：

> 讲到这点，我要请你们相信我：
> 读书人不可能称赞我们女人，
> 除非他们称赞的是位女圣人——
> 对于其他的女人就没这回事。（III.689—691）[①]

正巧她最宠爱的第五任丈夫詹金"一度曾在牛津大学里学习"（III.527），喜欢给她读那些笑骂恶妇的故事段落，这不可避免地导致了后来他俩之

[①] 本文所引《学者的故事》中译文主要参考了黄杲炘翻译的《坎特伯雷故事》，略有改动。

间戏剧性的冲突。作为朝圣客的学者恰好也来自牛津，因此很难想象他会对巴斯妇的冷嘲热讽无动于衷。他并不是个生性好斗的人，所以并没有跟她当面吵起来。然而趁旅店老板请他讲故事的机会，学者却毫不犹豫地试图反驳巴斯妇的谬论。细读原文，我们可以看到学者在下面这两个关键问题上直接批驳了巴斯妇的观点。

关于妻子在美满婚姻中所扮演的角色，巴斯妇斩钉截铁地认为她应该对自己的丈夫具有主宰和支配权。她相信丈夫只有完全屈从于妻子的意志之后，才能期望在婚姻中获得平静和幸福。她在故事的引子中列举了自己五次婚姻的个人经历来反复论证这一观点。其中最有说服力的是她第五个丈夫，后者经常虐待打骂她，曾经一巴掌击穿了巴斯妇一只耳朵的耳膜，但最后终于向她屈膝投降，并且用她自己的话说，"从那天以后，我们再也没争论"（III.822）。巴斯妇的故事讲的是一个犯了强奸罪的骑士被王后赦免了死罪，条件是骑士必须在一年之内找出"女人最想要的是什么"（III.905）。直到故事的结尾处，他才从一位丑老妪那儿得到了关于这个问题的正确答案：原来女人在所有事物中最想得到的是对丈夫和情人的支配及主宰权。骑士最终臣服于丑老妪的意愿，跟她结了婚，并且真的获得了一个娇妻和美满的婚姻。

而学者想要传递的是一个截然不同的信息。他故事中作为世人楷模的妻子格丽希尔达与巴斯妇所宣扬的那位丑老妪个性恰恰相反。格丽希尔达忍辱负重，委曲求全，完全服从于丈夫的意愿。在学者的眼里，这似乎是一种理想的夫妻关系：

> 结果，他们俩似乎只有一颗心，
> 因为她无论丈夫有什么意愿，
> 总把实现这意愿看得最要紧，
> 谢天谢地，其结果倒也很圆满。
> 作为妻子，面对世界上的纷乱，
> 她出于自愿，不肯有什么主张，
> 除非这主张就是丈夫的愿望。（IV.715—721）

在成功地经受住丈夫的各种堪称苛刻、过分的考验之后，格丽希尔达果然苦尽甘来，获得了最终的荣誉和幸福。

学者反驳巴斯妇观点的另外一个重要方面就是刻意强调了爱情的主题，后者则把两性之间的情爱看作是获得财富和婚姻幸福的一种手段。巴斯妇在其故事的引子里反复强调了她自己的观点，即男人必须能满足她自己的情欲，给她提供富足的生活条件，更重要的是还必须听命于她，才能够成为她的丈夫。根据这些必要条件，她将自己前后嫁过的五个丈夫一个个地排队比较，分出了三个好丈夫和两个坏丈夫，但即使是那三个好丈夫也不能满足她自己的欲望：

> 真的，他们那点活不在我眼里。
> 他们给了我他们的钱财、土地；
> 所以我不必对他们毕恭毕敬，
> 不必为博得他们的爱而费心。
> 天知道，他们爱我爱得很真挚，
> 所以，对他们的爱我并不珍视！（III.203—208）

与巴斯妇的看法相反，学者坚持认为脱离了世俗考虑的爱情和夫妻双方对彼此的忠贞才是婚姻关系的坚实基础。侯爵沃尔特当初选择贫女格丽希尔达并不是出于政治或金钱的考虑，而是因为爱慕她纯洁沉静的气质和异常高贵的品性：

> 她的容貌和举止都这么年轻，
> 侯爵的心感受到女性的温柔，
> 感受到姑娘超越常人的德性；
> 虽然说美德很难被眼睛看透，
> 但侯爵深信这姑娘品行优秀，
> 而且他已暗暗把决心下定了：
> 如果要娶亲，非娶这姑娘不可。（IV.239—245）

尽管如此，侯爵后来作为丈夫那种近乎病态的试妻方式在常人眼里还是不可取和令人难以接受的。关于这一问题，我们在后面会有进一步的深入讨论。

作为一个基督教的圣女，格丽希尔达本人也是把爱情和妻子对丈夫的忠贞视为高于一切的。在每一次厄运降临时，都是对于丈夫深深的挚爱，以及对于上帝坚如磐石的信仰，才使得格丽希尔达能忍受打击，渡过难关，转危为安。这跟上述巴斯妇的自述和所作所为形成了鲜明的对比。

二

当然，《学者的故事》并不仅仅是乔叟用作对《坎特伯雷故事集》中任何一个其他故事的正面或侧面回答。作为一个中世纪末期曾在欧洲广泛流传的民间传说，该故事本身对于当时的许多人肯定具有一种普遍的吸引力。据调查，在乔叟的众多故事中，它曾是15世纪英国最受欢迎的两个故事之一，这另一个故事便是《坎特伯雷故事集》中的《修女院院长的故事》，二者都曾被人转述过六次以上（Pearsall, 1985: 301）。虽然人们可以对中世纪读者理解文学作品之深层蕴意的程度持保留态度，但《学者的故事》作为虚构作品或道德劝诫的特质和价值却是毋庸置疑的。

关于格丽希尔达的故事源远流长，所以在对它做深层分析之前我们有必要了解乔叟本人对于原故事所做的贡献。J. B. 西弗斯在《乔叟〈学者的故事〉之文学渊源》（1942）一书中对此问题做了详尽的调查。他将乔叟的故事与其可能的原始出处，如薄伽丘的《十日谈》（1353）的意大利文本、彼特拉克的拉丁文改写本（1373—1374）和菲利浦·德梅齐尔的法译本（1383—1389）等进行了仔细核对之后，发现乔叟的重要贡献在于使故事更加现实化、更令人信服，人物的心理描写更为细腻（Severs, 1942: 342-350）。因此，让我们先弄清这一点，这对于进一步揭示《学者的故事》的深层蕴意可以说是至关重要的。

举侯爵沃尔特为例，他对妻子格丽希尔达的粗暴对待经常被评论家们说成是毫无动机的。然而乔叟给原故事增添的某些微小的细节恰恰为解释侯爵古怪行为的社会或心理动机提供了线索，使上面这种说法不攻自破。我们只要回顾一下历史背景，就不难看出沃尔特在《学者的故事》中的所作所为具有深邃的社会学含义。

在故事的开头，作为叙述人的学者就告诉我们，侯爵婚前过着公子哥儿的放荡生活。他不情愿结婚是因为有一种惧内的不安全感，或称结婚恐惧症：

　　我这人对于自由一向很倾心，

> 但一旦结婚就很难再有自由，
>
> 那时候我就不再有这种享受。（IV.145—147）

然而强大的政治压力迫使他要为自己的臣民选择一位侯爵夫人。他之所以匆忙地娶了格丽希尔达这样一位身份卑微的乡间女子，除了真的爱情之外，部分原因可能也是想要避免他所畏惧的婚姻束缚。他求婚的场景简直是对中世纪"优雅爱情"样式中骑士精神的莫大亵渎。这位在其领地上可谓权力无限的封建君主居高临下地站在一个双膝跪地、惊惶战栗的贫女格丽希尔达面前，声色俱厉地向她提出十分苛刻的结婚条件。他这样做的主要目的当然是确保他作为主人的社会地位和作为丈夫的家庭特权。这些要求未来妻子无条件服从的严苛条件为他后来的粗暴行为投下了浓重的阴影：

> "我要问你，是不是你真的愿意
>
> 以我的任何意愿为你的意愿；
>
> 不管我想法使你难受或欢喜，
>
> 你无论白天黑夜都不会抱怨，
>
> 也不会坚持同我相反的意见——
>
> 对我的决定不会皱眉和拒绝？
>
> 对此发了誓，我们就缔结婚约。"（IV.351—357）

当婚姻中这种不平等的夫妻关系确立之后，侯爵便可肆无忌惮地用各种方式来试探自己的妻子，其无理和霸道程度令人发指，就连作为故事讲述者的学者也不得不谴责这位唯我独尊的醋坛子郎君。

无论其内心如何因权欲而失去了平衡，但侯爵的行为却绝非普通意义上的精神变态。在试妻的整个过程中，沃尔特其实都是能控制住自己情绪的，从而将格丽希尔达玩弄于股掌之中。如他用把初生女婴从母亲怀里夺走的方式来试探格丽希尔达的反应时，后者并没有因此对他显露出任何违逆之意：

> 侯爵听了这回答，心中很得意，
>
> 却觉得好像心里感到不舒服，
>
> 等到他快要离开这间卧室时，

举止和神色更显得有点恼怒。(IV.512—515)

当警卫官前来向他报告格丽希尔达如何默默忍受失去女婴这一重大打击，并将女婴呈上给沃尔特看时，后者也曾闪现过恻隐之心：

这时侯爵的神色中流露怜悯，
但他并没有让他的计划变更，
因为王公贵人的心肠硬得很。(IV.579—581)

这句话很显然是对这位自负而虚伪的贵族一针见血的批评。

与此形成鲜明对比的是，乔叟通过对一系列不幸事件的渲染，着重强调了格丽希尔达对丈夫的挚爱及其温顺、坚忍和谦恭的品格。作为从底层贫女爬上来的侯爵夫人，格丽希尔达极有自知之明。从沃尔特向她求婚之时起，她就明白自己与未来丈夫之间有一道不可逾越的阶级鸿沟，正如她后来所承认的那样，"我没有自认为是这儿的女主人，/ 觉得只配做爵爷卑下的婢女"(IV.823—824)。此外，她超凡的自控能力也表明了一种以柔克刚的坚毅性格。例如在故事的第五部中，侯爵在假装剥夺了格丽希尔达的一对子女之后，还要跟她离婚，打发她回乡下的老家。更有甚者，在临走时他还要求她脱去所有的外衣，只穿着内衣离开。至此，侯爵对于她忠贞和忍耐力的考验几乎已经达到了极限，但她仍然保持了难以置信的自制力。最后，当沃尔特确信妻子经受住了考验之后，又以自己要举办婚礼为由，将她重新召回王宫之时，后者仍然显得神情自若，荣辱不惊，

她心怀谦恭，脸上显露出欢快，
奉命而来，见到了侯爵便跪拜；
她没有丝毫的骄气或是怨气，
而是恭敬得体地祝侯爵大喜。(IV.949—952)

必须指出的是，在刻画人物性格上，乔叟并没有落入俗套，给格丽希尔达的坚忍性格做公式化的刻板描写，而是根据故事情节的发展，细致地刻画了女主人公的情绪波动和变化，从而反衬出她性格之坚毅。如在前面第五部中，她表示愿意回到父亲那儿去的一段讲话就流露出了一

种微妙的反讽语气。正如西弗斯所指出的那样，乔叟对原故事情节所增添的那些诗行带有明白无误的责难口吻：

> "天主啊，回想我们结婚时的你——
> 那天你说话时的口气和神态，
> 让人感到多么的高贵与和蔼！（IV.852—854）
> ……
> "我这身子里孕育过你的儿女，
> 如果让我在你的臣民前走过，
> 如果让我赤裸裸暴露无遗，
> 这种不光彩的事，想你不肯做。
> 所以请别让我像爬虫般赤裸。
> 我最亲爱的夫君，请你要记得，
> 我曾经是你妻子，尽管不够格。"（IV.876—882）

格丽希尔达这番言辞激烈的请求将故事情节推向了高潮，与此同时，它也充分表现出了女主人公的强烈个性。乔叟笔下的格丽希尔达是一个有血有肉的人物形象，而绝不是有些评论家所想象或描写的那么消极被动和性格单一。

三

《学者的故事》尽管基本描写手法逼真，但格丽希尔达的圣洁形象却仍然给现代读者一种极为矛盾的感受，即便是与乔叟同时代的人也不例外。为了理解这一特定人物形象的真实蕴意，我们不必完全拘泥于这部作品字面上的描写，而是有必要探讨一下该故事的深层蕴意。这也正是乔叟要求读者做的。在该故事的结尾，作为叙述人的牛津学者一语点破了解读该故事寓意的正确方法：

> 讲这个故事，并非要每个女性
> 都学格丽希尔达的那种谦恭，
> 哪怕愿意学，学起来也太费劲，
> 而是要人人明白自己的地位，
> 哪怕在逆境中也要坚定无悔……（IV.1142—1146）

这种由表及里、由此及彼的阐释方式涉及了一个根深蒂固的中世纪文学作品解读传统，后者通常被称作"四重诠释"，即认为一般文本都可能具有四种层次不同的意义。这种特定的解读方式最早是被基督教教父们用来阐释《圣经》。早在公元 4 世纪，希波的圣奥古斯丁就曾经指出，《旧约》可按历史、原因论、类比和讽喻等类别区分出四种不同层次的含义；另一位中世纪神学权威托马斯·阿奎那后来对这一理论做了更为系统的修正。他运用一些超前的现代术语，将宗教作品的内蕴分别描述为字面的、讽喻的、伦理的和神秘的这四个层面的意义（Adams and Searle, 2005: 151）。然而这种解读方法并不局限于宗教作品。随着法国诗人纪尧姆·德洛里斯的《玫瑰传奇》第一部分在 13 世纪 30 年代的问世，世俗爱情诗歌中的讽喻性描写已经变得越来越普遍，其结果就是对深层次蕴意的强调最终成了中世纪欧洲文学作品的一个主要因素。在这种时代背景下，但丁试图将"四重诠释"的理论应用于普通文学作品的做法也就不足为奇了。他在著名的批评论著《飨宴》中几乎原封不动地借用了原有的批评术语，但却以更为直截了当的方式对于文学作品的解读理论进行了精辟的阐发：

> ……文学作品能够，也应该主要用四种不同观念来进行阐释。第一种称作字面意义，即受原文字母严格限制的观念层次；第二种称作讽喻意义，它经过故事伪装，是隐藏在一个美丽谎话下的真理……第三种是伦理意义，教师们为他们自身和学生的利益，在精读作品时尤其应该寻找它……第四种是被称作神秘意义，它无法用普通概念来说明，意指心领神会，即使是字面意义上最普通的事物也可以暗示天国永恒的无限荣光……[①]（Adams and Searle, 2005: 154）

在分析《学者的故事》时，我们有必要充分认识这个具有普遍意义的中世纪解读传统，注意寻找出作品各个意义层次之间的密切联系，这样才能避免阐释中的混乱，并能领略各种暗示或讽喻的深层蕴意。由于篇幅有限，本文不会面面俱到，试图去寻找和分析所有这四种不同层次的意义。但如果把《旧约·约伯记》中的故事拿来跟《学者的故事》进行一番比

---

① 此处中文译文由本文作者翻译。

较和剖析，就足以揭示出乔叟笔下的沃尔特和格丽希尔达这两个人物的行为举止为何看起来是如此的极端。归根结底，乔叟本人在《坎特伯雷故事集》中反复强调了这一特定的讽喻传统："我们的《圣经》上说，'凡是写下来的，其目的都是为了让我们受教益。'这正合吾意。"（X.1083）

约伯本是一个富裕的犹太人，耶和华的忠实信徒。"他生了七个儿子，三个女儿。他的家产有七千羊、三千骆驼、五百对牛、五百母驴，并有许多仆婢。"（《约伯记》1：2—3）但祸从天降，一下子就打破了他生活的平静。耶和华对约伯起了疑心，派撒旦①下凡去试探约伯对上帝的忠诚。于是约伯的牲畜被示巴人所掳，仆人被杀；羊和仆人被突降的天火烧死；骆驼也被迦勒底人抢走；而且狂风吹倒了房屋，压死了他的儿女们。面对着突如其来的灾难，约伯显示出了极大的忍耐力和对耶和华的信任和忠诚：

> 约伯便起来，撕裂外袍，剃了头，伏在地上下拜，说："我赤身出于母胎，也必赤身归回。赏赐的是耶和华，收取的也是耶和华，耶和华的名是应当称颂的。"（《旧约·约伯记》1：20—21）②

读到这儿，我们不禁恍然大悟，格丽希尔达对于丈夫沃尔特的无条件信任和忠贞原来跟约伯对耶和华的态度如出一辙。沃尔特为了试探妻子的忠贞，从她手中夺去了一对儿女，而且还以迎娶新欢为由，要把结婚多年、尽心尽力服侍他的妻子扫地出门。更有甚者，他还要她交还所有的衣服和首饰珠宝。对如此荒唐无理的要求，格丽希尔达不仅百依百顺，而且所说的话语也跟约伯几乎一模一样：

> "现在我向你交还所有的衣饰，
> 同时也永远交还这结婚戒指。
> 你所赏给我的其他所有珠宝，
> 我可以保证全都留在你屋里；
> 当初我光着身子离家，"她说道，
> "就必须也同样光着身子回去。"（IV.867—872）

---

① 撒旦在叛逆之前曾是天国的大天使和耶和华的信使官。
② 本文中有关《约伯记》的引文均出自《新旧约全书》。

同样，刚愎自用、乖张多疑的侯爵沃尔特似乎也是以《约伯记》中的耶和华为原型的。在他自己的领地上，沃尔特就是一个至高无上权威的存在。他在试妻一事上的所作所为酷似试探约伯的耶和华，动辄极限施压，完全不顾及对方的感受和社会行为规范。

有趣的是，在《约伯记》中，耶和华在首次试探约伯之后跟撒旦有过一次辩论。起初是耶和华向撒旦询问约伯在遭受家庭不幸后的表现。在得知约伯对他依然表示忠诚之后，其得意之情溢于言表。撒旦趁机说，约伯这么做是因为灾难尚未伤及他自身，"人以皮代皮，情愿舍去一切所有的保全性命。你且伸手伤他的骨头和他的肉，他必当面弃掉你"（《约伯记》2：5）。于是耶和华便对撒旦说，约伯任凭他处置，只要留其性命便可。对比沃尔特与耶和华的试探方法，我们得知后者远甚于前者。沃尔特从格丽希尔达手中夺走了她的一对儿女，谎称要应民众的要求弄死他们，但他并没有真的这么做。他后来又谎称要娶新欢，因此不仅要退婚格丽希尔达，而且还要求后者作为女仆来服侍新的侯爵夫人。这些做法虽然非常过分，但都不是真的。而耶和华试探约伯的做法则是刀刀见血：约伯的庞大家产转瞬间灰飞烟灭，他的十个孩子和众多的男女仆人也都随即死于非命，就像碾死蚂蚁那么简单。侯爵试妻，仅限于心理折磨，可耶和华试探约伯，则让他伤筋动骨，"使他从脚掌到头顶长毒疮"（《约伯记》2：7）。从纯世俗的角度看，这确实有点像暴君的做法，令人难以接受；但是从基督教的宗教角度看，耶和华是造物主，而人和家产等均是造物主的创造或馈赠，造物主本人自然有权随意处置。

忍耐和忠诚是沃尔特与耶和华试探手段的对象和目的，同时它们也是格丽希尔达和约伯的共同性格特征。在这一方面，约伯的性格显得比较外向，而格丽希尔达的性格则很内向。这跟他们的境遇和社会环境有关。

约伯有三位好友，分别是提幔人以利法、书亚人比勒达和拿玛人琐法。他们得知约伯遭遇飞来横祸之后，便一起来到他家，看望和安慰他。约伯在命运的严厉打击下，信仰曾有所动摇，开始诅咒自己的生日，并且想到了一死了之。于是这三位朋友便开始轮流斥责和开导他。他们告诉约伯："神所惩治的人是有福的，所以你不可轻看全能者的管教。因为他打破，又缠裹，用手医治。"（《约伯记》5：17—18）"神必不丢弃完全人，也不扶助邪恶人。他还要以喜笑充满你的口，以欢呼充满你的嘴。"
（8：20—21）约伯起初并没有被说服，他自以为有冤情，因为很多恶人
藐主反享平康，而他自己作为守义之人却反遭惩治，说着便与三位朋友
辩论起来并使后者陷入了无语的状态。这时一个名叫以利户的布西年轻
人也加入了进来，警告约伯不要妄议神的所作所为，而是要信服神之威
能奇妙。最后，耶和华跻身于旋风之中，与约伯直接开展了一场对话。
耶和华以造物之妙和禽献之性来诘问约伯，终于使约伯充分感受到了自
身的卑贱，并对神认罪自责。他以这种方式终于守住了底线。

相比之下，格丽希尔达的性格截然不同。从头到尾，她都没有朋友或
闺蜜来帮自己排忧解难。因丈夫试探她而遭遇了这么多的不公和心理折
磨，她的心里肯定也是有冤屈的，但她选择了独自默默忍受，没有怨恨，
也没有诉苦。这正是中世纪圣徒传记中典型的圣女形象，因为忍耐和忠诚
是基督教教义中的美德，而格丽希尔达将这些美德发挥得淋漓尽致。

正因为约伯和格丽希尔达都凭借忍耐和忠诚经受住了考验，所以他
们的故事都以传统的大团圆结局告终。耶和华的慷慨馈赠使得约伯有了
比以前加倍的家产，人丁也跟以前一样兴旺："他有一万四千羊、六千骆
驼、一千对牛、一千母驴。他也有七个儿子，三个女儿。"（《约伯记》42：
12—13）不但如此，他的三个女儿还是当地最漂亮的。约伯本人也得以
福寿延年，四世同堂，又幸福地活了一百四十年。《学者的故事》也是如
此，沃尔特在故事结尾处向格丽希尔达坦白了他所隐瞒的一切，把一对
已长大成人的儿女重新交还给她，并且重新恢复了她宫廷女主人的尊贵
身份。此后许多年，他们相亲相爱，和谐安宁，过了一段富裕而幸福的
生活。女儿嫁给了一位贵族，儿子后来也继承了父亲的爵位，并娶了一
位贤惠的妻子。

结　语

通过以上的分析，我们认识到，格丽希尔达那种表面上对丈夫的一
味顺从，实际上是一种以柔克刚的有效方法，最终征服了那位刚愎自用
的侯爵沃尔特。她的圣洁美德，在坚信上帝的力量和甘愿忍受痛苦等方
面与基督教英雄主义品德实际上是相一致的。弥尔顿在《失乐园》中把
这种精神称为"更为崇高的刚毅"，其深邃意义反映在亚当在诗歌结尾处

的一段告白：

> 因此我体会到最好的品德是服从，
> 爱慕和敬畏唯一的上帝，随时随地
> 都好像侍奉在他身旁，永远遵循
> 他的意志，平生只依靠他的恩赐，
> 对他所有的创造物都普施慈悲：
> 永远以善治恶，还要以表面的弱者
> 战胜世间的强者，并且以朴拙
> 来战胜世间的智巧……（《失乐园》12: 561—569）①

这最后三行诗也可用以概括乔叟笔下女主人公格丽希尔达的超常坚毅性格。她的坚定信仰和处惊不乱的毅力使她能勇敢地面对逆境的考验，并最终赢得她那位暴虐夫君的尊敬。她是一个从细微之处着手来完成大事业，并且以弱胜强、以拙制巧的光辉典范。

引用文献【Works Cited】

Adams, Hazard, and Leroy Searle, eds. *Critical Theory since Plato*. 3rd ed. Boston: Thomson Wadsworth, 2005.

Bronson, Bertrand H. *In Search of Chaucer*. Toronto: U of Toronto P, 1960.

Corsa, Helen Storm. *Chaucer, Poet of Mirth and Morality*. Toronto: Forum House, 1970.

Hammond, Eleanor Prescott. *Chaucer: A Bibliographic Manual*. New York: Macmillan, 1908.

Hinckley, Henry Barrett. "The Debate on Marriage in *The Canterbury Tales*." *PMLA* 32.2 (1917): 292-305.

Hughes, Merritt Y., ed. *John Milton: Complete Poems and Major Prose*. New York: Macmillan, 1985.

Kittredge, George Lyman. "Chaucer's Discussion of Marriage." *Modern Philology* 9.4 (1912): 435-467.

---

① 此处中文译文由本文作者根据 Hughes（1985）所编版本翻译。

Lumianski, R. M. *Of Sondry Folk: The Dramatic Principle in* The Canterbury Tales. Austin: U of Texas P, 1955.

Pearsall, Derek. *The Canterbury Tales*. Unwin Critical Library. London: G. Allen & Unwin, 1985.

Scala, Elizabeth. "The Women in Chaucer's 'Marriage Group'." *Medieval Feminist Forum: Journal of the Society for Medieval Feminist Scholarship* 49.1 (2009): 50-56.

Severs, Jonathan Burke. *The Literary Relationships of Chaucer's* Clerkes Tale. New Haven: Yale UP, 1942.

Whittock, Trevor. *A Reading of the* Canterbury Tales. Cambridge: Cambridge UP, 1968.

乔叟，2011，《坎特伯雷故事》，黄杲炘译，上海：上海译文出版社。

罗曼·英加登，1988，《对文学的艺术作品的认识》，陈燕谷译，北京：中国文联出版公司。

1989，《新旧约全书》，南京：中国基督教协会。

（特邀编辑：郝田虎、张炼）

中世纪英国文学在民国时期的"旅行"①

张亚婷

内容提要: 中世纪英国文学在民国时期得到了较好的译介和研究。本文旨在梳理和呈现不同年代的推广进程和主要观点,探讨民国时期学人在处理材料中遵循的原则和模式,以观照其中出现的偏好。研究发现,虽然相关成果产出地区不平衡,但民国时期学人具备跨文化意识,多遵循线性模式和类比原则,概述和定性同行。从偏好模式来看,他们多选择译介乔叟诗作,评论、撰写或翻译文学史,传递观点时能结合中国现状反思,具有一定的连续性和系统性,偏好序列有一定强度,认知宽度和深度逐渐增强。

关键词: 中世纪英国文学;乔叟;民国时期;接受;偏好

作者简介: 张亚婷,陕西师范大学外国语学院教授,主要从事中世纪英国文学研究,著有《中世纪英国文学中的母性研究》(中央编译出版社,2014)和《中世纪英国动物叙事文学研究》(北京大学出版社,2018)。本文为国家社科基金后期资助重点项目"盎格鲁-诺曼语文学史"(21FWWA003)的阶段性成果。

Title: "Travel" of Medieval English Literature in the Republic of China Era

Abstract: Medieval English literary works have been well compiled, translated and studied in the Republic of China era. This paper aims to examine and showcase their promotion and the dominant ideas in different decades and generalize the scholars' principles and patterns when they deal with the materials so as to find out their

---

① 本文为作者应位于牛津大学的中世纪语言与文学研究会(Society for the Study of Medieval Languages and Literature)斯蒂芬·平克(Stephen Pink)博士之邀,于2020年9月8日至10日在Zoom线上参加国际学术会议"Dark Archives: A Conference of Medieval Unread & Unreadable"的发言稿"Digitalization and Practicalities of Medieval English Studies in China"的第一部分。

preferences. As is shown, the relevant production is regionally unbalanced, but the scholars have cross-cultural consciousness and follow the linear pattern and analogical principle when they generalize with the qualitative research. As for their preferences, they mainly choose to compile and translate Geoffrey Chaucer's poems, make comments and write or compile the literary history. They usually respond to the contemporary situation when passing on their ideas, which are obviously continual and systematic with a certain intensity of preference ordering and a gradual intensification of both breadth and depth of their understanding.

Key words: medieval English literature, Chaucer, the Republic of China era, reception, preferences

Author: Zhang Yating is a professor at the School of International Studies, Shaanxi Normal University, specializing in medieval English literature. She has published *A Study of Motherhood Represented in the Literature of Medieval England* (Central Compilation & Translation Press, 2014) and *Animal Narrative in Medieval English Literature* (Peking University Press, 2018). Email: zhangyt@snnu.edu.cn

在中国，中世纪英国文学从民国初期的零星译介到 21 世纪的多样化研究已超百年，经历了一个复杂多变的运动曲线。国内学人已对古英语文学、1978 年后中世纪英国文学的研究、乔叟（Geoffrey Chaucer）[①]及《坎特伯雷故事集》（下文简称为《坎》）的译介和学术史都有相关总结。[②]需要指出的是，民国时期学人并未局限于对中世纪英国个别作家或作品的引介和评论，他们通过不同媒介向读者传递和扩散信息，在全面推介和研究方面做出了不可忽视的贡献，其建立起的知识体系和建立过程中的方法互鉴、对基本概念的界定与观点反思既通过时空与欧美学界达成共识和对话，又为后来的译介、研究和方法提供了基本模型。

[①] 中世纪英国作家姓名和作品题目翻译不一致，本文采用现在学界公认的名字和名称，人名注出英文名，中世纪英国作家作品的引文注明作品和诗行，不再另注。

[②] 按照发表或出版时间顺序：杨开泛（2011, 2012）、曹航（2013）、郝田虎（Tianhu Hao, 2015）、王荣（2017）、张炼（2019a, 2019b, 2021）、肖明翰（2019）、张炼（Lian Zhang, 2020）。

一、20 世纪 10 年代和 20 年代

目前可及文献显示，"中世纪"这一说法 1909 年在国内出现（哈门德, 1909: 14-16），也被称为"中古"或"中世"（乐天, 1941: 8）。虽然民国时期学人对"中世纪"的时间节点划分存在分歧（郑振铎, 1924a: 1; 乐天, 1941: 8; 东资, 1949: 32），但中世纪英国文学能被引介到中国是西学东渐历程和国内对西学的提倡以及国际关系格局发展需求的结果。19 世纪，中国人自认为在文化和物质上能自给自足，认为国外的东西都很低贱且国际交往没有任何价值（Lynch, 2010: 7），还持有偏见，把"英吉利"人及其国王威廉称作"红毛"，古代布立吞人被看作比钟馗还狰狞十倍的野蛮人。[①]17 世纪和 19 世纪来华传教士指出语言阻碍中西交流，李提摩太（Timothy Richard, 1845—1919）提出派人游学、出国读书、立报馆、译西书、建书院、增科目和加大人才培养力度等建议。[②]事实上，中国人很快意识到学习英语的重要性。吴肇基的文章表明，青年学子认为学习英语既可获取知识，又可为民族谋福祉（Wu, 1915: 135-136）。国内大学成立相关组织或社团以加强英语学习。[③]熊月之指出，19 世纪的西学书籍在中国的译介和传播多以宗教类和非文学类著作为多（熊月之, 2011: 385）。中国人认为，要学西方先要学日本，19 世纪末形成留日热潮和日文西书翻译热，而"欧美→日本→中国"成为 20 世纪初新学源源不断传入中国的主通道，面广量多，令中国学术界眼界大开（熊月之, 2011: 523）。[④]民国时期学人群体经历了科举制废除和清王朝覆灭，不少人除了在国内接受新式学校教育外，还留学欧美接受过西方高等教育，对西方学术文化比较了解，并有自己的研究领域和社会职业，可谓近代知识分子（郑大华, 2020: 21）。史学教材的编写旨在讲述东西各民族文化的

---

① 《东西史记和合：英吉利撒孙朝》（1834: 89 上）；《东西史记和合：元纪（英吉利哪耳慢朝）》（1834: 125 下）。

② 利类思、安文思和南怀仁（1669: 256-2, 256-4）；李提摩太（1897: 13-16）。

③ 《北大成立英文学研究组　德文学组亦筹备就绪》（1926）；《北大第一次英语竞赛昨在二院举行》（1936）；《师大英语辩论　题目拟定　报名者十余人》（1935）；《女院英语赛结果公布》（1936）；《几个有关英语教学的中等教育问题　教部长王世杰广播讲演》（1937）；《教部谋提高英语程度决组英语教学研究会　总会设南京各地设分会》（1945）。

④ 1915 年留日人数达 4500 人，参见《记载：中国留日学生总数》（1915: 129）。

盛衰和民族互动关系，了解当时国际形势，认识中国在世界上的地位以唤起自觉心（郑昶，1933：1）。大量期刊的出现为引介和研究提供了有效媒介（宋应离，2000）。欧阳哲生指出，民国学术是中国传统学术向现代学术转型的历史时期，传统学术的通识特征对新文化人纵横驰骋于不同学科提供了强有力的知识资源支持（欧阳哲生，2020：5），而民国学术研究方法具有引进、消化、融合和创新的过程（薛其林，2003：120-123）。就中世纪英国文学在国内的译介和研究而言，其"旅行"过程既有文学评论家或文学史家的推进，也有学院派的阐释，他们确定了译介和研究范式，话语体系和欧美中世纪研究开始接轨。

正是在这种大背景下，20世纪10年代，乔叟和《贝奥武甫》（下文简称为《贝》）分别出现在下列刊物中：《小说月报》《丞社丛刊》和《学生》。关于乔叟在中国最早的引介学者和时间，黄杲炘（1999：15）、曹航（2013：89）和王荣（2017：54）均有讨论，但张炼进行修正后定位到商务印书馆编译所负责人、从1908年起陆续把欧美作家介绍到中国的清朝秀才孙毓修（1871—1922）和1913年《小说月报》第4卷第1期（张炼，2019a：302；Zhang，2020：5）。孙毓修介绍了乔叟的文学地位和贡献，认为他洞察世故，把故事编译起来，英国人"因其古"而尊之，但其意在教化作用。这对乔叟的作者身份、作品价值和社会功能做了简短说明（孙毓修，1913a：7）。1913年，他编译了《坎》之《卖赎罪券教士的故事》，指出英国戏剧始于1100年前后，分为奇迹剧和神秘剧（孙毓修，1913b：47）。林纾和陈家麟合译的《坎》的故事中只在"林妖"题目下注明"英国曹西尔（即乔叟）原著"（曹西尔，1917：1-4）。关于《贝》，目前可及文献显示，启明（周作人笔名）率先在1915年的《丞社丛刊》中介绍了《贝》。他指出，史诗出自民歌，叙说壮举，英国诗歌开始于7世纪，凯德蒙（Cædmon）前有著者，但不知其名和年代，多残缺不全，谈到《贝》时指出，"欧洲史诗，舍希腊的二首外，此为最古亦最有价值者"（周作人，1915：5），并概述了其主要内容。[1]1917年，《贝》以两页现代英文介绍故事情节的形式出现在《学生》上，作者署名是位于开封

---

① 感谢郝田虎教授，他在2021年3月26日致笔者的电邮中明确提醒了周作人的这篇文章及其来源。

的政府预备学校（即河南留学欧美预备学校，后来的河南大学）的 K. C. Chu（Chu, 1917: 147-148）。①该刊目标读者是中学生。这说明，当时的英语教学已不再局限于语言使用，而是在人才培养方面注重文学和文化素养的提升和接轨。

20 世纪 20 年代起，国内学人有明确的文学批评意识和实践活动（刘诗诗, 2020: 10-18）。吴宓指出，中国人能读西书者甚少，虽作者笔墨辩论中述经据典，但读者因未读原著，并不能洞见论据是否合理，强调"欲谈文学，必须著译专书"（吴宓, 1921: 28）。这可以说是为文学研究和西方接轨提出了方法和途径。他列举的必读书目就包括《圣经及中古文选》和 40 年代被翻译的穆迪（W. V. Moody）的《英国文学史》（吴宓, 1923: 1-9）。我们发现，中世纪英国文学出现在对欧洲文学史或英国文学史的整体梳理和评论系统之中，显示出民国时期学人从对欧洲的宏大认识体系掌握逐渐转向更为细化和有深度的挖掘和研究之中。他们以通识为目的，沿袭了一套比较认同的话语，对民族史表现出兴趣的同时在文本和作家的选择取舍中出现偏好序列，也反映出他们的历史意识和开放姿态。正如任博德所言，1905 年，科举考试被废除，其结果之一就是被严格遵守的司马迁编年史风格消失，欧洲史学观取而代之，尤其是在民国期间，20 世纪初期欧洲的历史编纂学受孔德（Auguste Comte）和马克思（Karl Marx）所发展的实证主义历史编纂学的深刻影响（任博德, 2017: 291, 274）。

首先，我们来看各种刊物的推介和认识。英语刊物以"英文概述＋中文脚注"的方式把《贝》讲给读者（Vane, 1925: 702-703; Zan, 1929: 205）。人们对于中世纪的认识持"美的时代"和"黑暗论"两种论调，后一种论调自意大利学者彼特拉克（Petrarch）14 世纪早期提出，持续了近 7 个世纪。施蛰存认为，在中世纪"对于宗教的反动之表现在文学上就是多量传奇故事之产生"，把这些传奇故事和宋代流行于市井的"说话"相比，中世纪充满浪漫意味，是"美的时代"，鼓励把中世纪时期欧洲的传奇和中国唐宋传奇比较（施蛰存, 1928: 540-545）。郑振铎尤其关

---

① 1912 年，河南留学欧美预备学校在清代开封国家贡院旧址创办，与当时的清华学校（今清华大学）和上海南洋公学（今上海交通大学）呈三足鼎立的局面。该校每年派出留学人员 20 名，参见《指令河南教育厅留学预备学校毕业各生应准一律应考文》（1918: 78）。

注意大利、英国和德国文学，在分析历史和文化语境的基础上肯定了本笃会教士在保留古代文化遗产方面的贡献，认为在圣奥古斯丁（Saint Augustine）之后欧洲文学史上没有重要事迹可记，但认为各国民间史诗恰在这个黑暗时期完成，强调吟游诗人和宫廷诗人在文化发展和传播中的作用。英国方面，他提到历史学家比德（Bede）和哲学家洛格·培根（Roger Bacon），认为编年史家傅华萨（Jean Froissart）是"历史传奇"的代表，乔叟是英国诗歌之父，曾遇彼特拉克，《坎》受《十日谈》影响，每个故事都"极有神色"，指出乔叟的贡献在于以英国话作诗而获成功，使后来者不得不用他们本国的语言作诗与文。关于乔叟使用英语方面的开拓性贡献、善辩之才、知识渊博和辞藻之美，其实 15 世纪乔叟派诗人霍克利夫（William Hoccleve）就给予了高度肯定（Hoccleve, 1999: 96, 185）。显然，这种观点从英国辗转时空"旅行"到了中国。郑振铎提及兰格伦（William Langland）和高厄（John Gower）及其代表作，介绍了马洛礼（St. Thomas Malory）的《亚瑟王之死》（下文简称为《亚》）和它对斯宾塞（Edmund Spencer）、弥尔顿（John Milton）和丁尼生（Alfred Tennyson）创作产生的影响。应该说，他把对中世纪英国的认识置于整个欧洲文学史框架之内，拓宽了读者对中世纪晚期英国经典作家的了解，肯定了他们的贡献和对后世文学的影响。郑振铎具有跨文化视野，在谈及中世纪中国诗歌时指出，中世纪欧洲文学处于"黑暗时代"，重要作家极少，不朽之作除了《神曲》和各国民歌之外并不多见，但中国文学却产生了不少重要诗人和不朽名著（郑振铎, 1924b: 94-116）。曾虚白认为，要谈英国文学史，"从乔叟以至今日"，"跳不出条顿性和拉丁性的乘除消长，互为起伏"（曾虚白, 1928b: 1）。他点出了英国文学和欧陆文学之间的文化渊源和互动关系，第一次使用国内学界现在通用的"乔叟"这一译名。《金陵女子大学校刊》上的文章认为，盎格鲁-撒克逊文学充满想象与活力，以古英语诗歌鼓励人们要勇敢地为生命而战（Tseng, 1929: 116）。

其次，国内学人自撰的著作采用类比原则和时序组织对中世纪英国文学进行描述、阐释或定位，在信息筛选和传递方面呈现较一致的偏好。周作人在"异教诗歌"标题下对《贝》的标题、情节、基督教和异教精神进行了简述（周作人, 1922: 4）。关于诺曼征服之后的英国文学，他在

"骑士文学"部分谈到亚瑟王故事书写的三位作家，即蒙茅斯的杰弗里（Geoffrey of Monmouth）、莱亚门（Laȝamon）和韦斯（Wace），提到马洛礼。"文艺复兴之前后"部分谈及乔叟、兰格伦和威克里夫（John Wycliffe）的写作和贡献。王靖指出《贝》的故事来源、讲述方式和接受过程，提到塞尼伍夫（Cynewulf）、莱亚门、比德和《圣经》解经文本《奥姆鲁姆》；说明 14 世纪英国作家和文学特点，涉及曼德维尔（Sir John Mandeville）、威克里夫、乔叟、兰格伦、高厄和卡克斯顿（William Caxton）。他指出，英国人称曼德维尔为"英国散文之祖"，称马洛礼为小说家，称乔叟为"大诗家"，引用丁尼生的话称乔叟为"英国韵文之祖"，坚持乔叟创作三分法（王靖，1927: 1-7）。这部著作采用 19 世纪末德国学者布林克（Bernhard ten Brink）确定且被学界广泛认可的三分法（转引自肖明翰, 2019: 167）。这在后面不同时代仍被采用。曾虚白指出，中国当时没有一部像样的英国文学史,而英国人用 20 世纪新眼光做的文学史还不曾看到，认为英国人按照历史事件划分文学时代失当，英国人的文学眼光比较学究，重古轻今，而文学史要突出整体而非个人。他指出，他要在引用德莱顿（John Dryden）、阿诺德（Matthew Arnold）和泰纳（Hippolyte Taine）等大批评家时表达个人看法，把第一章"初创时代"分为三部分：盎格鲁-撒克逊时期、诺曼人占领时期和乔叟。他认为，盎格鲁-撒克逊时期文学虽多不可考，但流传下来的作品是"英国文学里面珍奇的古董"。他把诗歌分为四类叙事诗：吟游诗人写的短诗、凯德蒙轮诗（Cædmonian Cycle）、塞尼伍夫轮诗和《贝》，并认为《贝》全篇充满"爱自由、重法律的精神，充分地表现出它的民族性"（曾虚白，1928a: 2）。他指出，诺曼征服对英国文学产生了极大影响，受法国凯尔特人同化的诺曼人把喜幻想的性质和撒克逊人的沉着融合在一起，给英国文学奠定了坚实基础。这个时期的叙事诗分为四类：亚瑟王和他的武士、查理曼和他的贵族、亚历山大大帝和特洛伊的英雄，《寻找圣杯》和《高文爵士与绿衣骑士》是最著名的两篇，能代表所有作品的当推莱亚门的《布鲁特》。他认为，兰格伦的《农夫皮尔斯》（下文简称《农》）旨在反抗社会不公，提倡人类互助，是精神力量产生和宗教改革的先声；曼德维尔的游记汇集了各种怪事；高厄的《情人的坦白》各篇结构大同小异。在交代了乔叟的生平经历之后，他认为乔叟有机会接触文艺复兴的发源地意大利，因此坚持沿用乔叟作品的三分法做法，强调欧洲大陆文学对他的影响。他从民族性格考虑，认为乔叟在《坎》中把撒克逊人的端庄和诺曼人的轻盈融为一体，"他视察人性视野的广阔，足够当莎士比亚的先驱而无愧"；强调乔叟在诗歌中流露出的文艺复兴精神，"他是统一英文的第一人"，他用的"中英土白"成了英国国语，"他可以算是用我们看得惯的英文写作品的第一人"（曾虚白，1928a: 1-6）。

最后，译著把国外的观点引进来，和国内自著著作相得益彰。欧阳兰编译的《英国文学史》前三章按照时间顺序标为"英国古代的文学""诺曼征服后文学"和"十四世纪英国文学"，并未以"乔叟"单独命题，概括了《贝》的内容，介绍了凯德蒙和塞尼伍夫等，谈论了盎格鲁-撒克逊散文和阿尔弗烈德大王（Alfred the Great）及他翻译的《哲学的安慰》，把他称作"英国散文的鼻祖"，介绍了莱亚门的《布鲁特》，提到了蒙茅斯的杰弗里和韦斯的写作，把有关亚瑟王的故事看作当时最伟大的作品，还介绍了《奥姆鲁姆》和《修女指南》。第三章在讨论14世纪英国文学及背景的基础上谈到了曼德维尔和兰格伦，把《农》称作史诗，肯定了威克里夫把《圣经》译为英语的贡献，引用丁尼生的话指出乔叟是"英国诗歌的鼻祖"和"第一等的英文作家"，是"14世纪最高的光荣"，因为他改良了英国文学，从而使它达到文学的境界。他指出，乔叟非原创，而是"编译"，虽受薄伽丘影响，但能显示自我人格，而他的诗歌是法语和撒克逊语的混合。[①]他引文证明乔叟注重诗歌的语言和节律美，称高厄为"道学先生"，其诗歌虽具音乐性，但大多枯燥无味（欧阳兰，1927: 7-35）。这部译作涉及宗教作品、史诗和寓言等不同体裁，和20世纪10年代孙毓修的观点比起来，同样说乔叟是"编译者"，但更强调诗歌本身的艺术性和诗人的原创性。

关于英国文学史，自著或译著在原则和方法上较为一致和趋同，以线性方式布局，方法接近；以经典作家和作品为要绘制中世纪英国文学全景，经典作家基本包括其中，涉及诗歌和散文，但在散文发展和个别

---

① 2013年2月15日，笔者去剑桥大学拜访海伦·库珀（Helen Cooper）教授，提出学界认为乔叟是编译者这一看法时，她起身从书架上拿出一本书。此书把《坎特伯雷故事集》和《十日谈》的对应诗节双栏展示，表明乔叟在《十日谈》的基础上通过压缩或拓展做了个人创新。

作家（涉及阿尔弗烈德大王和曼德维尔）的贡献认定方面较有分歧。近几年，随着学界对中国形象的热议，曼德维尔引起了国内文学界和史学界的关注。

二、20 世纪 30 年代

20 世纪 30 年代，抗日战争爆发。有编者把当时的中国比作中世纪黑暗时代的欧洲，人民生活颠沛流离，没有发展知识学问的机会与能力，文化进步停滞，学术现状不容乐观。[①]但就有报纸宣布持国民中立立场，抱服务社会文化之心（燄生，1934: 1）。关于中世纪英国文学，刊物文章和著作的产出方面并不逊于 20 年代，相应成果增多。人们对于中世纪欧洲有较为清醒的认识，"中世纪一千年间（自 5 世纪到 15 世纪），前半称黑暗时期，虽旧文化似扫荡无余，也可说新文化正在酝酿，因而有后半期古典文化的复兴，和现代文化的孕育"。这篇译文表明，人们把中世纪看作是全黑时代，是为大错。[②]

首先，各类刊物仍以不同方式介绍中世纪英国作家和作品。值得注意的是，人们用英文介绍或评价或引用乔叟。《英语周刊》选刊了《坎》中几则故事，以"英文概述情节＋原文节选＋中文夹注"的形式介绍。[③]耕野持"黑暗论"，指出中世纪欧洲诗人写作的心理动机，因为封建势力和基督教的压迫，人们的情绪和思想多半充满幻想和寓意；诗歌主要为抒情诗和叙事诗，提到《贝》《罗兰之歌》和《尼伯龙根之歌》等，认为它们"种下了 14 世纪的文艺复兴的种子"（耕野，1936b: 24）。葛传椝指出了乔叟诗歌的措辞和语法，认为要理解乔叟不仅要看，还要读出来，节选了《坎》的《骑士的故事》部分原文并注以脚注（Ké, 1931: 380-381），强调阅读和朗读的重要性，而当时读者可在脚注协助下读中世纪英语原文。无息在长达两千字左右的评论中尤其对乔叟进行了全方位评价。他

---

① 《编后：我们可把今日的中国比为中世纪黑暗时代的欧洲》（1932: 872）。

② 《开明外国史讲义：第二篇　中古史，第二章　欧洲中世纪之前期：黑暗时代》（1933: 55）。Höffdiny（1936: 70）。

③ E. G. Chow, "Story from Famous Books: Stories from Chaucer's *Canterbury Tales*,"《英语周刊》1935 年第 141—150 期，页码分别为 1088—1091、1130—1133、1172—1175、1209—1212、1247—1249、1292—1294、1328—1331、1368—1371、1406—1409、1447—1450。

指出，"在以抄袭为满足的诺曼文学及不打果结实的撒克逊文学底长期的虚弱中，出现了久弗里·乔叟这个闻名之人"，高度肯定他的创造力，认为他虽为译者，但却有独见。他游历广泛且有各种角色和头衔，与彼特拉克和薄伽丘会话，像"两手满满的珠宝商"，把来自东西方的素材"安排起来，由此造出眩眼的装饰物"，"能够由中古底公共古林之中寻出故事们与传奇们，移植于他自己底土地，使它们发出新芽"，说明乔叟在传承的基础上具有整合和创新能力。他认为，乔叟不同于莎士比亚和但丁，他的想法是外感官的奇思怪想，浪漫且轻快，但人物塑造遵从人物气质和自我感知力，极具个性和典型性；讽刺有趣且自然，喜剧场面自由生动，达到娱乐之效。关于叙事，他指出，乔叟不同于薄伽丘，他研究各部分关系，这是当时所未闻见的，"我们看见现代小说底胚胎，先于比任何它国而出现……有统一效果底预算，使它活灵活现的"。（无息，1935: 1-2）这是对诗歌中出现的连续性和有机性的肯定。他强调乔叟从法国文学和古代文化思想中受益，但会独自观察人类。在所附节译为散文的《总引》开头，他认为"楔子"（即《总引》）最能表现乔叟描写的"神技"，"是十四世纪人物底博览会，是当时英国社会底照妖镜"，"楔子虽不曾告诉我们以'事件'，但它是告诉了我们以'人'；最艺术的作品，也只是示人以'人'而已"。（无息，1935: 3）Wang Pang-Chieh 的 "Geoffrey Chaucer" 一文提出"酒商之子如何进入宫廷"的问题。该文作者认为，乔叟的父亲和王室有关系，从而为他谋得了好职位，虽其生平不可知，但他富有智慧，性格受人欢迎，所以在王室中倍受器重。作者同样坚持三分法，认为《总引》和《骑士的故事》是《坎》中最佳的部分（Wang, 1936: 28-29）。这种解读是传统的传记研究法，也是其他研究中广泛采用的方法。灭魔节译了乔叟的两首短诗（Chaucer, 1934: 无页码）。开明（周作人）编译了《巴斯妇人的故事》，称乔叟为英国散文之始祖，以幽默著名（Chaucer, 1935: 410-413）。段洛夫对乔叟生平和三个时期主要诗作进行了分析概括（段洛夫，1938: 107-109）。郭贞叔以诺曼征服为界把中世纪英国文学分为两个时期：早期有凯德蒙体诗歌、塞尼伍夫诗歌和《贝》；诺曼征服后的文学有四种英雄叙事诗，即亚瑟王和他的武士、查理曼大帝和他的贵族、亚历山大大帝、特洛伊，并提到了莱亚门的《布鲁特》。他认为，在 14 世纪出现的伟大作品的代表人物就

是乔叟；他坚持作品三分法，说明乔叟诗歌中具有文艺复兴精神。(郭贞叔, 1937: 27-28)

其次，著作方面传承 20 年代的思路并进行阐述。徐名骥认为，从完整性和伟大性方面来说，《贝》不逊于荷马史诗，但贝奥武甫被神话了；他肯定乔叟是"英国文学的始祖""英国诗歌之父"和"英国最大的叙事诗家"，指出《坎》受《十日谈》影响，诗人高厄和兰格伦与他比起来"自然是觉得渺小的"。(徐名骥, 1934: 2-3) 他在介绍戏剧时认为，"在他（莎士比亚）之前英国好像没有什么了不起的戏剧作家和作品"(徐名骥, 1934: 93)。他坚持文学影响论，但忽视了理查逊时期其他诗人的贡献和戏剧的重要性。张越瑞把中世纪英国文学分为"盎格鲁-撒克逊时期"和"诺曼侵入至乔叟时代"两章，认为"（贝奥武甫）是民族的福星，更是国内一切上下阶级的人们的领导者。巨龙的个性似乎暗示一种贪念，或一种不法行为，那恶毒的格兰德以及他那可怕的母亲似乎是代表一种愚昧，一种迷信，代表邪僻的习俗"(张越瑞, 1934: 3)。这些评价凸显其隐含的政治隐喻，以英国史诗观照国内民生。难能可贵之处是，他谈到了古英语谜语诗、宗教诗和《盎格鲁-撒克逊编年史》（下文简称为《盎》），肯定了阿尔弗烈德大王在文化保护方面所做的贡献。他首次在国内谈到第一位法语女诗人法兰西的玛丽（Marie de France）、拉丁语编年史家马姆斯伯里的威廉（William of Malmesbury）、亨廷登的亨利（Henry of Huntingdon）和"珍珠"诗人（The "Pearl" Poet），阐释了辩论诗《猫头鹰与夜莺》的象征意义；还谈到莱亚门、威克里夫、曼德维尔、兰格伦和乔叟。这本著作包括了用古英语、盎格鲁-诺曼语、拉丁语和中世纪英语写作的作家，比较全面。另外，在金东雷所著的《英国文学史纲》中，张士一、傅彦长和金东雷的序言指出了国内读者的期待视野、目标读者和撰写目的。金东雷把中世纪英国文学分为四章阐述：盎格鲁-撒克逊时代（分三节）、盎格鲁-诺曼时代（分三节）、乔叟时代（1350—1385，分四节）和民间文学（分两节），明确指出他在进行"研究"，强调理解作品前了解社会背景的必要性。这本著作在前人基础上首次谈到《丹麦王子哈夫洛克》《华威的盖伊》和《汉普顿的比维斯》等作品和苏格兰诗人亨利森（Robert Henryson）和邓巴（William Dunbar）(金东雷, 1937: 13-74)，凸显了他对骑士文学、民间文学和苏格兰文学的重视。需要注意的是，当时在武汉大学任教的方重指出，《贝》具备文化移植特点（方重, 1939: 48）。

最后，在译著方面，林惠元翻译、林语堂校对的《英国文学史》在回顾英国被征服史、英语发展史和生活史的基础上，指出《贝》是盎格鲁-撒克逊文和韵律方面宝贵的材料并分析了它的构造；认为蒙茅斯的杰弗里使亚瑟王故事复兴，文化中心从温切斯特转换到伦敦之后，作家们，尤其是乔叟，采用伦敦的英语写作并使其发扬光大。基督教文化输入后，英国和拉丁基督教国家与意大利文化有了接触。作者谈到比德、塞尼伍夫和"盎格鲁-撒克逊宗教诗的鼻祖"、宗教史诗的开创者凯德蒙，认为阿尔弗烈德大王是"英国散文鼻祖"。诺曼征服对散文和诗歌发展在体裁、题材、语音、韵律、文法等方面影响极大。在谈到亚瑟王系列故事时，作者指出，莱亚门使凯尔特故事可用英文讲述，法国小说和传奇可在英国本土讲述，因为英国领土当时横跨海峡，肯定了英国的法语文学，尤其是《玫瑰传奇》。高厄被称作道学家，这个看法和乔叟把他称作"Moral Gower"（道德家高厄）（Chaucer, 2008: 585）（*Troilus*, V.1856）有关。国外学界至今仍持此观点（Yeager, 1984: 87-99）。被称作改革家的兰格伦写出了无产阶级的穷苦和资本家的不公平及教会的腐败，肯定了威克里夫翻译《圣经》的功绩，尤其谈到"平民主义的故事"《罗宾汉》，还涉及曼德维尔的作品。关于乔叟，作者指出，"他（乔叟）是第一位写实者，比 Shakespeare 还早一些的现代诗人。因为他的描写人物正依他的眼光所看见的，解释人生及其奇异正依他所看到的……达到现代的写实主义和个人主义"（Delmer, 1930: 35）。乔叟被称作叙事诗人，幽默家，第一个纯粹以故事本身为目标的英国人，英国文学上第一个工于诗艺的名家，第一个有自觉的文人和有所建树的批评家，"Langland 代表道学的人生观；而 Chaucer 代表文艺复兴时代的纵欲观念"（Delmer, 1930: 46）。作者对乔叟的诗歌坚持三分法，指出其和欧陆文学的渊源关系，"虽然他是封建时代和学究时代的人，但他能从普通生活，普通人和普通事情中看出诗意来"，并从平常人（酒商之子）身份、从多重身份中积累经验和文学创作不拘惯例方面分析乔叟。（Delmer, 1930: 59-60）显然，这些传统研究方法强调历史与文学、个人生平和文学思想、英格兰与欧陆之间的密切关系。

20 世纪 30 年代翻译或编译国外史学著作活动比较活跃，而中世纪英国文学作为文化言说中的一部分出现其中，是文史不分家这一思路的表现，更从史学角度观照到中世纪英国文学及英语语言的发展史。何炳松编译的《中古欧洲史》在谈论"古代英文"时提到凯德蒙所著的最古老手稿、《贝》和《盎》及其对后来欧陆文学产生的影响，简论了亚瑟王和圆桌骑士诸传奇及其中彰显的冒险精神和骑士忠勇；短篇小说（即市民文学）以诙谐的手法描述日常生活；寓言类故事重在攻击牧师和修道士的恶习，以列那狐故事为最（何炳松，1932: 230-233）。卡尔登·海士和汤姆·蒙认为，英语文学当推《坎》《农》和马洛礼的著作（海士、蒙，1934: 211-212）。汤姆森指出，《贝》和《盎》对于研究历史和语言具有重要意义；中世纪英国文学史上最重要的人物是乔叟，他的时代比法国和意大利的文学时代晚，他应该研读过法国和意大利文学，《坎》就可证明他是非常有技巧和创造力的真正诗人（汤姆森，1940: 418-419）。何鲁之谈到英语史时指出，乔叟以中世纪英语写故事，威克里夫以此译《圣经》，莎士比亚和弥尔顿使之充实（何鲁之，1937: 83-84）。

三、20 世纪 40 年代

20 世纪 40 年代的相关产出比之前减少，但仍有进一步推进和拓展。首先，刊物方面，苏采在谈及中世纪欧洲代表性作品时指出，除了亚瑟王故事之外，还有动物故事、寓言诗和抒情诗（苏采，1943）。方重1943 年翻译出版了全本散文体译本《特罗勒斯与克丽西达》。这是中世纪英国文学作品的第一部完整中文译本。方重在《引言》中指出，乔叟是英国最伟大的诗人的第一位，虽生平和作品年限无法确定，但可据内容相关性和来源定论（方重，1943b: 3）。他在评价此诗时认为，研究乔叟使用的素材方能洞悉他的艺术和技巧；以强调忠于爱情与道德为要，乔叟写出了英国文学史上第一篇情诗，在莎士比亚的《罗密欧与朱丽叶》之前未见其匹。他还指出这首诗和薄伽丘的《爱的摧残》互文，并强调理解时代背景在赏诗方面的重要性。在女主角的塑造方面，方重进行比较后指出，中世纪苏格兰诗人亨利森通过改写使女主角受到惩罚，这个故事在乔叟那里发展为完美阶段，莎士比亚把她描述为轻佻女子则成为一种变调。他指出以"力求忠实"为翻译原则（方重，1943b:

5-12）。[1]方重对乔叟文学地位的肯定、对《特罗勒斯与克丽西达》的定位与分析、对历史语境的强调、对文学书写传统和渊源关系的比较与20世纪30年代的相关研究一脉相承。

方重在1946年出版的《坎》的《代序》中强调故事的有机性、来源和体裁的包容性时指出，14世纪的英国借用欧洲大陆的法文和已失去生机的拉丁文，乔叟的出现奠定了数百年文字的基础，指出了一个伟大民族文风的定向，而该诗是14世纪最忠实的一幅生活画，社会史家可以此为最佳史料。他认为，乔叟把自己看作人生的记录员，《堂吉诃德》和《战争与和平》都缺乏它的优美性（方重，1946: 1-12）。方重选译了其中的六个故事。[2]值得注意的是，乔叟的名字在20世纪40年代之前有不同译法：孝素（1913, 1927）、曹西尔（1917）、乔叟（1924, 1928, 1930, 1934, 1935, 1937）、却塞（1924）、乔沙（1927）、绰塞（1934, 1940）、乔索（1935）、巧塞（1937）和乔塞（1938, 1947），认可度较高的译名为"乔叟"。黄杲炘指出："单是看作者姓氏译乔叟，书名译《坎特伯雷故事》而不译《坎特伯雷故事集》，就显出他（方重）考虑之周到：用'叟'象征其英国文学始祖地位；不用'集'则可区别于一般的短篇小说集，强调作品的整体性与内在的有机联系。"（黄杲炘，1999: 15）但方重采用的译名处于20世纪20年代已有的译名传统之列。方重指出了这部诗作的产生背景，并通过比较强调其艺术价值和现实意义。他的观点也是19世纪到20世纪初英美学界研究乔叟秉持的文学思想和批评方法的结论（肖明翰，2019: 145-178, 197-202）。需要说明的是，乔叟本人在《坎》之《总引》中指出，他如实说出了朝圣者的身份和衣着（Chaucer, 2008: 24, 34-35）（"General Prologue," I.40—41, I.715—717），强调故事复述中须尽量复述原话（I.725—740）。显然，关于人物塑造和故事叙述本身，乔叟从人物身份的真实性、现实性和语言准确性方面进行了说明。因此，学界对其"现实主义特点"

---

[1] 该译本在1946年再版，古今出版社设计的封面上，心形配图下的文字标题为《爱的摧残：屈罗勒斯与克丽西达》，注明"英乔叟著"，未标译者名字，后新文艺出版社（1955）和上海文艺出版社（1959）再版。

[2] 这些故事译文曾陆续于1946年前在《时与潮文艺》《民族文学》和《世界文学》上发表。《代序》的内容先后公开发表，参见方重（1943a: 108-114）；方重（1947: 63-70）。

的认识部分源于乔叟本人不断强调的真实性，但这种看法 20 年代就已在国内出现。张毕来叙述了《贝》的故事情节并肯定了其贡献，说明《亚》是据法国诗人特里提安（Chrétien de Troyes）而来，并认为乔叟是"近代英国文学的始祖"。他从文字和文风方面分析时指出，许多道学夫子认为乔叟把古典和《圣经》的东西混为一谈显得"淫秽"，但他认为这就是乔叟成为文艺复兴先驱的原因所在（张毕来，1948: 92-95），为乔叟正了名。

值得注意的是，柳无忌和曹鸿昭翻译的《英国文学史》信息量明显比之前的著作丰盈。他们在谈及翻译此书的必要性时指出，"在中英关系更加密切，我们对于英国民族更需深刻认识时，英国文学的介绍显得绝对的重要"（柳无忌、曹鸿昭，1947: 1）。[①]这本非常详细的译著与前面提到的英国文学史的思路和叙述模式相似，但在某些观点上不同于前文所提。例如，在古英语散文的创作方面，原文作者认为，散文作家阿尔弗里克（Ælfric）的贡献要大于阿尔弗烈德大王；而盎格鲁-撒克逊文学的流传归功于手抄本在意大利和英格兰得以保存。诺曼征服之后的文学体裁和题材更加丰富，文学的流传靠誊写员和吟游诗人，韵文传奇表达的对女性的崇拜是圣母玛利亚崇拜的表现，而亚瑟王和部分圆桌骑士成为英法德作品中的核心角色。他们讲述了宗教传奇《世界的主宰》和理查德·罗尔（Richard Rolle）的神秘主义作品，还有三首宗教诗《爱情曲》《珍珠》和《身体与灵魂之辩》，强调了头韵体复兴背景下诗作具备的双重性特点，因为诺曼征服之后，英格兰的"文化是属于大陆的、国际的"（Moody and Lovett, 1947: 29）。作者还指出，改变乔叟看法的是意大利之行和他的好奇心及远见，作品内容显示他意欲和意大利诗人竞争。16世纪之后英语在读音上发生变化，人们把乔叟看作粗鄙之人，但作者认为乔叟是工于诗艺的艺术家，因为那时的文学材料是"公共的产业"，乔叟有自己特有的"思想、文笔与组织技能"，像《巴斯妇的故事》和《总引》就属原创（Moody and Lovett, 1947: 40）。乔叟已超越时代，但高厄却墨守中世纪抽象概念和死板思想，兰格伦诗作研究需涉及版本考证，苏格兰国王詹姆士一世（James I）的《国王书》采用君王诗体。作者还

---

① 关于英文版，参见 Moody and Lovett (1902)。直到 20 世纪 60 年代，国外中古英国文学史的撰写内容和思路相似，区别在于细化程度和分时期出版，可参见 Anderson (1966)。

指出，15 世纪英国缺乏有才之人，大量庸俗文学是实用主义思想的产物，但推崇散文体作品《亚》和《圣约翰·曼德维尔游记》。

结　语

　　由上可见，民国时期学人已涉及中世纪英国许多作家和不同体裁的作品，但在散文发展的作家贡献认定方面仍存在分歧。虽然他们在人名或作品名翻译方面不一致，但在文学史撰写模式和文化发展影响论的基调方面基本保持一致。读者以现代英语，甚至以中世纪英语阅读原作节选部分。从空间分布来看，这些成果产出地多集中在长三角。中世纪英国作家和文本选择大多基于时代精神、作者生平和代表性作品进行布局，翻译和研究呈现连续性特点，材料处理时描述和定性结合，在认知逐渐拓宽的基础上选择出现差异性微调，恰在知识的系统性和完整性方面得以互补，但文本的析取具有模仿性，在观点上逐渐呈现拓宽和加深趋势。英美学界的观点被传播和移植到中国，而国内学人能结合当时语境进行一定的针对性回应。可见，中世纪英国文学在民国时期的译介、传播、接受和研究体现了民国时期学人作为接受者、传播者和解码者的历史选择和使命感，观照了当时读者群的期待视野和知识储备路径。虽然历史前进的步伐有时会出现延迟或暂时停滞，但认识的脉络仍然存在。今天，国内有关中世纪英国文学推介和研究的各类成果产出渐增，研究更加深入和全面，形成了较为稳定的学者群，既保持了和国际中世纪研究一定的交流和互动，又和民国时期的思路形成一种呼应。

引用文献【Works Cited】

Anderson, George K. *Old and Middle English Literature from the Beginnings to 1485*. A History of English Literature. Ed. Hardin Craig. New York: Collier Books, 1966.

Chaucer, Geoffrey. "General Prologue." *The Riverside Chaucer*. Ed. Larry D. Benson. 3rd ed. Oxford: Oxford UP, 2008. 23-36.

---. *Troilus and Criseyde. The Riverside Chaucer*. Ed. Larry D. Benson. 3rd ed. Oxford: Oxford UP, 2008. 473-585.

Hao, Tianhu. "'What's Past Is Prologue': Medieval English Studies in China in

Recent Decades (1978—2014)." *Journal of British & American Studies* 35 (2015): 183-202.

Hoccleve, Thomas. *The Regiment of Princes.* Ed. Charles R. Blyth. Kalamazoo: Medieval Institute Publications, 1999.

Lynch, Michael. *China: From Empire to People's Republic 1900—1949.* 2nd ed. London: Hodder Education, 2010.

Moody, W. V., and R. M. Lovett. *A History of English Literature.* New York: C. Scribner's Sons, 1902.

Yeager, R. F. "'O Moral Gower': Chaucer's Dedication of *Troilus and Criseyde*." *The Chaucer Review* 19.2 (1984): 87-99.

Zhang, Lian. "Chaucer in China: A History of Reception and Translation." *The Chaucer Review* 55.1 (2020): 1-31.

《北大成立英文学研究组　德文学组亦筹备就绪》,《益世报-北京》1926 年 4 月 17 日第 7 版。

《北大第一次英语竞赛昨在二院举行》,《益世报-北京》1936 年 6 月 7 日第 8 版。

《编后：我们可把今日的中国比为中世纪黑暗时代的欧洲》,《清华周刊》1932 年第 38 卷第 7/8 期，第 872 页。

《东西史记和合：英吉利撒孙朝》,《东西洋考每月统记传》1834 年 2 月卷，第 89 上—89 下页。

《东西史记和合：元纪（英吉利哪耳慢朝）》,《东西洋考每月统记传》1834 年 5 月卷，第 125 下页。

《几个有关英语教学的中等教育问题　教部长王世杰广播讲演》,《益世报-北京》1937 年 1 月 28 日第 8 版。

《记载：中国留日学生总数》,《学生》1915 年第 2 卷第 5 期，第 129 页。

《教部谋提高英语程度决组英语教学研究会　总会设南京各地设分会》,《益世报-北京》1945 年 12 月 14 日第 4 版。

《开明外国史讲义：第二篇　中古史，第二章　欧洲中世纪之前期：黑暗时代》,《开明中学讲义》1933 年第 4 卷第 3 期，第 55—63 页。

《女院英语赛结果公布》,《益世报-北京》1936 年 5 月 2 日第 8 版。

《师大英语辩论　题目拟定　报名者十余人》,《益世报-北京》1935 年 11

月 27 日第 9 版。

《指令河南教育厅留学预备学校毕业各生应准一律应考文》，《教育公报》
　　1918 年第 5 卷第 7 期，第 78 页。

Chaucer，1934，《给罗莎蒙》《向空荷包诉苦》，灭魔译，《红豆月刊》第 2
　　卷第 1 期，无页码。

Chaucer，1935，《巴斯妇人的故事》，开明（周作人）译，《论语》第 56 期，
　　第 410—413 页。

Chow, E. G., 1935, "Story from Famous Books: Stories from Chaucer's *Canterbury
　　Tales*," 《英语周刊》第 141—150 期。

Chu, K. C., 1917, "Story of *Beowulf*," 《学生》第 4 卷第 6 期，第 147—148 页。

Delmer, F. Soften, 1930，《英国文学史》，林惠元译，林语堂校，上海：北
　　新书局。

Höffdiny, 1936，《文艺复兴与中古时代》，彭基相译，《中法大学月刊》第 9
　　卷第 2/3 期，第 69—74 页。

Ké, Hertz C. K.（葛传槼），1931, "Regarding Chaucer as a Poor Speller," 《英
　　语周刊》第 819 期，第 380—381 页。

Moody, W. V., and R. M. Lovett, 1947，《英国文学史》，柳无忌、曹鸿昭译，
　　上海：商务印书馆。

Tseng, Suh, 1929, "My Impression of Anglo-Saxon Literature," 《金陵女子大
　　学校刊》第 11 期，第 116 页。

Vane, S. W.（范春水），1925, "How Beowulf Fought for the King," 《中华英文
　　周报》第 12 卷第 306 期，第 702—703 页；第 307 期，第 735—736 页。

Wang, Pang-Chieh, 1936, "Geoffrey Chaucer," 《高级中华英文周报》第 30
　　卷第 747 期，第 28—29 页。

Wu, Chaochi（吴肇基），1915, "The Study of Foreign Languages," 《学生》
　　第 2 卷第 5 期，第 135—136 页。

Zan, Tseu Yih, 1929, "Great Books and Their Stories: IX. 'Beowulf'," 《英语
　　周刊》第 710 期，第 205 页。

曹航，2013，《乔叟在中国的译介与研究》，《外语教学》第 3 期，第 89—
　　92 页。

曹西尔，1917，《寓言：林妖》，林纾、陈家麟译，《小说月报》第 8 卷第 3 期，

第1—4页。

东资，1949，《常用名词浅释：中世纪》，《知识（哈尔滨）》第10卷第4期，第32页。

段洛夫译，1938，《英国中世纪第一诗人：乔塞评传》，《世风半月刊》第5期，第107—109页。

方重，1939，《英国诗文研究集》，上海：商务印书馆。

---，1943a，《乔叟和他的康妥波雷故事》，《时与潮文艺》第2卷第1期，第108—114页。

---，1943b，《引言》，载乔叟《屈罗勒斯与克丽西德》，方重译，重庆：古今出版社，第1—13页。

---，1946，《乔叟和他的康特波雷故事（代序）》，载乔叟《康特波雷故事》，方重译，上海：云海出版社，第1—19页。

---，1947，《乔叟的地位和他的叙事技能》，《浙江学报》第1卷第2期，第63—70页。

耕野，1936a，《中世纪的欧洲文学》，《中国学生（上海1935）》第2卷第20期，第25页。

---，1936b，《中世纪的欧洲文学》，《中国学生（上海1935）》第2卷第21期，第24页。

郭贞叔，1937，《英国文学之演变》，《前导月刊（安庆）》第2卷第1期，第27—31页。

哈门德，1909，《欧洲宪政成立之历史：第十三章　中世纪各邦族》，《大同报（上海）》第11卷第8期，第14—16页。

卡尔登·海士、汤姆·蒙（Carlton J. H. Hayes and Parker Thomas Moon），1934，《中古世界史》，伍蠡甫、徐宗铎译，上海：世界书局。

何炳松编译，1932，《中古欧洲史》，上海：商务印书馆。

何鲁之编著，1937，《欧洲中古史》，上海：商务印书馆。

黄杲炘，1999，《译者前言：为什么我要译〈坎特伯雷故事〉》，载乔叟《坎特伯雷故事》，黄杲炘译，南京：译林出版社，第1—16页。

金东雷，1937，《英国文学史纲》，上海：商务印书馆。

乐天，1941，《名词浅释：中世纪》，《自修》第194期，第8页。

李提摩太，1897，《新政策一卷》，阙名辑，上海广学会刊行，武昌质学会用原刻本重刊。

利类思、安文思和南怀仁，1669，《西方要纪一卷》（清康熙刻昭代丛书本），张潮辑，诸殿鲲校。

刘诗诗，2020，《民国时期报刊术语研究》，《海南师范大学学报（社会科学版）》第 2 期，第 10—18 页。

柳无忌、曹鸿昭，1947，《译者序》，载 W. V. Moody and R. M. Lovett《英国文学史》，柳无忌、曹鸿昭译，上海：商务印书馆，第 1—2 页。

欧阳兰编译，1927，《英国文学史》，北京：京师大学文科出版部。

欧阳哲生，2020，《民国学术之历史定位》，《史学理论研究》第 1 期，第 4—8 页。

乔叟，1946，《康特波雷故事》，方重译，上海：云海出版社。

任博德，2017，《人文学的历史：被遗忘的科学》，徐德林译，北京：北京大学出版社。

施蛰存，1928，《缅想到中世纪的行吟诗人："屋卜珊和尼各莱特"译本序》，《文学周报》第 301—325 期卷，第 540—545 页。

宋应离主编，2000，《中国期刊发展史》，开封：河南大学出版社。

苏采，1943，《欧洲中世纪的几种代表诗作》，《中央日报扫荡报联合版》3 月 13 日第 6 版。

孙毓修，1913a，《欧美小说丛谈》，《小说月报》第 4 卷第 1 期，第 1—8 页。

---，1913b，《欧美小说丛谈（续）：英国戏曲之发源》，《小说月报》第 4 卷第 7 期，第 47—51 页。

汤姆森，1940，《西洋中古史》（下），陈受颐、梁茂修译，长沙：商务印书馆。

唐幼峰编译，1932，《外国史纲要》，重庆：重庆书店。

王靖，1927，《英国文学史》（上编），上海：泰东图书局。

王荣，2017，《〈坎特伯雷故事〉在中国的经典化》，《杭州电子科技大学学报（社会科学版）》第 6 期，第 54—60 页。

吴宓，1921，《再论新文化运动（答邱昌渭君）》，《留美学生季报》第 8 卷第 4 期，第 13—38 页。

---，1923，《西洋文学入门必读书目》，《学衡》第 22 期，第 1—9 页。

无息，1935，《乔叟——英国文学之父》，《红豆月刊》第 3 卷第 1 期，第 1—3 页。

肖明翰，2019，《乔叟学术史研究》，南京：译林出版社。

熊月之，2011，《西学东渐与晚清社会》，北京：中国人民大学出版社。

徐名骥，1934，《英吉利文学》，上海：商务印书馆。

薛其林，2003，《学术兴盛与方法创新：论民国时期学术研究方法问题》，《中州学刊》第 1 期，第 120—123 页。

餤生，1934，《开场的话》，《七日谈周报》第 1 卷第 1 期，第 1 页。

杨开泛，2011，《国内古英语文学研究综述》，《世界文学评论》第 1 期，第 296—300 页。

---，2012，《国内古英语文学研究 30 年述评》，《理论月刊》第 8 期，第 81—86 页。

曾虚白，1928a，《英国文学 ABC》，上海：ABC 丛书社。

---，1928b，《英国文学的鸟瞰》，《真美善》第 2 卷第 5 期，第 1—12 页。

张毕来，1948，《欧洲文学史简编》，上海：文化供应社。

张炼，2019a，《乔叟在中国》，载肖明翰《乔叟学术史研究》，南京：译林出版社，第 302—315 页。

---，2019b，《乔叟在中国的接受与场域竞争》，博士学位论文，湖南师范大学。

---，2021，《台湾地区的乔叟接受状况》，载郝田虎主编《中世纪与文艺复兴研究（三）》，杭州：浙江大学出版社，第 52—74 页。

张越瑞编译，1934，《英美文学概观》，上海：商务印书馆。

郑昶，1933，《编辑大意》，载郑昶编，张相、金兆梓校，《新中华外国史（全一册）》，上海：新国民图书社，第 1—2 页。

郑大华，2020，《要重视对民国学人群体的研究》，《史学理论研究》第 1 期，第 20—23 页。

郑振铎，1924a，《文学大纲（九）：中世纪的欧洲文学（附图）》，《小说月报》第 15 卷第 10 期，第 102—124 页。

---，1924b，《文学大纲（十）：第十三章　中世纪的中国诗人上（附图）》，《小说月报》第 15 卷第 11 期，第 94—116 页。

周作人（启明），1915，《英国最古之诗歌》，《叒社丛刊》第 2 期，第 4—8 页。

---，1922，《欧洲文学史》，第 3 卷，上海：商务印书馆。

（特邀编辑：张炼、王瑞雪）

香港地区的乔叟接受状况

张　炼

内容提要： 香港地区的乔叟接受状况与香港地区的地理位置、政治环境、经济发展和文化生态密切相关。兼容并包的文化氛围使香港地区的乔叟接受状况具有中西文学精神交融的特点，汇聚了西方以及大陆和台湾地区的影响。

关键词： 香港地区；乔叟；接受

作者简介： 张炼，博士，浙江大学外国语学院"百人计划"研究员，主要研究中古英语文学。本成果受浙江省教育厅科研项目资助（项目编号 Y202043885）。

Title: The Reception History of Chaucer in Hong Kong

Abstract: The reception history of Chaucer in Hong Kong is reflective of the region's geographical position, political condition, economic development and cultural ecology. The readings of Chaucer here, determined by the region's inclusive cultural environment, are enriched by both Chinese and western literary perspectives, and share characteristics with those of the west, the Mainland and Taiwan as well.

Key words: Hong Kong, Chaucer, reception

Author: Zhang Lian, Ph.D., "One Hundred Talents Project" researcher at the School of International Studies, Zhejiang University. Her research field is mainly Middle English literature. Email: zhanglian_hn@zju.edu.cn

　　香港地区的乔叟接受是中国乔叟接受史的一部分。香港地区的政治环境和文化空间与内地相比有所差异，因此乔叟在香港地区的接受状况也与在内地的状况有所不同。基于目前发现的资料，本文拟研究香港地区的乔叟接受状况，从中探讨接受史与香港地区社会文化生态的相互制约和促进。如布尔迪厄所言，文化、经济、社会资本的相对价值是由每一个场决定的，甚至是由同一个场内的连续状态决定的（布尔迪厄，1997：143）。香港地区作为中西文化接触的桥头堡，注重中西交流，将乔叟视为介绍西方文学以丰富中国文化的渠道。因此，中国和西方阐释方式都是学者赖以占据位置、建构文学场的文化资本。香港地区的乔叟接受也呈现出中西合璧的特点。

香港地区的乔叟接受自诞生之日起就与香港地区的社会状况紧密联系，是当地文学场与社会场相互影响的直接印证。20 世纪 30 年代前后，内地战事连绵，一部分知识分子逃往香港地区躲避。他们的到来促成了香港地区新文学的诞生，香港地区从此开始有大量文学作品发表和印刷。南来作家推动了香港地区文坛的活跃和水平提高，同时，由于他们仍与内地文坛有密切联系，香港地区的文学与内地的文学形成了互补和互相延伸的关系（刘登翰，1997：5-19）。此时的香港地区在经济文化各方面都与内地来往十分频繁，这种文学场、社会场域里兼容并包的局面也体现在香港地区的乔叟接受上。

"五四"思潮的影响使得南来的知识分子都接受了新文学的熏陶。从此，白话与文言创作并存的局面出现在香港地区文坛，西方文学和新诗都开始登载在香港地区的期刊上。鲁迅、胡适等文人先后来香港地区讲学甚或定居，大量文学刊物在香港地区涌现，促进了香港地区文学界的繁荣，也推动了香港地区对乔叟的初步接受研读。在此背景下，1933年，《红豆月刊》由这批来港的文人在香港地区创办。这个刊物既刊载左翼文学作品，又发表现代诗歌，还特别致力于介绍西洋文学，将介绍西方文学视为"任务与愉悦"，西方文学被他们当作将中国新文学萌芽培养成大森林的"营养"。①从这个期望可以看出，香港地区的学界希望将中西方传统结合以促成新的文学局面，改变文学场的建构，促成当地文学场和社会场的变革。

此后，《红豆月刊》刊载了一系列对中古英语文学的介绍和研读。

---

① 原文引自《红豆月刊》1935 年第 3 卷第 1 期张宝树《英国文坛的漫游》一文之前的编者按语，无页码。本文此处亦参看了王剑丛（1995：9-10）。

1934 年，乔叟的两首短诗节译《给罗莎蒙》和《向空荷包诉苦》发表在《红豆月刊》上，都标明由"Chaucer"作，由"灭魔"译（Chaucer, 1934）。①由于是节译，译作结构并不与原诗结构对等，两首的长度都仅为原诗的一半。语言采用的是白话诗体，诗行都为长句。虽然是节译，但主题内容得到了保留，其中《给罗莎蒙》里对女子诙谐的倾诉、《向空荷包诉苦》里调侃式的抱怨都传达得淋漓尽致。《给罗莎蒙》本是一首三节联韵诗，诗人对于宫廷爱情这种体裁进行了温和而风趣的揶揄。诗人先是盛赞女子的美貌和舞姿，然后诉说自己为爱所伤仍不沮丧，最后将自己比喻为浸泡在香汁中的鱼、像"特里斯坦"那样愿为爱情的忠仆。诗中表现了诗人对女子的美和善良的敏感，以及对她们的弱点的认知。现代学者多否认有"罗莎蒙"其人，其名字意为"rose of the world"，因此应是概指某位美貌女子。至于《向空荷包诉苦》，现代学者一般认为是乔叟写给新王亨利四世的怨诗，提醒后者向他发放自理查二世时期他就享有的年金。这也是一首三节联韵诗，诗人将他的请求也写作为一个对宫廷爱情范式的调侃。他将自己的空钱包当作宫廷爱情里的一位女士，抱怨自己的爱情被对方辜负，用"你如此轻""重起来吧"等双关语来同时喻指钱包和爱情的变化。由此可见，两首短诗都有一些共同的特点。它们都融自我嘲讽和道德情感于一体，目的虽严肃，但语气却轻松。这样的风格和这两首诗的主题使得它们较容易被当时香港地区的学者和读者接受。因此，虽然两首短诗翻译完全未保留原诗的诗律，但因它们融合中西风格，也就成了香港地区最早的乔叟研读文本。

在 1935 年第 3 卷第 1 期的《红豆月刊》里，乔叟在封面上被列为"英国文学十杰"之首。此期还有无息②用白话文撰写的一篇文章《乔叟——英国文学之父》，赞扬乔叟"有创造之力""有独见"。随文还附上了节译为散文体的"《康德伯里故事》底楔子"，指出这个楔子（即《总引》）告诉我们，"最艺术的作品，也只是示人以'人'而已"（无息, 1935: 3）。此后《红豆月刊》陆续刊载了对《贝奥武甫》《罗兰之歌》以及中世纪罗曼司等中古文学作品的介绍和简短翻译。这些文章开创了香港地区

---

① 原诗名分别是"To Rosemounde"和"The Complaint of Chaucer to His Purse"。"灭魔"当为笔名。

② "无息"当为笔名。

学界研读英国中古文学的先河。总体来看，这些文章都已经采用新文化运动提倡的白话文来书写，而文章中如"示人以'人'"这样的评价则表明香港地区学界已经接受了现实主义思潮和"人的文学"的观念。此时的香港地区学人引入以乔叟作品为代表的优秀西方文学作品，是希望开启民风，进而塑造中国的新文学。可以说，香港地区的乔叟接受虽然此时刚刚萌芽，在接受时间上要比内地迟了二十年，但在解读方式上却与内地几乎是同步的。

　　香港地区的乔叟接受虽有一个不俗的开端，此后几十年却少有大发展。1941 年，日军偷袭珍珠港，太平洋战争爆发，香港地区沦陷，香港地区的学术出版业陷于停顿状态。直至 1997 年回归祖国以前，香港地区处于英国的殖民统治下，接触英国文学的机会比内地多，可是中世纪研究却仍然极为少见。自 20 世纪 70 年代起，香港地区经济起飞，迅速成为世界级的金融商贸中心。新兴的现代都市产生了新的文化形态，模糊和消解了 1949 年后香港地区存在的政治派别分歧和中西对立。随着香港地区的社会走向多元化，香港地区的文坛迎来了开放和融合的新阶段。社会场里的中西融合塑造着中西合璧的文学场，继而影响着乔叟接受。从 60 年代开始，香港地区发行的期刊、报纸上开始陆续登载少量简短文章介绍乔叟和他的作品，[①]其中包括 1980 年龙应辉介绍方重翻译《乔叟文集》的文章。这也表明，香港地区学界对内地乔叟研究的动向一直有所关注。

　　这些资料表明，香港地区的学界当时已经认识到乔叟在英国文学史上的重要地位和他作为文化资本的价值。目前少有材料证明乔叟在香港地区的课堂讲授情况。1963 年，陈张美美（Chan Mimi）将撰写的硕士

---

① 这些期刊文章如下：傅宁，1962，《乔叟的含蓄讽刺》，《文艺世纪》第 66 期，页码不详；黄克亮，1965，《英国诗学之父：乔叟和他的坎特伯雷故事集》，《中国学生周报》12 月 31 日，第 4 版；孙述宇，1966，《中古英语文学之四——乔叟以外的中古英语文学》，《大学生活》第 1 卷第 3 期，第 10—12 页；孙述宇，1966，《中古英语文学之四——乔叟以外的中古英语文学（续）》，《大学生活》第 1 卷第 4 期，第 13—14 页；殿信，1974，《乔叟手稿拍卖》，《海洋文艺》第 1 卷第 3 期，第 89 页；龙应辉，1980，《介绍方重译的〈乔叟文集〉》，《开卷月刊》第 3 卷第 5 期，第 22—23 页；《乔叟杰作曾被誊抄员篡改》，《香港作家》2004 年第 4 期，第 32 页。

论文《乔叟的诗歌用语研究》提交给香港大学，此文当属香港地区乔叟研究领域最早的毕业论文之一。从论题可以看出，此文作者已经在按照西方阐释传统研读乔叟，分析的是他的作品的基本文学要素，而不是此时内地学界盛行的对文学作品的马克思主义研究。西学在香港地区占据重要位置，香港地区学者在习性和场域的相互作用下，在调整着自己的场域位置。此后，陈张美美又撰文说明乔叟的作品翻译成中文在用词和修辞方面遇到的挑战和问题，并提到了方重的翻译。她认为，将原作的诗体译为对应韵律的中文诗体是不可能的，但也许乔叟的短诗可以尝试这样做。陈张美美认为，方重 1955 年译的八首短诗在表现原作的格律上很大程度是成功的（Chan, 1977: 39-51）。这表明，香港地区学者时刻记忆着中国文学阐释传统，希望将中西方阐释方式进行对比研究，他们对内地的话语阐释尤为重视。这也是香港地区的文学场域里中西两种阐释方式并存且相互融合的表现。

由于区域面积小且专业学者较少，香港地区的乔叟研究极少。但它在乔叟传播过程中始终有一个重要作用不可忽略。香港地区是晚清政府最早开放的通商口岸之一，且又被英国殖民统治多年，历来是西方文化进入内地的窗口，是中西文化碰撞的交汇点。这样的地理条件和政治情况使得香港地区产生了独特的社会文化建构。由于开放程度高，香港地区兼收并蓄的文化特点使此地具备了独有的优势地位。首先，香港地区成为大量西文文学书籍在中国的首发地。时至 20 世纪 90 年代，香港地区出版界更趋国际化，多家国际出版公司在港设立分部。有好几个外籍作者改编的乔叟作品现代英文版是在香港地区和内地城市同时发行的。如迈克尔·韦斯特（Michael West）的《坎特伯雷故事集》改写本就被上海译文出版社和在香港的朗文出版亚洲有限公司同时出版（乔叟，1997）。又如，德里克·塞伦（Derek Sellen）的《坎特伯雷故事》改写本也被华东师范大学出版社和商务印书馆香港分馆同时出版（Chaucer，2004）。其次，由于香港地区的图书市场与内地交流频繁，内地的出版社发行的多个方重和黄杲炘的翻译版本、中国学者改写的多个翻译版本在香港地区图书市场和各大图书馆都能查阅到。此外，香港地区学界与台湾地区学界的交流颇多，台湾地区发表的多篇中世纪研究的期刊文章和出版的书籍在香港地区的图书馆都有收藏。如此开放的文化局面甚至吸引了海外的中国留学生。比如，曾在哈佛大学师从拉瑞·本森（Larry D. Benson）修读中古英语文学专业博士学位的冯象，就曾将论文发表在香港地区的期刊上（冯象，1987: 77-88）。因此，可以说香港地区在乔叟作品出版方面发挥了它作为中西文化碰撞交流之桥头堡的作用，汇聚了中西两种传统。

以上接受情形表明，乔叟在香港地区的接受史与香港地区的文化环境和政治生态密切相关。香港地区的社会场域结构是中西交融的，这种结构也在左右着文学场的运转。反过来，文学场的局面也影响着社会场的建构，促使香港地区社会文化更为包容。香港地区的乔叟接受因此深受影响，具有继承中西两个文学传统的特点。

香港地区的乔叟接受和多个译本的出现是乔叟在中国接受史的重要组成部分，也表现出了其独有的特点。总体而言，香港地区的乔叟接受是中西合璧的。香港地区学者的习性养成深受中西两个阐释传统的影响，同时也是学者基于其自身所处的特殊的地理背景和历史文化条件做出的选择，更是这个地区在近百年的特殊时代背景下的产物。文学场的竞争或融合，就是外部社会场的状况的反映。中西之间的博弈，内地与香港地区之间的政治、经济、文化等社会各个分场域的交流，既影响着乔叟接受的状况，决定着外国文学意义的重新生产，同时也证明了文学场受社会权力场的支配。用布尔迪厄的话说，就是作品作为"社会炼金术"被社会生产和重构。

引用文献【Works Cited】

Chan Mimi（陈张美美）. "On Translating Chaucer into Chinese." *Renditions* 8 (1977): 39-51.

---. "Studies in Chaucer's Poetic Diction." Postgraduate Thesis. The University of Hong Kong, 1963.

Chaucer, Geoffrey. *The Canterbury Tales*. Adapted by Derek Sellen. Black Cat Reading. Shanghai: East China Normal UP, Hong Kong: The Commercial P, 2004.

---, 1934，《给罗莎蒙》《向空荷包诉苦》，灭魔译，《红豆月刊》第 2 卷第 1

期，无页码。

皮埃尔·布尔迪厄，1997，《文化资本与社会炼金术——布尔迪厄访谈录》，
　　包亚明译，当代思想家访谈录，包亚明主编，上海：上海人民出版社。

冯象，1987，《书评〈乔叟与但丁〉》，《九州学刊》第 2 期，第 77—88 页。

刘登翰，1997，《论香港文学的发展道路》，《文学评论》第 3 期，第 5—19 页。

杰弗雷·乔叟，1997，《坎特伯雷故事集》，迈克尔·韦斯特改写，庄和玲译，
　　上海：上海译文出版社，香港：朗文出版亚洲有限公司。

王剑丛，1995，《香港文学史》，南昌：百花洲文艺出版社。

无息，1935，《乔叟——英国文学之父》，《红豆月刊》第 3 卷第 1 期，第
　　1—3 页。

张宝树，1935，《英国文坛的漫游》，《红豆月刊》第 3 卷第 1 期，无页码。

（特邀编辑：厚朴）

莎士比亚与文艺复兴文学研究

Studies of Shakespeare and Renaissance Literature

与莎士比亚的际遇：十四行诗的教学志

邱锦荣

内容提要： 本文介绍在中文语境的课堂上如何带领大学生克服文化鸿沟，与莎翁建立有意义且个人化的关系。课堂以莎翁的商籁（十四行诗）诗串为学习英文的范例，课程设计模拟工作坊的形式，注重精读、跟读、商籁的格律分析与写作操练，以及协力编辑商籁日志。工作坊类似艺文沙龙的对谈交流，可以激发参与者分享观点和经验，逐渐内化商籁成为个人的语库。

关键词： 莎士比亚；十四行诗；商籁诗串/诗集；教学

作者简介： 邱锦荣，台湾大学外国语文学系荣休教授，主要研究领域为莎士比亚和人文教育。

Title: In Search of Shakespeare via His Sonnets—A Pedagogical Travelogue

Abstract: In this paper, I would like to share with you my experiment with a group of undergraduates who established meaningful and personal contact with the Bard despite temporal distance and cultural differences. Much in the nature of a workshop, my course renovated the way we learn English by offering a concrete model—Shakespeare's sonnet sequence. I emphasized close reading, paying attention to the sonnet form, and we kept a sonnet journal. The workshop was designed to be interactive and collaborative throughout, like a small world café or salon discussions, to best elicit and use the different ideas and experiences of the participants.

Key words: Shakespeare, sonnet, sonnet sequence, pedagogy

Author: Chiu Chin-jung is Professor Emerita of English at Taiwan University. She has conducted research projects on humanities education, Freud on Shakespeare, and pedagogies based on teaching/learning Shakespeare. Email: jung@ntu.edu.tw

> 赖山德　唉！从我过去读到的一切书籍中，
> 　　　　或是我听过的所有故事与史实里，
> 　　　　真爱的道路向来崎岖不平；
> 　　　　要不是门第不相当……
> 何蜜雅　可恨哪，尊贵要向低贱拜倒！
> 赖山德　要不就是年纪不相配……
> 何蜜雅　可惜啊！妙龄怎可匹配老朽！
>
> 　　　　　　　　　　　　（《仲夏夜之梦》，1.1.132—138）

以上摘选的恋人唱和多少呼应了我们与莎士比亚的因缘际会，这段移植中文的思维到莎翁的英语土壤，并且跨越四个世纪的时间鸿沟的追求旅程"向来崎岖不平"。个人尝试通过阅读商籁，内化莎翁的语言。这篇报告是一篇教学旅程志，记载教学现场的实际运作。

一、概　述

商籁（sonnet，现译为"十四行诗"，本文主要使用"商籁"这个译名）起源于意大利，是以十四行文字写成的短诗、小歌谣，于 13 世纪逐渐成为一种定型的诗体。14 世纪的诗人彼特拉克（Francesco Petrarch，1304—1374）以商籁向他仰慕的女性劳拉（Laura）倾吐爱慕之情，这段恋情充满挫折，苦求而不得，而其诗作成了意大利商籁的代表。在中世纪的欧洲大陆，贵族之间流行"宫廷之爱"（courtly love），歌颂骑士与城堡中君夫人之间幽微而禁忌的情愫，流风所及，商籁所歌咏的理想女性经常是高不可攀的贵妇或冷若冰霜的仙子。典型的商籁本是情诗，由第一人称的男性向其爱恋的女士诉说渴慕，抒发衷情。此一诗体后来传播到欧洲各国，17 世纪 50 年代英国盛行商籁以及合为诗集的商籁诗串（sonnet sequence），中间隐含叙事，其中以莎士比亚的 154 首商籁诗集为冠冕，1609 年以四开本问世。

莎翁商籁的第 1—126 首是献给一位年轻男性，诗人称之为"my lovely boy"；第 127—152 首则写给 Dark Lady（黑发女士）或 Mistress（女士、姑娘）；最后两首描写月神狄安娜的使女潜入爱神丘比特寝室，熄灭爱的火焰以解救凡人苦恋的种种情欲病根。换言之,商籁诗集的绝大部分聚焦于一位美少男,学者因此对莎翁的性倾向充满了想象和臆测。王国维《人间词话》云:"词至李后主而眼界始大,感慨遂深。"(王国维,2012: 17)流传到英国的商籁在莎翁笔下也有类似的嬗变:商籁诗体的内容由情诗扩大到对生命多方面的关注,如伤逝、忏悔、美学、情欲等,题材的样貌丰富多变,尤以性别的流动最令人瞩目。诗歌在文学中本是最神秘、隐私的一种文类,一般认为诗歌与诗人有紧密的联系,因此许多学者认为莎翁的商籁诗串有自传的况味,试图通过诗串分析莎翁的人格品质及其生平,并且作为了解他所写的 38 出剧本的途径。莎翁商籁的神秘深邃吸引后世研究者不断地解读他情感的归属,拼凑他生命的梗概。

(一)商籁的迷津——诗中人物与诗串的排序

由于诗集扉页标示"献给 Mr. W. H.",关于美少男的身份,所有考据都环绕姓名之谜,多数猜测指向南安普顿伯爵亨利・赖奥思利(Henry Wriothesley)(Harrison, 1952: 1592; Evans, 1997: 1839—1841)。当时皇室、贵族给予作家赞助是一项文雅惯例,尤其是在 1592—1594 年,瘟疫肆虐,伦敦的剧院悉数关门歇业,剧作家和诗人寻求贵族金援的可能性极高。据达顿(Richard Dutton)考察,伯爵雅好文艺,年少清秀,有画像为证;他也是莎翁赞助者中确实留下历史记录的一位(Dutton, 1996: 36-49)。诗集中出现的另一位诗人,较少学者论及。有人猜测是马洛(Christopher Marlowe, 1564—1593)(Dutton, 1996: 44-45);电影《莎翁情史》(*Shakespeare in Love*)的编剧家所见略同,安排数个场景让两位剧作家同框。马洛与莎翁同年生而略长两个月,是位早慧型的剑桥才子,在莎翁尚未成名前,马洛已经誉满伦敦剧场界。两人是否有交流,不得而知;至于二者之间的瑜亮情节倒不失为有趣的联想。至于黑发女士的身份,几乎没有任何线索,但她被取名露西(Lucie),根据诗串改编的戏剧通常采用此名,如英国广播公司(BBC)的电视剧《爱欲情愁》(*A Waste of Shame*)(Boyd, n.p.)。但是有关角色的臆测都仅止于拼图游戏,至今皆无定论。此外,商籁诗串的顺序也是迷雾:索普(Thomas Thorpe)的 1609 年四开本是否具有连续性?编辑的顺序是否可信?解谜者不乏其人,学者如坎贝尔(S. C. Campbell)认为四开本的编序有诸多谬误,他另行梳理顺序，整理出一则动人的悲情故事，诗人的隐私面隐然浮现（Campbell, 2009: i-xxiv）。虽然类似的考辨可以自成一套逻辑，在教学上我选择从众，依循四开本的排序。

（二）商籁格律

英式商籁每行十个音节，节律为轻重五个音步（iambic pentameter），结构为：三节（stanza），每节四句，结尾的对偶句（couplet）常被比拟为笑话的"哏"（a punch line），带出峰回路转的一笔惊讶，与前面诗节形成显著的反差。商籁的格律、押韵皆有规范，是定型诗，其中英式商籁一般的韵脚是 abab cdcd efef gg。但随着历史的演变，格律也有些改变。商籁简短而意义完整，非常适合朗诵与锻炼英语表达，朗读时须注意每一词的轻、重音节以及行尾的押韵。读诗不求甚解，也不可能有完全的理解，而宜享受音韵的悦耳，咀嚼辞藻之美，沉浸在音节起伏的律动中。"Sonnet 18"的诗体工整，适合模拟：

Shall I compare thee to a summer's day?	a
Thou art more lovely and more temperate:	b
Rough winds do shake the darling buds of May,	a
And summer's lease hath all too short a date;	b
Sometime too hot the eye of heaven shines,	c
And often is his gold complexion dimm'd;	d
And every fair from fair sometime declines,	c
By chance or nature's changing course untrimm'd:	d
But thy eternal summer shall not fade,	e
Nor lose possession of that fair thou ow'st;	f
Nor shall Death brag thou wander'st in his shade,	e
When in eternal lines to time thou grow'st.	f
So long as men can breathe or eyes can see,	g
So long lives this and this gives life to thee.	g

我如何能把你比作夏日？
你比它更加可爱而温婉：

疾风无情击打五月娇蕊，

夏季的租期如昙花一现；

有时天庭之眼照耀炽烈，

刹那它的金光转为阴暗；

一切美好不免凋零消谢，

听凭机缘或时序的摧残：

唯君永恒长夏永不凋零，

君之花容青春永驻长存；

死神难夸你徘徊其阴影，

因你定格在永恒的诗文。

但凡世间存气息鉴文采，

此诗长存君亦与之同在。（作者自译）

诗人提醒爱慕的人韶光易逝，人生如寄；一生的岁数犹如租约，期满终需归还给造物者；时光实非个人恒产，仅供短暂使用。诗人在结尾的对偶句中，自诩他的诗行可以超越时间的破坏力，心上人的美好容颜可以永存不朽。

二、中文语境下的商籁教学

塔特洛说："任何一个与莎翁文本的际会必然都是跨文化的。"（Tatlow, 2001: 5）在英语为外语的情境里研读莎士比亚必然是一项跨文化的投资。多年以来我致力于莎剧研究以及教学，回首来时路，多所颠簸窒碍。经过多方的摸索，我尝试了解莎士比亚的语言，舞台上的人物，从伊阿古（Iago）到普洛斯彼罗（Prospero）；想象奥菲利娅（Ophelia）在随水沉落那一刻心中的残念；以弗洛伊德精神分析的视角诊断"奥瑟罗症候群"。但是，即使没有语言和文化的隔阂，掌握他戏剧里形色各异的角色也绝非易事。我开始认真思考如何能借着自身的经验帮助学生挪去求学路上的障碍，而实验另类方法——绕道转进莎翁的商籁。

相较于莎剧舞台的众声喧哗，商籁诗集只有诗人单一的声音，人物仅有四个。中年诗人抒发私密领域里赤裸的感受：爱与愁，流光与变迁，美丽与凋残，羞辱与颓丧，诗中甚至宣叙放浪形骸、云雨悲欢的感官际遇。每一种情动（affect）都是一般人能与自身经验呼应相连的。如果莎翁戏剧是一个国际大都会、一块吸引各行各业进驻的磁石，那么他的商籁诗串就像一条乡间小道，亲切却不单调。就学者而言，诗集本身也是迷津，其中的人物或许可考但都未定案，然而每一首诗可以独立自成一局，四百年来逐行逐句的阅读，带给读者极大的愉悦。基于这个原因，我并不企图对商籁诗集建立定论，而是通过诗人的视角观看他情感的投射，并与莎剧中的人物比对联结。著名莎剧演员爱泼斯坦（Jonathan Epstein）说："通过十四行诗我们体验诗人现身说话。即使是世间最善于表达的人也不一定能触摸到自我情感的真相。"（Epstein, n.p.）莎翁诗集可贵之处正在于此，诗中的主人公并不等同于莎翁本人，而是他笔下创造的"诗人角色"（poetic persona），但此一角色与莎翁的距离似远又近。这部诗集可视为诗人角色的日志，他自述如何与内在情欲争战、与外在环境搏斗，如何与人生这项大课题进行一连串的对话。如此阅读，诗集成为既饶有趣味又能实际应用的导览指南。通过诗集，我们不但能观察人性的情绪光谱，也能穿越时空与文化的隔阂与莎翁际会。商籁诗串很可能成为一个通关密码，帮助我们解锁庞大的戏剧文本。

2018 年，我第一次开设"莎士比亚十四行诗"课程，七成英文主修学生，三成外系生。除了例行性的阅读与讨论之外，我在课程中加入了新的成分：十四行诗的写作练习。当时摸着石头过河，实无远见可言。经过课堂的实务操作以及与学生的互动，在教学相长中，这门课程逐渐成形。那年期末，绝大部分的学生不但与"莎士比亚"建立了个人关系，而且可以写商籁，进步的奇妙超出我（甚至他们自己）的期待。我也自觉融入轻重五音步的节奏，师生同享诵读与习作之乐，逐步攻克语言的关卡。

2021 年春，英国莎剧演员、80 岁高龄的帕特里克·斯图尔特爵士（Sir Patrick Stewart）在社群媒体展开"每日一商籁"（a sonnet a day）计划。他朗诵的第一首诗是"Sonnet 116"。这首诗颂赞真爱，英语地区的婚礼中经常被引用作为爱情的告白。粉丝们在防疫的幽闭之中热烈地呼应爵士的录影，短短四天之内点阅的人次超过 457000。当时我正在规划秋季第二度执教的十四行诗课程，也感受到相当大的激励。因为有前次的经验，对于课程走向和前景有较好的掌握。课程目标定为：跟着莎翁学英文；执行方式：强调精读、细读，熟悉商籁的格式，要求每一学生记录个人的商籁日志（sonnet journal）。

开学前三周，我首先做导论，考察商籁诗体历史纵深的脉络，接着使用网络的影音资源，导读几首诗，如劳伦斯·奥利弗（Laurence Olivier, 1907—1989）男爵和约翰·吉尔古德（John Gielgud, 1904—2000）爵士等的资源。学生追随这些著名的莎剧演员做跟读（shadow reading）：学习者在听名家朗诵两个音节之后，亦步亦趋地跟着诵读。先求正音（每一字的辅音、元音、重音要精准）；其次模拟音调（intonation）；最后，通过观察名家的音色表演，揣摩他们对商籁的诠释，如停顿、声腔、高亢低回的吐字表情等。这门课程以工作坊的形式设计，全程都以参与式及互动式进行，教室类似艺文沙龙。不高举学术为目标，但求激发参与者不同的眼光和亮点。作为英语学习者，我们的首要目标是把莎翁的辞藻、文采内化，收在记忆库里，无论用以申述理念或抒发感情，可以随时活用，不至于词穷羞涩。通过揣摩诗人角色，我们也企图捕捉莎翁对于情感、他人以及周遭环境的感知。我们讨论商籁可以令所爱的人永垂不朽是否可信，或更精确地说，商籁本身作为一个爱的言说（discourse of love）是否能够超越时空的变迁。

以下分享个人的教学旅程志，记载师生寻找莎士比亚的跨文化之旅。长途跋涉的旅行者需要有个愿景引领前行，我勾勒出这幅图景：与莎翁同行，信步海滩边，聆听他的心言，虽是异国语言却不违和；读者与作者建立信赖的关系。

（一）与莎翁同行

南非共和国的第一位黑人总统曼德拉（Nelson Mandela）认为，教育是改变世界最强而有力的方法。20世纪南非黑人的识字率仅有一成，曼德拉呼吁：阅读书写的能力就是教育的基石，他坚信："人无语言，无法与别人对话，了解别人；无法参与他人的希望与向往、他们的历史，也不能欣赏他们的诗歌。"（Mandela, n.p.）关于曼德拉激励人心的一生，其中有则小故事鲜为人知。2016年全球纪念莎翁去世四百周年时，英国的《卫报》（Guardian）登载了一篇文章《莎士比亚改变世界的十个面向》，内有一则故事：

　　2012 年大英图书馆展示了一本罕见的书，这本书吸引了媒体的关注，报道的声量不下于古腾堡活字印刷的《圣经》。这本书不过是大量印刷、平淡无奇的普及版，却是曼德拉曾经持有的书，里面充满了他的亲笔标注，曼德拉放在床边逾二十年，支撑他度过牢狱中阴暗的岁月。他经常大声朗诵给同室的狱友听。（McCrum, n.p.）

这书并不是宗教经文，而是《莎士比亚全集》；曼德拉的听众大部分不识字，但是莎士比亚却在他们之间自然地流动。谁能相信莎翁曾经陪伴、支撑在牢笼中煎熬的曼德拉？这份关系是如此的沉静甘甜，犹如空谷足音划破死寂。曼德拉出生于南非东部地区的一个酋长家庭，与英国的地理位置相距六千英里，英文从来不是他的母语。然而论及莎翁全集，他说："莎士比亚总是有话对你我说。"我甚愿每一年对每一班的学生重复传讲这个逸事：关于两条生命的平行线跨文化之旅的故事，中间有着巨大的语言落差和地理隔阂，因缘际会而成为双向交流的通道——患难的灵魂在莎翁文本中找到慰藉，而莎翁也因为这位隔世的知音，从灰烬中复活。

不久前我在"网飞"平台看了一出电视连续剧《叫我系主任》（The Chair），背景设在美国东部一所虚拟常青藤大学的英文系，其中有一幕令人感动。一位明星级的教授不慎卷入学生抗议风波而遭停职处分，在院方举办的申诉会上，他并没有捍卫自己的权利，反而做了一段看似不着边际的独白。他说：

　　作为一名英文教师，你必须喜爱故事，喜爱文学。你永远要从另外一个人的角度看待事情，设身处地，换位思考。当你处在故事的进行式中，尽管我们深陷实际人生的困境，前面总有无尽的可能性展开。

他如此描述我们与文本、与诗的关系：

　　文本是活的存在，是一首双人舞曲、一场与你持续进行的对话。你或许喜爱一首诗如此之深，每一遍阅读开启新的对话，生命被触动；这是难以描述但又忠实的关系。

活的文本属于你我他，是每一个人的资产。敞开心扉与它对谈，作品有

江河的生命涌流。这是曼德拉与《莎士比亚全集》交互的见证，如同
"Sonnet 18"中诗人对他深爱的对象宣告：诗文能够超越夏日的租期，
令其生命不朽。但可以争辩的是：不朽的是作品本身，而非美少男；诗
人对于夏日美好的描绘吸引我们的深情寄托。文本之所以长存系于历时
历代人继续地阅读，只要人尚能呼吸或目尚能睹视（"So long as men can
breathe or eyes can see"）。

　　如同《叫我系主任》中的那位教授，我经常反省自己在大学作为英
文教师的职责：关于教职有一项不变的核心价值，即启发学生与琢磨英
才。对此，先人早有智慧的洞见。人类还没有发明火柴之前，我们的先
祖从两块火石互相撞击生火的现象得到灵感，发明了钻木取火，但是可
能历经数十次钻木行动才偶得火苗。史前时代的那一瞬间之得，维系了
生命温饱的供应链。还有儒家关于教育方法的理论。《礼记·学记》十八
章云："玉不琢不成器，人不学不知道。是故古之王者，建国君民，教学
为先。"从钻木取火到战国晚期的琢玉成器的论述，点出人类文明进展的
关键态度无非是坚持二字。我们岂可轻忽人文教育的潜能？一个坚持不
断琢磨的态度造就了整个人类文明的前进。

　　迈入 21 世纪的第三个十年，面对数字化、全球化各种剧烈的变迁，
我不禁反思：人文教育有没有为 Z 世代的学生，即所谓"天然数字人"，
在大学里奠定核心技能的基础，培养成熟而丰富的生命呢？《叫我系主
任》里那个虚拟的英文系正面临招生大失血的危机，这样的氛围也是全
球与人文相关的学科此刻面临的严峻挑战。科技当道、人文没落造成一
连串的触发效应（trigger effect）：网络成瘾、去人性化（dehumanization）、
虚拟世界的犯罪与暴力等社会问题，在韩剧《鱿鱼游戏》中被放大渲染，
2021 年 9 月全球上线以来引起火热的回应，价值体系的颠覆可见一斑。
多年以来，我一直在寻找莎士比亚教学上新的可能性，是否可能把学生
导向人文化、文学 / 莎学普及化的另类价值体系，从感官的暴力刺激导
向感官美学的熏染和品味？于是在学院一方角落我尝试更新课程设计，
翻转教室，使传道授业的场所成为比较有趣的"游于艺"工作坊。活动
的设计针对增强学习动机，落实做中学（learning by doing）的概念，在
互动参与式的情境中激发学生的创造力，思考文学与艺术的价值，建构
伦理的判断。基于这些目的，我打造了一个友善的学习环境，强调实验

室的手作技能，规划人际互助的工作坊，分享技能与创作成果。

（二）与莎翁同工——商籁日志

这个工作坊性质的课程强调实作的练习，要求从被动型的学习（passive learning）逐步趋近创造型的学习（productive learning）。

一、每日一首商籁：利用网络资源做跟读，每天重复同一首诗直到熟练后进入下一首。

二、选择一首商籁改写为半片（half sonnet）：浓缩原诗成为一节十对偶句，共计六行的小诗。鼓励回收使用（recycle）原诗的修辞，犹如书法的临摹，从模仿中趋近范例。

三、翻译商籁为中文：诗、词、曲、新诗体。

我期待学生通过聆听诗人的声音而能理解其中蕴含的感情。莎翁的商籁诗集可以归纳为若干主题：欲望、情色、悲伤、忧郁等，但每一首诗却通过不同的视野发展出迥然不同的论点（West, 2007: 12-13）。如果试图在所有的论点之上做一总结，也许最重要的信息是：诗人渴望和一位理想化的对象交心，渴望通过诗文留住起初的爱。无论是对失落的他人、失落的过去的自己，书写犹如自我救赎的行动，在无望中重新获得力量。每一个人会读出不同的故事，最终学生可以交出一份以第一人称叙述的故事，记载他们各自与莎翁的际遇、独特的个人交流。这样读诗的方法不免勾起窥视人物的欲望，特别是诗人这个角色和他情感归属的暧昧性。非严谨的诠释自然不为学者们认可，然而我鼓励外行的想象。一学期我们阅读四十多首诗，超过诗集的三分之一。如果诠释建立在互文考察之上，而能够将诗集中的四个人物串联起来说一则动人的故事，与诗人的距离或许不远。

莎翁是一个棱镜，对每一位读者折射出不同的面貌，我们可以从中获取属于个人的潜文本。我设计商籁日志的共同笔记作为我们分享的叙述空间，学生各自需要撰写记录他们关于十四行诗的实作操练，举行如阅读、分析、创作、翻译等各种活动。为了便于交换观点，形成有效的反馈机制，日志设计为可以在网络上共同编辑的电子文档，如此我们可以同时编辑文案，观摩创作，互相激荡。当莎士比亚迈向全球化，与他同行的人就是跨文化的继承人。但是这项文学的投资，与莎翁深刻的际会能带给我们什么改变呢？我想到一则趣事。1882 年，尼采获得一个新的书写工具——一台打字机，有位作曲家朋友注意到尼采书写风格从此有了微妙的改变。对于朋友入微的观察，尼采如此回应："我们的书写工具也参与了我们的思考。"（Carr, n.p.）如果书写工具，如一支笔、一张纸、打字机或笔记本电脑，以及每样工具本身的品质都间接参与、形塑我们的思考，作为我们日常"主食"的莎士比亚岂非有更大的形塑力？叙事学包含许多成分：声音（节奏与押韵）、视觉（形、色、意象）、修辞、情感、哲学等。经过细嚼慢咽，转化他的文字、修辞技巧，在英文学习的旅程中自然脱胎换骨，获得丰富的莎味词语库。

三、结 论

莎士比亚研究历经四个世纪的发展，可谓全球品牌的国际企业。在这个场域中有不同形式的研究理论介入，从传统的治学方法如历史、考证、版本、语言学，到 19 世纪的心理学、表演学，再到 20 世纪的形式主义、结构主义、新历史主义、殖民理论、解构主义等的百家争鸣，持续到晚近的数字人文学，以及翻译与改编、各种专业的集合形成一个生生不息的循环：挪用、回收、再生、创新。这也许是莎士比亚留给后世最可贵的资产，不仅止于四开本与对开本的版本分析、庞大的莎学评论，以及历代挖掘莎翁作品的每一个角落，更在于不容忽视的另一面——莎学普及化：一名普通的读者，任何非英语母语的学习者也可以与之亲近，被激发而灵感涌现。著名的人文经典论述学者努斯鲍姆（Martha C. Nussbaum）指出：

> 公民想象力的基础必须尽早扎根。儿童开始探索故事、韵律、歌谣，特别是在他们信赖的成人陪伴之中，就被引导认识其他的同伴，培养敏锐的感知，同情他人的疾苦……古典希腊文化即因注重年轻人的道德教育而赋予希腊悲剧极重要的地位。（Nussbaum, 1997: 93）

在接近学期末的时候，我期待每一个学生自述与大师相遇的过程，跨文化之旅中所经历的喜悦和劳苦；编写以诗人角色为中心的剧本，诗人在爱与羞辱间的挣扎；诗人如何凝视内在的中年危机。除了文字作品外，我预期 Z 世代擅长的呈现方式：微电影、歌曲、舞曲、纸雕、绘图、广告文案。2022 年的冬天，曲终人散之时我将欣然恢复自己的身份——参与莎学马拉松长跑的选手，严肃地面对文本。学生所有的想象的故事、表演呈现，我锁进脑海任其悬浮。而我，选择拥抱诗人济慈对经验开放的"消极感受力"（negative capability），允许未知，搁置存疑，愿意把自己完全浸淫于当前的经验（Keats, 1980: 766-768）；同理，我接受莎翁商籁诗集的不确定性和神秘性，谨慎收敛起个人的经验判断。

这篇报告简述个人指导的十四行诗课程的互动工作坊形式，思考如何在中文语境中带领初学者接近莎士比亚和他的语言。通过商籁共同笔记，邀请学生在莎士比亚的遗泽上留下一枚指纹，成为莎翁的集体继承人。借由课程运作以及对学生的每一阶段实作的观察，我希望活化知识传递。学生们走过商籁的乡间小道，已有足够的基础出发探索莎翁戏剧的大千世界。如果有幸成为莎剧莎诗的终身乐学者，获得雅正的英文和文化素养，就可以期许未来在学术英语中存活并且茁壮成长。

引用文献【Works Cited】

Campbell, S. C. *Shakespeare's Sonnets the Alternative Text*. Cambridge: Cassandra P, 2009.

Carr, Nicholas. "Is Google Making Us Stupid? What the Internet Is Doing to Our Brains." *The Atlantic*, July and August 2008 issue. https://sdsuwriting.pbworks.com/w/file/fetch/83284144/03_Carr_google.pdf. Accessed 1 Oct. 2021.

Dutton, Richard. *William Shakespeare: A Literary Life*. London: Macmillan, 1996 (1989).

Epstein, Jonathan. "Jonathan Epstein's Sonnet Workshop." http://www.youtube.com/watch?v=iyZjGT2ZtuM. Accessed 10 Aug. 2020.

Evans, G. Blakemore, ed. "Sonnets." *The Riverside Shakespeare*. New York: Houghton Mifflin, 1997.

Harrison, G. B. "*Sonnets* and *A Lover's Complaint*: Introduction." *Shakespeare: The Complete Works*. Ed. G. B. Harrison. New York: Harcourt Brace, 1952. 1592—1594.

Keats, John. "Letter to George and Tom Keats, Dec. 1817." *The Oxford Anthology of English Literature.* Vol. II-A. New York: Oxford UP, 1980. 766-768.

Longino, Daniel Gray. *The Chair.* Winchester, CA: Netflix Studios, 2021.

Mandela, Nelson. "Top Nine Nelson Mandela Quotes about Education." https://borgenproject.org/nelson-mandela-quotes-about-education/. Accessed 17 Aug., 2021.

McCrum, Robert. "Ten Ways in which Shakespeare Changed the World." 17 April 2016. http://mseffie.com/assignments/shakespeare/10%20Shakespeare%20Changed%20the%20World.pdf. Accessed 10 Oct. 2020.

McKay, John. Dir. *A Waste of Shame: The Mystery of Shakespeare and His Sonnets.* London: BBC, 2005. DVD.

Norman, Mark, and Tom Stoppard. *Shakespeare in Love.* New York: Miramax Films/Universal Studios, 1998.

Nussbaum, Martha C. *Cultivating Humanity: A Classical Defense of Reform in Liberal Education.* Cambridge, MA: Harvard UP, 1997.

Stewart, Patrick. "Patrick Stewart—Instagram Photos and Videos." http://www.instagram.com/impatrickstewart. Accessed 4 April, 2021.

Tatlow, Anthony. *Shakespeare, Brecht, and the Intercultural Sign.* Durham: Duke UP, 2001.

West, David. *Shakespeare's Sonnets with a Commentary.* London: Duckworth Overlook, 2007.

黄东赫执导及编剧，2021，《鱿鱼游戏》（*Squid Game*），Winchester, CA: Netflix Studios。

王国维，2012，《人间词话》（1910），台北：师大出版中心。

杨世彭译，2001，《仲夏夜之梦》，台北：猫头鹰出版社。

（特邀编辑：郝田虎、王瑞雪）

卞之琳对 A. C. 布拉德雷莎学观的接受、批评与发展

张　薇

内容提要： 卞之琳接受 A. C. 布拉德雷注重文本事实的研究，对莎翁的《哈姆雷特》《奥瑟罗》《里亚王》进行了详尽的论述，但对布拉德雷的纯粹的文学内部研究、体验式审美和性格分析法的局限性有所批评。他秉承马克思主义的社会分析文艺观，既注重文学内部研究，也注重文学外部研究，发展了布拉德雷的莎学观。卞之琳对布拉德雷莎学观的接受、批评和发展，反映了中国学者在吸收西方莎学理论时的主体性，而非照搬照抄，盲目信从。

关键词： 卞之琳；布拉德雷；莎学研究；马克思主义；接受；批评；发展

作者简介： 张薇，上海大学文学院副教授，博士，哥伦比亚大学访问学者。主要从事莎士比亚研究。

Title: Bian Zhilin's Reception, Criticism and Development of A. C. Bradley's Shakespearean Study

Abstract: Accepting A. C. Bradley's Shakespearean criticism that paid attention to textual facts, Bian Zhilin exhaustively analyzed *Hamlet*, *Othello*, and *King Lear*, but he criticized Bradley's limitation of pure intraliterary research, experiential aesthetic criticism and character analysis. He insisted on the Marxist literary view of social analysis. He stressed not only intraliterary research, but also extraliterary research, which has greatly developed Bradley's Shakespearean criticism. Bian Zhilin's reception, criticism and development of Bradley's theory reflects the subjectivity of Chinese scholars when they accept the Western Shakespearean criticism, instead of copying it blindly.

Key words: Bian Zhilin, A. C. Bradley, Shakespearean study, Marxism, reception, criticism, development

Author: Zhang Wei, Associate professor of the College of Liberal Arts, Shanghai University, Ph.D. and visiting scholar to Columbia University. She focuses on the teaching and research of Shakespeare. Email: zhangweijinqiu@shu.edu.cn

卞之琳是我国著名的莎学家，他的莎译、莎评在 20 世纪对中国的莎学做出了重大贡献。卞之琳自述研究莎剧的路向："约略参考了苏联二十年代至四十年代和五十年代初期莎士比亚研究的成败、得失的经验、教训，有鉴别地吸取莫洛佐夫、前期的阿尼克斯特等人以及西方莎士比亚同时代人本·琼生、十八世纪歌德、十九世纪布拉德雷（A. C. Bradley）、二十世纪多弗·威尔孙（John Dover Wilson）、英美'新批评'派、考德威尔（Christopher Caudwell）等等的见解，进行自己的探索。"（卞之琳，1980: 38）[1]在此，卞之琳明确表示他受诸多国外莎士比亚研究者的影响，其中有布拉德雷。本文将着重论述卞之琳对布拉德雷莎学观的接受、批评和发展。

英国著名学者 A. C. 布拉德雷（1851—1935）是极具影响力的莎评家，他在牛津大学讲授莎士比亚，其讲稿后来被整理成书，名为《莎士比亚悲剧》（*Shakespearean Tragedy*, 1904）。他用纯粹审美批评的方法对莎士比亚的《哈姆雷特》《奥瑟罗》《里亚王》《麦克白斯》[2]进行了细致入微的解析，也正因为他选取并高度评价了这四部悲剧，以致后来有了莎士比亚"四大悲剧"之说，并被沿用至今。卞之琳基本上接受这种说法，但对把《麦克白斯》列入伟大的悲剧之列并不完全认同，理由是：该剧"效果上又是让反面人物压倒了一切。现实主义和浪漫主义在这里也是并用的，但是二者都更多从积极方面向消极方面发展，实际上落入了没有具体理想作指导的现实主义和没有具体现实作基础的浪漫主义的危险境地。失去了三部中心悲剧的恰到好处的平衡（或者紧张），粉饰或虚夸就会进一步抬了头"（卞之琳, 2007: 271-272）。在卞之琳的眼中，伟

① 卞之琳先生在文章中有的外国人名注英文名，有的不注。为尊重他，本文在引文里按照其作品的原样。
② 本文中莎剧的译名均采用卞之琳的译名。

大的悲剧应该是正面人物压倒一切，而不是反面人物，他强调理想、积极意义和现实基础；另外，伟大的悲剧应该有平衡感，平衡感不够，则不完美。因此，他曾想提出"三大悲剧"之说，但最后还是随了学界的共识，他说："从十九世纪以来已经被公认为莎士比亚的'四大悲剧'，尽管还有人（包括译者本人也曾一度）尝试撇开《麦克白斯》，终还不能否定其（'四'而不是'三'）为莎士比亚悲剧的中心作品以至莎士比亚全部作品的中心或转折点以至最高峰。"（卞之琳，2007: 287）这是卞氏对布拉德雷接受的第一步，并且他单单把四大悲剧翻译成中文。

布拉德雷的莎学研究影响了几代学人，奎勒-柯奇爵士（Sir Arthur Thomas Quiller-Couch）赞扬其为"第一流的批评，我们时代的真正光彩"（杨周翰，1985: 51）。H. B. 查尔顿称布拉德雷是"我们时代最伟大的莎评家"（Charlton, 1938: 174），为了向布拉德雷致敬，他也专门写作《莎士比亚悲剧》（*Shakespearian Tragedy*）。卞之琳先生非常钦佩布拉德雷，称"在 20 世纪开头出版的《莎士比亚悲剧》直到今天对英美莎士比亚批评界还是影响极大的一本书"（卞之琳，2007: 51）。布拉德雷的《莎士比亚悲剧》着重论述"四大悲剧"，卞之琳的《莎士比亚悲剧论痕》也聚焦"四大悲剧"，并在书中频繁引证布拉德雷的观点和材料，甚至在人物分析、结构分析、意象分析上也参照布拉德雷的，这是卞氏对布拉德雷接受的第二步，也是最重要的一步。不过，在大方向上卞之琳又与布拉德雷不同，他并非采用浪漫派的文艺观，而是秉持了马克思主义文艺观，显示了一个中国学者的主体性和创造性。

一、悲剧论

卞之琳接受布拉德雷把握莎翁悲剧实质的方法——注重文本事实。布拉德雷认为，要把握莎士比亚悲剧的实质，必须牢牢把握文本，依据剧中事实来论述，而不是游离剧本，也不是生硬地套理论。他说："我们不想用援引著名戏剧理论的方法来走捷径。因此在着手进行讨论的时候，最好是直接从事实出发，从事实中逐渐得出有关莎士比亚悲剧的观念。"（Bradley, 1924: 7）这里所说的事实，就是文本中的事实，如人物、意象、情节和结构等元素，而这一切中，人物性格是最重要的，"导致这些行为发生的主要因素是性格"（Bradley, 1924: 13）。基于这一认识，他花了大量篇幅，事无巨细、不厌其烦地分析人物性格，不仅分析主要人物，连次要人物也都涉及。他还认为，莎士比亚悲剧除了表现人物性格的行为以及剧中人物遭遇的苦难和情境之外，还有"其他因素"，大致有三种：一是异常的思想状态，如疯狂、梦游和幻觉。二是超自然的因素，如鬼魂、女巫，它们对已经发生并正在发生影响的人物内心活动是一种确认。三是偶然事件或意外事故影响了戏剧的进程，比如瘟疫、手帕丢失、海盗解救等。这三种因素处于附属地位，而主要因素在于由性格所产生的行为。卞之琳的《莎士比亚悲剧四种》的"译者引言"以及《莎士比亚戏剧创作的发展》里对悲剧的论述可以被视作卞氏莎士比亚悲剧论。在这一方面，卞之琳接受布拉德雷的"人物性格论"，接受"超自然因素论"，认为剧中出现的鬼魂、女巫是莎士比亚的噱头，是人物内外统一的表现，即人物内在的恐惧和担忧借用外化的形式表现出来，莎士比亚"为了烘托自己的高深命意，他使边鼓也融入了悲剧的主旋律"（卞之琳，2007：300）。卞之琳将鬼魂、女巫之类附属的因素戏称为"边鼓"，这些边鼓的加入增强了戏剧性，假如去除这些元素，那么戏剧效果将大打折扣。

卞之琳批评布拉德雷注重个人体验式的评论，拘泥于文本事实，纯粹进行文本研究。布拉德雷继承浪漫主义的个人体验式批评的传统，注重感觉体验，他习惯于说"我们觉得""给我们的印象"之类的话，这些话语是体验和主观性的表征。比如他说："他们无法逃脱的那种力量是冷酷无情、不可抗拒的——要是我们从来没有这些感觉(if we do not feel at times...)，那就是丢失了全部悲剧效果的一个重要部分。"（Bradley，1924：27）卞之琳不用"印象""体验""经历"的个人体验式的批评，而是用唯物主义文艺观的批评方法——"文学内部研究＋文学外部研究"，注重文本事实和历史事实，注重客观和理性。

卞之琳对布拉德雷悲剧论的发展有"理想现实冲突论"，"神、人、兽三层关系公式"论（卞之琳，2007：277）以及人文主义思想的观照。首先，卞之琳认为，四大悲剧中"占主导地位的是理想与现实的矛盾冲突"（卞之琳，2007：290）。"这些中心悲剧里表现理想与现实的矛盾，就是莎士比亚的人文主义理想和它烛照下的社会现实的矛盾。这还是从表面看。从深处看，这种主客观的矛盾就显出了主观上人文主义理想本身的矛盾：与封建贵族相对立，对封建贵族抱幻想；与人民大众相一致，与人民大众有距离；从个人主义的角度反对个人主义的发挥，以资产阶级倾向为最基本的倾向，反对以资产阶级倾向为最突出的表现的利欲熏心、不择手段的丑恶倾向。"（卞之琳，2007：279）卞之琳在此揭示了莎士比亚悲剧中理想与现实冲突的具体表现，赋予了社会含义，所用的是马克思主义的阶级分析的话语，这是对布拉德雷的发展。其次，布拉德雷用善恶论来分析悲剧根源。"在莎士比亚悲剧中，产生痛苦和死亡的激变的主要根源绝不是善，正相反，主要的根源在每桩事例中总是恶。"（Bradley，1924：34）卞之琳并没有采用布拉德雷的善恶论的表述，而用"神、人、兽"以及正面人物和反面人物的表述。他认为，在莎翁悲剧里，从社会关系看，是非颠倒；从个人品质看，"神""兽"颠倒。再次，关于人文主义及其危机，布拉德雷在书中只字未提，而卞之琳在论述中，将其置于莎剧研究的重要位置而大书特书。"莎士比亚最基本的创作倾向的实质是——当时在封建关系和资本主义关系交叉发展面前的最开明的资产阶级倾向的两面性。也就是这种两面性规定了莎士比亚的人文主义在这里发生了深刻的危机。"（卞之琳，2007：262）

　　对比二者对莎翁悲剧的看法可以发现，他们都肯定莎剧中附属因素的戏剧效果，但布拉德雷突出性格论，而卞之琳注重社会论，并上升到人文主义哲学意义的层面。在卞之琳眼里，社会环境、社会思潮是第一位的，人文主义是莎剧的核心思想，性格则是第二位的。布拉德雷和卞之琳的论著像两面镜子，镜像中所呈现的莎士比亚样子有同有异，这跟他们各自的美学观有关，布拉德雷传承的是西方美学，而卞之琳更多地秉承了中国的马克思主义唯物论美学观以及苏联马克思主义莎评的观点。文艺复兴时期的人文主义是一个历史概念，也是一个思想体系，它强调以"人"为本，而不是以"神"为本，这一点已体现出唯物色彩，关注实实在在、真正存在的人，而不是虚无缥缈的、想象中的神。人文主义注重维护人的尊严，肯定人的价值，尊重人性和人权，要求个性解放，反对禁欲主义。人文主义思潮蕴含着唯物论的哲学思想。唯物论客观地认识天地万事万物，其中作为万物之灵长的人是认识的重中之重。马克思在《1844 年经济学哲学手稿》中把"自由地发挥自己的体力和智力"（马克思，2002：270）当作人的类本质，这一点与人文主义有一脉相承的关系。

莎士比亚剧中的年轻人追求理想、追求爱情，反对现实社会中的封建包办婚姻制和昏庸的王权，并与命运抗争，维护自己的正当权益，这是一种唯物的姿态。卞之琳并非单纯地只研究莎士比亚文本，也吸收了布拉德雷莎评的精华，过滤掉了他所不认同的观点，并将其研究向前推进。

二、对《哈姆雷特》的解读

卞之琳接受了布拉德雷关于哈姆雷特性格的核心问题是"忧郁"（melancholy）的论断。布拉德雷花了两讲讨论《哈姆雷特》，他采用纯粹审美批评，详细地分析了剧中的每一个人物，能发幽于细微处，并提出真知灼见。布拉德雷指出："我以上用了大量的篇幅来谈论哈姆雷特的忧郁，这是因为从心理学的观点来看，它是悲剧的核心。假如疏忽或低估了它的重要性，莎士比亚的这个故事就无法理解了。"（Bradley, 1924: 127）学界对哈姆雷特不听从鬼魂的吩咐立即去复仇的原因争论不休，布拉德雷不赞同莎评界的"外部障碍论""多愁善感论""良心论""不善行动论""延宕论""软弱论""无法胜任论"等解释，也对托马斯·汉默和约翰逊的解释不以为然，但对施莱格尔和柯尔律治的"沉思悲剧论"则基本认同，不过，他修正了因果关系。布拉德雷认为，整个故事取决于主人公独特的性格——忧郁，他说："直接的根源是由特殊的情况造成的一种极不正常的思想状态——一种压抑忧郁的状态。"（Bradley, 1924: 108）布拉德雷剖析了哈姆雷特的忧郁，他认为：第一，这是一种性情。第二，这是一种敏锐的情感，这种情感被称为"道德"，"哈姆雷特敏感的道义感中无疑潜藏着一种危机。生活中任何重大的打击都会使他受到强烈的震动。这样的打击甚至会导致悲剧的产生。事实上，如果说《哈姆雷特》是一出'思虑的悲剧'，我们同样可以称它为一出'道德理想主义的悲剧'"（Bradley, 1924: 113）。第三，"过度的思虑是忧郁的表现，而不是造成他忧郁的原因"（Bradley, 1924: 108），它会作为这种病态的症状之一，以颓废的面貌再现出来。笔者梳理一下布拉德雷的逻辑思路：忧郁—思虑—复仇迟疑，这就是哈姆雷特不立即复仇的原因。第四，父死母嫁，尤其是母亲匆忙改嫁，给哈姆雷特以巨大的打击，他厌恶整个人世，忧郁愤懑，以至于想自杀。第五，哈姆雷特装疯，但又担心他无法完全把这些心事压抑住，这种状况病理学家称之为忧郁，这种忧郁乃产生病态的厌世感之源，与疯狂大相径庭。

卞之琳接受布拉德雷的"忧郁论"，认为忧郁是哈姆雷特性格的核心。卞之琳指出："延宕问题，软弱问题，悲观问题，装疯问题，残酷问题，以及到最后还得碰上的所谓命运问题，这些问题实际上又都是环绕着一个基本问题：忧郁。"（卞之琳，2007: 42）卞之琳在此列举的一系列问题都是布拉德雷曾涉及的。但对忧郁原因的解析不同，卞之琳认为，"理想幻灭，造成了'忧郁'。哈姆雷特开始怀疑到'人'，怀疑到'女人'，怀疑到社会，怀疑到人生"（卞之琳，2007: 31）。父死母嫁，同学背叛，恋人误解，理想忽然遭受现实的沉重打击，精神危机正是哈姆雷特进一步忧郁的基本内容。"哈姆雷特的装疯发泄了忧郁，可是在装疯中放手思考了问题的时候，他的忧郁也愈来愈深。"（卞之琳，2007: 32）这一点与布拉德雷的观点一致。

卞之琳对布拉德雷的宿命论有所批评。布拉德雷评论《哈姆雷特》说："当我们考虑这出悲剧的这样一些特点，我们就会承认这一种看法，即《哈姆雷特》尽管自然不能被称为特定意义上的'宗教戏剧'，但比起莎士比亚的任何其他悲剧来，它还是包含了更自由地运用了民间的宗教思想和更明确地暗示了一个关注着人间善恶的至高无上的力量的存在这样两个方面。"（Bradley, 1924: 174）这一出戏"最能使我们同时深深感受到灵魂的浩渺广袤，以及制约着那种无穷的浩渺并看起来是它的必然归宿的最终厄运"（Bradley, 1924: 128）。在此，布拉德雷将哈姆雷特的悲剧归结于宗教观和宿命论（这是布拉德雷的《黑格尔的悲剧理论》中的重要观点）。卞之琳批评布拉德雷的这一观点："他在这本书里，讲哈姆雷特，讲到底还是只好说仿佛冥冥中还有一种更大的力量支配了哈姆雷特的悲剧，说悲剧里有一种命定的感觉。资产阶级唯心论，解释不了问题，终于还得拉出宗教来帮忙。布拉德雷虽然也不承认《哈姆雷特》是'宗教剧'，终还是向宗教观念去找了解答。"（卞之琳，2007: 51）笔者认为，这里有几点值得注意：第一，布拉德雷在整个文本分析中并没有突出宗教问题，只偶尔提了几句。第二，布拉德雷指的是普罗大众的宗教（popular religion），而不是官方宗教——正统的基督教，这种普罗大众的宗教包含民间所说的命运观，一种神明统摄的命运（但没有确指哪一个神明，只说是"上天的正义"，就像我们民间所说的"老天有眼"）。

在《莎士比亚悲剧》的第一讲中，布拉德雷说："这个问题不应该用'宗教的'语言来回答。因为虽然这个或那个登场人物可能谈到众神或上帝，谈到恶魔或撒旦，谈到天堂和地狱，虽然诗人可能向我们显示阴间的鬼魂，这些观念在实质上并不影响他对生活的表现，他也没有用它们来阐明生活中悲剧的秘密。伊丽莎白时代的戏剧几乎是完全非宗教性的；莎士比亚写作的时候，实际上把他的视野局限于从非神学的角度观察和思想的世界，因此，不论故事发生在基督教以前的时代还是基督教时代，他大体上是用同样一种方式表现这个世界的。"（Bradley, 1924: 25）第三，卞之琳不赞同布拉德雷的命运观，把它定性为资产阶级唯心论，并否定以这种宗教观念来分析《哈姆雷特》。笔者认为，卞之琳的这番话是从广义的宗教观去理解的，把民间的宗教观与正统的基督教观念都归为宗教。卞之琳是一个唯物论者，自然否定布拉德雷把一切归之于命运的观点。不过，笔者认为"命"的说法并不是资产阶级才有的，因此卞之琳用阶级论来下定论有失偏颇。另外，用命运来解释一些无法用理性来解释的现象，这是人类通常的做法，我们不能用"唯心论"来妄加定性。"命运观"是人类的共识。莎士比亚在很多戏剧中不止一次地透露出命运影响人的思想，如《罗密欧与朱丽叶》《麦克白斯》等。哈姆雷特在决定参加"比剑"前，霍拉旭曾劝说其不要应战，哈姆雷特说："我们不用怕什么预兆。一只麻雀，没有天意，也不会随便掉下来。注定在今天，就不会是明天；不是明天，就是今天；今天不来，明天总会来：有准备就是一切。"（第五幕第二场）（莎士比亚, 2016: 208）这里哈姆雷特表达了浓重的宿命论思想。哈姆雷特也好，莎士比亚也好，对命运都有敬畏之心。

尽管卞之琳接受了布拉德雷关于哈姆雷特性格的"忧郁论"，但他对《哈姆雷特》的分析在广度上有所发展。卞之琳首先专门用一讲来论述莎士比亚写作《哈姆雷特》的创作背景和社会原因：圈地运动给人民造成的苦难，埃塞克斯事件，王室、资产阶级与劳动人民的矛盾，封建基础崩溃和资本主义生产关系兴起，剧坛上弥漫着阴惨的气氛等，是从文学的外部去研究，是社会分析法。布拉德雷主要从人物性格论的角度去剖析，而卞之琳站在社会的高度、时代的高度去审视，更有气魄和宏观视野，这跟他一贯坚持马克思主义文艺观的理念是分不开的。这是卞之琳的莎学观与布拉德雷的莎学观最大的差异，也可以说是对布拉德雷莎学观的发展。其次，卞之琳考察《哈姆雷特》创作的前后时期，认为这部作品在莎士比亚的整个创作中是一个转折点，"是两大创作时期之间的桥梁"（卞之琳，2007：23），在它之前，着重宣扬个性发展，在它之后，着重批评极端个人主义。再次，卞之琳考察该剧的材料来源（布拉德雷并没有考察），除了指出 12 世纪末丹麦历史学家萨克索·格拉姆玛提库斯（Theodore Grammaticus）写的《丹麦史》是该剧的材料来源外，还指出 1589 年左右伦敦舞台上出现过一个以哈姆雷特故事为题材的悲剧。

三、对《奥瑟罗》的解读

卞之琳接受布拉德雷对《奥瑟罗》的时代性的判断。虽然《奥瑟罗》的材料源于意大利作家金乔 1565 年出版的《百日谈》第 3 辑第 7 篇小说，但莎士比亚推陈出新时，既沿用原来的故事和人物，又赋予作品以文艺复兴时代的气息。卞之琳在脚注里引用布拉德雷的话说明，这部作品刚面世的时候"差不多是一出当代生活的戏剧，因为土耳其攻击塞浦路斯的日期是 1570 年"（卞之琳，2007：139）。金乔小说里只提到塞浦路斯调换驻军将领，也不可能提到土耳其进攻。所以这部剧掺杂了莎士比亚时代的事件，这个细节是莎士比亚加入的，是莎士比亚的创造。布拉德雷断言："《奥瑟罗》是一部时代风俗剧；在它首次上演时，几乎称得上当代风俗剧。人们熟悉剧中的人物，而且拿该剧来'套'我们的生活显然也比用《哈姆雷特》或《里亚王》更为恰当。"（Bradley，1924：180）过去的故事加当代的事件和观念，这是莎士比亚创作的一贯做法，也是莎士比亚成功的法宝。如果他只是复制原故事，那他绝对成不了世界戏剧伟人。在这一点上，卞之琳首肯布拉德雷的观点。

卞之琳接受布拉德雷对该剧人物属性的判断。这部剧涉及种族人和社会人，到底哪一个更重要？学术界有争论。布拉德雷看淡这部剧的种族问题，他说："我不是说奥瑟罗属何种族毫无意义……但就其对人物性格的本质而言，种族就谈不上重要了。"（Bradley，1924：187）在这一点上，卞之琳与布拉德雷有相似之处。卞之琳认为："莎士比亚笔底下的奥瑟罗首先也还是社会人，其次才是种族人。换句话说，《奥瑟罗》剧本首先表现了人文主义的一般性的进步思想，其次才包含了种族平等的特殊性的开明观念。"（卞之琳，2007：144）有意思的是，即便讨论种族问题，布拉德雷谈及种族时只讨论奥瑟罗的肤色是黑色还是棕色（在笔者看来，这没有本质区别，卞之琳也觉得是多余的），并没有论述种族歧视、种族自卑，跟现在许多学者大刀阔斧地批评剧中种族歧视的文章截然不同。卞之琳对剧中的种族歧视问题虽然论述得不多，但比布拉德雷的深刻，他说："亚果的种族歧视比什么人的都更露骨，更突出。"（卞之琳，2007: 171）

　　卞之琳批评布拉德雷对《奥瑟罗》结构的判断。布拉德雷认为，该剧布局先松后紧、先扬后抑，他指出："这部剧情结构冲突开始较晚，然而却不停顿地加速发展，直至灾难结局发生，这是造成气氛紧张的主要原因。"（Bradley, 1924: 177）布拉德雷认为，该剧主要冲突到中间才一涌而出，从此一泻千里。但卞之琳不赞同这一观点，认为："效果上实际是差不多一开始就是如此，决不是开头先停滞不动，舒展不开。"（卞之琳，2007: 198）不是前松后紧，而是此起彼伏，一环扣一环，冲突不断。开始时奥瑟罗与布拉班旭的冲突是次要冲突，后来奥瑟罗与苔丝德摩娜的冲突是主要冲突，"先经过一种冲突的紧张，再接另一种冲突的紧张，一波未平，一波又起……两种冲突性质不一样，结果也不一样。描写发生在舞台以外而看不见的大风暴的谈话正好就用作前一种冲突的尾声，同时又用作后一种冲突的前奏曲"（卞之琳，2007: 199）。笔者赞同卞之琳对该剧结构的判断，第一幕就开门见山，剑拔弩张，冲突激烈。值得注意的是，奥瑟罗与苔丝德摩娜的冲突双方并不是对等的，而是一方绝对性地压倒另一方（这在莎剧中是罕见的），苔丝德摩娜被迫卷入冲突的漩涡中，她对冲突的缘起莫名其妙，甚至欲委曲求全，化解冲突，但无奈奥瑟罗过于偏执、强势，这种冲突的极端不平衡性导致苔丝德摩娜像一只无辜的羔羊般被献祭了。

　　卞之琳对布拉德雷的发展还体现在对《奥瑟罗》的人物分析上。布拉德雷纯粹从人物性格维度去解析，他认为奥瑟罗有浪漫秉性，有诗意，但头脑简单，不善于观察，从不反思，也不勤于内省，感情常激发他的想象，但又使他糊涂，钝化了他的理智。奥瑟罗不容易嫉妒，但一旦嫉妒，会变成失控的洪流；一旦证实，他会毫不留情，立刻报复；一旦醒悟，他会对自己严惩不贷。而卞之琳从社会斗争的全局去看问题，他认为："奥瑟罗只看到外部的敌人，看不到内部的敌人。"（卞之琳，2007: 149）这个判断是正确的。的确，在奥瑟罗眼中敌方就是土耳其，他率军前往塞浦路斯岛就是要打退土耳其人；他做梦也没有想到在自己的军队中有阴谋家、伪君子。可怕的不是外在的敌人，而是内部的敌人，隐蔽、伪善。奥瑟罗是一个头脑简单的理想主义者，对人世的复杂性根本没有参透，容易轻信，被人耍弄。布拉德雷坚持"人物性格论"，卞之琳则更多地从社会人的角度把人物性格和社会环境结合起来考察。

卞之琳对布拉德雷论述亚果的部分进行了发展。布拉德雷花了整整一讲来专门讨论亚果，他认为莎士比亚对亚果的罪恶刻画得淋漓尽致，超过了对理查三世的刻画。他不完全赞同以往莎评中的"恶棍论"，即亚果"具有非凡的能力，而且心狠手毒"（Bradley, 1924: 209）。他认同柯尔律治所创立的"无动机之恶意"说，即"亚果恨善只因为它是善，他爱恶只因为它是恶。他的行为并没有复仇、忌妒或野心之类的明显动机，仅出自'无动机之恶意'，即以他人痛苦为乐的非利己性动机。奥瑟罗、凯西奥不过是供其发泄取乐的对象而已"（Bradley, 1924: 209）。亚果的心理不像一个正常人，把他摆到《浮士德》之类的象征主义诗篇里也许更合适些。虽然剧中详细地展现了亚果阴谋的步骤，但布拉德雷反对将这部剧看作"阴谋悲剧"，认为性格仍然占主导地位，"亚果的阴谋是亚果这个人物性格的具体表现；它建立在对奥瑟罗的性格了如指掌的基础上，否则，便绝无成功的可能"（Bradley, 1924: 179）。也就是说，奥瑟罗易轻信和易嫉妒的性格给了亚果可乘之机。卞之琳对亚果的评析是从社会学的角度去考察，亚果代表了是非颠倒的社会黑暗势力。卞之琳认为，亚果所表现的尽管不是马基雅维利本人的全面思想，却基本上就是莎士比亚时代一般英国人所了解的"马基雅维利主义"。这种"马基雅维利主义"，带有资产阶级思想的特色，却和没落的反人民、反人道的封建主义正好同流合污、狼狈为奸。在这一点上，卞之琳与布拉德雷背道而驰。卞之琳透彻地分析了亚果的极端个人主义："亚果到剧本临了，显出了他的极端个人主义怎样登峰造极地见之于行动。他陷害了奥瑟罗和苔丝德摩娜，不但陷害而且直接刺伤了凯西奥，为了卸责而陷诬与他太不相干的妓女，为了灭口而刺死他的工具洛德里科，最后刺死了自己的老婆。"（卞之琳，2007: 178）这种极端个人主义的危害性巨大，造成了悲剧性的灾难。卞之琳的结论是：剧情表明，亚果作恶并不是没有动机。这一点与布拉德雷和柯尔律治的论断截然相反。他从马克思主义文艺观的立场指出："莎士比亚的现实主义艺术表现出来了他（亚果）的基本动机就包含在他同奥瑟罗和玳丝德摩娜基本倾向的矛盾里；他根本不能容忍他们和他们的发展。"（卞之琳，2007：179）具体的动机就是亚果字面上说出来的，如升官的野心、在黑人手下做事心存不满、种族歧视、疑心奥瑟罗与自己的妻子有暧昧关系。卞之琳认为，基本动机与具体动机二者相互结合，并不矛盾。

卞之琳也发展了布拉德雷对玳丝德摩娜的评价。布拉德雷把玳丝德摩娜看成"最可爱、最令人敬慕的女子，童稚般地纯真，圣徒般地富于勇气和理想，天使一样心地纯洁"（Bradley，1924：201）。而卞之琳把玳丝德摩娜视为人文主义理想的化身，"是一个敢于摒除一切偏见、摆脱一切束缚、要求自由发展个性、全面发扬人格、追求宽阔壮丽的生活目标的文艺复兴时代人"（卞之琳，2007：160）。布拉德雷与卞之琳都褒奖她，但所使用的话语迥异，前者纯粹从神、人关系的角度形容玳丝德摩娜的美德，后者是从社会人的角度提升玳丝德摩娜的形象，带有政治色彩。

四、对《里亚王》的解读

卞之琳对《里亚王》的解读大部分赞同和接受布拉德雷的观点，比如对该剧结构上双重情节线以及人物分类的判断。布拉德雷指出："我们讨论双重情节问题。从严格的剧情要求来看，这样的安排的确有不少益处。作者或许正是出于纯戏剧性方面的考虑才决定这样做。副线情节能使一个本身稍嫌单薄的故事变得丰满，并在副线人物与主线人物之间形成最有效的反差，使得后者的悲剧力度和气势在前者的映衬下得以升华。可是，情节副线的主要价值却在别处，它不仅体现在戏剧效果方面，而且还表现为一个更重要的事实——它只能在无与伦比的莎士比亚笔下实现，即副线完全重复了主线情节的主题。"（Bradley，1924：262）布拉德雷认为，《里亚王》的双线情节总使人觉得好像置身于一种普遍意义的冲突之中，代表着世界上的两股力量——善与恶。他顺着两条线索把人物分阵营，"要是撇开里亚、格罗斯特和阿尔巴尼三人，《里亚王》里其余的人物可分成泾渭分明的两方，相互形成鲜明的对照：考黛丽亚、肯特、艾德加和弄人为一方，戈奈丽尔、芮艮、艾德孟、康瓦尔和奥斯瓦尔德为另一方。……一方仁爱宽厚，另一方残忍自私……双方人员之间的差别则是浓墨粗画，界域分明"（Bradley，1924：263）。卞之琳对该剧的结构持相同看法，根据主副情节所表现的情况，除里亚和格罗斯特以外，主要人物也截然分成了正反两类人物。"在主要情节里，以考黛丽亚为一方，以戈奈丽尔和芮艮为一方，当然是对立的两面。在副情节里，对立的两面当然是艾德加和艾德孟。"（卞之琳，2007：211）

卞之琳接受布拉德雷对《里亚王》中借用动物意象来揭示莎士比亚写作的寓意。布拉德雷在讲稿中详尽地论述了该剧的意象，他指出："该剧一再提到下贱的兽类，并把人与动物相比较。综观全剧，这样的比拟比比皆是，好像莎士比亚满脑子都是这些形象，每写一页就非得提它一下不可。剧中提到的动物有狗、马、牛、羊、猪、狮、熊、狼、狐、猴、鼬、麝、鹈鹕、猫头鹰、乌鸦、红嘴山鸦、鹪鹩、苍蝇、蝴蝶、老鼠、青蛙、蝌蚪、壁虎、水蜥、蚯蚓——品种之多，不胜枚举，而且有些还被一再提起。"（Bradley，1924：266）布拉德雷把剧中所有涉及的动物全部列举出来，以丰富的实例来证明该剧区别于其他莎剧的醒目特征，言之凿凿，令人信服。布拉德雷分析这些动物意象的目的是挖掘它们的隐喻作用，他曾说莎士比亚"隐喻成癖"（pestered with metaphors）（Bradley，1924：73）。戈奈丽尔被比作苍鸢，她的忘恩负义像毒蛇的牙齿，咬碎了父亲的心；她长着狐狸脸，又像秃鹫般凶狠，用尖利的牙齿残酷地啄食父亲的胸膛。对丈夫，她是饰金的美女蛇；对格罗斯特，她残忍如野猪的利齿。两姐妹是噬人的虎豹，钩心斗角，犹如蝰蛇相争，她们肉体上长的是兽皮。奥斯瓦尔德是杂种老母狗生出的小杂种，又是鹊鸰和鹅，惯于向权势顶礼膜拜，动辄吓得脸色发白。阿尔巴尼在妻子的心目中，像牛一样胆小怕事。"人们读着这些，似乎觉得野兽的灵魂一步步地侵入了各个角色的体内。恶人的毒辣、凶暴、贪婪、欺诈、懒惰、残酷和污秽，令人发指。善人的孤弱单薄、赤身裸体、无力自卫、双目失明，催人心碎。"（Bradley，1924：267）西方意象派批评家斯珀津也认可布拉德雷的意象分析，她在《莎士比亚的意象及其意义》一书中多次提到布拉德雷对意象的论述："大量的动物意象及其在剧中的作用常常被人注意，尤其是布拉德雷的《莎士比亚悲剧》。"（Spurgeon，1968：342）卞之琳无疑受布拉德雷的影响，指出《里亚王》的语言里充斥了禽兽虫豸的意象，"这些意象，有目共睹，最适用于描绘或者渲染戈奈丽尔、芮艮之流的人物形象，贴到他们的发言人艾德孟这个道地'马基雅维利主义者'的身上，更能使这个人物形象闪闪发光"（卞之琳，2007：237）。动物意象的隐喻活画出人物形象，使那些狼心狗肺的男女遭人诅咒，也使主题深化，凸显良善，鞭挞邪恶，伸张正义。

卞之琳批评布拉德雷以宗教的观点看待《里亚王》。卞之琳说："布拉德雷在 20 世纪初年提出《里亚王》可以叫作《里亚王的救赎》。"（卞之琳，2007：207）布拉德雷的原话是："将《里亚王》的剧名改成《里亚王的救赎》更为恰当。神的启示，在这里既非惩罚里亚，也不激起其满腔悲愤。它引导里亚渡过绝望和失败的茫茫苦海，抵达人生真谛的彼岸。"（Bradley，1924：285）卞之琳认为："《里亚王》悲剧这一类作品，从爱憎分明的社会反映里体现出来的不断向前突进的时代精神、探索精神，首先就不符合维护道统的基督教精神、蒙昧精神。"（卞之琳，2007：230）卞之琳用阶级性去分析该剧本，认为这部悲剧里正反人物的冲突归根结底是新旧社会力量的冲突，里亚王就是两种社会力量交攻的战场。他对这两种相互冲突的社会力量并非中立，而是前后各有所偏，开头他代表封建统治的腐朽力量，偏向以艾德孟为发言人的一派，后来转向以考黛丽亚为旗帜的一派。发生在暴风雨场景里的大转换是翻天覆地式的，里亚由生杀予夺者沦为一无所有的乞丐，由此感同身受，同情平民，同情受苦受难者。

卞之琳对布拉德雷关于该剧人物的分析有所发展。他运用马克思主义阶级分析的方法来论述，认为剧中在青年贵族男女古色古香的外形下，实际上表现了当时社会上尚未定型的资产阶级，随着它的发展，由于它本身的两面性，分裂成两派。"一派开始与上层贵族结合，形成臭味相投的反动力量，一派继续与下层平民接近，形成声气相通的进步力量。由于本身共有的两面性，前者和上层贵族总还有对立冲突；后者和下层平民总还有距离、矛盾。前者就是以艾德孟为首的一种有形集团所代表的社会力量，后者就是以考黛丽亚为首的一种无形集团所代表的社会力量。"（卞之琳，2007：213）卞之琳超越布拉德雷之处在于他没有局限在剧本内部，而是引申出这两类人的普遍意义和象征意义，探索莎士比亚塑造这两类人的深刻性、普遍性，因此他的分析站得更高远，具有马克思主义的思想深度和广度。

结　语

卞之琳在论述《哈姆雷特》《奥瑟罗》《里亚王》时，无疑是深入研读过布拉德雷的著作的，有选择性地接受了布拉德雷的观点和方法，他接受布拉德雷注重文本事实的原则，接受性格分析法，接受对意象的分析等。但他批评布拉德雷只重文本内部研究，脱离历史现实，没有从生活环境、社会条件、时代特点，更没有从阶级立场等方面来探讨莎士比亚悲剧的实质，因此视野稍嫌局限；也批评布拉德雷的宿命论。卞之琳对布拉德雷莎学的发展体现在用马克思主义文艺观将人物放置在社会背景中考察其阶级性，注重文学外部研究，将文学内部研究与外部研究相融合；从人文主义思想的维度去探讨莎士比亚悲剧的社会根源。其论述视野宏大，有深度和广度，思想上倾向于"阶级论""社会论"，是马克思主义文学分析的典范。

为什么莎士比亚投射在布拉德雷和卞之琳身上的镜像有所不同？这是因为布拉德雷的西方美学的背景，他传承的是亚里士多德和黑格尔的美学观念，视人物冲突为研究的重中之重，所以他会对莎剧中的人物格外关注；而且他继承了英国浪漫主义的批评传统，"他们企图从人物的一言一行中发现作者深刻的、首尾连贯的戏剧意图，并且根据内心规律来解释人物的一切表现。他们依靠自己的艺术直觉阐明了莎士比亚，显示了他在手法和人物刻画方面的惊人天才。英国这种对莎士比亚的纯粹审美的唯心主义的批评传统，为十九世纪后期的亚·查·史文朋、爱·道顿以及二十世纪初年的安·塞·布拉德雷和华·雷里爵士继承下来。其中以布拉德雷的成就最为突出"（曹葆华语，见：杨周翰，1985: 51）。而卞之琳在新中国成立前后主要受苏联马克思主义莎评的影响，尤其是阿尼克斯特、莫罗佐夫的影响，同时受我国马克思主义美学观的影响，在这样的背景下，他从莎剧中更多地看到社会斗争、阶级冲突，这是时代氛围和意识形态所决定的。为什么卞之琳从布拉德雷的镜像中又照见许多心仪的东西？这是因为卞之琳还是有西学背景的，民国时期他在北京大学西语系学习西方文学，尤其精通英国文学、法国文学。除了译莎之外，他还翻译了法国现代派的诗歌，并出访过英国、美国，因此，他对西方的艺术精髓心驰神往。卞之琳作为诗人，重主观感情，对布拉德雷的浪漫主义解读也心领神会。

卞之琳对布拉德雷的接受可以看作本土文化对外来文化的镜像折射，看作一种受制于本土文化语境的想象和选择性的投射。卞之琳选择性地接受了布拉德雷的莎学观，对布拉德雷的观点有肯定，有批评，更有发展。同时我们也应看到：卞之琳对布拉德雷莎学观的选择性接受，体现了中国学者的主体性，没有对西方莎学盲目膜拜，人云亦云，而是有自己的立场判断和独立思想。在此，特别值得一提的是，卞之琳运用中国戏剧来阐释《哈姆雷特》《奥瑟罗》《里亚王》中的主角，饶有趣味。他说，按年龄顺序，"丹麦王子的青年——威尼斯摩尔将军的中年——远古不列颠老王的暮年，程式化脸谱（借用中国旧剧舞台术语，作比喻说）也应是小生式白净脸（带点苍白的）——净角式大黑脸——多血质（虽然白发苍苍的）大红脸"（卞之琳，2007：294）。这一类比新颖别致，妙不可言，绝妙地体现了卞之琳的诗性气质和深厚的中西文化素养。

引用文献【Works Cited】

Bradley, A. C. *Shakespearean Tragedy: Lectures on* Hamlet, Othello, King Lear, Macbeth. 2nd ed. London: Macmillan, 1924.

Charlton, H. B. *Shakespearian Comedy*. London: Methuen, 1938.

Spurgeon, Caroline F. E. *Shakespeare's Imagery and What It Tells Us*. Cambridge: Cambridge UP, 1968.

卞之琳，1980，《关于我译的莎士比亚悲剧〈哈姆雷特〉：无书有序》，《外国文学研究》第 1 期，第 38—50 页。

卞之琳，2007，《莎士比亚悲剧论痕》，合肥：安徽教育出版社。

马克思，2002，《马克思恩格斯全集》第三卷，中共中央马克思、恩格斯、列宁、斯大林著作编译局编译，北京：人民出版社。

莎士比亚，2016，《哈姆雷特》，卞之琳译，杭州：浙江文艺出版社。

杨周翰主编，1985，《莎士比亚评论汇编》下册，北京：中国社会科学出版社。

（特邀编辑：郝田虎）

新历史主义视角下《亨利六世》中的颠覆力量探析

许 展

内容提要：新历史主义视角下，莎士比亚历史剧中意识形态错综复杂，其文本内的社会存在不是单一的声调，不是统一、稳定的存在，而是多种声音的复调；它们是多种历史现实和意识形态相互交会、争斗的角斗场。正因为莎士比亚戏剧呈现了历史与文本、不同意识形态之间相互抵触、相互竞争的"历史的交会"，将其放置于社会语境与其他文学文本和历史文本的坐标中，可以更好地探讨莎士比亚的戏剧所呈现的历史与文本的互动。从此视角来审读莎士比亚的《亨利六世》，可以看出，其文本中的互动不仅仅传达了关于政治秩序的观念，更是融合了当时的历史思想，产生了颠覆性的力量。

关键词：新历史主义；莎士比亚；《亨利六世》；意识形态；秩序；颠覆

作者简介：许展，博士，洛阳理工学院讲师，研究方向为英国文学。本文系国家社会科学基金项目"莎士比亚英国历史剧的历史叙事研究"（17BWW006）的阶段性成果。

Title: A Study of the Subversive Power in *Henry VI* from the Perspective of New Historicism

Abstract: From the perspective of New Historicism, the social existence in Shakespeare's history plays contains not a single tone but a polyphony of multiple voices and the ideologies represented in the text are so complicated that a variety of historical realities and ideologies meet and intersect with each other. Precisely because Shakespeare's plays present such an "intersection of history" in which history and text, and different ideologies contradict and compete with each other, placing the plays in the social context of history, other literary texts and historical texts, enables one to better explore the interaction between history and text represented by Shakespeare's plays. From this perspective, we can see that the interactions in Shakespeare's *Henry VI* not only convey the concept of political order, but also integrate the historical thoughts at that time and produce some subversive power.

Key words: New Historicism, William Shakespeare, *Henry VI*, ideology, order, subversive power

Author: Xu Zhan, Ph.D. in English language and literature; lecturer in Luoyang Institute of Science and Technology; major research field: English literature. Email: xu10zhan@163.com

一、引　言

　　15 世纪，英国的封建统治遭受了一系列沉重的打击，统治阶级内部矛盾日益尖锐。在法国，英国所占领的属地丧失殆尽，英法之间的百年战争继续进行；在英格兰本土，兰开斯特王族和约克王族之间展开了一场旷日持久的争夺统治权的"玫瑰战争"，这就是莎士比亚早期历史剧《亨利六世》（上、中、下）所涵盖的主要内容。对很多批评家来说，包括历史主义学派代表人蒂利亚德（E. M. W. Tillyard）都认为，《亨利六世》及《理查三世》在内的四部曲是莎士比亚响应"都铎神话"的主题而创作的（辛雅敏，2016: 90）。作为官方意识形态主导下的一种史学传统，都铎神话将都铎王朝之下的英国视为一个黄金时代，把从理查二世到亨利八世的英国历史看成一种特定的模式，并认为这种模式体现了上帝的正义和惩罚（蒂利亚德, 2016: 171），即兰开斯特家族必须为亨利四世的篡位付出代价。虽然亨利五世以自己的强大延拓了这一过程，但亨利六世幼时继位，国家大政由大贵族把持，导致派系纷争和海外领土尽失，最终国家倾覆，理查三世篡位，直到亨利七世统一红白玫瑰家族，才迎来黄金时代——都铎王朝。这种都铎神话在莎士比亚历史剧中体现为固定的政治主题——"关于秩序和混乱，关于政治上的等级分明和内战，关于罪恶和惩罚，关于上帝的仁慈最终调和其正义，关于上帝对待英格兰的这种方式的信仰"（蒂利亚德, 2016: 225）。但以新历史主义的观点来看，这种结论值得商榷。首先，新历史主义认为，文本并不是一种稳定的、统一的文化和思想结构，任何文学文本的分析和解读都应该在其历史语境中进行，同时文学文本对历史现实也具有一定的形塑功能。其次，新历史主义认为主导意识形态常常决定了历史现实如何进入文学艺术，但是同时，文学艺术也可能作为残余意识形态或新兴意识形态的表述生成为意识形态的对抗性力量。就此，新历史主义的代表人物格林布拉特（Stephen Greenblatt）在其《隐形的子弹》一文中提出了"颠覆"和"抑制"这两个相对的关键词。"颠覆"是对统治秩序的主导意识形态的颠覆，而"抑制"则是对这种颠覆力量的抑制。具体来说，当统治阶级要巩固自己的力量时，都会激起某种颠覆性的力量，而这种颠覆性又会被权力所遏制，在这种交互中，权力最终确立起自己的权威（Greenblatt, 1988: 30）。

从新历史主义的视角来考察莎剧，可以发现，莎士比亚的历史剧正是在文艺复兴背景下与历史交融、被历史影响，同时又影响历史的典型代表。莎士比亚的历史剧创作既为了迎合观众趣味，又参与了王权贵族的权力建构，同时又对历史产生了影响，是消弭历史叙事与文学虚构之裂隙的绝佳范本。莎士比亚戏剧所体现的社会存在不是统一、稳定的存在，它们是多种意识形态相互交会、相互竞争的角斗场。莎剧文本中更是存在着多种颠覆力量，这种颠覆并不是指在现实世界中推翻现存的社会制度，而是在文化思想领域对社会制度所依存的权威意识形态加以质疑，进而发现被压抑的异质的反抗因素，从而揭示错综复杂的社会文化中政治意向的曲折表达方式以及从属意识形态对掌握权力话语的主导意识形态的抵触和竞争。在此视角下考察《亨利六世》可以看到，虽然《亨利六世》反映的是 15 世纪的历史事件，但在这部可能是他最早的戏剧作品中，莎士比亚似乎更专注于描绘政治图景。从《亨利六世》（上）的第一个场景开始，莎士比亚戏剧化地反复打断、违反和破坏历史和政治的纪念性时刻，呈现从属或边缘意识形态对主导意识形态运作疆域的抵触和颠覆，通过冲突和反讽来质疑编年史书和政治想象所勾勒的社会层级秩序，具体体现为派系斗争对有序仪式和权威的颠覆、女性对父权制英雄价值观的颠覆和普通民众对权力规制下社会层级秩序的颠覆。

二、派系斗争对有序仪式和权威的颠覆

历史剧有一种内在的能力，尽管它似乎只涉及过去，但能够唤起、评论和影射当时的时政话题，如朝廷重臣的政治生涯、宫廷政治的基调、时事大事和人民的利益等，都可能被反映在戏剧当中。其产生不仅是当时政治与历史、舞台与宫廷的行为，也是民众政治、民间谣言与戏剧表演之间的非常复杂的相互作用。正因为如此，历史剧提供了一个完美的工具来传达某些政治信息，同时也给我们提供管窥剧作家创作时的历史侧面的机会。

《亨利六世》（上）第一幕第一场中，亨利五世的葬礼在西敏寺举行，有序的仪式尚未完成就让位于护国公格罗斯特公爵和温彻斯特主教之间的互相攻讦和谩骂，贝德福德试图平息他们的愤怒，但刚刚要开口，使者报英军在法国战事失利。这出戏一开始，对英格兰未来福祉的关注就被封建王族的尔虞我诈和对权力的攫取所取代；英国征服的荣耀的丧失甚至在其伟大的国王还未被安葬之前就已经注定了；皇室继承人明显缺席，教会似乎与王权背道而驰。因此，这部剧的三个主题：幼主无能、派系政治、法国土地的丧失在一开始就显露出来。第一个信使公开指责贵族们的个人和派系斗争——"醒来吧，醒来吧，英格兰的贵族们！"（莎士比亚，2014: 17）第二个信使带来了英国在法国属地尽失的消息，第三个信使带来了英国将军、勇士塔尔博特被法国俘虏的消息（莎士比亚，2014: 17）。事实上，直到亨利五世死后七年，英国在法国的统治地位才逐渐开始瓦解，而信使所报的事情更是分散发生在亨利五世逝世后二十多年的时间里。莎士比亚通过对史料的压缩呈现，营造了仪式不断被打断的持续效果，这种累积凸显了终结感和国际性的巨变。这一场景的最后，温彻斯特暗自谋划："他们各有各自的岗位和职能，只有我被抛在一边无事可做，可我才不打算就这样永远受冷落。我准备把国王从埃尔塔姆宫轰走，自己来坐江山把持国政当舵手。"（2014: 21）温彻斯特的话暴露了贵族们的内部纷争、阴谋诡计：争相把持国政来争权夺利。《亨利六世》的开场戏剧性地揭开了隆重的皇家葬礼的仪式感与贵族们的纷争和阴谋之间冲突的本质：国家仪式的脆弱性和政治的高度戏剧化。所有这些都不祥地预兆了与法国的战争。在其后的戏剧中，这样的结构模式经常被重

复，直到政治外交和国家礼仪的尊严和意义在各个方面都被颠覆。

如果只从当时大的历史背景来看《亨利六世》，人们也许会产生疑惑：莎士比亚创作《亨利六世》期间，英国打败了西班牙的"无敌舰队"，取得了海上战争的胜利，英国人信心激增。"无敌舰队修辞"的流行似乎需要一部歌颂政治成功的戏剧，而不是一部以亨利五世的死为开头，进而戏剧化英国损失的戏剧。为了更好地理解戏剧文本里发生的事情，我们需要更深入地去探索当时的政治现实。这出戏中的贵族和军事指挥官之间的内部分裂、个人纷争和冲突，与伊丽莎白时期宫廷政治的氛围有着直接的时代共鸣。在 16 世纪 90 年代早期，伊丽莎白宫廷中的精英成员之间出现了激烈的矛盾。伊丽莎白的宠臣、莱斯特伯爵的继子埃塞克斯伯爵，与许多宫廷中的追随者都渴求军事上的荣耀，更希望与西班牙对抗到底，而以女王的重臣罗伯特·塞西尔和伯利男爵为中心的派系，则以和平和稳定为主要诉求。埃塞克斯伯爵坚持视塞西尔为敌人，在宫廷中形成派系之争。这成为伊丽莎白女王执政晚期的突出问题，也制造了许多纠纷、贿赂与机会主义者（威尔，2014: 579）。除此之外，埃塞克斯伯爵和一些年轻贵族，既为了奉承年老的女王而争风吃醋，也为了争夺军事指挥权和荣誉多次产生激烈矛盾。有时，激烈矛盾差点演变成暴力，埃塞克斯曾一度发起挑战，与年轻贵族决斗。这一点也加剧了政治派别的对立。

派系斗争并非剧作与历史环境之间唯一或最明显的相似和共鸣。剧中上演的一些最壮观的军事行动发生在围攻鲁昂期间。杰弗里·布洛（Geoffrey Bullough）在详细考察了莎士比亚的剧作与其戏剧来源后指出，《亨利六世》（上）与"1591 年年底的热门话题"相关，即英格兰派兵对鲁昂的围攻（Bullough, 1957: 24-25）。就在这部戏剧创作和演出的同时（1591 年年末和 1592 年年初），伊丽莎白支持信仰新教的纳瓦拉的亨利登上法国王位。1591 年秋天，她派出埃塞克斯伯爵协助法军攻打鲁昂。而埃塞克斯伯爵的军事行动最终以失败告终。英国军队在为一个新教王位候选人争取法国王位的失败努力中遇到的问题，与第一个信使对埃克塞特提出的巴黎和鲁昂是否由于"诡计"而失陷的反应密切相关：

　　没有什么诡计，只因缺丁少银。

　　士兵们都在私下里悄悄议论，

说你们这儿派系分歧，意见不一；

大战临头，披挂上阵才是正经，

诸公却还在为遣将用兵举棋不定。

一位主张少花些钱延拓战争，

另一位恨不能生出双翅飞腾；

第三位则主张不花分文，

幻想凭花言巧语赢得和平。（莎士比亚, 2014: 17）

这里信使的评论影射了埃塞克斯伯爵军事行动的一些困难。伊丽莎白女王摇摆不定，多次召回又重新派遣埃塞克斯出征，且不愿意为这次战役支付额外的经费；埃塞克斯则希望通过海外战争来为自己争取军事声誉，证明自己是一位伟大的指挥官，将自己皇室宠儿的身份转变成一个战争家和事务家，但他却十分不明智地与军队的将领们不断地发生争执与龃龉；议会也对与这次出征相关的外交政策分歧很大。总之，由于"缺丁少银"，这次围攻鲁昂的军事行动并不成功，埃塞克斯回到了英国。我们从围城初期女王给伯爵写的一系列信件中得知，女王对这次战役的结果非常愤怒，认为几乎是浪费时间和金钱（Watson, 1990: 40）。《亨利六世》没有直接涉及这些当时的问题，但却在戏剧中隐晦地暗指。莎士比亚从其所处时代时事政治的角度看待过去的事件，并有意地暗合了亨利六世统治时期的一些事件，表明了莎士比亚对历史的双重性的理解，以及当代历史与戏剧文本之间的巨大张力。

《亨利六世》指出了内乱的危害，以勇士英雄的死亡作为开始和结束，暗示了当时的政治政策、朝臣们争宠导致的派系纷争对国家有序仪式和权威的颠覆。然而，莎士比亚对这些政治事件的兴趣主要在于利用它们在舞台上呈现那些导致国家不稳定的错误的选择和政策、个人和国家行动领域内价值观的扭曲和颠倒。这种问题意识使得历史文本与政治现实之间充分互动，戏剧从历史出发阐释了当代政治如何运作。

三、女性对父权制英雄历史的颠覆

在《亨利六世》中，围绕着对法战争，塔尔博特的美德与贞德相对立，拥有恶魔般超自然力量的贞德与精于"阴谋算计"的法国贵族结盟最终打败和杀死了塔尔博特。然而，这一对立全然与历史不符，是莎士比亚的虚构，因为历史上贞德和塔尔博特的生涯并无任何重合。实际上，贞德早在塔尔博特建立赫赫战功之前就已经被处死（1431年），而塔尔博特则死于1453年，但莎士比亚有意使得塔尔博特和贞德的军事生涯在时间上更加紧密地平行，并编排了双方之间的多次战斗（Shakespeare, 2000: 23-25）。这组对立使不少评论家将该剧解读为一部政治英雄史，其中塔尔博特"代表了英格兰和正义的力量"，贞德则是"邪恶的法国力量"（Riggs, 1971: 105）。然而，如果仔细研究，我们会发现，虚构的贞德和塔尔博特的对立结果并非为了歌颂英格兰的政治英雄历史，相反，贞德颠覆了"英国骑士精神"的传统，解构了"理想贵族军事荣誉和精神"。贞德颠覆英雄传统的行动有两个层次：一方面，军事行动中，她通过战斗将英国人从法国赶出；另一方面，她用生动的语言抨击了英雄价值观。

在《亨利六世》第一部中，正如塔尔博特是英国事业的化身一样，贞德是法国事业的化身。这出戏以亨利五世的葬礼开始，在葬礼上，贝德福德暗示死去的国王将在历史上占有一席之地，甚至比裘力斯·恺撒的事迹更为辉煌。贝德福德试图找回英雄过去的努力被贞德打断，贞德自称是亨利五世英雄遗产的"终结者"：

> 我此番前来讨伐英格兰人是上苍所差，
> 今晚我就一定要将奥尔良之围解开。
> 既然有了我前来参加这一场殊死决战，
> 圣马丁夏日和太平盛世便可翘首以待。
> 光荣就如同水面上的一朵浪花，
> 它会不停地一圈一圈越扩越大，
> 直到无法再大而最终归于毁灭。
> 亨利驾崩，英格兰的圆圈到了尽头，
> 圈内的光荣也必随之玉殒香消。
> 而此刻我就像那艘傲笑汹涛的小舟，
> 正载着恺撒和他的好运逢凶化吉。（莎士比亚, 2014: 26）

贞德颠覆英国英雄历史的努力首先是在军事层面上。历史上从来没有记载过贞德与英国将领肉搏战的描述，然而，在《亨利六世》中，莎士比亚不仅安排了贞德与男性将领直接比武，而且还通过剧中人物之口，把贞德描述成"亚马逊女战士"的形象。亚马逊人是古代希腊神话中的一个女战士种族，在荷马的《伊利亚特》中，这些亚马逊女战士以英勇无畏的姿态加入了特洛伊战争，帮助特洛伊人对抗希腊联邦。在传统的神话中，往往都是由男性英雄（例如大力神赫拉克勒斯、忒修斯和阿喀琉斯）最终打败这些异族的女性战士，将英雄的胜利与捍卫父权制的历史记录联系起来。贞德自称是被圣母显灵选择来"解救法国的大难大灾"（莎士比亚，2014: 24），首次见到法国王太子查尔斯便自告奋勇通过格斗来展现她的勇气和能力。王太子接受了这个挑战，但不一会儿就躺在贞德脚下高喊："住手！住手！您真算得上是巾帼英雄，使起剑来如底波拉，让人无招架之功。"（2014: 24）

贞德在与塔尔博特的第一次交锋中同样令人生畏，同样是单打独斗。舞台说明把这次战果描述成"贞德追逼英军"。塔尔博特同样被她非比寻常的力量所打败："我的头脑就像陶匠的旋盘一样在打转；这是在哪儿，在干些什么我全不知道。"这场战役中，贞德就像"当年摆火牛阵的汉尼拔一般"，而英军则像是"小狗，只能一边嗥叫一边逃走"。（2014: 36）。

其次，贞德始终被赋予了超越世俗传统之外的现实理性。作为反传统的女性，她不断地对事件的深层价值进行质疑。贞德对理想主义的不懈解构体现在她跟勃艮第公爵的对话之中。勃艮第公爵支持英国攻打法国，并赞美塔尔博特的"丰功伟绩将如一座勇敢者的纪念碑"，贞德则迫使勃艮第睁开眼睛看到了一幅完全不同的画面："看看你的国家，看看这肥沃的法兰西，再看看被眼前这些残酷的敌人 / 蹂躏得满目疮痍的名城大邑，且像母亲看着死神令她已奄奄一息 / 的婴儿合上娇嫩的眼睛一样，看看法兰西吧，它已是遍体鳞伤！"勃艮第被贞德雄辩的演讲所说服，回归法国，贞德评论道："真不失为法兰西人——说变卦就变卦。"（2014: 77）与和勃艮第的对话同样重要的是贞德对骑士精神的讽刺。得知塔尔博特已经去世，寻找塔尔博特的信使威廉·露西爵士背诵了一大串塔尔博特的荣誉称号：

　　我要找的是战场上的阿西底斯，

> 英勇的塔尔博大人什鲁斯伯里伯爵，
> 由于赫赫战绩曾被册封为
> 伟大的瓦希福、沃特福及瓦伦斯伯爵、
> 古德立克与厄琴菲尔德的塔尔博勋爵、
> 布拉克米的斯特兰治勋爵、阿尔顿的魏尔顿勋爵
> 温菲尔的克伦威尔勋爵、舍菲尔的佛尼瓦尔勋爵
> 战无不胜的福康勃立治勋爵；
> 曾获圣乔治、圣迈克尔及金羊毛
> 各项勋章的崇高骑士称号；
> 亨利六世御前统领法兰西
> 境内所有战事的大元帅——他在哪里？（莎士比亚，2014: 102）

露西将塔尔博特的军事荣耀与其英雄的父系传统相结合，而贞德则剥离了这些长串头衔与实际意义的真实关系："真是好一堆啰啰唆唆的头衔！拥有五十二个王国的土耳其苏丹，也开不出这样一大串乏味的头衔。你用这么多头衔来吹捧的那个人 / 正躺在我们的脚边冒臭气逗苍蝇。"（2014: 102）贞德话语中的讽刺平衡了露西的戏剧性夸张，同时揭掉了任何试图将战争浪漫化的侠义伪装。露西虽然是来向贞德索要塔尔博特的尸体的，但仍然虚张声势："但愿我能让死难者复活，这样就足以吓坏你们法兰西全国！只需把他的画像悬在你们中间，就将让你们最傲慢的人心惊胆战。"（2014: 103）贞德指责他是如此的傲慢无礼和咄咄逼人，就像"塔尔博特的灵魂"。贞德对他的请求做出的反应，更凸显出她对敌人蔑视的怪诞幽默："且让他运走尸体，留在这里，也只能发臭污染空气。"（2014: 103）虽然塔尔博特是剧中表面上的英雄，但是贞德最有力地揭示了所有英雄价值观的虚荣肤浅，体现了非正统的人文主义观点。

总体来说，半虚构的贞德是非传统的。作为女性，她有足够的勇气和资源在战斗中战胜塔尔博特，并用生动的语言颠覆以塔尔博特为代表的传统骑士荣誉观。其他法国男性军事领导人与之相比，黯然逊色。她身体上的现实理性抵制了英国人创造历史的努力。同时，贞德演讲中丰富的修辞拒绝了任何"民族自我代表"所能唤起的男性英雄理想。

四、普通民众对社会层级秩序的颠覆

在诗歌或小说中，下层边缘人物很容易用叙述的手法来解决，锡德尼（Sir Philip Sidney）笔下的侠义王子和斯宾塞（Edmund Spenser）笔下的阿泰格尔与塔鲁斯以暴力手段消灭了下层反叛分子，对他们冷嘲热讽，重申了贵族的优越性。但在舞台上，下层民众很难被简单地描绘成无名、无姓、无人性的群体，下层阶级在戏剧中的存在拓展了社会的定义，扩大了思想斗争的舞台。《亨利六世》第二部中，平民这一政治要素格外突出。莎士比亚通过引入陌生化的普通民众和贫民，突破了编年史书只通过贵族来呈现英国历史的局限性，并打破了贵族视角在意识形态上的排他性。当那些地位低于国王和贵族的普通市民、农民一上台，与贵族们在阶级、财富、服饰、风度等方面的不对称立即显现出来，这些差异就变成了鲜明的对比。很多时候，这种对比导致了喜剧，但喜剧的效果不仅仅局限于嘲笑下层阶级在财富和文化方面的劣势；更重要的是，当下层边缘人物成为戏剧活动的一部分时，由于戏剧的本质，会使人们更容易感知到统治阶级意识形态对资源的操纵，从而激发出对权威的审问和对现存阶级秩序的颠覆感。

戏剧一开始，下层民众群体以三个明显的序列出现：彼得和霍纳，辛普考克斯一家，凯德的叛乱。这些民众都有名有姓，就像活生生的社会中的人，虽然前两个纯属剧作家的虚构，但仅仅是命名就赋予了他们人性和个体化的特色。此外，这些场景都有自己的矛盾共鸣。每一个都凸显了人民内部对社会的不满情绪、强权阶级的各种剥削手段，以及穷人和无权者根本无缘政治舞台的社会现实。凯德的叛乱是一个极端的例子，杰克·凯德的反叛是约克公爵一手操纵和策划的。随着约克公爵派系的壮大，他煽动凯德和他的工匠们造反，为凯德设计了一个虚假家谱，试图扶持凯德叛乱来牟取私利：

> 我已经怂恿了一个刚愎的肯特人，
> 此人真名叫阿什福的杰克·凯德，
> 要他化名为约翰·摩提默，
> 尽其所能地制造骚乱。

······

> 我要叫这鬼家伙变成我的傀儡；
>
> 因为他相貌、步态、言谈都酷似
>
> 早已死掉了的约翰·摩提默。
>
> 用这个法子我可以窥测百姓的心思，
>
> 了解他们对约克家族及其主张的反应。
>
> 万一他得逞——大有可能得逞，
>
> 那我就可以从爱尔兰率兵前来，
>
> 将这坏蛋播下的种子结出的果实采摘，
>
> 汉弗瑞一死——他是必死无疑，
>
> 亨利一废，下一个就轮到我登基。（莎士比亚, 2014: 192-193）

这段独白十分耐人寻味。约克称凯德为"鬼家伙"，显示凯德不过是约克的傀儡和替代品，是被约克及其贵族联盟操纵利用从而为其伺机篡位服务的。约克公爵在早些时候向他的盟友沃里克伯爵和索尔兹伯里伯爵做了详尽的解释，声称他对王位的权利（约克的母亲是摩提默家族，父亲是金雀花家族）。当凯德自称他也有这样的父母，他的父亲是摩提默家族，他的母亲是金雀花家族时，迪克屠夫在旁悄声揭露，他的父亲是个不错的泥瓦匠，他的母亲是一个接生婆。实话实说的迪克揭露了凯德作为王位继承者的说法是谎言。无产阶级对于贵族家系的模仿讽刺了阶级等级制度的虚伪性，更揭示了所谓的王室谱系不过是贵族们玩的血统游戏。

在约克的秘密鼓励下，凯德领导叛军起义。"阶级"一词在伊丽莎白时代还没有真正出现，但在凯德以及他的追随者的呼吁中确实有一种早期的阶级意识（Chernaik, 2007: 36）。社会等级制度被认为是人民的敌人。一名反叛者声称："自打绅士们得势后英格兰就不再是一片乐土了。"因此，凯德用一个假设来吸引他的追随者——爵爷、绅士都是他的敌人，所有节俭老实、鞋掌上有钉子的人都是他的天然盟友（莎士比亚, 2014: 218, 224）。然而，不仅是绅士成为敌人，所有学者也成了凯德及其盟友的敌人。雄辩的人道主义者赛伊勋爵，以文明和法治的代言人的形象，与凯德面对面地对质。他刚开始用拉丁语说他的自卫演讲，就听到凯德的喊声："把他拉出去，把他拉出去！他还唠叨什么拉丁文哩。"（2014：232）凯德对赛伊勋爵的指控之一是，他们的祖先除了记账的刻痕标签，别无其他书籍，但赛伊却使印刷术大行其道。根据凯德的说法，赛伊建造纸厂的行为也背叛了这个国家的年轻人（2014：231）。

实际上，凯德造反的时代造纸厂和印刷机还没有在英格兰出现，但这并不重要，重要的是凯德意识的来源，语法学校把他从刻痕计数的世界中带走，强迫他进入印刷书籍的世界。他接下来的话将教育和法律程序等同于不正当的特权，提出对权威价值观的审问：

> 我可以当面向你证实，你身边的那些人张口就是什么名词动词，以及诸如此类叫基督徒的耳朵不能容忍的可恶的词汇。你委任了大堆大堆的地方治安法官，这些人动不动就传讯穷人，问一些他们根本答不上来的事情。而且，你还把他们投入大牢，因为不识字，你便把他们吊死，其实，正因为如此，他们才是最配活的人。（莎士比亚，2014：231）

认为罪犯识字就应该被赦免的想法是疯狂的，但是凯德抗议的正是当时的英国法律：如果一个被定罪的罪犯可以通过阅读《圣经》的《诗篇》来证明他是识字的、具有一定文化程度的，那么他就可以获得神职人员的特权，受没有死刑的教会法院的管辖（Greenblatt, 2004：171）。正是这种逻辑使得法律被扭曲，通过"受教育"这种上流社会的福利特权，懂得读写的人在被起诉犯罪时可以申请某些豁免权甚至被免除死刑。结果，在大多数情况下，是有文化的小偷或杀人犯逍遥法外。因此，凯德的演讲一开始是为反对学习的盲目无知辩护，后来变成了对一个延续特权和不公正的社会制度的批判。凯德对封建社会制度的批判不但影射了现实政治，还产生了巨大的颠覆效果。在戏剧世界里，统治者与被统治者、地主阶级与人民、博学者与未学习者之间的等级关系在凯德那里被颠覆。他试图建立一个由自己独断统治、人们可以在那里永久狂欢的乌托邦：

> 我谢谢你们，善良的人们——我将取消货币；大家吃喝都记在我的账上，我还要让大家全都穿上同样的服装，以便让他们和睦相处得

如同兄弟一样，进而拥戴我为他们的主上。（莎士比亚，2014: 220）

凯德表达了反叛者的社会目标，他们的愿望是退回到文明前人人劳动、平等的状态。马里奥特指出，杰克·凯德对这个乌托邦的描述给了我们"有史以来最优秀、最狡猾的'自我追求'的共产主义者肖像"（Marriott, 1918: 192）。实际上，凯德及其追随者所设想的乌托邦，即便无法在现实社会中成真，也为大众提供了一个本质上具有颠覆性的想象疆域。

在《亨利六世》第二部中，凯德叛乱既体现了底层民众们具有颠覆性的狂野的乌托邦幻想，也呈现了无政府、反传统、不受控制的暴力形式，这种暴力主要针对社会等级和造成阶级分化的文化制度。戏剧展现了底层人民的颠覆性品质是如何不断积累的，这种品质促使人民在集体行动中对政治施加影响，并试图通过暴动在政治舞台上占有一席之地；而导致这些暴乱的真正原因是普通和底层民众对他们所受的剥削和不公平、不公正待遇感到由衷的不满。

五、结　语

《亨利六世》三部曲揭示的政治问题比编年史家揭露的要严重得多：英格兰对外战争失利，国内贵族党派纷争，国家功能失调，下层民众民不聊生，暴动起义。莎士比亚从其所处时代现实政治的角度看待过去的事件，并有意地暗合了亨利六世统治时期的一些事件，表明了莎士比亚对历史的双重性理解，以及历史与戏剧文本之间的巨大张力。戏剧展现了被主流意识形态压抑的不安定因素对现有秩序和层级意识的颠覆，其中包括贵族斗争对王室权威的颠覆、女性对父权制英雄主义的颠覆，以及普通民众对社会秩序的颠覆。这些情节是对黑暗、邪恶的现实政治的影射，既揭示了政府的无能，也反映了无政府状态的混乱。观看戏剧的观众们发现，他们不仅在观看历史，而且还带着恐惧和焦虑用反乌托邦式的眼光在审视现实的政治。尽管在戏剧中，世界分裂成历史碎片，残缺不全的仪式被暴力和邪恶所干预，以及其他所有破坏性的混乱力量破坏了秩序，但是这种残缺的秩序正是戏剧通过艺术对日常世界的对抗，使得观众能够成功地从这种复杂和颠覆的混乱中找到有意义的中心。

引用文献【Works Cited】

Bullough, Geoffrey. *Earlier English History Plays: Henry VI, Richard III, Richard II*. Vol. 3 of *Narrative and Dramatic Sources of Shakespear*. London: Routledge & Kegan Paul; New York: Columbia UP, 1960.

Chernaik, Warren. *The Cambridge Introduction to Shakespeare's History Plays*. Cambridge: Cambridge UP, 2007.

Greenblatt, Stephen. "Invisible Bullets." *Shakespeare Negotiations: The Circulation of Social Energy in Renaissance England*. Los Angles: U of California P, 1988.

---. *Will in the World: How Shakespeare Became Shakespeare*. New York: Norton, 2004.

Marriott, J. A. R. *English History in Shakespeare*. London: Chapman & Hall, 1918.

Riggs, David. *Shakespeare's Heroical Histories: "Henry VI" and Its Literary Tradition*. Cambridge, MA: Harvard UP, 1971.

Shakespeare, William. *King Henry IV Part One*. Ed. Edward Burns. London: The Arden Shakespeare, 2000.

Watson, Donald G. *Shakespeare's Early History Plays: Politics at Play on the Elizabethan Stage*. London: Macmillan, 1990.

蒂利亚德，2016,《莎士比亚的历史剧》，牟芳芳译，北京：华夏出版社。

莎士比亚，2014,《亨利六世（上篇）》，覃学岚译，载方平主编《莎士比亚全集（第八卷，历史剧卷二）》，上海：上海译文出版社，第1—126页。

艾莉森·威尔，2014,《伊丽莎白女王》，董晏廷译，北京：社会科学文献出版社。

辛雅敏，2016,《二十世纪莎评简史》，北京：中国社会科学出版社。

（特邀编辑：郝田虎、王瑞雪）

论《仙后》第一卷中的寓言性空间

阮 婧

内容提要： 在《仙后》第一卷中，红十字骑士经历一系列的艰险和磨砺后，终于获得神圣这一美德并成长为一名受人尊敬的基督教骑士。本文认为，埃德蒙·斯宾塞巧妙地将红十字骑士为获得神圣这一美德而经历的成长过程设计并安排进三种空间框架中。简而言之，这三种空间包括自然空间、建筑空间和伊甸园空间。本文将探讨这三种空间的寓意及其在红十字骑士成长为代表神圣美德的基督教骑士中的作用。此外，本文也将讨论斯宾塞神圣观念的源起、历史文化语境及意涵，从而揭示斯宾塞的神圣观与其在《仙后》第一卷中的寓言性空间建构的相关性。

关键词： 寓言性空间；《仙后》；神圣；埃德蒙·斯宾塞

作者简介： 阮婧，台湾成功大学博士在读，绍兴文理学院元培学院讲师。主要从事英国文艺复兴时期文学研究。

Title: The Allegorical Spaces in Book I of *The Faerie Queene*

Abstract: In Book I of *The Faerie Queene*, Red Crosse experiences a series of trials and tribulations before he attains holiness and becomes a respectable Christian knight. The present paper argues that the whole process of Red Crosse's journey of bildungsroman towards holiness is designed and arranged ingeniously by Edmund Spenser within three types of spaces, which are natural space, architectural space and Edenic space. By exploring the allegorical connotations of the spaces and their functions in assisting Red Crosse to become a true Christian knight who embodies holiness as a virtue, this paper also attempts to discuss the source, contexts and implications of Spenserian holiness as well as the correlation between Spenserian holiness and the construction of allegorical spaces in Book I of *The Faerie Queene*.

Key words: allegorical spaces, *The Faerie Queene*, holiness, Edmund Spenser
Author: Ruan Jing (Ph.D. student, Cheng Kung University) is a lecturer in Shaoxing University Yuanpei College. Her research field is the English Renaissance literature. Email: 392702398@qq.com

1. Introduction

The Faerie Queene, a masterpiece of epic poetry in six volumes, has guaranteed its writer Edmund Spenser (1552—1599) a position in British literary history as "the poet's poet." The first book of *The Faerie Queene* is a legend of holiness, in which the knight Red Crosse is commissioned by Gloriana, the Queen of Faerie Land, to accompany Una to the kingdom of her parents and to deliver them from the scourge of the dragon. Though a knight by whom Spenser attempts to "expresse Holynes" (Spenser, 1978: 16), Red Crosse does not manifest holiness at his initial appearance in the book. Instead, at the outset of the book, he is "a tall clownishe younge man" (17), "pricking on the plaine" (I.i.1.1) and seeking for "straunge aduentures" (I.i.30.4). Thus, the first book of *The Faerie Queene* can be regarded as a bildungsroman of Red Crosse on his path to holiness, during which he has to encounter and experience a series of trials and tribulations before he can attain holiness.

In his essay "The Structure of Imagery in *The Faerie Queene*," Northrop Frye points out that "He [Spenser] thinks inside regular frameworks—the twelve months, the nine muses, the seven deadly sins—and he goes on filling up his frame even when his scheme is mistaken from the beginning" (1961: 110). In line with Northrop Frye's argument, this paper proposes that spaces in the first book of *The Faerie Queene,* which can be categorized into natural space, architectural space and Edenic space, are frames that not only reveal the psychological or spiritual bildungsroman of Red Crosse, but also point to Spenserian holiness allegorically through their distinctive means and connotations.

Space in *The Faerie Queene* is not an unexplored arena. Coleridge considers Spenser's Faerie Land as a "mental space" (qtd. in Smith, 2008: 86). Other critics also highlights the immaterial dimension of the Faerie Land by calling it as "pure wonderland," "dreamwork," "transitory world," "a dream of empire" (86). D. K. Smith himself stresses the simultaneity between Spenser's creation of *The Faerie Queene* and England's "burgeoning confidence in cartographic precision" (75). By reading *The Faerie Queene* as a process of allegorical cartography, Smith argues that Spenser "effectively superimposed a very particular memory of the English people onto a *locus* as large as all Faerieland, creating not so much a theater of memory as a national poetic map of memory" (116). Besides, Christopher Burlinson, in his monograph *Allegory, Space and the Material World in the Writings of Edmund Spenser*, studies how the emergence of materiality in the Elizabethan era is infused into the narrative and physical space of Spenser's writing in *The Faerie Queene*. However, previous studies show insufficient attention to space in Book I of *The Faerie Queene*, especially when it comes to the correlations between its allegorical connotations and Spenserian holiness.

Based on the argument proposed above, this paper will follow a road map of first discussing the Spenserian concept of "holiness" within its cultural, social and historical context, and then exploring the three types of spaces to figure out their allegorical connections to the "holiness" that Spenser meant to express through Red Crosse.

2. Spenserian Holiness

Holiness, an abstract term, is dramatized, explored and concretized into specific meanings through its embodiment in Red Crosse, who is referred to as the "Patron of true Holiness" in the argument stanza of Canto I, Book I. In addition, the initial appearance of Red Crosse wearing an armour with "a bloudie Crosse" (I.i.2.1) on his breast has already hinted at the connection between knighthood and Christianity in interpreting the possible meanings of "holiness" to Spenser. In the following, we will narrow down the scope of our study upon "holiness" from its historical and cultural sources to its possible connotations in Spenser's *The Faerie Queene*.

The history of knighthood starts from the period of ancient Rome when Romulus selected a thousand men from his people "for war and called them knights" (Bumke, 1982: 22) after he founded the city of Rome. Around the 11th century, church and chivalry became "two great ideologies of medieval Europe" (Wise and Scollins, 1984: 4) and "came together as one in the Holy Land" (4). Knighthood attained its full prosperity around the 13th and 14th century, but was on the wane during the 16th century, when knights were gradually supplanted by professional soldiers in standing armies. It is recorded that "[b]y the time Edmund Spenser published his *Faerie Queene* (1590—1596), chivalry was a remainder of 'antique times'" (54-55). However, the fact that Spenser still employed a Christian knight to embody the virtue of holiness may not only be attributed to his well-acknowledged attachment to the medieval inheritance and knowledge of the literature of antiquity and of Renaissance Italy and France, but also to the possibility that the historical linkage between Christianity and knighthood could be endowed with new meanings in the transitional period of the Elizabethan Era.

The age in which Spenser lived is an age of magnificence, an age of discovery as well as an age of reformation for England. The 16th-century England witnessed the high period of the European Renaissance. In addition, during the reign of Elizabeth I, new continents and oceans were explored, and a colony was established.① It is an age that marks England's ambition to expand

---

① According to Lenman, the first colony of England was established on Roanoke Island in 1585, and "the queen had given the incipient colony little beyond the use of her name in the allusive form of Virginia" (2001: 93). Sir Water Raleigh, one of Elizabeth I's favorites, supported the colony and even set up "the city of Raleigh in Virginia under the governorship of the artist John White" (93) in 1587 when he sent the third group of colonists there. However, the colony proved its failure in 1590. Besides, Alan G. R. Smith accounts that "Elizabethan explorers also made new initiatives, notably attempts to found colonies in North America as well as efforts to discover and exploit the vast continent which was then generally believed to occupy the whole southern part of the globe" (1984: 155).

its imperial territory.^① Moreover, Queen Elizabeth's determination to remain separate from the Roman Catholic Church and to strengthen the Church of England had brought her and her nation threats and isolation from "the great Catholic continental powers, particularly Spain" (Heale, 1999: 4). Nevertheless, Edmund Spenser, a zealous Protestant, staunchly espoused and worshipped the Virgin Queen and dedicated his epic romance to celebrate her rule.

Elizabeth Heale and Anthea Hume highlighted the Protestant dimension of Spenserian holiness. Heale quotes from John Calvin's *Institute of the Christian Religion* to illustrate that to pursue holiness is an obligation for the Elect because "'God is holy' (Lev. xix.1; Pet. i.16)" (qtd. in Heale, 1999: 21). Holiness forms the linkage between God and the Elect. Likewise, Anthea Hume claims that "[i]n the Protestant conception of human nature the only 'true' holiness is that of Christ, imputed to the sinful human being *sola gratia, sola fide*" (2008: 73). In this sense, the path to holiness requires insistent human faith in the grace of God.

Following the track of Protestantism, Macdonald claims that Spenser's Red Crosse demonstrates limited human agency compared with the Calvinist beliefs on human depravity (2015: 114). Besides, he points out that "[b]y presenting George as a saint who combines reformed spirituality with English tradition, Spenser furnishes an idealized basis for Elizabeth's rule by offering holiness as the root of her princely state" (126). In saying so, Macdonald has suggested the parallel between the spiritual transformations of Red Crosse and the tortuous Reformation that Elizabethan England was going through, so that the Spenserian holiness is endowed with historical implications.

Morgan, however, studies Spenser's holiness by exploring and expanding the connotations of Spenser's word choice "holiness" etymologically. He

---

① According to Ken MacMillan, "English knights such as Francis Drake, Martin Frobisher, Humphrey Gilbert, John Hawkins and Walter Raleigh travelled the oceans in search of new lands and trading opportunities" (2011: 646). Henceforth, though "origins of the British Empire are to be found in later centuries" (646), still explorations in the reign of Elizabeth I laid foundations for England's expansion hereafter.

proposes that holiness should be defined "principally (as we are assured it will be in the *Letter to Raleigh*) in relation to a scheme of Aristotelian moral analysis (mediated by Aquinas)" (2004: 453). Besides, he points out that "holiness" is a more circumspect word choice than "religion" as a virtue in the case of *The Faerie Queene* because the word "holiness" represents "not only such acts as devotion and adoration, but also acts of fidelity, courage, and humility such as are required in the exercise of religion" (453). Moreover, he warns about the easy equation between "faith" and "holiness or religion" and explains that whereas "faith" is a theological virtue which points to God, holiness is a moral virtue that points to the worship of God (451-453). In this manner, Morgan provides a more exact and comprehensive explanation of Spenserian holiness.

To sum up, the connotations of Spenserian holiness can be categorized into four aspects. First, holiness embodied by knights not only indicates the inextricable connections between knights and their ardent pursuit of Christian chivalry in the Middle Ages, but also demonstrates the courage, bravery, righteousness, endurance and bellicosity that England desperately needed in its years of Reformation. Second, as the first virtue that is embodied by Red Crosse who will ultimately grow to be St. George and the patron of England, holiness is to be pursued and cherished by England as it goes through various historical and religious tests. Third, in Spenserian holiness, human agency is admitted and highlighted. Fourth, as the sovereign queen to be glorified in the poem, Elizabeth I is also an emblem of holiness who has abandoned the Roman Catholic Church and chosen the Church of England for her people and her land.

3. Allegorical Spaces

The Faerie Queene is explicitly acknowledged by Spenser to be "a continued Allegory or darke conceit" (Spenser, 1978: 15) in his letter to Raleigh. In fact, allegorical meanings of *The Faerie Queene* have been unearthed for centuries, which testifies to the complexity and profundity of the book. To be brief, C. S. Lewis considers *The Faerie Queene* as an allegory of love (2013: 371-450). Jason Crawford elaborates the allegory of enchantment in *The Faerie Queene* as a modern poetics (2017: 138-174). Donald Stump parallels *The Faerie Queene* with the history of Elizabeth's period, and studies *The Faerie Queene* as a historical allegory (2019), to name just a few.

Nevertheless, our focus here is the allegorical space in Book I of *The Faerie Queene*. In the following, we will try to explore Spenser's design of spaces in this book, studying how the three types of spaces, namely, natural space, architectural space and Edenic space, function as frames to present Red Crosse's path towards holiness through changes of geographical spaces, while at the same time, demonstrating Spenserian holiness in its various dimensions.

3.1 Natural Space

Spenser spent nearly half of his life span serving in Ireland, which inevitably imprinted a deep mark upon his literary creation. Indeed, most of his literary productions were completed in Ireland. C. S. Lewis comments that "we can call *The Faerie Queene* an Irish product" (1998: 125) because Spenser's life and work in Ireland guaranteed him time and energy to sink into his imaginative literary writings. In fact, Ireland not only provided Spenser with the serenity that creation demands, but also proffered him multifarious inspirations for writing.

Ireland in the 16th century was covered with large areas of forests, which provided natural images for Spenser to create the scenes and spaces in *The Faerie Queene*. To quote from C. S. Lewis, "Keats in his sonnet 'To Spenser' speaks of one who loved *The Faerie Queene* as 'a forester deep in thy midmost trees'. There is forest, and more forests, wherever you look: you cannot see out of that world, just as you cannot see out of this" (136). Spenser's forest has various functions in Book I of *The Faerie Queene*; it can be common scenery, or the dwelling of witches, satyrs, nymphs and beasts, or the place that germinates the seed of love for Queen Gloriana in Arthur's dream, or a habitat that is filled with productive powers. Here, we are concerned with how the forest as a natural space could enwrap allegorical functions that are resonant with the theme of holiness shining at the end of this Book.

The forest is tinted with moral and psychological implications from the inception of Book I. To seek shade in a bright summer's day, Una and Red Crosse enter the grove where

> loftie trees yclad with sommers pride,
> Did spread so broad, that heauens light did hide,
> Not perceable with power of any starre. (I.i.7.4—6)

In an area where God's light is nearly unable to penetrate, Una and Red Crosse soon lose their road among trees of different types. The catalogue of trees, which echoes Vigil, Ovid and Chaucer, also indicates a diversity of choices that are confusing and undiscernible in the dark shade that blocks the light of God. Cheney considered the catalogue of trees as "evidence of man's confident moral dissection of his universe" (qtd. in Burlinson, 2006: 175), even though men themselves are often ironically lost within it.

In addition to the misleading shade of trees, there are also Error's den and Archimago's hut in the forest. The monster Error, together with its stinky and filthy vomit "full of bookes and papers" (I.i.20.6), indicates the insidious hazards from stale, misleading and poisonous religious pamphlets or theoretical writings. Archimago, on the other hand, represents the hypocrisy of the Roman Catholic Church. In Canto I, though Una's shout "[a]dd faith unto your force" (I.i.19.3) can assist Red Crosse in defeating Error "with more then manly force" (I.i.24.6), yet Red Crosse still falls into the snares woven by Archimago's cunning schemes and vile magic, which will result in his depravity and loss of virtue.

Moreover, the bleeding trees in the forest symbolically suggest the cost one has to pay if he/she is beguiled and misled by false religions of the Roman Catholicism represented by Duessa. In Canto II, Fradubio and his lady Fralissa are transformed into trees by Duessa's witchcraft because Fradubio is beguiled by Duessa to abandon his lady Fralissa and later incidentally sees Duessa "in her proper hew" (I.ii.40.6). When his motive to slip away is detected by Duessa, he is "enclosd in wooden wals full faste" (I.ii.42.8), just as Duessa has done to his lady Fralissa previously. When discussing the scene of the bleeding trees, Campana notes, "Spenser invokes a literary history of bleeding trees in order to think through the relationship governing pain and imagination, on the one hand, and beauty and violence, on the other, in the wake of the Reformation" (2012: 48). In this sense, through the trope of bleeding trees, Spenser may insinuate that Roman Catholicism, behind its superficial and deceitful grandeur, is malicious and wicked to the core. Besides, the means that Roman Catholicism employs to avenge and punish its apostates or opposing religionists could be harsh, cruel and even nefarious.

After describing the cost and pain suffered by those who have religiously strayed away or become lost, Spenser does not forget to point out the road of salvation. In Canto II, Fradubio tells Red Crosse the only solution to break Duessa's witchcraft or spell is "bathed in a living well" (I.ii.43.4). Evidently, the living well refers to baptism, manifesting that the grace of God offers ultimate salvation to erring humans.

While it is able to test erring humanity as well as one's faith in God, the forest also demonstrates sympathetic and redemptive powers. For example, in Canto III, a lion comes to the feet of lonely Una, serving her, protecting her and dying for her. In Canto VI, when Una is threatened by Sansloy's beastly lust, fauns and satyrs come to her aid and scare Sansloy away.

In fact, through the inhabitants of the forest, mainly the fauns and satyrs who are half-goat and half-human savages, Spenser probably expresses his political as well as religious insights and considerations. In the poem, after saving Una from the hands of Sansloy, "[t]he woodborne people fall before her flat, / [a]nd worship her as Goddess of the wood" (I.vi.16.1—2). It is quite possible that they have sensed the divinity within Una since she represents the True Church. In that sense, Una seems to assume the role of missionary. Moreover, it is described in the poem that

> During which time her gentle wit she plyes,
>
> To teach them truth, which worshipt her in vaine,
>
> And made her th'Image of Idolatryes;
>
> But when their boodesse zeale she did restrayne
>
> From her own worship, they her Asse would worship fayn. (I.vi.19.5—9)

Here, the doctrines that Una preaches to the wood people have invoked their passionate worship and idolatry. However, Una refuses to be treated as the image of idolatry by these wood people because she is aware that even though she tells the Truth, she is not God. Then, the wood people even expose willingness to worship Una's ass after Una rejects their idolatry. Such passion exhibited by these wood people towards the preaching of the True Church ostensibly expresses their eagerness to be converted to Christianity. Henceforth, Spenser was probably illuminating that, along with England's discovery of the new land, its Church of England could be spread to cultivate, enlighten and "tame" native peoples there.

In fact, it is noteworthy that when Spenser wrote *The Faerie Queene*, England was busy embarking on its road to explore the new world. English knights including Sir Walter Raleigh "circumnavigated the globe, explored the coasts of Africa, America, the Caribbean and Russia, engaged in trade, piracy and slavery, and attempted to establish English colonies in North America" (MacMillan, 2011: 646). Virginia is known to be named after the Virgin Queen Elizabeth I. It is imaginable that travelers to America had brought back descriptions of their sights of the new land, a land with a vast expanse of virgin forests where they could restore the lost paradise and build a new Garden of Eden, and also those native Americans who looked, dressed and lived differently. If we parallel the English people's imagination about North America then with Spenser's writing about the woodland people living in the forest in Book I, we may discern the message that Spenser was projecting the ambitions of Elizabethan England while constructing his forest. Indeed, Christianity spread around the world with similar steps of European nations' colonization.

In addition to the forest, the Cave of Despair can be considered as another natural space in Book I. After physical recovery from imprisonment in Orgoglio's dungeon, Red Crosse encounters Trevisan and is brought to the Cave of Despair, where "carcases were scattered on the greene, / And throwne about the cliffs" (I.ix.34.5—6). By showcasing the images of grave and death, Spenser indicates the destructiveness of Despair to human life since it may dissolve one's hope and faith in God's grace and salvation. Furthermore, by identifying Despair as a "False Prophet," Mallette notes that "[a]s a distorted version of the Reformation preacher, Despair incarnates Antichrist, at loose abroad in Roman Catholic forces threatening to undo the godly work of the English Church" (Mallette, 1997: 41). Fortunately, the prompt and powerful homily delivered by Una triumphs over the "inchaunted rimes" (I.ix.48.8) of Despair's speech and rescues Red Crosse out of the Cave safe and sound.

In a word, as a natural space, the forest, though perilous and misleading from time to time, is responsive to the Grace of God. The Cave of Despair, however, allegorically points to the distinction between repentance and despair, which will be essential knowledge for Red Crosse to move towards holiness.

3.2 Architectural Space

In Book I, the architectural spaces pertinent to holiness include the House of Pride, the dungeon of Orgoglio and the House of Holiness. Hume insightfully points out that "Book I is chiefly concerned with the attainment of a 'true' holiness by the Redcross Knight, which paradoxically means a discovery of his own sinfulness and of his dependence on divine grace for personal transformation" (2008: 89). Indeed, the three spaces here gesture to the three phases of Red Crosse's spiritual journey, in which the House of Pride contains the seven deadly sins, the dungeon of Orgoglio represents hell, and the House of Holiness is a space for redemption as well as salvation.

The House of Pride appropriately emerges on the scene when Red Crosse abandons his service to Una and comes to the side of Duessa. This change of service suggests Red Crosse's apostasy of faith. Morgan writes, "[t]o apostatize or desert God is called the beginning of pride" (2004: 460). Therefore, the House of Pride runs parallel to the stage of Red Crosse's spiritual transition. In Canto IV of Book I, the House of Pride is described as a concrete and material building that is splendid in appearance but fickle in nature. Likewise, the sin of pride will cause people to be arrogant and self-satisfied in attitude and behavior but inane, shallow and spiritless to the core. Thus, at the time when Red Crosse steps into the House of Pride, he not only enters an architectural space, but also moves into a phase in which his erring humanity is tested.

Orgoglio's dungeon witnesses Red Crosse's harrowing experience in hell. In Canto VIII, Red Crosse is defeated by Orgoglio, who embodies human vanity, and thrown into the dungeon where he will be imprisoned for three months before Una and Arthur set him free. Heale mentions that Orgoglio "seems not only to signify earthly rebelliousness, but also to act as an omen or a sign of God's wrath" (1999: 39). Before encountering Orgoglio, Red Crosse has multiplied his sin through abandoning Una, accompanying Duessa, entering the House of Pride, and drinking the cursed fountain water that can fill the drinker with sloth. Thus, Red Crosse is destined to purge his sins by suffering in Orgoglio's dungeon. According to Hume, Protestant writers are inherently influenced by the Lutheran analysis of Christianity in terms of the parity between Law and Gospel, so that the condemnation of sinners is also combined with the forgiveness of sinners (2008: 97). Henceforth, Orgoglio's dungeon is not less important than the House of Holiness in terms of a Christian's journey towards Holiness.

The House of Holiness is distinct from the House of Pride in both aspect and content. In contrast to the broad pathway to the House of Pride which is "[a]ll bare through peoples feet, which thither traueiled" (I.iv.2.9), the road to the House of Holiness is "so few there bee, / That chose the narrow path"

(I.x.10.3—4). Besides, in contrast to "[a] stately Pallace built of squared bricke" (I.iv.4.1), the House of Holiness is "an auntient house" (I.x.3.1). However, it is in the House of Holiness that Red Crosse will be taught the tenets of holiness by the three daughters living in the house, namely Fidelia (faith), Speranza (hope), and Charissa (love or charity). Moreover, it is in this house that Red Crosse will be led by the godly aged Sire to see "the new Hierusalem, that God has built / For those to dwell in, that are chosen his" (I.x.57.2—3), and to know his true birth as "springst from ancient race / Of Saxon kings" (I.x.65.1—2) as well as his identity to be the national saint, that is, St. George of England. Thus, in the House of Holiness, Red Crosse discovers where he comes from, who he is and where he is going.

In conclusion, the architectural spaces in Book I are more psychological than material, since they perfectly manifest the phases of a psychological journey towards holiness. Moreover, the House of Holiness allegorically enlightens readers about the religious content of holiness as well as its significance as a virtue.

3.3　Edenic Space

The kingdom of Una's parents is commonly considered as Spenser's reference to the Garden of Eden not only because of the parallel plots including the imprisoned king and queen, the sprawling dragon which represents the evil force of Satan and the familiar trees—the tree of life and the tree of knowledge of good and evil, but also the explicit description of Una's father as "most mighty king of Eden faire" (I.xii.26.1). Thus, we name this space as Edenic Space and propose that this space points to holiness from two aspects. On the one hand, Red Crosse overcomes the dragon eventually by the help of God's grace; on the other, Red Crosse is finally engaged to Una, which represents his bond with the One True Church.

In the Bible, the Garden of Eden is the original place that God designated for the human beings he created, hence, it is originally a holy space where humans encounter God. In Spenser's version of the Garden of Eden, Adam and Eve are "captiue parents" in "their forwasted kingdome" (I.xi.1.2—3), threatened by the dragon, which is described as a "huge feend" (I.xi.3.3). Therefore, it seems that the mission of Red Crosse is to restore holiness to the land. In the story, Red Crosse fights for three days before he kills the dragon. In a much-cited sentence, "Then God she praysd, and thankt her faithfull knight, / That had atchieu'd so great a conquest by his might" (I.xi.55.8—9), the vague pronoun "his" is often discussed as to whether it refers to Red Crosse or God. The answer usually stays on a middle ground between God and Red Crosse. In other words, it is certain that without God, Red Crosse cannot win the battle with the dragon. However, it is Red Crosse's faith that invokes the strength of God's grace to his aid. Therefore, when using the word "his" Spenser may emphasize the combined force of God and Red Crosse in overwhelming the dragon which stands for Satan in Book I.

In addition, the Well of Life and the Tree of Life are not only emblematic of the land of Eden but also the manifestation of God's regenerative powers. The Well of Life indicates baptism, whereas the balm from the tree of life symbolizes Holy Communion. During his three days of fights with the Dragon, Red Crosse is healed and restored by the well of life and the balm of the tree successively, which again reflects the force of human agency blessed with the grace of God. Besides, Weatherby comments that baptism at the end of Book I is "as much a triumph over an old life as the beginning of a new one, less the undertaking of a quest for holiness than its completion" (1987: 302). Henceforth, alongside the restoration of the kingdom of Eden, Red Crosse also consummates his journey towards holiness.

Moreover, in Canto XII, Red Crosse and Una hold their engagement party in the Edenic space, which not only symbolizes the official union of Red Crosse with the True Church or the Church of England, but also ceremoniously puts an end to Red Crosse's journey towards holiness. In the following, Red Crosse will embark upon his new journey back to the Faerie Court to fulfil his promise to Queen Gloriana, which suggests that holiness, as a virtue, should be practiced in concrete missions.

In summary, the Edenic space, which covers the last two cantos of Book I, is a consummation of Red Crosse's holiness. The land of Eden, as the first land designated by God to human beings, is eventually restored. The movement of Red Crosse in space towards the virtue of holiness in Book I is completed in the Edenic land, which indicates that it is in the garden where God first creates human beings that holiness can be regained and re-established.

4. Conclusion

Rooted in the Protestantism of the 16th century, Spenserian holiness highlights human faith, will and agency in practising the worship of God. Besides, Spenserian holiness responds to the historical and political requirements of its time. As a virtue, it is expected to guide England through its age of Reformation. As a religious belief, it motivates England in its discovery of the new world. Spenser's spaces in Book I are allegorical ones, since each of them echoes the spiritual stages of Red Crosse's development of holiness and reflects the mediation of God. Traversing through these spaces, Red Crosse finally grows to be a holy knight who will restart his journey and spread his holiness in new missions.

Works Cited

Bumke, Joachim. *The Concept of Knighthood in the Middle Ages*. Trans. W. T. H. Jackson and Erika Jackson. New York: AMS P, 1982.

Burlinson, Christopher. *Allegory, Space and the Material World in the Writings of Edmund Spenser*. Cambridge: D. S. Brewer, 2006.

Campana, Joseph. *The Pain of Reformation: Spenser, Vulnerability, and the Ethics of Masculinity*. New York: Fordham UP, 2012.

Crawford, Jason. *Allegory and Enchantment: An Early Modern Poetics*. Oxford: Oxford UP, 2017.

Frye, Northrop. "The Structure of Imagery in *The Faerie Queene*." *University of Toronto Quarterly* 30.2 (1961): 109-127.

Gravett, Christopher. *Tudor Knight*. Illus. Graham Turner. Oxford: Osprey, 2006.

Heale, Elizabeth. The Faerie Queene: *A Reader's Guide*. 2nd ed. Cambridge: Cambridge UP, 1999.

Hume, Anthea. *Edmund Spenser: Protestant Poet*. Cambridge: Cambridge UP, 2008.

Lenman, Bruce. *England's Colonial Wars, 1550—1688: Conflicts, Empire and National Identity*. Harlow: Longman, 2001.

Lewis, C. S. *Studies in Medieval and Renaissance Literature*. Ed. Walter Hooper. New York: Cambridge UP, 1998.

---. *The Allegory of Love: A Study in Medieval Tradition*. Cambridge: Cambridge UP, 2013.

Macdonald, J. S. "The Redcrosse Knight and the Limits of Human Holiness." *Spenser Studies: A Renaissance Poetry Annual* 30 (2015): 113-131.

MacMillan, Ken. "Exploration, Trade and Empire." *The Elizabethan World*. Ed. Doran Susan and Norman Jones. London: Routledge, 2011.

Mallette, Richard. *Spenser and the Discourses of Reformation England*. Lincoln: Nebraska UP, 1997.

Morgan, Gerald. "'Add Faith unto Your Force': The Perfecting of Spenser's Knight of Holiness in Faith and Humility." *Renaissance Studies* 18.3 (2004): 449-474.

Smith, Alan G. R. T*he Emergence of a Nation State: The Commonwealth of England, 1529—1660*. London: Longman, 1984.

Smith, D. K. *The Cartographic Imagination in Early Modern England: Rewriting the World in Marlowe, Spenser, Raleigh and Marvell*. Burlington: Ashgate, 2008.

Spenser, Edmund. *The Faerie Queene*. Ed. Thomas P. Roche. London: Penguin Books, 1978.

Stump, Donald. *Spenser's Heavenly Elizabeth: Providential History in* The Faerie Queene. Cham: Palgrave Macmillan, 2019.

Weatherby, Harold L. "What Spenser Meant by Holinesse: Baptism in Book One of *The Faerie Queene.*" *Studies in Philology* 84.3 (1987): 286-307.

Wise, Terence, and Richard Scollins. *The Knights of Christ: Religious/Military Orders of Knighthood 1118—1565*. London: Osprey, 1984.

（特邀编辑：张炼）

著译者言

Editor's/Translator's Preface

海内莎学知音　天涯君子传书

——写在《云中锦笺：中国莎学书信》出版之际

李伟民　杨林贵

作者简介： 李伟民，浙江越秀外国语学院特聘教授，四川外国语大学莎士比亚研究所教授，中国外国文学学会莎士比亚分会副会长，《中国莎士比亚研究》主编；杨林贵，中国外国文学学会莎士比亚分会副会长，东华大学外语学院教授。

Title: Foreword to *Selected Chinese Shakespeare-Related Epistles*

Authors: Li Weimin is vice president of Chinese Shakespeare Research Association and professor of Shakespeare Study Institute at Sichuan International Studies University, editor-in-chief of the *Study of Shakespeare in China*, professor of Zhejiang Yuexiu University of Foreign Languages. Email: 83517459@163.com; Yang Lingui is vice president of Chinese Shakespeare Research Association and Professor of English, Donghua University. Email: l-yang@dhu.edu.cn

为了解西方国情，林则徐在鸦片战争前夕请人译述了英国人慕瑞（Hugh Murray）的《地理大全》（*Encyclopædia of Geography*），并编辑成《四洲志》，纳入《海国图志》出版。由于书中介绍了包括莎士比亚在内的四位文学家，①莎士比亚就此传入中国，并开始为中国人所知晓。此后，历经晚清、民国、新中国三个时期，莎士比亚及其戏剧已经成为外国文学、戏剧的经典代表，为中国人所熟知，并被不断地进行翻译、演出和研究。

进入 20 世纪 80 年代，中国莎学研究发展很快，取得了长足的进步，已经引起了世界莎学研究界的惊叹。毫无疑问，这些非凡的成绩凝聚了几代中国莎学研究者的心血。乘改革开放的春风，中国莎士比亚研究会（简称"中莎会"）经中华人民共和国文化部批准，于 1984 年 12 月正式成立于上海。中莎会成立后，先后于 1986 年、1994 年和 2016 年举办了三届莎士比亚戏剧节和多次国际性、全国性的莎学学术研讨会，极大地推动了中国莎士比亚研究、演出和翻译工作的不断发展，引起了学界的瞩目。

但是，20 世纪 90 年代以后的很长一段时间，中国莎学研究显得较为沉寂，举行的学术活动不多。很多老一辈莎学研究者目睹这一局面，忧心如焚，担忧日甚一日。但是，他们仍然积极开展莎学研究，联络同仁，努力推动着中国莎学研究的发展，期望中国莎学能够薪火相传。莎学研究者分散于全国各地，他们担心中国莎学研究的发展：如何促使中莎会健康发展？如何举办莎剧节？如何研究莎学？他们经过鱼书雁礼，夙夜晨夕之商讨，以书信方式进行了多方面的探讨，并广泛征求各方面的意见。通过相当频繁的书信往还，他们贡献出的对中国莎学研究和如何办好中莎会的种种设想，为中国莎学研究做出了不可磨灭的贡献。

---

① 参见郝田虎（2010: 66-74），杨周翰提到，"莎士比亚的名字是由传教士在 1856 年介绍到中国的"，见《百科知识》1979 年第 4 期，第 5—11 页；后来的《中国大百科全书·外国文学卷》第 1 版、第 2 版仍然采用这一提法。郝田虎在考订一些提法后指出此说有误："莎士比亚等人的名字于 1839—1843 年被介绍到中国。更确切地说，是林则徐和魏源等将英国文学的代表人物，包括莎士比亚等，介绍给了中国人。"（郝田虎，2020: 19）李伟民提到："1838 年，林则徐被道光皇帝任命为钦差大臣，往广东查禁鸦片，从 1839 年 3 月到 1840 年 11 月，林则徐一直进行组织和翻译工作，翻译英国人慕瑞所著《世界地理大全》，并整理编译成《四洲志》……莎士比亚的名字最初传入中国发轫于中西文化的交流与碰撞中，出于中国人渴望'睁眼看世界'，以改变贫弱中华帝国的现状，出于中国人自觉与自愿了解世界的愿望主动去'拿来'。"（李伟民，2006: 10-11）

　　一樽浊酒，满目青山，且任君心洗流水。这些或透露着真知灼见或透露着尚不成熟构想的学者之间的倾诉，在时光里慢慢点染浸开，其中既有从翻译角度探讨莎剧翻译应该异化还是归化，散文化还是诗化；也有从演出角度探讨莎剧是写实还是写意，是直喻还是隐喻；更有从研究角度阐释莎剧是现代还是后现代，是现实主义还是浪漫主义。而弥漫于书简之中的爱国主义情怀和对民族文化的自信心，始终是鞭策学者们前行的不竭动力。这些书简从思想理论层面和文艺实践层面，反映了时代脉搏的跳动。阅读这些信件，有时真有山重水复、柳暗花明、茅塞顿开之感。音书过雁，蓬莱不远，有历史才有现在和未来。书简的价值何止万金，让我们缓缓地打开秦帝国一个普通家庭的宝贵家书。咸阳古道音尘绝，西风催衬梧桐叶。公元前 223 年，秦国拉开灭楚战争的大幕，这是秦灭六国中最艰苦的灭楚之战。烽火连天，金戈铁马，夜摇碧树红花凋。秦军中的小卒，二哥、三弟兄弟俩"惊"和"黑夫"求军中书吏先后给自己的大哥"衷"寄去家书。战火中价值万金的家书抵达八百里外的故乡——秦国南郡安陆（今天的湖北孝感云梦县），成为我们今天能见到的中国历史上最早的书信实物——"云梦睡虎地秦简"。黑夫在信中写道，"二月辛巳，黑夫、惊敢再拜问衷，母毋恙也"①。他问候母亲大人，向母亲请安，母亲身体还好吗？征战在外，要求母亲寄夏衣或钱来，关心搏命换来的军功，官府落实了"爵位"奖励没有？惊在给大哥的信中，催促母亲寄钱，要钱"五六百"，布料"二丈五尺"，兄弟俩现在是借钱生活，连用"急急急"告急，云：再不还钱就要死了。安慰家人即使占卜得到了凶兆，不过是我居于"反城"中罢了。惊嘱托妻子，好好孝顺老人，嘱咐哥哥多费心，好好管教我那女儿，女儿还小，注意安全，担心自己的新媳妇，叮嘱大哥不要让她去离家太远的地方捡柴火。信中充满了对亲人浓浓的思念之情和对家人的关爱。但是家里却实在拿不出十件夏衣

---

① 在"睡虎地四号墓木牍释文""木牍甲（M4：11）""正面"记载"二月辛巳，黑夫、惊敢再拜问中，母毋恙也？"在"木牍乙（M4：6）""正面"记载"惊敢大心问衷，母得毋恙也？家室外内同……以衷，母力毋恙也？""反面"亦有"衷教""衷令""衷唯母方行新地，急急"字样。见：湖北孝感地区第二期亦工亦农文物考古训练班，1976，《湖北云梦睡虎地十一座秦墓发掘简报》，《文物》第 9 期，第 51–61 页。本文从"衷"。

的救命钱，而惊和黑夫却在等待音信中战死沙场。两封写在木牍上的家书使我们今天有幸窥见秦帝国底层民众的血泪、悲哀与家国情怀。忆秦娥，西风残照，箫声咽。从"云梦睡虎地秦简"中，我们感受到历史沉重的足音，触摸到历史烁金的温度。为历史留下记录，为当下留下真实，为未来留下今天，为中国莎学璀璨的星空留下真情的记录和那些已经定格的远去身影，这就是我们编纂《云中锦笺：中国莎学书信》的初衷。

从这些信件中，我们可以看到老一辈莎学学者对莎学和世界优秀文化的挚爱，对莎学研究的执着。因此，把这些已经成为中国莎学研究史料绝响之一的书信编辑出版，就显得尤为急切和必要了。随着时代的变迁、社会的变化、联系方式的改变，《云中锦笺：中国莎学书信》在中国莎学史上重要的文献价值和学术价值将愈加凸显。万壑松涛携翠雨，一片红霞随君去。"莎学书信"记录了处于时代脉搏中的中国莎学研究事业在不断克服各种困难中所取得的辉煌成就。这些书信同时也是学者们真性情的流露，是学术史的真实记录。

早在 20 世纪 90 年代，鉴于孟宪强先生对中国莎学的贡献，就有一些学者建议我们写一写孟宪强教授，当时作为被邀请撰写者之一的李伟民也几次征求过孟老师的意见。但孟老师非常谦虚，要求首先应关注莎学研究本身，至于写他，还不到时候，与一些大师相比他还需要不断深入研究莎学，以便最终将莎士比亚之石攻成东方之玉，在中华大地上建立莎学研究的中国学派，使中国莎学在世界莎学研究领域占有一席之地。因此，李伟民虽然发表了评孟老师主编的《中国莎士比亚评论》的论文（1993），评孟老师主编的《中国莎学年鉴》的论文（1997a），以及评孟老师撰著的《中国莎学简史》的论文（1997b），但始终没有敢于动笔去写孟老师。"人的天职在勇于探索真理"，2002 年，李伟民的《光荣与梦想：莎士比亚在中国》一书出版，孟老师对他鼓励有加，他说："李伟民先生以他的激情、勤奋、踏实以及孜孜不倦的追求精神所凝结而成的莎学华章，为 20 世纪末的中国莎坛锦上添花。……李伟民先生的莎学文集是一座两面神雅努斯式的里程碑。"（孟宪强，2002：6）这可以说是老一辈莎学研究者对他的莫大鼓励和无限期许，孟老师就是我们年轻学者学习的榜样。

轻舟一路绕烟霞，更爱山前满涧花。时间转眼就到了 21 世纪的第一个 10 年，此时，李伟民的《中国莎士比亚研究：莎学知音思想探析与理论建设》在四川外国语大学得以立项。由于要集中反映中国莎学研究者的研究思想、研究经历，因此必须对中国莎学研究者的莎学研究思想进行较为整体的梳理。看万里湖山，谈经云海花飞雨。研究当代中国莎学史，论述必然涉及孟老师的莎学研究经历和思想。在这本书中，李伟民对包括孟老师在内的著名莎学家进行了比较全面的研究，同时也再次捧读了与孟老师交往的十多年里孟老师写给他的一百多封信。他在该书中这样写道，孟老师的"这些信件篇篇都离不开莎学，堪称一部资料丰富的'莎学书简'。在 2011 年的苦夏中，我将这些书简再次翻阅了一遍。俯首书案中，青春恰自来，往事历历在目，碧落星辰，曾来一夕听风涛。在适当的时候，如果能将包括孟宪强、张泗洋、孙家琇、袁昌英、方平、王元化、杨周翰、李赋宁、王佐良、顾绶昌、卞之琳、朱生豪、梁实秋、孙大雨、裘克安、刘炳善等先生的这些'莎学书简'出版，毫无疑问，对莎学界了解 20 世纪到 21 世纪的中国莎学历史是有重要价值的"（李伟民，2012：381）。可以说，那时，他就产生了编辑一本《云中锦笺：中国莎学书信》的设想。

随后，在杨林贵与李伟民对中国莎学的研讨中，这件事终于得到了杨林贵的肯定、支持和有力推动。尤其是 2012 年，由杨林贵、殷耀主编的《中国莎学走向世界的先导——孟宪强纪念文集》出版了。这本《文集》的出版不仅是对孟宪强先生莎学研究思想比较全面系统的梳理与研究，而且书中还收录了孟老师早年发表的一些珍贵的莎学论文。对于中国莎学研究来说，出版研究专辑的学者，孟老师是第一位。在编辑这本书时，我们感觉到，由于书的篇幅有限，孟老师的许多论文和书信都无法收进去，如果我们不能出版这些书信，无疑是中国莎学研究中无法弥补的重大损失。为此，我们多次讨论，先设想是否可以编辑出版一部《孟宪强先生莎学书信集》，后经多次讨论，觉得编辑出版一本汇集中国莎学学者的书信集更有意义，也更具全面了解中国莎学研究的学术价值。

而孟老师本人又是一位谦谦君子，博观约取，厚积薄发，在平易中透露着深邃，包容中蕴含着真诚。他时刻关注着中国莎学的发展，有信必回，信中往往蕴藏着大量的信息，如莎学专著的出版、莎学论文的发表、莎剧演出、莎剧节、中莎会的学会建设、国内外莎学动态等等。千山之外，梅花远信。在莎学界，孟老师写信勤、写信多是出了名的。李伟民与孟老师交往较晚，但也保存了孟老师的一百多封来信。犹记得，那时他给孟老师去信后，就翘首以待：在月照寒林之际，鸿雁几时到？我们在进一步深入商讨中认识到，书信的搜集还可以扩大到全国莎学界，覆盖面的扩大将能够更完整、更全面地通过史料的汇集，反映中国莎学研究所走过的曲折历程。编辑出版《云中锦笺：中国莎学书信》，把所能觅到的莎学学者的书信汇集为一书，把目前所有能够搜集到的莎学研究者的往还书信尽可能给予出版，在学术研究上价值更大，更有守正创新的意义。一花一世界，三摩三菩提。出版一本覆盖 20 世纪以来莎学研究者的集体书信集，更易使读者通过这些莎学书信了解中国莎学的发展历程，因此我们也初步商定把该书定名为《云中锦笺：中国莎学书信》。

为了把这件事赶快做起来，2017年，我们决定先在中莎会的会刊《中国莎士比亚研究》（《中国莎士比亚研究通讯》）上发出征求莎学书简的征稿启事。我们的目的是在尽可能全面征集"莎学信件"的基础上精选那些凝聚着前辈学者博学、审问、慎思、明辨的智者之言，以及对中国莎学研究最有价值、最具史料意义的素笺，并尽早公开于学界。弦歌别绪，断肠移破秦筝柱。"莎学书信"的出版目的是通过莎学学者之间倾吐真性情的书信，为中国莎学研究留下一份真实的学术记录。同时，我们也相信，"莎学书信"的出版，能够为中国的外国文学、莎学研究留下一份不可多得的学术记录。这样的书信甚至可以为中国的外国文学、莎学研究提供新的学术研究方向。同时，出版"莎学书信"在外国语言文学研究界、莎学研究领域也堪称具有承前启后作用的创举。这些莎学学者在通信中展露了他们学术研究的心路历程，满怀激情地讨论着中国莎学研究事业的未来。我们相信，选取的这些莎学信件本身就是中国莎学研究不可或缺的有机组成部分。

周虽旧邦，其命维新。在编辑过程中，每当我们打开这些尘封多年、已经泛黄发脆的信函时，我们就可以感受到老一辈莎学学人为情而造文，抒怀以命笔，那一颗颗跳动着的滚烫之心的清英珠玉之言，以及他们热爱祖国、热爱人民、热爱莎学研究、热爱外国文学研究事业的一腔热血。这些"莎学书信"的出版，必将为深入研究中国莎士比亚传播史提供翔实而珍贵的文献。

物有本末，事有终始。知所先后，则近道矣。毫无疑问，这些"莎学书信"在中国莎士比亚研究史上具有非常重要的史料价值。故君神游香草远，雄姿人去大江东。可以认为，"莎学书信"的编选是中国莎学史研究中的重要史料建设工作，对于中国莎学史的编撰和中国莎学思想的流变研究具有重要意义。同时，我们也看到，相对于源远流长的文学史而言，这些"莎学书信"出现的时间较近，因此往往容易为研究者所忽略。但是随着时代的变迁、人们联系交往方式的根本改变、住房的搬迁、人员的迁徙，这些鲜活的、蕴藏着莎学研究价值的书信，很可能随着老一辈莎学研究者的谢世被随手丢弃，甚至会被永远毁灭掉。今后再要寻觅这些书信，就几乎是不可能完成的任务了，即使能偶尔找到一些，也很难为读者提供系统研究的文献。

这些书信的作者几乎均为在中国莎学史上著名的翻译家、学者、导演、表演和莎学活动家，他们经历了中国莎学史的发轫期、繁荣期、沉寂期与崛起期。他们的莎学研究与他们所生活的时代、社会、历史、政治、经济、文化、文学、戏剧都有着千丝万缕的联系，特别是由于他们个人思想、情感和识见的不同，这些书信反映了不同的性格特征和不同的学术见解，是他们内心真性情的反映。只有向内心审视的人才懂得清醒，在这些书信中我们看到，尽管他们对待莎士比亚、莎学研究、莎作翻译、莎剧演出的观点有颇大的差异，但是这种差异也正反映出莎士比亚的经典价值所蕴含的无穷魅力。

水参如是观，月喻本来心。"书信"中绝大部分是当时学者们往还的私人信件，由于这些信件并不是作者要在公开场合发表的，那么也就更加真实可信，这些书信也就更加真实准确地透露出他们研究莎士比亚的心路历程、莎学思想、对中国莎学发展所经历的种种曲折的忧心、担心。华夏春夜，水镜渊渟。学术价值往往体现在某件信函的写作细节之中，体现在书信中透露出来的研究思路和对中国莎学整体格局的把握之中。交错迭代的"书信"，构成了研究中国莎学史、莎学家必须参考的不可多得的文献资料。因此，"书信"具有明显的史料价值，为莎学研究真问题的解决奠定了坚实的基础。

眉睫之间，晨夕相濡，卷舒莎学风云之色，满腔热血酬知己。莎学研究者之间的书信往还，是研究他们的莎学思想和中国莎士比亚研究规律的重要佐证。彩笺尺素，山长水阔。我们在中莎会会刊上发出"中国莎学书信"的"征稿启事"后，许多学者积极响应，不把这些书信据为私有，而是积极热情地把自己手中珍贵的书信毫无保留地贡献出来，愿意向莎学界公开这些书信，以助这些书信能够及时结集出版。例如，当已故的中国莎士比亚研究会副会长孙福良教授得知我们为了给中国莎学研究留下一份真实的记录，探讨近一个世纪以来中国莎学家的心路历程及中国莎学发展过程，决定出版《云中锦笺：中国莎学书信》时，专门给我们寄来了一批曹禺先生、香港莎协等人和组织的重要信件，以助力《云中锦笺：中国莎学书信》更加完美（李伟民，2018: 80-87）。落霞孤鹜，芳草斜阳。这些"书信"表面上看来是学者之间的私人通信，但是联系起来，进行全面审视，我们认为这些"书信"的史料价值、学术价值绝不仅仅局限于此，因为从这些"书信"中，我们能够清晰地感受到 20 世纪 80 年代以来中国莎学积极进取、共同谋划、团结协作，勇于理论探索和艺术实践的拳拳之心。

人生如寄，留得踏雪鸿爪，一溪桃李，四野花田。如果说《傅雷家书》只是父亲与儿子之间心曲真情流露的关爱之言的话，那么《云中锦笺：中国莎学书信》则在更为广阔的社会语境中和更多学者之间架设起了学术交流的桥梁，它清晰而真实地勾画出中国莎学发展的昨天、今天，并期盼着辉煌的明天。千岩迤逦，万树凝烟。在当今的信息时代，书信这种古老的通信方式已经显得越来越珍贵了，《云中锦笺：中国莎学书信》这份学术遗产理应得到我们的珍视，出版《云中锦笺：中国莎学书信》是时代赋予我们这一代中国莎学学人的历史重任；我们必须担当起这一沉甸甸的任务，因为出版这些"书信"本身就带有抢救莎学史料的重要意义和重大学术价值，它的出版必将为 21 世纪中国莎学的进一步繁荣与发展奠定坚实的基础。

引用文献【Works Cited】

郝田虎，2010，《弥尔顿在中国：1837—1888，兼及莎士比亚》，《外国文学》第 4 期，第 66—74 页。

---，2020，《弥尔顿在中国》，文艺复兴论丛，杭州：浙江大学出版社。

李伟民，1993，《先行者的足迹——评〈中国莎士比亚评论〉》，载《中国文化与世界》第 1 辑，上海：上海外语教育出版社，第 401—412 页。

---，1997a，《评〈中国莎学年鉴〉》，《解放》第 2 期，第 78—86 页。

---，1997b，《他山之石与东方之玉——评〈中国莎学简史〉》，《人文学报》总第 21 期，第 92—102 页。

---，2006，《中国莎士比亚批评史》，北京：中国戏剧出版社。

---，2012，《中国莎士比亚研究：莎学知音思想探析与理论建设》，重庆：重庆出版社。

---，2018，《莎学书简》，《戏剧文学》第 5 期，第 80—87 页。

孟宪强，2002，《〈光荣与梦想：莎士比亚在中国〉序》，载李伟民《光荣与梦想：莎士比亚在中国》，香港：天马图书有限公司。

（特邀编辑：王瑞雪）

译者札记：莎士比亚诗剧体《牡丹亭》全译本

黄必康

作者简介：黄必康，文学博士，北京大学外国语学院教授。中美富布赖特研究学者（2003—2004），国家级精品课主持人（2005），英国杜伦大学高等学术研究院客座国际高级研究员（2017），美国福尔杰莎士比亚研究院客座艺术家基金研究员（2019）。著作出版：《形式与政治：莎士比亚历史剧的意象和意识形态》(北京大学出版社, 2000)、《虚构的权威：女性作家与叙述声音》（译著）（北京大学出版社, 2002)、《莎士比亚名篇赏析》（北京大学出版社, 2005)、《美国政治家及其演说述评》（北京大学出版社, 2013)、《莎士比亚十四行诗（仿词全译本)》(外语教学与研究出版社, 2017)、《英语散文史略》（外语教学与研究出版社, 2020)、《牡丹亭》(莎士比亚诗剧体全译本)（商务印书馆, 2021)。

Title: Translator's Thoughts on the English Translation of *Peony Pavilion* with a Shakespearean Flavor

Author: Huang Bikang (Ph.D.), Professor of English, School of Foreign Languages, Peking University. Fulbright Research Scholar (2003—2004); International Senior Fellow, Durham University (2017); Artist-in-Residence Fellow, Folger Shakespeare Institute (2019). His book publications include: *Politics in Form: Imagery and Ideology in Shakespeare's History Plays* (Peking University Press, 2000), *Fictions of Authority: Women Writers and Narrative Voice* (trans., Peking University Press, 2002), *Selected Readings in Shakespeare* (Peking University Press, 2005), *American Statesmen and Their Political Speeches* (Peking University Press, 2013), *Shakespeare's Sonnets in Classical Chinese Verse* (trans., Foreign Language Teaching and Research Press, 2017), *A History of English Prose* (Foreign Language Teaching and Research Press, 2020), *The Peony Pavilion* (trans. in reference to Shakespeare's poetic style, Commercial Press, 2021). Email: hbk@pku.edu.cn

【编者按】商务印书馆新近出版了由北京大学黄必康教授英译的明代伟大戏剧家汤显祖的名作《牡丹亭》（Huang, 2021）。美国福尔杰莎士比亚图书馆此前对此项目做了推文报道（French, 2021）。这部译作的显著特征是，译者采用莎士比亚的诗剧体语言进行翻译，为中国经典戏（曲）剧的英译做出了具有创新性的探索。作为莎士比亚学者，黄必康教授多年潜心于莎士比亚和中国古典戏曲（剧）的对比研究。在此译本中，他熟练地采用英语读者所熟悉的莎士比亚诗剧体语言，在译文（诗）过程中寻觅汤莎戏剧话语和文化契合，巧妙化用莎士比亚诗剧体和散文语言，尽可能忠实地再现了原作的语言细节、独特的审美意象、至情的诗意情感以及丰富的文化内涵。这样的译本英文文字体量增大，却能够让英语读者喜闻乐见，读来兴趣盎然。上述具有创新性的翻译方法涉及文学经典的互文诠释和戏剧艺术传统等诸多问题，旨在有助于《牡丹亭》等中国经典戏剧作品在英语文本中展现其独特的艺术价值，尤其是具有现代性的艺术价值与魅力。我们这里刊出黄必康教授的译后感言，希望读者对欣赏这部带有莎剧韵味的《牡丹亭》新译有所助益。

　　用优美流畅的英语文字翻译出汤显祖用梦幻般美的曲辞写成的名剧，让英文剧词在表意方面最大限度地表达出原作精练而富有古典诗意的语言所承载的语义内容和文化意蕴，同时仿用莎士比亚诗剧体语言，并化用莎剧中一些经典的语句来表述原文的细节和审美意象与不同人物的情感和心理过程，使译文读起来文学趣味浓厚，诗意盎然，并带有莎士比亚诗剧的味道和美感，以满足更多的英语读者和观众的异文化间理解和文学审美需求，这是我在学习英语和英美文学的早期就萌生的一个梦想。几十年东风吹梦流年去，经过时断时续的积累和努力，这一梦想部分变成了现实。望着打印机里吐出来的一大摞译稿，我除了瞬间的兴奋和释然，不免想起促成这项译事的一些人生往事、思想轨迹和译事感想，在此借《中世纪与文艺复兴研究》中的栏目，简略写下来与读者分享，也借此机会求教于我国译界同仁和广大的文学翻译爱好者。

　　回想起来，莎士比亚戏剧和中国古典戏剧，这是我学术生涯的两大基石。我在高校从事英语语言文学教学与研究 40 余年，除了广泛阅读英美文学作品，研读文学批评和文化研究理论，也一直都站在这两大基石上营造着自己的精神家园。

由于 20 世纪 60—70 年代特殊的社会政治环境，我错过了学习外语的最佳年龄；蹉跎青春岁月后，20 多岁才从头开始学习英语。好在我的父亲是英语语音学教授，对我的英语语音语调有着近乎苛刻的要求，教习间时而吟诵莎翁诗句，以示纯正英语发音对未来欣赏英语文学经典作品之重要。不过，我对莎士比亚真正产生兴趣，并且接触到中国古典戏剧，还是在高校的学习环境中。1981 年，我在四川大学外文系学习，没课时便喜欢到邻近的望江楼公园，在翠竹掩映的亭子中大声朗读和背诵英文诗歌和莎士比亚的十四行诗，久而久之便也对莎翁诗句抑扬顿挫的音律音效美感有了些许自发的感悟。时任川大外文系主任的是朱生豪先生的胞弟朱文振教授。朱先生承兄遗愿，曾试图用中国古典戏曲的体式续译朱生豪先生未译完的 6 部莎士比亚历史剧。一次，我偶然在阅览室读到朱先生《仿戏曲体译莎几个片段》（1981）一文，感到十分好奇和新颖，觉得朱先生用仿中国古典戏曲的词句和腔调翻译过来的莎剧台词读来有滋有味，与莎翁的素体诗在语言的音效上有一种异文化间共振的感觉。我当时想，反之亦然。这便种下了我学业生涯中的一颗种子。

1985 年，我受业著名莎学家水天同教授念硕士。水先生提倡莎学本土化，指导我从事莎士比亚戏剧和中国古典戏剧的比较研究，这与我的学业兴趣和阅读积累对上了口。水先生在哈佛大学师承西方新批评派先驱瑞恰慈（I. A. Richards），特别注重文本细读，要求我们必须暂时搁置当时已经十分热门的比较文学理论以及浩繁的莎学系谱考据和五花八门的莎评话语。水先生认为，只有专注莎士比亚戏剧语言，力求读懂、读深、读出味道来，做到了然于胸，才能真正感受和理解莎士比亚戏剧的艺术世界和魅力，从而为日后的莎学研究提供真正的文本支撑。我至今仍保持着对莎士比亚戏剧语言敏锐的感悟力（sensitivity），而且对一些脍炙人口的名篇，也能够做到了然于胸，虽久不传习，亦能朗朗上口，不漏一字。这是莎剧研究的基本功。水天同先生同时要求我加强中国古典文学语言的训练，广泛研读中国古典文学，特别是元曲、元杂剧和明清传奇剧，在历史化语境中去发现不同文本表达的文化契合，并加以阐释，以期在大量占有文本的基础上进行平行比较和理论归纳。循此路径，我逐步拓展和深化了此方面的学习和研究，硕士论文集中比较研究了莎剧《特洛伊罗斯与克瑞西达》（*The Tragedy of Troilus and Cressida*）与孔尚任的《桃花扇》的社会悲剧意识，其精简版也发表在上外《外国语》杂志（1991）。1995 年，我入北京大学，在李赋宁先生门下攻读博士学位，论文做的还是莎士比亚。在李先生的指导下，我的博士论文承继新历史主义和文化唯物主义的研究路子，进一步深入莎士比亚语言的肌理，在语言文本和时代历史事件之间穿梭梳理，对莎士比亚历史剧中的诸多文化意象做出历史政治化的解读。如此浸润于文本本身的研究方法无疑为我本人内化莎剧语言和历史文化意象，在莎士比亚的文化语境和戏剧视界中准确而又细致地解读和翻译中国古典戏曲提供了深层次的中西语言文化基础。该博士论文不久后由北京大学出版社出版。李赋宁先生是西方语言文化大师，也是浸透了中国古典语言文化的学者。先生在表演京剧唱段时字正腔圆的唱词和物我两忘的神情让我至今难以忘怀。人生如梦，戏剧人生。回首向来梦境处，这些人生求学经历也就促成了我的译事梦想：用莎士比亚诗剧体移译中国古典戏剧，让汤显祖的名剧在英语读者的心目中产生文学审美快感、文化理解和诗意共鸣。①

以下简略谈谈我对用莎士比亚诗剧体翻译《牡丹亭》大致的过程和一些思考。

2016 年是汤显祖和莎士比亚逝世 400 周年纪念年，一年之内，中英学界和戏剧界举办了一系列学术讲座和盛大的演出活动，共同纪念这两位世界文坛上伟大的戏剧家和诗人。这场持续一年多的汤莎盛会，表达出中国莎士比亚学者和艺术家对中国文学经典世界化和当下化的诉求。2017 年 6 月，我应邀到英国杜伦大学高等学术研究院从事了 3 个月的研究，其间受汤莎研究启发和鼓舞，用宋词的形式，借用 91 种词牌翻译了莎士比亚 154 首十四行诗，并由外语教学与研究出版社出版。这算是我反过来用莎士比亚诗剧体翻译《牡丹亭》的一次成功的尝试。在此期

---

① 采用莎士比亚诗剧体互文移植（intertextual transplantation）中国古典戏词和叙事的做法，译者在《牡丹亭》（莎士比亚诗剧体全译本）开头的 "Translator's Introduction"（Huang, ix-xxiv）列举了一些具体的想法和描述；亦可参见国外有关博文的介绍和讨论（French）。

间，我还重读《牡丹亭》，搜集参阅现有英译本，试译选段并着手一些有关读者反应的调研。这些工作为日后用莎士比亚诗剧体翻译《牡丹亭》奠定了基础。2019 年 6 月起，我在美国福尔杰莎士比亚研究院做客座研究员 3 个月，其间又针对英译中国经典文学做过一些英语读者问卷调查，并对重译《牡丹亭》做过一些反思。

我认为，汤莎并举，借船出海，也许是讲好中国经典文学故事，让汤显祖的戏剧文学经典"走出去"的一条有效的途径。然而必须看到，莎士比亚丰富多彩的戏剧语言和天才诗情创造出了英语民族最伟大的戏剧精品。这些精彩的作品随着 18 世纪中叶西方工业革命以来大英帝国的海外殖民扩张而远播世界各地，几百年来保持着世界性的持续影响，形成了具有世界文化意义的经典文学价值和意识形态意义。相比之下，明清帝国衰微，积贫积弱，其优势文化也就未能得以彰显和发扬，汉语自然也就没有获得像英语全球扩张那样的历史机遇。如此，莎士比亚在当今世界文学中的地位和影响远超汤显祖，也是不争的事实。总体而论，历史造成的中国经济和科技的弱势，导致汉语语言权力较之英语的不对等，也是今天中国经典文学走进世界文学的最大的难点。克服这一劣势，是摆在中国经典文学翻译者面前的长期的、艰巨的任务。

不过，汤显祖的戏剧作品中展现出来的具有前瞻意义的时代精神，深厚的人文底蕴和人性洞察、独特的审美传统和鲜明的艺术创新精神，在深度和广度上与其同时代的莎士比亚戏剧遥相呼应，显现出不同社会文化语境中人类在不同程度上步入现代性过程中的行为和思考。汤显祖"临川四梦"剧本中诗意盎然的古典语言和大量典故中凝聚着中华文化的精华成分，在中国文化语境中无疑占据着戏剧审美的最高峰，其文学思想和戏剧审美价值也具有尚未充分描述和阐释的世界意义。然而，我们如果仅仅在中国学术语境中，循西方理性传统，借用西方文化研究和中西比较文学的理论话语，从时代意义、哲学意蕴、思想深度、人性诠释和艺术审美诸方面高扬汤显祖戏剧的思想意义和审美价值，或立足于中国传统的戏曲的形式，通过对汤莎戏剧的相互改编、艺术拼贴或融合，在舞台上力图展现中国古典诗词和戏曲的魅力，是难以在语言文化的深层次上达到在世界文化的大舞台上全面弘扬中国古典文学艺术之目的的。对于汤显祖用典雅华丽的古典汉语和历史文化典故写成的戏剧诗文和曲辞，西方读者在读不了、读不懂，或因为译本中存在一些细致场景、人物塑造和心理描写未能准确表达等问题而读来无趣的状态下，则难以认同汤显祖与莎士比亚比肩的文化意义和审美价值。

同时，我们必须看到，莎士比亚广博丰富的戏剧语言经过 18 世纪中叶，尤其是 19 世纪初浪漫主义莎士比亚偶像化以来几个世纪在全世界范围内持续不断的文化再生产和流通，已经成为西方戏剧文化中经典的话语形式，为英语国家受过教育的英语读者和观众所熟悉，成为他们心理内在的文化构成，莎剧中有些经典台词和词语甚至已成为西方社会文化生活的不同场景中自然而然的表达方式。正如哈佛大学莎学家马乔里埃·加伯尔（Marjorie Garber）指出的那样："莎士比亚是我们大众生活的组成部分。'莎士比亚'成了当今人们互相交往，谈论政治、伦理道德和社会问题等话题的表达方式之一。人们在议论哲学家莎士比亚、历史学家莎士比亚、心理康复师莎士比亚、伦理学家莎士比亚等等。莎士比亚戏剧中一些简短的话语被人们信手拈来，用于谈资。可以毫不夸张地说，在美国大众生活中，只有《圣经》才比得上莎士比亚的人气。"（Garber, 29）在今天的英美社会里，人们对莎翁十四行诗中的一些诗句，或名剧中的一些台词耳熟能详，遇到选择则会想到 "To be, or not to be, that is the question"，感叹戏剧人生则会随口而出 "All the world's a stage / And all the men and women mere players"，赞美友情则立即想到 "Shall I compare thee to a summer's day"，叹息命运既定、人生徒劳而荒诞时则会引用 "There's a divinity that shapes our end, / Rough-hew them how we wil"，感到人性不可测时又会脱口而出 "We are such stuff / As dreams are made on; / And our little life is rounded with a sleep"。现实中这样的例子，举不胜举，甚至一些名气不大的早期莎剧中最不起眼的台词也会在严肃的政治场合中被政治人物随意引用，以引起人们普遍的共鸣。例如美国一位参议员在 "9·11" 恐怖袭击的第二天发表悲愤演讲，引用了莎剧《错误的戏剧》中一句台词："Grief hath changed me since you saw me last."（Garber, 29）这么一句简单的莎剧话语表达了当时普遍的社会意识和情绪，竟然具有预言式的影响："9·11" 恐怖袭击事件造成的震撼和悲痛，的确改变了此后美国社会的政治和文化心理。可见，在跨文化交流中充分考虑文化接收者的社会话语行为及其文化构成，适应对方的语言文化传统和话语习惯，实现文化输出的语言"软着陆"，是值得译者注意的问题。尤其是古典文学作品的翻译，译者必须充分考虑目标语阅读者的文学话语能力和审美习惯，在翻译过程中实现跨文化交流中的语言借力效应。

为此，在翻译策略上，应该以经典对经典，为英语戏剧爱好者和文学读者提供一种新的译本，使之在语言细节、具体意象、诗意情感、人物心理和个性语言表达上最大限度地呈现出汤显祖原作的文本内容，并且使译入语读者和观众获得文化心理上的同感，同时在艺术话语表现形式上为他们所喜闻乐见，读起来又似曾相识、兴趣盎然。这也许也是当今中国汤显祖研究者和译者的一个有意义的课题。换言之，中国古代文学经典作品好的译本应该是一种既充分尊重原作历史语境和文化精神，表现原作文学形象细节和诗意情感，又能融入译入语读者和观众的语言文化心理和戏剧艺术审美趣味的译品，是一种尽可能趋向钱锺书先生所谓"化境"的语言文字结晶。

当然，这样的译法不仅仅是一个文学翻译的异化或归化的问题，它涉及汉英两种完全不同体系的语言转换而引起的文字体量大小、文学经典的互文诠释和戏剧艺术传统等诸多问题。这里着重就汉英两种语言在表达同一思想或意念时显现的不同文字体量问题举例说明一二。我们知道，汉语是表意符号体系，它由成千上万具有表意和表音功能的汉字组成。比起英语这样的拼音文字来说，汉字及其组成的词组的表意密度相对要大得多，表达诗意情感的古典汉语更是如此。例如，汤显祖写到牡丹园中，几个秀才赏花，每人都极尽文采，赞美盛开的牡丹，其中一人用带韵的曲辞如此赞美不同种类的牡丹花争奇斗艳的风姿：

【原文】谁种？鹤顶移鞓，檀心倒晕，旋瓣重瓤争茸。渲紫生绯，袍带寿安围拥。

此处短短 26 个字，吟唱出了 5 种牡丹花各自的色彩和形态，显示出说话人熟知唐代牡丹文化，身为当朝状元而才高八斗的心态。这是一个具有文化象征意义的场景：园中牡丹名花竞相开放，赏花秀才们也各显文华，文墨露才，形成戏剧象征。如此重彩画面，在莎士比亚戏剧中也是少有的，而且，这样的场景与紧接而来的戏剧冲突对比鲜明，形成戏剧性铺垫作用。如果译者要真正忠实地向英语读者传达其中的审美意象和文化内涵，同时又不失其诗意气质，就不得不推敲每个汉字的表意和文化寓意，顺势利用莎士比亚素体诗流畅自如的诗剧体，同时顾及说话人特殊的身份和心理，以及其与剧情进程的关联，译出说话人炫耀才学的意味来。于是可做如下译文：

> Wonderful peonies! Who has them so planted!
>
> Mark, this one boasts a special red color,
>
> Like that on the top of a fair crane's head,
>
> With a tint of brown like that of a leather belt.
>
> That one, look you, is called "Sandalwood Heart",
>
> With the petals of faint color near its calyxes,
>
> Its curling petals spreading out to contend
>
> For beauty with its pistil of a hundred folds.
>
> Ah, here we have this one named "Painted Purple"
>
> Which generates a faint cloud of bright crimson.
>
> They are hailed by other beauties around
>
> Such as these ones which are named "Belt on Robe"
>
> And those ones there called "Long and Tranquil Life".

如此译文，近 5 倍于原文，文字体量十分地不对等，但在语意、语气、诗意和文化寓意诸方面都贴近了原文，应是对原作最大的忠实的译文显现。文中除了第一句承上启下的感叹句外，其间并无实质性的"创译"表现，也就是说，文字体量和形式的不对等换来的是较为理想的动态语意和诗意对等。

关于译文的体量问题，还有另外一个方面：对于原作中文化积淀深厚，形式十分隐蔽，但又十分"有戏"的词句，则必须在译文中向英语读者说明。一般情况下，译者可能做个注解，说明其典故出处或文化含意。但我以为，这样做的结果打断了读者对剧情的感知，让理性消解了形象思维和审美过程，是帮了倒忙。在此类情况下，译者必须发挥主体审美意识，在译文中适当地"创译"，以有效还原原作的文化隐喻意义，使英语读者在不自觉中领悟中国文化的精神。以下通过比较不同译者的处理方式和结果，对此问题做出一点说明。而且，我认为，回译能够在一定程度上有效地检验译文表意的正确度，因而在每一译例后加以回译，读者对比自明。

《牡丹亭》最后一出，杜丽娘的父亲杜宝与中了状元的秀才柳梦梅一同上朝，到皇帝面前对质。此时，身居宰相（平章）大位的杜宝对柳梦梅嗤之以鼻，拒不认他为女婿，坚信他是一个应该受到严惩的盗墓贼。而柳梦梅自恃新科状元，卖弄才气，故而引用宋代诗人卢梅坡的《梅雪》中的头两句"梅雪争春未肯降，骚客阁笔费平章"，以反唇相讥。意思是说，梅花与白雪各有其美，梦梅状元与白丁宰相各有其位，无须在皇帝面前争宠，正如梅花和飞雪争春，各美其美，难以分出胜负一样。所谓"梅须逊雪三分白，雪却输梅一段香"，其间孰优孰劣，是历代文人墨客皆难以用语言评判清楚的。汤显祖有意把卢梅坡原诗中的"评章"改为"平章"（宰相），所指更为明朗。这里展示的，是一个极具戏剧性的场面，具有明显的喜剧效果，既表现了作为权势大臣的杜宝不言怪力乱神、不屑于浪漫情事的务实形象，也表现了柳梦梅后来居上、洋洋自得、舞文弄墨的文人性格。"梅雪争春"是中国人耳熟能详的意象和文化比喻。面对可能未解其意的英美读者（观者），翻译这样文化厚重的诗句，又要表现出当下的戏剧场面和讽刺意蕴，译者必须具有主体阐释自由，把其载负的文化含义展开讲明，同时还要用有节奏有韵的语言表现出说话者柳梦梅得理不饶人、卖弄语言技巧的文人气质（在莎士比亚戏剧里，更多地表现为弄人和小丑的文字游戏）。如果译者偏重形式对等而做硬性直译处理，则只能部分地传达原文的表层意义，不能达到向读者最大限度地传达原作文化内容和诗意精神的目的。

【原文】梅雪争春未肯降，骚客阁笔费平章。

【译例 1】[①]

　　When plum and snow **vie for** the prize of spring,

---

① 此处列举的 3 个译例皆出自己经出版的《牡丹亭》英译本。译例 1 出自外文出版社 2001 年版的《牡丹亭》英译本，译例 2 出自上海外语教育出版社 2014 年版的《牡丹亭》英译本，译例 3 出自美国印第安纳大学出版社 2002 年版的《牡丹亭》英译本。

Poets drop their pens to counsel each other.

【评点】此译例是形式和文字体量基本对等的直译；counsel each other 是误译。

【回译】

> 梅和雪为了春天的荣耀而争夺，
> 诗人们放开他们的笔互相商量。

【译例 2】

When snow and plum blossom **vie to** win spring grace,

The poet lays down his pen to settle the case.

【评点】句式和用词与译例 1 大同小异，末尾为了押韵而强行译成 settle the case，曲解了原意。

【回译】

> 雪与梅花为了赢得春天风雅而争夺，
> 诗人放下他的笔来解决这个案例。

【译例 3】

Apricot bloom and snowflake

　　　　vied to crown the spring,

and the poet laid down his brush

　　　　to administer their dispute.

【评点】此译例跳出前两个译例的时间状语结构的叙事结构，以获得诗意表达，其间突出梅花和雪花意象，有诗意传达，但理解有误，且末尾表达公文化，有伤诗意。此外，译者此处采用过去时态，与说话人强调本诗句普遍意义的意图不匹配。

【回译】

> 梅花和雪片，
> 　　曾经互相争夺春天的桂冠；
> 诗人当时放下了毛笔，
> 　　来解决他们的争端。

比起译例 1 和译例 2，译例 3 进了一步。译文略加解释而直译出，用词地道而加入了诗的节奏，增加了读者的文化理解，并且为此诗句加注（此处略），表现了译者对英美读者文化理解需求的关注。但此译者仍被原句的形式结构捆住了手脚，英美读者读来仍然费解。而且，译者对"费平章"（费思量，费评判）这样的传统语句理解有误，造成误译。上述三个译例都未能突破原文的思维定式，亦步亦趋，照直逐翻，只接触到原文的表层意义，因未能深挖原句的文化意蕴而失去了戏剧场景中人物的拟态和反讽意味。而且，这三个译例都毫无例外地忽略了原文中梅雪争春不分胜负（"未肯降"）这个关键的信息。此外，三个译例的句式和主要动词也互相参照，概无新意。但它们有一点是共同的：力图控制译文文字体量，并力图在形式上和表层意义上求得对等。

如果我们放弃形式对应，重视向读者传达此句中中国文化之意蕴，同时关注英语读者的话语认同和文化契合，即可发挥译者主体的文化理解和翻译的文化补偿功能，贴近译入语文化思维，并做适度"创译"，还原原诗的整体意义，并展示人物的剧中形象。于是我大致用英雄对偶体试译如下：

> In their rivalry for the beauty in spring
> Neither plum petals nor snowflake wins,
> For the fragrance of the plum that flows
> Replaces not the whiteness of the snow.
> To say who contributes more to the spring,
> Many a poet finds it hard to judge and sing;
> They put aside their pens and ruminate:
> What learned words could nature imitate?

这四个大致的双行对偶句回译过来是：

> 为争夺春天之美奂，
> 梅花雪花互不相让；
> 梅花虽幽香飘天外，
> 却不如雪花那般白。
> 谁能够胜出添新春，

> 诗人们谁都说不准；
>
> 他们无奈搁笔遐想：
>
> 文字岂能模仿自然？

这样带有解释性的译文，在连续的阅读过程中，让英语读者重建诗意意境，领悟梅雪各有所性，各有所长，难以替代，互不相让，难以评判的拟人情状。同时，类似莎士比亚素体诗或对偶韵句给西方读者增加了话语的亲近感，而"诗人的文字难以模仿自然"这样的解释性"创译"是原句中蕴含的意念，也让习惯以"艺术模仿自然"理论思考艺术问题的西方读者读来有文化上的贴近感。此外，"骚客"（诗人）作复数理解，加深了此诗的普适意义，易于历代传诵。我个人认为，这样带有适度"创译"的翻译是文学翻译中译者优势的体现，也是一种以尊重原作文化意义、以读者为中心的翻译理念和策略。我译出的《牡丹亭》既以此翻译观为理念，如此的译例便也俯拾即是，呈现出这部译作的独特的翻译艺术。如此说来，就汤显祖的《牡丹亭》一个剧本，如果以此最大限度忠实原意和文化寓意而英译出来的文字体量大概是 5 个莎士比亚剧本的长度，也就不足为奇了。

总之，站在沟通不同文化体系、融通文学审美体验、促进文化交流的高度看，我认为译者不仅应是异文化之间的语言桥梁，而且在一定程度上也是沟通不同历史文化心理、审美习惯和话语范式的阐释者和重建者，这对于文学译者，特别是中国古代经典文学作品的翻译者，提出了一个更高的要求。唯有如此，中国文学典籍的译本才不会被西方读者束之高阁，"东方的莎士比亚"这样的提法才不会被视为中国在国际上提升国家文化软实力的手段之一；也唯有如此，像《牡丹亭》这样优秀的中国文学经典才能在保持自己的文化个性的同时，在不同的话语结构和文化体系中展现出它的现代性价值和世界性意义。

引用文献【Works Cited】

French, Esther. "Translating the Chinese Classic 'The Peony Pavilion' with a 'Shakespearean Flavor.'" Folger Shakespeare Library: Shakespeare in the

World. 28 Feb. 2020. https://shakespeareandbeyond.folger.edu/2020/02/28/peony-pavilion-tang-xianzu-shakespearean-translation/. Accessed 23 Nov. 2021.

Garber, Marjorie B. *Shakespeare after All*. New York: Anchor Books, 2004.

Huang, Bikang, trans. *The Peony Pavilion* (Translated in Reference to Shakespeare's Poetic Style) 牡丹亭. Beijing: The Commercial Press, 2021.

黄必康，1991，"Tragic Disillusionment in *Troilus and Cressida* and *Peach Blossom Fan*: A Comparative Study," 《外国语》（上海外国语学院学报）第 5 期，第 49—54+17 页。

朱文振，1981，《仿戏曲体译莎几个片段》，《外语教学》第 3 期，第 46—50+25 页。

（特邀编辑：郝田虎）

书 评

Reviews

走进克里斯托弗·马洛的语言世界

——评华明译《马洛戏剧全集》

冯 伟

内容提要： 华明教授和商务印书馆推出的《马洛戏剧全集》对于我们深入解读马洛戏剧有着重大而深远的意义，这也是新中国成立以来马洛批评史上具有里程碑意义的文化大事。《马洛戏剧全集》汉译本的问世，尤其有助于我国读者以动态、辩证的角度理解马洛戏剧的艺术成就，避免标签式、扁平化式解读马洛戏剧人物，深入理解马洛与莎士比亚、琼生，乃至古典文学和《圣经》传统之间的复杂关系，特别是有助于我们直接领略马洛雄浑的语言风格和舞台艺术。

关键词： 克里斯托弗·马洛；戏剧；早期现代英国；《帖木儿大帝》

作者简介： 冯伟，东北师范大学外国语学院教授、博士生导师。解放军外国语学院学士（英语文学，1999），北京大学博士（英美文学，2009）。美国耶鲁大学富布莱特研究学者、东北师范大学"仿吾青年学者"。

Title: A Commentary on Hua Ming's *Translation of the Complete Plays of Christopher Marlowe*

Abstract: The publication of Hua Ming's translation of the complete plays of Christopher Marlowe by the Commercial Press is of great significance for the reception and criticism of the dramatist in China. Due to his short but controversial life, Marlowe still remains an enigma today. With the Chinese translations available, more and more Chinese readers and critics alike will be finally in a position to explore his works and appreciate his "mighty lines."

Key words: Christopher Marlowe, drama, early modern England, *Tamburlaine*

Author: Feng Wei is a professor of English at Northeast Normal University. He obtained his Ph.D. (early modern English drama) from Peking University and B.A. (English language and literature) from PLA Foreign Languages University. He has been a Fulbright research scholar at Yale University (2018—2019) and most recently he is nominated as Fangwu Scholar at NENU. Email: fengw160@nenu.edu.cn

　　克里斯托弗·马洛（Christopher Marlowe, 1564—1593）是早期现代英国著名的"大学才子"派（University Wits）戏剧作家，其代表作品《帖木儿大帝》《浮士德博士的悲剧史》《马耳他的犹太人》等都是英国戏剧史上的杰作。从童年时代开始，马洛就在当时的文法学校接受严格的拉丁文教育。文法学校的日常教学以填鸭式的机械灌输为主，要求学生大量的死记硬背，学习生活单调而乏味。每天的课程从早上六点或七点开始，晚上七点结束，每周六天，周周如此。星期日和其他节假日则用来做礼拜或其他宗教活动。按照当时国王公学校长约翰·格雷斯普（John Gresshop）的说法，文法学校的学生到 12 岁左右就要掌握所有拉丁语法，并"熟知每个动词和名词的全部变位形式"（Riggs, 2004: 40）。进入剑桥大学以后，清苦的大学生活也是为毕业生未来从事神职做准备。在伊丽莎白一世及詹姆士一世时期，宗教常常与政治纠葛在一起，效忠女王往往被等同为效忠上帝，外表行为上的驯服与内心信仰的虔诚也被混淆不分。对于宗教和政治"顺服"的要求使得英国的宗教政策和教育体制都在一定程度上表现出强制性的特征。如戴维·里格斯（David Riggs）指出，"克里斯托弗·马洛是（早期现代英国）接受古典主义普及教育的第一代人"；马洛代表了早期现代英国教育中"最糟糕的案例"，是英国古典主义教育和基督教神学之间悖论的充分体现。（Riggs, 2004: 62）颇为反讽的是，正是这个所谓失败教育的案例，却造就了克里斯托弗·马洛独特的戏剧艺术。

　　由于种种原因，国内的英国文学史研究对于马洛的关注往往停留在标签式的简单描述层面，或充其量选取马洛《帖木儿大帝》或《浮士德博士的悲剧史》中的少数选段，将其作为欧洲"文艺复兴人"的典型代表，然后统统将之归为早期现代英国戏剧或莎士比亚戏剧的"先驱者"，似乎马洛的存在就是为了迎接莎士比亚的到来。作为文学史研究，这本无可厚非，然而作为深入、全面的马洛戏剧研究，这些显然远远不够。进入 21 世纪以来，评论家们大多不再局限于马洛作为先驱者或文艺复兴人的狭窄理解，马洛研究也因其作品中大量有关暴力、种族、帝国政治和同性恋等众多"当代"话题而焕发出新的生机和活力。有鉴于此，华明教授和商务印书馆推出的《马洛戏剧全集》对于我们深入解读马洛戏剧有着重大而深远意义，这也是新中国成立以来马洛批评史上具有里程碑意义的文化大事。《马洛戏剧全集》汉译本的问世，尤其有助于我国读者以动态、辩证的角度理解马洛戏剧的艺术成就，避免标签式、扁平化式解读马洛戏剧人物，深入理解马洛与莎士比亚、琼生，乃至古典文学和《圣经》传统之间的复杂关系，特别是有助于我们直接领略马洛雄浑的语言风格和舞台艺术。本文仅以华明译《马洛戏剧全集》中《帖木儿大帝》为例加以简要分析，旨在管窥马洛戏剧独特的语言美学。

需要指出的是，马洛在短短的一生中，无论是创作思想还是写作风格，都处在不断成熟和发展过程中。摘取作品中的某一片断或某一人物，孤立、静止地评判作家马洛及其剧作都难免有失偏颇。换句话说，从马洛进入剑桥大学开始，他就没有停止过对于道德、政治、宗教、文学等诸多问题的思考，而马洛的作品本身，包括他的译作、诗歌、戏剧，直接见证了一个青年作家、学者的思想轨迹。《帖木儿大帝》（上篇）是马洛独立创作的第一部成熟作品，也是唯一一部在他尚在世时出版的剧作。该剧在 1587 年一上演就引起了伦敦剧场的轰动。如彼得·贝雷克（Peter Berek）指出，从 1587 年至 1593 年，仅英国剧场中流传下来的38 部戏剧作品中，至少有 10 部作品明显受到《帖木儿大帝》的影响。《帖木儿大帝》（上篇）给伦敦观众带来了一种前所未有的全新体验，一时间效仿者众，直接模仿或映射马洛及其作品的剧作家包括莎士比亚、本·琼生（Ben Jonson）、乔治·查普曼（George Chapman）、托马斯·德克（Thomas Dekker）、约翰·福德（John Ford）等。同年稍晚，马洛又继续创作了《帖木儿大帝》（下篇）。马洛首先成熟使用的五音步抑扬格也令英国观众耳目一新，并为后来莎士比亚的戏剧创作奠定了坚实基础。马洛的传记者帕克·霍南（Park Honan）甚至把《帖木儿大帝》引起的轰动效应称为"帖木儿现象"。（Berek, 1982: 58）

马洛从创作《帖木儿大帝》开始，就非常清楚地意识到他正在与整个漫长的中世纪戏剧传统告别。正是在这样高度自觉的创作意识之下，才会有《帖木儿大帝》的著名开场诗。华明教授的译文生动地捕捉了"先驱者"马洛的语言风格：

> 告别押韵合辙的轻松语调，
> 以及自得其乐的滑稽表演，
> 我们将带你进入威严的军营，
> 你将在那儿听见斯基泰的帖木儿
> 以刺耳的话语威胁世界，
> 并用征服之剑一路横扫列国。
> 请用这面悲剧的镜子来观看他的形象，
> 然后尽情地为他的丰功伟绩大声喝彩。（马洛，2020: 136）[①]

帖木儿虽然出身寒微，却凭借着无比的力量与超人般的胆识，从一个普通牧民成长为雄霸一方的征服者。马洛使用了一种雄浑的语言风格，塑造出一个冲破传统中世纪宗教与伦理规范的尚武英雄，五音步抑扬格的诗体与征服者形象完美地融为一体。

> 我是一个贵人，我的行为将会证明；
> 虽然我出生在一个牧羊人家庭。
> 但是，夫人，这张漂亮的脸和美丽的肤色
> 将给此人的床第增添荣耀，他注定将征服亚洲，
> 震惊这个世界，
> 扩展他帝国的疆土
> 向东向西，沿着福玻斯的行进路线。（第 1 幕第 2 场）（150）

帖木儿的形象如此光彩照人，以至于剧中所有人物在他的面前都黯然失色，而马洛对于语言的敏锐把握，也让征服者的雄浑风格与被征服者的软弱形成了鲜明对比。在强大的帖木儿面前，迈锡提斯的语言更加暴露他的懦弱无能：

---

① 后文引用时只括注页码。

> 科斯柔弟弟，我觉得自己很憋屈，
>
> 无法正常表达，
>
> 好兄弟，把事情告诉我的王公贵族们，
>
> 我知道你比我更加睿智机敏。（第 1 幕第 1 场）（137）

另一人物，巴耶塞特浮夸、空洞的语言风格则代表着与迈锡提斯截然相反的另一个极端：

> 你们都知道我们的军队战无不胜；
>
> 我们拥有那么多行过割礼的土耳其人，
>
> 以及众多放弃信仰的勇武基督徒，
>
> 就像月亮开始吹响
>
> 她的半圆号角之时，大西洋或者地中海拥有的
>
> 所有小水滴的汇集；
>
> 我们不会撤回我们的围攻，直至希腊人屈服，
>
> 不是勇敢地面对外国军队，
>
> 就是在城墙之下倒地而死。（第 3 幕第 1 场）（190-191）

乍一听上去，巴耶塞特似乎与不可一世的帖木儿在语气上并没有区别，不过前者很快就暴露出了内心的胆怯：

> 告诉他，你的主公土耳其皇帝，
>
> 非洲、欧洲和亚洲的霸主，
>
> 伟大的君王，希腊的征服者，
>
> 包括大西洋、地中海、黑海，
>
> 全世界的最高统治者，
>
> 要求与命令，（不要说我恳请）
>
> 绝不要把他的脚踏上非洲，
>
> ……
>
> 但是如果他想滥用他愚蠢的武力，
>
> 疯狂到向我用兵的话，
>
> 那么你就阻止他，比如说，我命令你这样做。（第 3 幕第 1 场）
>
> （191-192）

对于一个稳操胜券、不容置疑的征服者而言，括号中的插入语部分既显得画蛇添足，又是"露怯"的标志。巴耶塞特在下达命令以后，甚至还要再次重复，"比如说，我命令你这样做"，这显然又是发号施令的军事主将不自信的表现。相比之下，帖木儿的语言在今日看来虽不免显得简单浮夸，不过他不会流露半点犹豫不决。在帖木儿面前，整个世界都是他欲征服的对象，其果敢、骄横、跋扈像极了罗马帝国的缔造者——恺撒大帝。恺撒之名句"我来，我见，我征服"（拉丁文 veni vidi vici 在文法上是三个动词，"来""见""征服"的第一人称完成式），成就了恺撒无往不摧的战神形象，而马洛笔下的帖木儿最常用的两个情态动词"will and shall"则有异曲同工之妙。

> 离开你的国王，加入我的队伍，
> 我们将（will）战胜全世界；
> 我要用锁链紧缚住命运之神，
> 用我自己的双手转动成功的舵轮；
> 除非太阳（shall）从天穹陨落
> 帖木儿才会被杀死或者征服。（第 1 幕第 2 场）（157-158）

帖木儿的语言不但征服了世界，而且还获得了美人的芳心，且看他向奇诺科拉特的求爱场面：

> 奶白色的雄鹿拖曳着象牙的雪橇
> 将你带到冰封的极地，
> 登临冰山的绝顶，
> 你的美丽将消融冰雪。（第 1 幕第 2 场）（153）

《帖木儿大帝》中"雄伟的诗句"（mighty lines）以摧枯拉朽之势一扫都铎王朝时期英国间插剧（interlude）的乏力文风，对其后包括莎士比亚在内的早期现代英国剧作家的语言风格有着深远影响。尤其在莎士比亚的早期戏剧创作中，常常可以看到马洛体的诗歌语言。例如在《威尼斯商人》中，鲍西娅的三个求婚者之一，摩洛哥亲王很可能就是"马洛式"语言的生动再现：

　　凭着这一柄曾经手刃波斯王，并且使一个三次战败苏里曼苏丹的波斯王子授首的宝剑起誓，我要瞪眼吓退世间最狰狞的猛汉，跟全世界最勇武的壮士比赛胆量，从母熊的胸前夺下哺乳的小熊；当一头饿狮咆哮攫食的时候，我要向它揶揄侮弄，为了要博得你的垂青，小姐。可是唉！即使像赫拉克勒斯那样的盖世英雄，要是跟他的奴仆赌起骰子来，也许他的运气还不如一个下贱之人——而赫拉克勒斯终于在他的奴仆的手里送了命。（第 2 幕第 1 场）（莎士比亚，1994: 23）

只要把这段"求爱"修辞与帖木儿征服奇诺科拉特的名段稍作对比，马洛式语言的影响即不言自喻。不过，到了莎士比亚创作《威尼斯商人》时，曾经风靡一时的马洛式诗歌语言很有可能已经变得落伍，甚至让人感到浮夸、矫情，或不够"自然"。[①] 在《帖木儿大帝》中，这种语言是征服者和胜利者的语言，而在《威尼斯商人》中，摩尔人已然再无可能如法炮制，或借此赢得鲍西娅的爱情了。

　　与《帖木儿大帝》一样轰动伦敦剧场的另一部作品，基德的《西班牙悲剧》也遭遇了相似的命运（Kyd, 2014）。该剧中霍罗尼莫式的语言也在伦敦剧场获得巨大成功，成就了"基德式悲剧"的风格。随着英国舞台艺术的不断发展，基德、马洛等英国戏剧的"先驱者"们也开始走向僵化，但其开创性贡献仍然值得肯定。需要指出的是，帖木儿的语言和雄辩并不是华兹华斯等浪漫主义诗人所主张的强烈情感的自然流露（Wordsworth, 2005: 237）。相反，语言是帖木儿征服世界的工具，人要驾驭语言，而不是语言驾驭人。紧随在帖木儿向奇诺科拉特求爱之后，他就尽力消除特切里斯的疑虑（"怎么回事？堕入爱河？"），"特切里斯，女人必须加以奉承"。也可以说，帖木儿对于语言和雄辩的"自觉"意识是马洛语言艺术的重要特征。

　　哈里·莱文（Harry Levin）是 20 世纪以来最重要的马洛评论家之一，其研究著作《僭越者：克里斯托弗·马洛研究》今日读来仍然不乏真知灼见。莱文认为，马洛戏剧中的主人公都是"僭越者"形象。这些人物

---

① 《威尼斯商人》同样在诸多方面受到马洛创作的《马耳他的犹太人》的巨大影响，读者可参见 Shapiro（1991）。

精力旺盛、永不满足，总是追求难以企及的事物，如帖木儿崇尚武力，渴望征服世界；浮士德博士追求无限的知识；巴拉巴斯富于计谋，追求无尽的财富，最终带来自己的灭亡；爱德华二世贪恋同性之爱，最终丢了性命和王位；狄多女王也因为追求不可能得到的爱情而自杀身亡（Levin, 1967）。不过，马洛笔下的"僭越者"形象固然让人过目不忘，但这并不代表剧作家只是某种单一价值观念的传声筒或宣传机器。综观《帖木儿大帝》《浮士德博士的悲剧史》《马耳他的犹太人》等马洛成熟作品即不难发现，马洛在成功塑造这些"僭越者"形象的同时，也会对这些人物进行多维度的展现，进而使其戏剧作品呈现出具有"多声部"的复调特征。在《帖木儿大帝》中，我们不但看到了一个出身寒微的牧羊人如何通过"自我形塑"，把自己打造成为一个骁勇善战的马上英雄的故事，同时也看到了这个有着无限雄心的英雄在其被征服者和旁观者眼中的另一张面孔。例如，在该剧第 2 幕开场，米纳夫向科斯柔这样描述帖木儿的形象：

> 他身材高大，腰杆挺直
> 如同他的志向那样，耸立、超凡；
> 四肢健硕，关节强壮，
> 双肩宽阔，可比背负天穹的巨神阿特拉斯；男子汉的颈上，
> 一颗世所罕见的头颅，
> 在其中以奇特的掌控艺术，
> 固定着锐利的双目
> 炯炯有神的眼球之中
> 一对超凡脱俗的瞳孔，
> 引导他迈向宝座的脚步与行动
> 那里是被庄严授予的荣誉；
> 他的肤色雪白，充满激情，
> 渴望得到至高无上的权力和军队的爱戴；
> 他高傲的眉毛皱起时意味着死亡，
> 舒展时则意味着和睦与共存；
> 一头琥珀色的浓发，

卷曲盘绕，就像凶猛的阿喀琉斯那样，

上面洋溢着神的气息

与无拘无束的威严共舞；

他的臂膀与手指修长有力，

预示着勇气与无穷力量——

这个每一部分都比例匀称的男子汉

将让整个世界臣服于他帖木儿。（第 2 幕第 1 场）（164）

在米纳夫的眼中，帖木儿大帝犹如天神，就像一件不可复制的审美艺术作品。值得注意的是，在这段描述中频频出现了有关审美创作活动的词语，如 fashioned、knit、placed、fixed、wrought、encompassed 等。剧中米纳夫与其说是在描述战场上的勇士，不如说是在欣赏一座完美的勇士塑像。换言之，当米纳夫以一种审美的目光注视和打量这位征服者时，后者的伦理或道德批判反而变得无足轻重。尤其是剧作家还刻意使用这些词语作为每一诗行的结尾，例如，"他身材高大，腰杆挺直"一句的英文原文为：Of statue tall, and straightly fashioned；"四肢健硕，关节强壮"一句的英文原文为：So large of limbs, his joints so strongly knit；"一颗世所罕见的头颅"一句的英文原文为：A pearl more worth than all the world is placed。不难看出，这几句诗行都分别以 fashioned、knit、placed 结尾，旨在刻画帖木儿的审美维度。然而，鉴于中英文法的内在差异，如果译者只顾传达原文句法结构，反而会让译文显得生硬、蹩脚，故而中译文虽未完全传达出原句的微妙含义，但却在相当程度上保证了译文的自然、流畅。奇诺科拉特则为观众展现了帖木儿更为人性化的一面：

如同太阳照射尼罗河一泻千里的河流，

或者清晨将它拥抱怀中，

我也这样看待我高贵的爱，英俊的帖木儿；

他的谈吐远比缪斯女神们的歌声甜蜜。（第 3 幕第 2 场）（196）

帖木儿利用波斯王的弟弟推翻了波斯王，在登上王位后又杀害了波斯王的弟弟，然后帖木儿马不停蹄地战胜了土耳其君主，并将他关入囚笼示众。这个嗜血成性、权迷心窍的牧羊人最后越发残暴和疯狂，直至暴病而亡。随着征服者残暴程度的不断升级，奇诺科拉特的父亲成为其个人野心不断膨胀，最后走向灭亡的见证者和批评者：

> 在我的感觉中，我们像墨勒阿革洛斯那样前进，
> 身边簇拥着阿耳戈号船上的勇士们，
> 前往捕杀那凶猛的卡莱顿野熊，
> ……
> 一只五十万颗头颅的怪物，
> 集抢掠、劫夺与破坏于一身，
> 人类渣滓，上帝的仇恨与皮鞭，
> 在古埃及所在地口出狂言，惹恼了我们；
> 我的上帝，这就是血腥的帖木儿，
> 一个凶恶的惯犯，一个卑贱的盗贼。（第4幕第3场）（229）

如乔尔·奥尔特曼（Joel B. Altman）所指出的，尽管在《帖木儿大帝》开场诗中，剧作家说观众需要用"这面悲剧的镜子"观看帖木儿的故事，然而与传统意义的悲剧完全相反，该剧并没有以暴君或征服者的陨灭，而是以征服者接二连三的凯旋告终。那么，帖木儿的"悲剧"在什么意义上称得上是一部悲剧？剧作家显然对此并没有交代。而且从《帖木儿大帝》（下篇）的开场诗中不难看出，马洛在创作第一部故事时，最初很可能无意续写后来的第二部同名作品。"《帖木儿大帝》登上舞台之后／受到了普遍欢迎；／这促使我们的诗人续写他的第二部。"（Altman, 1978: 323）无论如何，正是通过多视角的展现方式，马洛才能最终塑造出一个集"天神""柔情"和"血腥"等多种性格特征于一身的帖木儿形象。

除了通过雄辩的语言烘托帖木儿的征服者形象，采用多点透视的叙事策略表现征服者的不同维度外，马洛还在《帖木儿大帝》中出色地运用了戏剧独白（soliloquy）的艺术手法来展现马洛式英雄的最终宿命。[1]下面

---

[1] 迄今为止，笔者尚未发现有关马洛的戏剧语言，尤其是戏剧独白的专门研究，而有关莎士比亚对于戏剧独白手法运用的研究则不乏重要著作，如 Clemen（1987）、Newell（1991）、Hirsh（2003）。

的选段是帖木儿大帝咏叹奇诺科拉特的美貌乃至一切超验之"美"：

> 啊，美丽的奇诺科拉特！——圣洁的奇诺科拉特！
> 对你来说美丽是个错误的形容——
> ……
> 如果所有诗人们握过的笔
> 都蘸满了它们主人的感情，
> 和产生于他们心中的每一种甜蜜、
> 思绪，和对美好事物的冥想；
> ……
> 如果这些已经凝成一首完整的诗篇,将美的价值全部包含在内,
> 那么至少有一种思想、一种优美、一种奇迹,
> 将在他们的头脑中永无休止地回旋,
> 无法融入语言。（第 5 幕第 1 场）（249）

　　由于篇幅所限，本文此处只引用了其中一小部分，原文中这段独白则有 56 行之多。与《哈姆雷特》《麦克白》等莎士比亚戏剧中"独白"的舞台效果不尽相同，帖木儿的独白以夸张的手法见长，但这一大段独白同样非常符合独白者的性格特征。帖木儿在骨子中是不可一世的军人，有着征服世界的无限野心，这样一个"僭越者"根本不可能接受命运的束缚，然而他却在奇诺科拉特的面前发现了语言的无能为力，"美丽是个错误的形容""至少有一种思想、一种优美、一种奇迹""无法融入语言"。如果说语言和雄辩象征了帖木儿的武力征服和无限野心，那么可以说，即便在马洛续写帖木儿暴病身亡的悲剧结局以前，这个僭越者已经走到了不可征服的世界的边缘。

　　尤为值得一提的是，马洛在《帖木儿大帝》的开场诗中就对韵体极尽讽刺，并改之以无韵体诗演出。伊丽莎白时代的英国剧场上，演员站在突出舞台的中央，面对着环绕于三面的观众，再以流利的无韵体诗朗诵出长篇独白，对观众听觉上的震撼可想而知。哈罗德·布鲁姆（Harold Bloom）即这样描述马洛戏剧的舞台效应："马洛的夸张语言通过演员阿莱因慷慨激昂的宣泄式朗诵，剧场里几千观众为之神迷、为之倾倒。英国戏剧表演史出乎人们意料地翻开了新的一页。"（布鲁姆，

2006: 26）华明教授译《马洛戏剧全集》生动、准确地传达出了马洛独特的语言风格，也为我们进入马洛的语言世界打开了一扇门。

引用文献【Works Cited】

Altman, Joel B. *The Tudor Play of Mind: Rhetorical Inquiry and the Development of Elizabethan Drama*. Berkeley: U of California P, 1978.

Berek, Peter. "Tamburlaine's Weak Sons: Imitation as Interpretation before 1593." *Renaissance Drama* 13 (1982): 55-82.

Clemen, Wolfgang. *Shakespeare's Soliloquies*. Trans. Charity Scott Stokes. New York: Methuen, 1987.

Hirsh, James E. *Shakespeare and the History of Soliloquies*. Madison: Fairleigh Dickinson UP, 2003.

Kyd. Thomas. *A Norton Critical Edition of* The Spanish Tragedy. Ed. Michael Neill. New York: Norton, 2014.

Levin, Harry. *The Overreacher: A Study of Christopher Marlowe*. London: Farber & Farber, 1967.

Newell, Alex. *The Soliloquies in* Hamlet. Rutherford: Fairleigh Dickinson UP, 1991.

Riggs, David. *The World of Christopher Marlowe*. New York: Henry Holt, 2004.

Shapiro, James. *Rival Playwrights: Marlowe, Jonson, Shakespeare*. New York: Columbia UP, 1991.

Wordsworth, William, and Samuel Taylor Coleridge. *Lyrical Ballads*. Ed. R. L. Brett and A. R. Jones. London: Routledge, 2005.

哈罗德·布鲁姆，2006，《影响的焦虑》，徐文博译，南京：江苏教育出版社。

克里斯托弗·马洛，2020，《马洛戏剧全集》，华明译，北京：商务印书馆。

莎士比亚，1994，《莎士比亚全集（二）》，朱生豪译，北京：人民文学出版社。

（特邀编辑：王瑞雪）

评朱世达译《文艺复兴时期英国戏剧选》

——兼论文艺复兴时期英国戏剧研究

徐 嘉

内容提要： 朱世达教授的译著《文艺复兴时期英国戏剧选》（第1、2、3辑）选材丰富，译文准确，展现了莎士比亚以外的文艺复兴时期戏剧的重要价值。文艺复兴时期戏剧家也并非只是莎士比亚的"参照"和"附庸"，而是具有鲜明的风格和重要的文学价值。而文艺复兴后期的英国戏剧目前"微不足道"的地位，不仅与莎士比亚研究的强势和莎士比亚戏剧外作品的译本缺乏相关，也与我国研究界对文艺复兴后期文学的历史定性有关。

关键词：《文艺复兴时期英国戏剧选》；朱世达；文艺复兴时期英国戏剧

作者简介： 徐嘉，北京理工大学外国语学院副教授，北京大学英语语言文学博士，研究方向为早期现代英国戏剧，曾在英国肯特大学英语学院、英国莎士比亚学院、美国耶鲁大学访问学习。出版专著《莎剧中的童年与成长观念研究》（外语教学与研究出版社，2016），译著《谈颜论色》（北京大学出版社，2020）、《莎士比亚百科》（英国 DK 出版社和电子工业出版社，2016）等 6 部，在《外国文学评论》等学术期刊发表论文 20 余篇。

Title: On Zhu Shida's *A Selected Translation of Renaissance English Plays*, with a Glimpse on the Study of English Renaissance Drama as a Whole

Abstract: *A Selected Translation of Renaissance English Plays* (Vols. 1, 2, 3), translated by Prof. Zhu Shida, is rich in selection of plays and accurate in translation, demonstrating the significance of non-Shakespearean Renaissance English plays. The dramatists of the Renaissance period, as a whole, were not "reference" and "vassal" of William Shakespeare, but had a distinctive style and literary value. The current "insignificant" position of late Renaissance English drama is not only related to the strong influence of Shakespeare and the lack of translations of non-Shakespearean works, but also has something to do with the attitude of Chinese researchers towards the later period of Renaissance drama.

Key words: *A Selected Translation of Renaissance English Plays*, Zhu Shida, Renaissance English drama

Author: Xu Jia, with a Ph.D. degree in English from Peking University, is an associate professor at the School of Foreign Languages, Beijing Institute of Technology. Her research interests are in early modern English drama. She has published a monograph *On the Childhood and Growth in Shakespeare's Plays* (FLTRP, 2016), 6 translated books such as *On Color* (Peking UP, 2020) and *The Shakespeare Book* (DK & Electronic Industry Press, 2016), and more than 20 journal articles. E-mail: xujia.sfl@bit.edu.cn

文艺复兴时期英国戏剧本身具有文学价值和研究意义，但大多数研究者似乎只将精力放在莎士比亚身上，以至于"莎士比亚戏剧"从文艺复兴时期戏剧中脱颖而出，而提起"文艺复兴时期戏剧"，人们反而特指"莎士比亚以外的文艺复兴戏剧"，将莎士比亚戏剧排除在外了。当然，如琼生所说，莎士比亚"不属于一个时代，而是属于所有世纪"，莎翁是英国文艺复兴时期文学史中最为明亮的一颗星，但这并不意味着文艺复兴时期戏剧就只属于莎士比亚。早在 1964 年，王佐良的《英国诗剧与莎士比亚》就曾对比了莎士比亚与马洛、琼生和韦伯斯特等的作品，指出除莎士比亚之外文艺复兴时期戏剧的重要价值："16、17 世纪英国诗剧中，作家辈出，好戏连台，应该说即使没有莎士比亚，它也要占英国文学史上光辉的一页。"（王佐良，1964: 13）而近年来，随着莎士比亚研究的不断深入，学术界不仅出现了对莎士比亚经典地位的反思（如对莎士比亚的作者性的质疑、对 18 世纪的莎士比亚经典化的考察等），而且将关注点延伸至莎士比亚同期的戏剧家和作家如马洛、琼生、斯宾塞、米德尔顿等的戏剧作品。这些努力已然取得一些成果，但相对于莎士比亚的知名度和研究深度，显然并不足够。正如郝田虎在 2015 年所指出的："1978 年是弥尔顿诞辰 370 周年，2011 年是钦定本《圣经》出版 400 周年。二者并未在中国学界掀起哪怕微小的波澜，这固然是因为莎士比亚的一枝独秀和宗教问题的敏感性,但也可以标示除莎士比亚外早期英国文学研究在以经济建设为中心的新时期中国事实上微不足道的地位。"(2015:3)

朱世达教授不仅是美国文学研究专家和译者,而且一直关注文艺复兴时期戏剧研究。对文艺复兴时期英国戏剧翻译的现状,朱教授一针见血地表示:"莎士比亚的作品在我国已经有多位翻译家做了翻译。但和他同时代或者稍后的戏剧家的作品的译介在我国仍然不尽如人意。"(2018:1)朱教授不仅注意到这"不尽如人意"之处,而且以一己之力,翻译了基德的《西班牙悲剧》、马洛的《浮士德博士的悲剧》、米德尔顿的《复仇者的悲剧》等五部剧,于 2018 年结集为《文艺复兴时期英国戏剧选》(上、下)出版(即《文艺复兴时期英国戏剧选》第一辑,作家出版社)。译事艰辛,翻译四百多年前的文艺复兴时期诗剧就更是如此,译者的勇气和付出可想而知。但正如朱教授在译者前言中所说,这项翻译并非出于任何功利目的,而是"还了一生的对于英国文学迷恋的心愿"(2018:11)。2021 年,朱世达教授又接连出版了《文艺复兴时期英国戏剧选》的第二辑和第三辑,收录了十四部文艺复兴时期英国剧作。

朱世达教授的这套译著选材丰富,内容广泛,第一辑包括基德的《西班牙悲剧》,马洛的《浮士德博士的悲剧》(第一版和第二版)、《马耳他岛的犹太人》、《爱德华二世》,米德尔顿的《复仇者的悲剧》五部剧;第二辑和第三辑除了莎士比亚"新作"《爱德华三世》,还包括马洛的《跛子帖木儿大帝》(第一部和第二部),芒戴的《托马斯·莫尔爵士》,米德尔顿和劳里(一译罗利)的《娘们儿小心娘儿们》(一译《女人提防女人》)和《假傻瓜蛋》(又译《掉包》《换儿》),米德尔顿的《齐普赛街上的贞女》,图纳的《不信上帝的人的悲剧》;博蒙特和弗莱彻的《菲拉斯特》,韦伯斯特的《白魔鬼》和《马尔菲公爵夫人》,查普曼的《布西·达姆布瓦的复仇》,琼生的《炼金术士》,德克的《鞋匠铺的节日》和马辛格的《新法还旧债》。译著基本包括了文艺复兴时期的重要作家和作品,读者从中可以一窥文艺复兴时期英国戏剧的美妙之处。

在形式上,译著以诗译诗,保留了文艺复兴时期戏剧的诗剧特色。文艺复兴时期戏剧之美,不仅在于其脍炙人口的情节,更重要的是它开创了"诗剧"的形式——无韵诗体的对话优美而流畅,给剧作增添了艺术性，受到读者的欢迎，并对以后的戏剧发展有很大的影响。朱世达教授也注意到了这一点，他在译者前言中就介绍了闻一多、卞之琳、孙大雨等前辈的以顿代步等翻译方法，在翻译实践中也始终注意补救、转换乃至移植英文的诗意。例如，在《爱德华三世》第二幕第二场中爱德华国王的一段独白：

> The quarrel that I have requires no arms
>
> But these of mine: and these shall meet my foe
>
> In a deep march of penetrable groans;
>
> My eyes shall be my arrows, and my sighs
>
> Shall serve me as the vantage of the wind,
>
> To whirl away my sweetest artillery.
>
> Ah, but, alas, she wins the sun of me,
>
> For that is she her self, and thence it comes
>
> That Poets term the wanton warrior blind;
>
> But love hath eyes as judgement to his steps,
>
> Till too much loved glory dazzles them. (Shakespeare, 2017: 2.2.65—75)

这段台词被翻译为：

> 我卷入的争执无需武器，
>
> 但需我的双手；用这双手
>
> 在长吁短叹声中去对付我的对手；
>
> 我的眼睛将是我的箭，
>
> 我的唏嘘
>
> 将是为我效劳的顺风，
>
> 送去我最甜蜜的炮火。
>
> 啊，但是，唉，太阳向着她，
>
> 因为她本身就是太阳，
>
> 太阳一照耀，
>
> 正如诗人吟唱的
>
> 一身英武的丘比特也眼花缭乱。

> 但爱情长有眼睛，
>
> 眼睛引导着它，
>
> 直到爱的光辉使他们昏眩迷乱。（朱世达, 2021a: 280）

译者注意到了这段台词中 arms（武器；双臂）的谐音双关，主人公爱德华望着双手长吁短叹"但需我的双手；用这双手 / 在长吁短叹中去对付我的对手"，不仅错爱之苦跃然纸上，而且台词朗朗上口，符合剧本演出的需要。此外，译者还以深厚的学术功底和对莎士比亚戏剧的广泛阅读，注意到 "she wins the sun of me" 对《爱的徒劳》第四幕第三场俾隆的一句台词："Advance your standards, and upon them, lords! / pell-mell. Down with them! Be first advised, / in conflict that you get the sun of them"（4.3.364—366）的互文性。朱生豪译为"但是先要当心，交手的时候哪个太阳是归你的"可能掺杂了意译成分，而朱世达译为"太阳向着她"，既让读者联想起国王、俾隆、杜曼和朗格维互相打气着向爱情冲锋，希望赢得（get the sun of）所爱女子青睐的场景，又秒懂爱德华（或是诗人本人）对习语 get the wind of（占上风）的巧妙"篡改"——在有情人眼里，爱人哪里是"风"，而绝对是炙热夺目的"太阳"——实在是妙趣横生。

如果说，作为一篇书评，总要提出些吹毛求疵的建议，那么该译著的一点遗憾之处也主要在于诗剧的诗意传达上：译文虽然采取了"以诗译诗"的方法，但诗意大多体现在断行的形式上，而这种断行也不同于原文的跨行（enjambment）停顿。如上文的"我的眼睛将是我的箭，/ 我的唏嘘 / 将是为我效劳的顺风，/ 送去我最甜蜜的炮火"实际上是将原文的 "and my sighs" 单列一行，强化停顿。虽然这里的断句别有韵味，但确也破坏了原诗的抑扬格五音步的流畅的节奏感。当然这并非译者之过，而是中英诗歌自身特点的不同和翻译的难度所注定的缺憾。

这套译著的最重要意义，我认为在于文艺复兴时期戏剧本身。

首先，只有了解整个文艺复兴时期的英国戏剧，才能更好地理解莎士比亚、莎士比亚的戏剧与他同时期的作家具有千丝万缕的联系。据考证，莎士比亚的《亨利八世》和《两位高贵的亲戚》是莎士比亚与弗莱彻合作完成的；《麦克白》中的女巫赫卡特出自托马斯·米德尔顿的《女

巫》；《冬天的故事》的素材来自格林的《潘多斯托》（1588）。莎士比亚
与同时代作家在戏剧内容与写作风格上的互文性，也给莎士比亚的作者
性带来了争议——米德尔顿的《约克郡悲剧》就曾被认为是莎士比亚的
作品。

其次，文艺复兴时期戏剧家也并非只是莎士比亚的"参照"和"附
庸"，而是具有鲜明的风格和文学价值。鲍蒙特和弗莱彻的《燃杵骑士》
是目前欧美学界研究较多的一部剧，它的开场充满了元戏剧特色，被认
为是英国戏剧舞台上第一个戏仿英雄风格的作品——该剧与塞万提斯的
《堂吉诃德》一样，抨击和嘲讽了中世纪的所谓骑士作风和冒险传奇。
城市喜剧的主要作家米德尔顿不仅是唯一一位得到莎士比亚剧团的授
权，在莎翁逝世后可以改编其戏剧的戏剧家，他本身在喜剧、悲剧和历
史剧领域也都成果斐然，有"另一位莎士比亚"（the Other Shakespeare）
之称，而他的作品几乎串联起了英国文艺复兴时期后期戏剧史——米德
尔顿的不少作品是与德克、福特、海伍德、罗利、莎士比亚或韦伯斯特
等合作完成的。其中，他与德克合作的城市喜剧《咆哮女郎》是笔者最
喜欢的文艺复兴时期戏剧之一，也是近年来欧美学术界讨论较多的一出
戏剧。这部戏剧生动地呈现了活力无限、大胆无畏的都市女郎莫尔·卡
特珀斯的生活，她如女游侠一般的形象，是文艺复兴后期戏剧中的一抹
亮色，而米德尔顿对伦敦市井生活的浓厚兴趣和洞察力，让人想起德克
的《鞋匠的假日》。据说该剧上演之时，莫尔·卡特珀斯的原型玛丽·弗
里斯（Mary Frith）还曾现场献唱，在当时的伦敦舞台上大获成功。

再次，了解文艺复兴时期作品还有助于破除读者对于这一时期文学
史的某些固化观念。比如，大多数读者知道罗伯特·格林，但对他的
了解大都仅限于这名"大学才子"对莎士比亚舞台成就的"酸葡萄"
式攻击——在自传性的《百万的忏悔换取的一先令的智慧》（*Greenes,
Groats-vvorth of Witte, Bought with a Million of Repentance*, 1592）中（知
道这个出处的人更少），格林讽刺莎士比亚："其中有一只暴发户式的乌
鸦，用我们的羽毛装点自己，用一张演员的皮包起他的虎狼之心；他写
了几句虚夸的无韵诗就自以为能同你们中最优秀的作家媲美：……恬不
知耻地以为举国只有他能震撼舞台。"（Greene, 1923: 45-46）这是伦敦文
艺界首次提到莎士比亚。在大部分文学史教材中，格林一生穷困潦倒、

怀才不遇，传说死于暴饮，但格林对文艺复兴时期文学的意义并不只如此。他熟练地运用无韵诗写作戏剧，达到了诗歌和戏剧的和谐统一；《詹姆斯四世》（1598）塑造了一位富有人情味的君主形象；《僧人培根和僧人邦格》（1594）极富想象力地设计了一道铜墙来保卫英国，传递出当时英国民众高涨的爱国情绪；另外，格林的《潘多斯托》（1588）是莎士比亚《冬天的故事》的重要素材，格林笔下的少女也影响了莎士比亚，尤其是莎士比亚早期浪漫喜剧中纯洁、天真、机智、可爱的女主角。

那么，文艺复兴后期的英国戏剧为何被低估？这个问题，同样值得思考。莎士比亚之外的文艺复兴时期作家作品的"微不足道"的地位，不仅与莎士比亚研究的强势和莎士比亚戏剧外作品的译本缺乏相关，也与研究界对文艺复兴后期文学的历史定性有关。文艺复兴后期的许多戏剧情节复杂离奇，对白机智诙谐，但道德观念淡薄，往往存在着大量荒谬和淫乱内容，常常招致评论家的抨击。在《英国诗剧与莎士比亚》一文中，王佐良指出，马洛是英国诗剧的"先驱者"和"奠基人"，他引导英国进入了一个繁荣时期，但他自己却在大门前面倒下了。马洛"洋溢着英国文艺复兴时期的新精神，歌颂人的伟大和生的快乐，然而他的戏剧艺术还是不够成熟"。但仅仅 25 年后，韦伯斯特却将"出色的诗才浪费在不必要的死亡描写上，善于写动人场景的戏剧才能却用来制造恐怖，而且是为恐怖而恐怖，这就表明剧作家和观众都处在怎样严重的病态心理之中，英国诗剧的危机已经出现明显的迹象了！"在韦伯斯特之后，英国诗剧的衰败之势更甚，"一批戏剧家更露骨地写凶杀戏和色情戏，这代表着一个伟大的诗剧时代的终点，而这种现象之所以产生，正是因为王室和贵族加强了对于戏剧的控制，即使在戏剧内部出现了对这一坏品位的抵制，但也无能为力"。（王佐良，1964: 5-9）王佐良、何其莘之后撰写的《英国文艺复兴时期戏剧史》也延续了上述观点。但有意思的是，进入 21 世纪后，这个看法也受到了挑战。如米德尔顿与罗利合作的 *The Changeling*（朱世达译为《假傻瓜蛋》）在 17 世纪二三十年代颇受欢迎，而后因为离奇的情节和对淫乱场景毫不避讳的描写而淡出文学批评视野，但近年来这部剧似乎又因为呼应了光怪陆离的现代社会生活而常被改编为电影，重获大众关注。

感谢朱世达教授的译本，让读者有更多机会接触到琼生、米德尔顿、德克、查普曼、鲍蒙特和弗莱彻等的风采。这些原本只在文学史或节选中出现的文艺复兴时期戏剧家，带着他们各自令人拍案惊奇的故事和强烈的个人风格来到我们面前，彰显出文艺复兴时期英国戏剧的璀璨夺目。期待见到更多文艺复兴时期英国戏剧的翻译和研究成果，期待朱世达译《文艺复兴时期英国戏剧选》的第四辑、第五辑和更多辑作品。

引用文献【Works Cited】

Greene, Robert. *Groats-vvorth of Witte, Bought with a Million of Repentance*. London: Bodley Head, 1923.

Shakespeare, William. *King Edward III*. Ed. Richard Proudfoot and Nicola Bennett. London: Bloomsbury, 2017.

---. *Love's Labour's Lost*. Ed. Richard David. London: Methuen, 1956.

郝田虎，2015，《改革开放初期中国的莎士比亚及早期英国戏剧研究述评》，《英语广场（学术研究）》第 5 期，第 3—7 页。

王佐良，1964，《英国诗剧与莎士比亚》，《文学评论》第 2 期，第 1—25 页。

朱世达译，2018，《文艺复兴时期英国戏剧选》（上下册），北京：作家出版社。

朱世达译，2021a，《文艺复兴时期英国戏剧选 II》，北京：作家出版社。

朱世达译，2021b，《文艺复兴时期英国戏剧选 III》，北京：作家出版社。

（特邀编辑：王瑞雪）

阿尔弗烈德大王的麻雀

——评《盎格鲁-撒克逊英格兰的时间观念》

史敬轩

内容提要：盎格鲁-撒克逊人皈依基督教，并不是因为他们的日耳曼传统中缺乏信仰。基督教围绕创世、耶稣和末日审判所构建的宗教时间框架为古英语使用者带来了有关时间未来性的新问题。皈依了的盎格鲁-撒克逊的文学作者们有意无意地都面临着如何把基督教的时间体系和传统的盎格鲁-撒克逊时间观念融合到一起的任务。在认知语言学的框架下，分析若干古英语中的时间词，可以看出，从皈依前的盎格鲁-撒克逊时代，到盎格鲁-撒克逊人的英格兰，到阿尔弗烈德大王的文艺复兴运动，清晰地体现出了一条由环形时间观到线性时间观再到螺旋形的时间概念的文化意识形态。对这种时间意识形态形成的分析既有助于深入理解古英语文学中基督教与异教之间的关系问题，也为英格兰民族性中的忧郁特征提供了一条新的解读思路。

关键词：盎格鲁-撒克逊人；环形时间；同位风格；永恒；荣耀

作者简介：史敬轩，男，重庆邮电大学外语学院教授，西南大学外语学院博士生；研究方向：莎士比亚、文艺复兴文学、古英语文学。本文为国家社科基金项目"英国文艺复兴时期戏剧阅读及其影响研究"（19BWW080）部分成果，重庆市社会科学规划项目"莎士比亚盎格鲁萨克森语本的现代数据挖掘研究"（2017YBWX095）的阶段性成果。

Title: Sparrow of King Alfred the Great: A Review of *The Concepts of Time in Anglo-Saxon England*

Abstract: The Christian conversion of the Anglo-Saxons is not for their lack of a religion in the German tradition. The linear time of biblical history from the Creation, the Resurrection, to the Judgment has some concepts about the *futurus* and the *æternalis* which are new to the Anglo-Saxons, who have had in Old English various linguistic means but any future tense to express the concept of future. Therefore, a very important task of Old English literature is to assimilate the Christian time framework into the Anglo-Saxon perception. In the context of cognitive linguistics, the analysis of time words in Old English shows that there has been a long evolution of time perception from the Anglo-Saxon cyclical, the Christian linear, to the euhemerized spiral time throughout the literary and historical writings of Old English. A study of this evolution will both help to elaborate the Christian-pagan relationship in Anglo-Saxon England and offer a new way to account for the melancholy in the English national character.

Key words: Anglo-Saxons, Cyclical Time, appositive style, eternity, glory
Author: Shi Jingxuan, a Ph.D. candidate of Southwest University, is a professor of the Foreign Language School in Chongqing University of Post and Telecom. His research fields cover Shakespeare, Renaissance, and Old English literature. Email: xiaomuxia@163.com

一

牛津大学博德林图书馆（Bodleian Library）所藏的一份《圣伯纳德箴言诗》（*Sayings of St. Bernard*）中有一句经典之问："我们之前他们在何处？"（Ubi sunt qui ante nos fuerunt?）[①]这句格言在英国文学史上曾被反复引用，一直流传至今。这句话既是对基督时代之前历史的追问，也透露出浓重的忧郁苍凉之感。作为文艺复兴时代的人，罗伯特·伯顿（Robert Burton）在他的皇皇巨著《忧郁的剖析》（*The Anatomy of Melancholy*）中，撇开中世纪教会的论调，也免不了问一句："那埃及四千城池今何在？那克里特一百城邦今何在？"（Burton, 1948: 75）这种情

[①] "Ubi sunt qui ante nos fuerunt" 见于牛津所藏约 1275 年 Ms Bodl. Digby 86, fol., 126v。此说法最早见于罗马波伊提乌所著的《哲学的慰藉》："Ubi nunc fidelis ossa Fabricii manent?"（Boethius, 1934: 43）后各种仿用不绝如缕，如莎士比亚笔下的哈姆雷特慨叹道："Where be your gibes now, your gambols, your songs, your flashes of merriment, that were wont to set the table on a roar?"（Shakespeare, 1996: 2057）

愫不是文艺复兴时代的独创，也不是中世纪神学思考的产物，而是来自托尔金所认为的古老的"格兰德尔的世界"，即《贝奥武甫》中的格兰德尔。打扰了格兰德尔沉睡的并不是鹿厅的喧嚣热闹，也不是丹麦国王赫罗斯加（Hrothgar）的傲慢无礼，而是"对于幽居在黑暗中的盎格鲁人的怪物来说，日月交替，时序生死, 毫无意义"；当人知道了这些，① 则通过诗歌成为一种可以传承的知识，从此将人和其他生灵区别开来，并作为"已有的诗歌和历史的知识被听者继承"（Tolkien, 2002: 123）。也就是说，《圣经》为前基督时代的盎格鲁-撒克逊人带来了有关时间的观念，这种观念通过文学作为一种知识被传承了下去。因此，这种时间观念，这种从没有未来时间概念的古代走向基督教义中的未来的变化也就产生出某种情感落差, 这正是盎格鲁-撒克逊人文化传统中最突出的要素，也是英国文学中被继承并萦绕不去的主题。德国乌兹出版社出版的古英语学者杨开泛所著的《盎格鲁-撒克逊英格兰的时间观念》（以下简称《时间》）敏锐地抓住了盎格鲁-撒克逊文化中的这个核心问题，由盎格鲁-撒克逊人的时间观念切入，作者发现了萦绕于古英语研究中一个长期被忽视的研究空白：基督教的思想观念是如何与日耳曼异教思想杂糅到一起的？

国外学界在传统上对于这一问题的研究始终纠结于基督教与异教之间的对立。例如古英语研究史上具有里程碑意义的《贝奥武甫手册》（*A Beowulf Handbook*）几乎收录了现代撒克逊学派②中所有的代表作品，其中几乎无一例外地、下意识地把基督教神学和日耳曼异教观念对等起来，用以考察史诗《贝奥武甫》中既有基督教要素，又有日耳曼神话要素的矛盾现象。在杨博士的书中，这个纠缠了古英语学界百余年的问题或许有了一条新的思路。可以说，该书就是盎格鲁-撒克逊文化和文学研究的一部"时间简史"。

---

① 指的是《贝奥武甫》中第 91—92 行吟游诗人依据《圣经·创世记》所唱的 "frumsceaft fira feorran reccan, / cwæð þæt se Ælmihtiga eorðan worhte"（人之初，远古遥 / 上帝言，大地造）（Heaney, 2000: 8）。

② 早期中世纪英国国际研究会（International Society for the Study of Early Medieval England）原名为：盎格鲁-撒克逊学者国际研究会（International Society of Anglo-Saxonists）。2019 年，该会出于政治正确性考虑，改为现名。

　　而中国的"撒克逊学派"向上可以追溯到《贝奥武甫》的第一个译者冯至先生、国内首部《英语史》的作者李赋宁先生以及当今沈弘、刘廼银、肖明翰等人。在他们笔下，对于西方的古英语研究传统既有继承，也表现出了鲜明的中国学派特点。

　　不过，古英语文学研究本身就是英语文学研究中的一座高峰，能够登顶者海内寥寥。坦率而言，对于试图寻找学术终南捷径的人来说，古英语和盎格鲁-撒克逊文化研究并不是一个很好的选择，因为要想在这个领域有所建树，必须面对以下三个障碍。

　　第一个挑战就是，研究者不仅要有良好的英文功底，同时还要修习古英语和拉丁语这两门罕用语言，否则，就谈不上任何成就。杨开泛博士的《时间》一书用英文完成，中国学者所写的英文著作能在欧洲出版，本身就足以证明该学者扎实的语言功底，同时，书中丰富而准确的古英语、拉丁语引文也使得该书即便在国外英美文学界也是难能可贵的。

　　第二个使得多数研究者望而却步的障碍就是该领域中研究文本的明显匮乏：有勇气进入古英语文学领域一窥堂奥的人首先面对的不是山积海量的铅字印刷书籍，而是笨重、脆弱、泛黄、珍贵的中世纪手稿。更为艰难的是，与深藏在欧洲各大图书馆或博物馆中弥足珍贵、难以触及的珍贵手稿相比，古英语手稿更加稀缺。截至目前，古英语诗歌完整手稿文献全世界仅存四册：牛津大学的朱利厄斯手稿（Junius XI）、意大利的维切利手稿（The Vercilli Book）、英国埃克塞特学院的埃克塞特手稿（The Exeter Book）和不列颠图书馆的包含《贝奥武甫》的科顿手稿（Cotton Vitellus A XV）。这其中抄成于公元 990 年前，可以算作英国国宝级的古英语手稿仅有 18 份——无论从这些文献的获取难度，还是从解读方面来看，古英语文学似乎都是一座不可攀登的终年积雪的高峰。但是，作者能有这样的勇气挑战"不可能"，除了他在康奈尔大学接受的扎实全面的学术训练，更有"在当今人文危机的背景下，本书尝试凭借数字人文技术提供的独一无二的资源来解决相关问题……计算机技术最大程度上消除了与手稿紧密关联的盎格鲁-撒克逊研究的障碍"（Yang, 2020: 185-186）。是的，在以前学者想都不敢想的数字图书馆技术的帮助下，深藏在世界各大图书馆和博物馆中的羊皮古卷得以让类似像杨开泛这样心怀热忱的学者与西方学者共享珍贵的资源。仅就这一点来说,《时间》一书的附录中包括《博斯沃思古英语词典》（*ASD*）、多伦多大学希列（Antonette diPaolo Healey）等人的《古英语词典语料库》（*DOEC*）、剑桥的"盎格鲁-撒克逊英格兰研究丛书"（CSASE）等在内的数据库就足以造福国内今后的古英语研究者。更不必说,《时间》一书结尾的参考文献足以承担起古英语研究的核心资源的分量,是任何研究者都绕不开的重要书单。

第三个摆在研究者面前的困难是:手稿学（paleography）本身就是一个非常特殊的研究学科。如果不懂手稿学,任何对于包括古英语在内的古典文学研究都不啻是隔靴搔痒。对于一个有勇气的学者来说,所需要学习的不仅仅是拉丁语或者古英语这么简单,还需要学习如何解码古拉丁语符号、古英语手稿的转写、各种不同的笔迹、羊皮纸的产地、流向;要具有"识别格式、核对签名、发现删节（包含错误或可能有违碍字句的书页）、明辨字号、追踪水印、分析插图及鉴别装帧"（Darnton,2003: 43）等烦琐而老道的学术经验。可以说,如果谙熟手稿学,就会"在相当程度上修正了文学史的书写,因为从前对印刷媒介的过分关注扭曲了文学史的真实图景"（郝田虎,2011: 81）。

但正因为障碍如冰封雾锁,这个领域也就成了一块尚待开发的蕴含着丰富资源的处女地。在古英语领域里面,无论从文学还是文化的角度切入,一旦掌握了进入宝藏的钥匙,任何一点锱铢之取都会为研究者带来巨大的创新价值。《时间》一书就是明证。

二

如开篇所述,盎格鲁-撒克逊人的日耳曼传统在遭遇了来自南方的基督教思想之后,也许并不是前人所想象的截然对立,但也不是我们想象的"润物细无声"。这其中可能充满了矛盾、龃龉、混乱、茫然,也或者是相互妥协,错综揖让。这种情况特别是当面对未知的来世时,表现得尤为明显。东盎格鲁国王的谋臣运用了一个生动的比喻:

> 这个世上的人生（与我们不可确知的不间断的时间相比）就像一只麻雀飞进屋里又很快地飞了出去一样:冬天,当您和您的首领、仆人们在吃饭的时候,它从一个窗口飞进来,接着又从另一个

窗口飞出去；客厅中间的火炉把屋子烤得一片暖和，可是外面却到处是风雪交加的冬天。一旦它飞进屋里，就感觉不出冬天的风暴雨雪的凛冽，可是经过一阵短暂的宜人气候之后，它又会从你们眼前消失——他从冬天里来，又回到冬天里去，我们的人生稍纵即逝，对那些在这之前和在这之后发生的事情，我们当然一概不知。（比德，1991: 134）

麻雀之喻并非第一次被学者注意到。但从时间观念这一维度探讨并发现了其中的特殊意义，《时间》一书却是第一次。一方面，在日耳曼文化形态中的时间表现为一种空间意象（Yang, 2020: 44-48）；另一方面，古英语语法颇为独特地缺少将来时态，这为具有线性时间观的基督教从将来时间概念渗入日耳曼异教思想提供了一个很好的切入点（Yang, 2020: 30-39）。

没有将来时态的古英语塑造了盎格鲁-撒克逊人的一种循环往复的环形时间意识（cyclical perception）。这意味着对于古代的盎格鲁-撒克逊人来说，现在只不过是对过去的不断重现，是循环往复，时间有如转轮（Time is Rotation）。这听起来会让习惯于用历史进程思考问题的人觉得匪夷所思。这并不是说盎格鲁-撒克逊人没有未来概念，他们的未来概念恰恰是因为他们的时间观念体现为一种空间隐喻，从而成了一种方向性认知（toweard）。换言之，前基督时代的盎格鲁-撒克逊人并没有《圣经》中的从创世到末日审判的宿命时间意识。因此，日耳曼文化中的时间是开放和无限的；基督教的时间观则是确定的有始有终的一段过程。但《时间》的作者更进一步注意到了基督教的时间观并不能和世俗的时间观相提并论。可以说，基督教世俗的时间观是有限的一段过程，但神圣的宗教时间却是永恒而无始无终的。"永恒"（eternity）与"未来"（future）紧密相关，而"永恒"这个词进入英语的时间甚至比"未来"还要晚。一直到乔叟将波伊提乌（Boethius）的《哲学的慰藉》（The Consolation of Philosophy）再次翻译成英语的时候，"永恒"（eternity）才出现在英语中。

不过这并不意味着乔叟之前的古英语使用者没有接触过拉丁语的"永恒"（œternalis）概念。只不过，当传统的环形时间意识受到拉丁线性时间永恒概念濡染的时候，在盎格鲁-撒克逊人的空间性（hall）时间观中，这种永恒成了一种类似于向前的运动，这和原本基督神学中"永恒"的超时间（timelessness）性是有所不同的。盎格鲁-撒克逊人的时间观念要从具体的自然时序进入包含未来概念的抽象时间观，例如，古英语文学中往往用 wintra 来代替"年"（geare）计时；而包含清晰的四季和明确的 365 天的"年"（geare）常常都和宗教历史或节历有关。这正是古英语文学的作者们所做的工作，

在《时间》的第三章，作者运用比德的作品以及《十字架之梦》《凤凰》等几部古英语作品详细解释了古英语文学的作者是如何把基督教的时间观与盎格鲁-撒克逊人的日耳曼异教时间糅合到一起的。这一个过程可以被简单地称为"移合"（euhemerize）：盎格鲁人的大神沃登成了诺亚的儿子——基督的十世孙（Niles, 1991: 135）。异教神话被基督教历史化。比德把《圣经》中从创世记到耶稣复活的明确的有始有终的线性时间纳入他的"八个纪"（Eight Ages）之中，盎格鲁-撒克逊人的王国历史是处在这一时序的第六纪。第七纪、第八纪都属于未来，属于永恒的时代。在《时间》的作者看来，比德的未来时代却并不是基督教的最后审判，而是盎格鲁-撒克逊人的环状回归——是重复盎格鲁-撒克逊荣耀的历史，是再次回到过去。基督教的末世时间只终结于第六纪。这一点在《十字架之梦》中更进一步被理解为现世的时间是"转瞬即逝的借用"（lœnan life）。由此，基督教的永恒观可以被盎格鲁-撒克逊人接受为"永恒的福祉"（singal blis）。所以，虽然《凤凰》的故事原型源于阿拉伯，因为盎格鲁-撒克逊人将未来理解为对过去荣耀的回归，古英语诗人却可以用凤凰死而复生式的环状轮回来很好地解释教义中的所谓"永恒的福祉"。这种"永恒的福祉"在古英语诗歌《流浪者》（Wanderer）的作者看来，足以劝诫人们放弃今世财富、亲情、友情的无常空虚，转而寻求上帝赐予的"荣耀"（are）和"安乐"（frofre）。

在《贝奥武甫》中，这种盎格鲁-撒克逊世俗时间观念和宗教时间观念的统一形成了罗宾逊（Fred C. Robinson）所谓的"同位风格"。《贝奥武甫》全诗始于丹麦国王谢尔德的葬礼，终于英雄贝奥武甫的葬礼，在《时间》的第四章，作者认为《贝奥武甫》全诗构成了一种从过去到现在的环形时间。但这种环形时间却由于诗歌中吟游诗人讲述王国部落之

间的恩怨情仇而产生了一种悲凉忧郁的气氛。这一气氛使得贝奥武甫的葬礼不再是简单的对过去荣耀的重现，它也变为了一种从过去而来的开始、一种特有的螺旋式的旅程（oðre siðe）。正因为盎格鲁-撒克逊人所理解的未来是"非过去"的，在基督教的框架里，这种未来时间观成了某种预言性的未来，它和盎格鲁-撒克逊人的过去荣耀的重现之间形成了一种张力。当伴随着荣誉和勇敢观念产生的是盎格鲁-撒克逊人王国间永无休止的冤冤相报时，这种一般人难以改变的宿命（wyrd）之环在基督教的上帝的未来那里找到了一种解脱的方法——世俗的荣誉变成了上帝的荣耀。至此，基督教的神学思想终于得以在日耳曼异教徒的头脑里落地，并开始生根发芽。

到了阿尔弗烈德大王（Alfred the Great）的时代，他的文艺复兴也就绝不是复兴那个盎格鲁-撒克逊英雄过去的荣耀，而是皈依了基督教的盎格鲁-撒克逊人的过去的荣耀。[①]所以，阿尔弗烈德大王的翻译运动也就不是为了复兴异教的历史文化，而是"致力于复兴教会文化知识的荣耀"（Yang, 2020: 148）。对他来说，基督教的时间观已经不是那茫茫的黑夜，他的臣民也不再是惶惶然穿越鹿厅的麻雀。在他看来，基督教的神学知识正如时间的车轮（hweol）轮毂，当时间的车轮滚滚向前的时候，离轮毂越近，也就越加静止不动，越加坚定稳固，离轮毂越远也就越如同圆环一样，循环往复。所以，越接近中心也就越接近永恒。阿尔弗烈德大王的"车轮之喻"代表着线性时间观念和环形时间观念的成功结合，并且，还使得基督教的永恒时间概念最终处在了盎格鲁-撒克逊文化的中心地位。这种思想形态使得两本古英语的历史书写，比德的《英吉利教会史》（*Historia Ecclesiastica*）和《盎格鲁-撒克逊编年史》（*The Anglo-Saxon Chronicle*），体现出了独特的风格。比德试图将盎格鲁-撒克逊人的历史嵌入基督教的时间进程中来体现时间的线性向前运动；而《盎格鲁-撒克逊编年史》的作者们则仅仅将基督教的时间年历用作记录历史事件的简便手段。比德尝试用这种方法来让历史承担宗教教

---

① 阿尔弗烈德大王在他翻译的《哲学的慰藉》中感叹："Hwær sint nu þæs wisan Welondes ban（睿智卫兰今何在）"（Sedgefield, 1899: 165）；卫兰是古代盎格鲁-撒克逊传说中的铁匠之神，擅造兵器盔甲，《贝奥武甫》中曾提到英雄贝奥武甫的盔甲是卫兰所造。

化的功能；而《盎格鲁-撒克逊编年史》的作者则显然把盎格鲁-撒克逊人作为了一个独立的族群整体，它的历史也就成了一个族群认同意识的构建文本。

最后值得一提的是，正因为盎格鲁-撒克逊人的时间空间化（spatialization of time）和环形的历史进程观，在《古德拉克 A》这首诗中，时间成了旅程，而经过这段旅程的人也就成了"穿越时间的人"（tidfara）。这种穿越时间之旅从来都不是对过去的再现，而是朝向未来的宗教飞升。

《时间》的作者不无审慎地认为：盎格鲁-撒克逊人的时间观念与"盎格鲁-撒克逊英格兰的忧郁情怀和人生苦短的情愫紧密相关。而追求永恒则是解开这一心结的方法"（Yang, 2020: 183）。所以，当我们重新回头来看文艺复兴时期的"忧郁的人"，文艺复兴也就绝不是复兴希腊或者罗马的辉煌荣耀，"核心问题不是追随希腊或者罗马人，而是追随什么"（Yang, 2020: 149）。假如我们理解了这一点，我们也就理解了《时间》的作者的思想观点。

不过，作者既没有把自己的观点硬塞给读者，也没有像珠宝店里的公牛一样直来直去。综观全书，作者在翔实的资料基础上，十分谨慎地得出每一步论断，凡有陈述，皆有所据，所谓"一点一笔不放过，一丝一毫不潦草。举一例，立一证，下一结论，都不苟且"（耿云志，1996: 903）。凭借扎实的英语、古英语、拉丁语及文献功底，作者引证丰富精当，观点得出处处令人信服；但文风却又自然流畅，全书读来绝不晦涩牵强，正是文如其人，想来作者为人也当有如沐春风之感。

《盎格鲁-撒克逊英格兰的时间观念》一书也正像春风中飞来的一只麻雀，啁啾声过后，该是撒克逊"麻雀们"的夏天了。

引用文献【Works Cited】

Boethius. *De consolatione philosophiae*. Ed. Wilhelm Weinberger. Vienna: OAW, 1934.

Burton, Robert. *The Anatomy of Melancholy*. Ed. Floyd Dell and Paul Jordan-Smith. New York: Tudor, 1948.

Heaney, Seamus, trans. *Beowulf: A New Verse Translation*. New York: Norton, 2000.

Niles, John D. "Pagan Survivals and Popular Beliefs." *Cambridge Companion to Old English Literature*. Ed. Malcolm Godden and Michael Lapidge. Cambridge: Cambridge UP, 1991. 126-141.

Robert Darnton, "The Heresies of Bibliography." *New York Review of Books*, 50.9 (2003): 43-45.

Sedgefield, Walter John, ed. *King Alfred's Old English Version of Boethius de consolatione philosophiae*. Oxford: Clarendon P, 1899.

Shakespeare, William. *The Riverside Shakespeare*. 2nd ed. London: Houghton Mifflin Company, 1996.

Tolkien, J. R. R. "Beowulf: The Monsters and the Critics." *A Norton Critical Edition: Beowulf a Verse Translation*. Trans. Seamus Heaney. Ed. Daniel Donoghue. New York: Norton, 2002. 103-130.

Yang, Kaifan. *The Concepts of Time in Anglo-Saxon England*. München: Utzverlag GmbH, 2020.

比德，1991，《英吉利教会史》，陈维振、周清民译，北京：商务印书馆。

耿云志、欧阳哲生编，1996，《胡适书信集（上）》，北京：北京大学出版社。

郝田虎，2011，《手稿媒介与英国文学研究》，《江西社会科学》第7期，第78—83页。

（特邀编辑：张炼、王瑞雪）

追 思

In Memoriam

世纪莎学　百岁人生

——缅怀先师张泗洋（1919—2021）、任明耀（1922—2021）

杨林贵

作者简介：杨林贵教授是国际莎士比亚学会执委、中国外国文学学会莎士比亚分会副会长。美国得克萨斯 A&M 大学博士，在美国高校执教多年，主讲莎士比亚研究等课程。现任东华大学特聘教授、莎士比亚研究所所长、外语学院副院长。国内外发表论文 40 余篇，出版著作类成果 10 余部，主编的《莎士比亚与亚洲》在美国出版。最近成果有"莎士比亚研究丛书"（5 册，商务印书馆，2020）等。

Title: In Memory of Zhang Siyang (1919—2021) and Ren Mingyao (1922—2021)

Author: Yang Lingui, Ph.D., Professor of English, Donghua University, Shanghai. He has previously taught at Texas A&M University and Skidmore College. His major research interest is Shakespeare. His recent book publications include *Shakespeare and Asia* (Edwin Mellen Press, 2010), *Shakespeare in Old and New Asias* (University of Lodz Press, 2013), "Chinese Shakespeare Studies" (7 vols., Northeast Normal University Press, 2014), and "Series of Shakespeare Studies" (5 vols., The Commercial Press, 2020). Email: l-yang@dhu.edu.cn

2021 年 4 月和 6 月，李伟民教授通过微信发来两则讣闻：

中国莎士比亚研究重要学者，中莎会会员，杭州大学（浙江大学）任明耀教授（1922—2021）于 2021 年 4 月 7 日逝世，享年 99 岁。任明耀教授生前著有《说不尽的莎士比亚》等著作多部，曾参加国际莎学研讨会。2004 年在参加杭州莎学学术会议期间，我组织杭州学术书店在大会期间展销莎学书籍。任明耀教授也送来了他的

《说不尽的莎士比亚》，赠送给每位参会者。【几年前，】杨林贵教授、郝田虎教授拜访任老师的时候，在他书桌的显赫位置摆放着《中国莎士比亚研究》，他说他每期都会仔细阅读。杨林贵教授任总主编的"莎士比亚研究丛书"（商务印书馆，2020）收录了任老师的文章。任明耀教授千古。

著名莎士比亚研究专家，吉林大学教授，中国莎士比亚研究会副会长张泗洋先生于温哥华时间【2021 年】6 月 15 日下午 1:08 去世，家人开了追思会。张泗洋教授生前著有《莎士比亚引论》《莎士比亚戏剧研究》《莎士比亚大辞典》等著作，为中国莎学研究做出了重大贡献！张泗洋先生晚年仍时刻关注中国莎学的发展，关照中国唯一的莎学刊物《中国莎士比亚研究》。我们永远缅怀张泗洋先生。张泗洋先生千古。

四年前，这两位中国莎学界的百岁老人还是我的一篇记事的主人公。2017 年 5 月和 8 月笔者曾经分别拜望了他们，并写了小文《中国莎学百年的见证》（发表于郝田虎主编的《中世纪与文艺复兴研究（一）》）。四年前的情景历历在目，而今他们与我们虽是阴阳两界，但他们的音容笑貌永驻我心。兹以此文对前篇记事略作补遗，追忆他们生前与我交错的特别片段，借以缅怀张泗洋、任明耀两位先师。

将近 30 年前张泗洋老师对我的教诲言犹在耳。1994 年年底，本人受张老师委托，带着《莎士比亚大辞典》（2001 年商务印书馆出版）手稿从长春赴京。当时电子稿还没有普及，所有书稿都是在方格稿纸上手工誊写。张老师担心邮寄出现纰漏，手稿丢失或者受损，决定派我乘火车赴京送稿。我扛着沉甸甸的书稿，更扛着前辈的嘱托，唯恐出现事故，手稿丢失，张老师及 12 位撰稿人的辛勤劳作的心血付之东流。我一路不敢怠慢，虽坐着卧铺车厢仍一夜不眠，直到把手稿送到王府井大街 36 号商务印书馆，交到责任编辑周陵生先生手上，才松了一口气，并当即打了长途电话告诉张老师手稿已经安然送到。他表扬我不辱使命，一向不苟言笑的张老师竟然跟我开了个玩笑。他说，给我送行时，看着我手中的两个大编织袋的手稿，他感觉"林贵此行好像进城打工的'农民工'"，因为这部两百万字的手稿装满了整整两个蓝白相间格子的编织袋，而编织袋是当时的"农民工"进城务工的旅行标配。接着，他严肃起来，说"我们就是要做学界的'农民工'"，要勤勤恳恳，吃苦耐劳，坐得住冷板凳，耐得住寂寞。的确，编写大辞典的时代，即 80 年代末 90 年代初，正是全民向商、人心浮躁的时期。当时甚至产生了"搞导弹的不如卖茶叶蛋的"，"当教授不如做买卖"等民间说法，甚至兴起了所谓的第二次"读书无用论"。年轻的我不免受到一些影响，硕士研究生毕业前一度想过弃学从商（当时很多外语专业毕业生都去做外贸了）。当时，张老师同孟宪强老师一道给了我最宝贵的教诲，我才没有随波逐流。他们让我静下心来，坚定地选择了自己喜欢和擅长的事业，甘于教书育人，并从中体味人生的价值和意义。我也因此在留校任教后，有更多机会向他们学习为人为学的真谛，并在辅助他们开展吉林省莎士比亚协会工作的同时，结识了中国莎学界的更多前辈学者。我作为《莎士比亚大辞典》的主要撰稿人之一，有幸全程参与了编撰工作，见证了张老师的勤恳、严谨和博学。

2017 年 8 月，杨林贵在温哥华拜望张泗洋教授

大辞典在我 1997 年赴美攻读博士学位几年后才正式出版。21 世纪开年，张老师耄耋之年还亲自给我去信讨论关于样书和稿费的安排，事事躬亲，细心认真，令我感动和敬佩。之后不久，他与子女团聚移居加拿大，

我在美高校工作，我们一度失去了联系。在恢复了通信联系后，我们讨论了大辞典的修订再版等事宜，他仍然对我进行关怀和鼓励。2017 年 8 月终于再次与张老师晤面，已是分别 20 年后，就是前文记叙的我对他的访问，此时的老人家虽年近百岁，仍然关注着中国莎学事业。

也如前文所述，我与任明耀老师的交往，让我领悟了另外一种为人的况味。老人的文风正如他笑眯眯的神态，也如他的一篇论文题目的关键词，一直是一种"情趣无穷"的状态，他总是笑对人生，笑对他人，豁达开朗，谦逊热情。与他交往轻松愉快，前文记述了任老师送我的"君子之交淡如水"的手迹的来历以及他款待我的东坡肉。题字是我 2017 年 5 月与郝田虎教授一道到任老家中拜访他之前两年的事；东坡肉的故事发生在 1989 年 4 月。有些难为情的是，我这个北方粗汉至今分辨不出红烧肉与东坡肉的区别，但老人家的热情细致令我至今感念至深，是我应该学习的为人之道。这里抄录的 2015 年老人写给我的这封信中，老人笔端无意而轻松地点画了的一些莎学交往和平实的人生瞬间，却令我至今读来几欲涕零。

> 杨林贵教授钧鉴：
>
> 寄来的中国莎士比亚论丛（第一系列共 8 册①）已经收到。谢谢，迟复为歉。
>
> 你们主编的这套丛书质量太高，花了不少心血，代表了中国学者研究莎士比亚的水平，值得赞赏。也收录了我的论文《情趣无穷的〈驯悍记〉》，十分感激！
>
> 其中不少老同志均是我的老朋友。其中贺祥麟教授久无消息，不知他还健在否？请通告。此兄十分活跃，我多次去信均无回音，不知怎么回事？
>
> 早年你来访时，在我家吃过东坡肉，你十分赞赏，这是我老伴做的，她已故世数年，如今我成了失独老人，十分孤寂。少年夫妻老来伴，这是真理。你还年轻，正当盛年，也请好好保护你的贤妻。
>
> 我无以为报，今寄上我最后一部著作《求真斋文存》，请你指

---

① 这里是写信者记错了，该论丛第一系列实际为 7 册。

教。如今我已94岁，记忆力严重衰退，已难以为文。这是自然规律，我一生平庸，无怨无悔，随时等待上苍的召唤，一旦召唤，我即离世，进入天国，和先我而去的亲友相聚，这也是一种幸福。

孟宪强兄是我的好友，比我年轻，怎么会先我而去，惜哉，大概他为莎士比亚研究太辛劳了吧！由此看来，凡事都需适可而止，不少老专家因笔耕太勤而离世了，这是重大的损失。而今我已封笔，以文化养生度过我的余生。平时阅读书报，约见朋友，有时练练书法，不再为文章。祝羊年大吉，创作丰收！

附上一些书法，请正学。

收到后请电复或函复，谢谢。

垂暮老人

任明耀

2015.11.6

这里就信中内容注解一二，再次回味任老师的为人之道，尤其是他的交友之道。他提到的"中国莎士比亚论丛"是笔者整理前辈成就，汇编再版的7本莎学专著和文集，2014年由东北师范大学出版社出版，其中一集里收录了任老师的大作《情趣无穷的〈驯悍记〉》。而本人总主编的新的"莎士比亚研究丛书"（5册）2020年由商务印书馆出版，其中也收录了任老师的文章。信中，任老师还惦念着与他同辈的贺祥麟等莎学学者，遗憾的是贺老已于2012年去世。我给他的信中说我仍然怀念30余年前在他家品尝的"红烧肉"，就是他回信中默默地纠正了的"东坡肉"。更让我体味无尽的是，他提到了一个为人的道理：要更加珍惜身边的人。这道理虽然平白，但任老以自身为例跟我提起却让我感到了深意。任老师把他的个人文集《求真斋文存》和他的书法作品赠送给我，它们是最为珍贵的礼物。他还表达了对我的恩师、亲人孟宪强教授的怀念，惋惜他的早逝，最后还分享了他的"文化养生"体会。整篇书信，虽时有提及哀伤之事，但最后总归于乐观和豁达，字里行间透露出他的大度和谦恭，以及对他人的关爱和温情。

前辈的真切教诲和温情不应仅存在个别人的心里，也不应因为他们的故去而被遗忘。所幸的是，我们可以用文字的形式记录过往，留存历史记忆。在本人与李伟民教授汇总、主编的《云中锦笺：中国莎学书信》

中收录了莎学前辈的一些珍贵的莎学书信，即将作为新的莎学研究论丛的一部分在商务印书馆出版。《书信》中不仅包括本文提到的张泗洋、任明耀、贺祥麟、孟宪强等前辈的莎学书信，还有曹禺、朱生豪、卞之琳、方平、屠岸、李赋宁、杨周翰、王佐良、陆谷孙等戏剧家、翻译家和外国文学大师关于莎学的书信、部分图片和手迹，也有年轻学者与前辈交流莎学体会的笔迹。我们希望以此留住真实的历史，以这种形式记录中国莎学的发展轨迹。这更是借助莎士比亚作品进行交流的关于人的历史以及人文时代的历史，因为这些书信除了总体上体现了可以被冠以"中国莎学"的东西之外，还承载着以莎士比亚为媒介对外文化交流的使命，展示了中国莎士比亚学者积极参与世界文化学术交流，中外汇通，参与构建人类命运共同体的文化生态。从这层意义上讲，或许这些书信在某种程度上与莎士比亚作品及中国文学作品一样，有写实与写意、抒情与载道兼备的功能。

1993 年 5 月，首届武汉大学莎士比亚国际学术研讨会。后排从左至右：曹树钧、任明耀（站立者）、杨林贵、美籍华人王裕珩教授、孟宪强等

最后说明一下，这篇纪念文章的完成，我要感谢我的同辈学者的提醒和邀约。我在"第三届上海国际莎学论坛"（2021 年 10 月 22 日—24 日）之前得到邀约，但当时忙于会前的准备。另外，2019 年出版的《中世纪

1992 年 4 月 19 日，上海戏剧学院中莎会纪念朱生豪诞辰 80 周年学术研讨会。

从左至右：孟宪强、张泗洋、阮东英、索天章、阮珅、方平、任明耀

与文艺复兴研究（一）》上发表的拜望散记中已经记叙了两位老人的成就和贡献以及我与他们的交往，我怕没有更多的东西可写，所以当时接受任务时尚有些犹豫。我犹豫的最重要的原因是，我最近有些怕回忆过往，恐怕触碰怀旧的情愫，触发伤感。然而，写到这里竟然发现对两位故去老人和其他前辈的仙逝不是伤感，而是庆幸，庆幸在他们生前与他们结下友谊，这友谊也随着莎学事业的发展延续下去，因为友谊的传递会让他们与我们同在。借用一位 80 后莎学小朋友的话说，这就是"中国莎学共同体"的力量，大家以莎会友形成的这个友谊的共同体，可以凝聚几代有共同志趣的学人，还可以让前辈的治学精神得以传承。

2021 年 11 月 2 日草

2021 年 11 月 4 日定稿

（特邀编辑：厚朴）

图书在版编目（CIP）数据

中世纪与文艺复兴研究. 六 / 郝田虎主编. —杭州：
浙江大学出版社，2022.5
ISBN 978-7-308-22580-9

Ⅰ. ①中… Ⅱ. ①郝… Ⅲ. ①中世纪文学—文学研究
—世界 Ⅳ. ①I109.3

中国版本图书馆 CIP 数据核字（2022）第 074924 号

中世纪与文艺复兴研究（六）
Medieval and Renaissance Studies（No. 6）
郝田虎　主编

责任编辑	张颖琪
责任校对	陆雅娟
封面设计	周　灵
出版发行	浙江大学出版社
	（杭州天目山路 148 号　邮政编码 310007）
	（网址：http://www.zjupress.com）
排　　版	浙江时代出版服务有限公司
印　　刷	杭州高腾印务有限公司
开　　本	710 mm×1000 mm　1/16
印　　张	16.25
字　　数	300 千
版 印 次	2022 年 5 月第 1 版　2022 年 5 月第 1 次印刷
书　　号	ISBN 978-7-308-22580-9
定　　价	56.00 元

版权所有　翻印必究　印装差错　负责调换
浙江大学出版社市场运营中心联系方式：（0571）88925591，http://zjdxcbs.tmall.com